A Deadly Encounter

(Book 1)

KR Bankston

KR Bankston

All rights reserved. No part of this book may be used or reproduced by any means, graphic, electronic or mechanical, including, photocopying, recording, taping or by an information storage retrieval system without the written permission of the author or publisher except in the event of quotes embodied in articles and reviews.

The work is a work of fiction. All of the characters, names, incidents, organizations, and dialogue in this novel are either the products of the author's imagination or are used fictitiously.

Copyright © 2008 KR Bankston. All rights reserved.

The views expressed in this work are solely those of the author and do not necessarily reflect the views of the publisher, and the publisher hereby disclaims any responsibility for them.

Printed in the United States of America
Kirabaco Publishing rev. date 03/01/2009

**Liberation is not a gift bestowed upon us
from our oppressor.
It is taken and owned by the decision that
NO ONE can keep them from it.**

For too long we've watched silently as we've been violated by our government at every turn. The rights and needs of the poor, minorities, and women have been ignored and trampled upon. It's time to stand up and say no. You have the power to make a difference and it is as simple as casting a ballot in your local, state, and federal elections.

If you haven't registered to vote, you may do so in the following ways:

- Contact your Secretary of State and request a voter registration form by mail
- Register at your Public Library
- Register at the DMV when you renew your license
- Register when you renew your TANF/Food Stamp benefits

Registering to vote doesn't automatically sentence you to jury duty. If you get a jury summons, don't avoid it! We need rational voices to keep our men and women from behind bars!

Convicted felons are not barred from registering! States such as Rhode Island, South Carolina and Utah automatically restore your voting rights upon completion of your sentence. Check your state laws for complete information on restoring your voting rights if you've been convicted of a felony.

To Report Voter Issues: call the Civil Rights Division toll-free at (800) 253-3931, or contact them by mail at:
Chief, Voting Section
Civil Rights Division
Room 7254 – NWB
Department of Justice
950 Pennsylvania Ave., N.W.
Washington, DC 20530

Your right to vote was secured through blood, sweat, and tears. Exercise it to the fullest without relenting. Social change and justice for people of color is not optional: it is mandatory. Make them know this by registering your voting voice today!

KR Bankston

Acknowledgements

Because there is none other worthy of this high honor, I give all thanks and praises unto Almighty God, without whom my destiny would never have been revealed or fulfilled. Thank you for the gift, the talent, the covering, the protection and the love. Without you I am nothing and I acknowledge you.

To my loving husband, thank you baby for telling me to "sit down and write something" (smile). Thank you for putting up with my moods, for dealing with my issues, for encouraging me, for supporting me, for holding me and protecting me, sometimes from myself. You are my heart and I love you dearly.

Big Dee Dee, my road dawg, my partner in crime, one of my best friends. Thank you for being who you are, a wonderful daughter, and a never ending source of joy. Thanks for all the goofy songs, crazy dances and strange facts you kept supplying me with. Thanks for being my second set of eyes, for always being honest with me and never letting me give up. You are my spirit, and long after I am gone, in you I'll ever exist.

A very special thank you Mr. E. Lynn Harris. Thank you for taking the time to answer all my questions and emails. For giving me sound wisdom and advice, for encouragement when I felt like giving up. Continue to keep the beautiful aura you have surrounding you. I am still very much an avid fan!

For my all my girlz who've had my back and pushed me forward, Thanks! Joni, my BFF, Cathy, my friend and e-mail partner in crime (smile), Nikki, my drum major of inspiration, The FishBowl crew, my personal cheering squad!

Thank you to NYCita and Urbanizd Skillz, for making all my joints unique and special. I really appreciate all of you.

Thank you to the fans, past, present and future for taking the time to read my novels and support my effort. I am eternally grateful and give you all the highest kudos realizing without you, the effort would be in vain.

Lastly, of course this wouldn't be complete without an acknowledgement to all the haters and naysayers. Thanks for all the whispering, for all the snickering when you heard me say I would be published one day. For all the negativity you spouted about the project and its success. You all fueled my fire and made yourselves my ladder and I thanked you with each step. Keep on hatin' and keeping on snickering, I still need more height on this ladder of success that I am climbing.

KR Bankston

*For you Big Daddy,
the sun that brightens my way,
and for you Miss Finesse,
the ocean that calms my spirit.*

The Gianni Legacy

A Deadly 1 Encounter

Today was busy like any other day at Le Bistro. The trendy upscale restaurant opened a couple of months ago. Adrian pleased with the pace, knew it meant more tips. He could really use them. Le Bistro featured an appetizing array of American, Italian, and Mediterranean cuisine. A favorite meeting spot for a few of the major power brokers, minor celebrities, those who exuded money. it also gave space to those who wanted to rub elbows with all of the above.

Dezi, one of Adrian's glanced at the woman sitting with her friend as Adrian poured his iced tea.

"Who is that?"

"That's Taea and Kayla. They're regulars."

Adrian answered while glancing toward the table where the ladies sat.

"Hmm, Kayla is a very sexy lady."

Dezi took in the woman's flawless complexion and wavy black hair. He and his partner, Eric Greene a.k.a. Dirty, were enjoying a casual lunch at the eatery.

"Yes, they're real cool ladies.".

Dezi Gianni, a.k.a. Devastator, could simply be described as a work of art. Standing a formidable 6'2", muscular build; an immaculate meld of Italian and black, with a sparkling smile that dipped into dimples as deep as pools. He was also the head of the most vicious crime cartel in the state. Unfortunately for Adrian, he wasn't interested in him at all. *Pity.* He would love to be this man's special friend. He sighed silently, going to the kitchen to pick up Devastator's order.

"I guess if I had to lose his attention to someone, I'm happy at least that it was to Kayla."

●●●

"Hey heffas," Adrian exclaimed playfully to the two beautiful sistahs seated in front of him.

"Who you calling heffa, heffa, " they both asked simultaneously, laughing out loud.

This was typical of Taea and Kayla, two of his favorite customers. They were always nice to him. Not making rude comments about him, like some of his other customers when they thought he was out of earshot. They always left him a great tip.

"There are a couple of big ballers checking y'all out from one of the VIP tables."

Adrian casually looked back over his shoulder.

"Oh, really? And how big of a baller would they be?"

The query came from LaTaea Shontrell Everett, the more outgoing of the two.

Taea wasn't afraid to ask questions or speak her mind, no matter the subject. Creamy, chocolate complexion; she sported a short-coifed style. She carried herself with pride, dignity, grace and plenty of attitude; but she wasn't mean like some sistahs could be. She also possessed the perfect hourglass figure.

Mikayla L'Nae DeWitt, the quieter one, was an exquisite combination of Hawaiian and black. She heralded beautiful long, black tresses that complemented her caramel complexion, and big, sparkling light brown eyes. The successful businesswoman of the two, Kayla was an independent broker who created her own capital; petite framed with everything in the right place. Kayla was sweet as can be, maybe too much for her own good sometimes.

They both made Adrian's day every time they came in.

"Well, they got it going on, I can tell you that."

He bantered back with Taea, still wishing it were him they were looking at instead.

"What exactly does that mean? They own something?"

"Yeah, they own a whole lot of stuff, and stacking plenty of paper."

"They ugly?"

"Oh my God, Taea, you are so crazy!"

Kayla almost spewing her iced tea across the table, laughing at her friend's question.

Taea gave her a look that said, what?

"They're both sexy as hell and, to be honest, I wish one of them would holla at me! Shoot."

Adrian somewhat petulant, added the warning.

"But I'ma be real with y'all, they're dangerous."

● ● ●

"Where the hell is that damn slow-ass waiter," Dirty complained.

He was second in command for the deadly cartel, referred to as The Clique. He earned his nickname from his days on the street. He would do anything to get by, undeterred by consequence. A little rough around the edges, Dirty was the opposite of Dezi; slimmer with a darker complexion.

"I need some more to drink and I want dessert."

This muthafucker is working on getting hurt.

"Relax, he's down there with the ladies," Devastator replied.

Dezi had been in the game since he was a youngster, hanging around the drug dons and mafia bosses of his old New York neighborhood. He left New York at 19, building quite an impressive empire in his short seven-year reign here in his new home.

He earned his nickname from several women who got their hearts broken after falling for his smile. He was also a cold-blooded killer who devastated many families over the years. Devastator always liked to kill three or more at a time, it mattered not which gender. He took pleasure in seeing the fear and pain of his victims as they watched their friends and loved ones die. Men or women, they were all the same to him. However, he drew the line with children because he did have a conscience. At least, that's what he told himself to keep himself sane.

Devastator sat back studying the object of his attention. She was totally captivating to him.

"I've got to get to know her a lot better."

Devastator chuckled, as he sipped his tea, looking her over again from head to toe. He contemplated how easy it would be to carry her around the room while he had sex with her.

•••

"Girl, can you get a good look at them?"

Taea questioned Kayla, who faced the VIP table. She wanted to make sure they were at least pleasant to look at. The last time they went on a blind date, the guys looked like a pair of gorillas. Not a nice memory at all.

"No, not really."

Kayla tried to casually look up at the table and see the occupants.

"All I can see is like a basic outline; they both look like they're fine as hell but looks can be deceiving."

They both laughed, thinking of the blunders and total losers of before. Taea and Kayla may have appeared to be two of the least likely people to be best friends; but they clicked and were like sisters, despite their differences.

Taea was all the family Kayla claimed. With her mother's side denying she exists and her father's thinking she branded First National Bank on her forehead, Taea was the only person who treated her well. She didn't ask for anything, and was always straight with her, even when it hurt.

Kayla was very leery of men when it came to romance. Put her in a boardroom or on the trade floor, and she was on. Love was something that always left her hurt, broken, and alone. She just dissolved a relationship a year ago that left her drained and guarded.

Kayla loved Chris with all her heart, thinking he was truly the one, even giving him her virginity. He was a broker like she was, ambitious and on top of his game. Good looking, athletic, cultured kind, and faithful. Well, at least Kayla thought he was faithful; until she caught him in bed with his office assistant. She thought she would never get past the pain and want to live again. She felt so stupid, but Taea was right there. She helped her cuss Chris out, berate him, and bleach his clothes. She laughed out loud. Taea looked at her like she was crazy.

"What in the hell are you laughing about girl?"

Kayla told her about the bleach incident and they both broke into long gales of laughter all over again. She often wondered what she would do without Taea being there for her. It sent a chill down her spine. It was a question Kayla didn't want to ever have to answer.

"Anyway, if you're done strolling down memory lane, do you want to tell Adrian to ask them what they wanna do?"

Kayla thought a moment.

"I'm a little curious."

"You should be, hell, you ain't had none in how long now?"

Taea laughed, teasing her friend.

"Oh shut up, will you? Good grief!"

But she was right, which made it even funnier.

"OK, when he comes back, we'll tell him to go see what's up."

●●●

"Sorry about the delay ladies." Adrian spoke, as he put Taea and Kayla's orders before them.

"You know it's cool Adrian," Kayla responded with a smile. "You all right? You look kinda upset," she asked gently.

His usual warm smile had been replaced with a cold, deep scowl.

"Who ass we need to kick," Taea chimed in.

Adrian smiled.

"I'm fine, just some personal stuff."

His thoughts going back to the phone call he just received from his lover.

"You can always talk to us if you need to Adrian. We're not just your customers; we want to be your friends too," Kayla said.

Adrian looked at her and then at Taea.

"Thanks, I'll keep that in mind. Now, what you two heffas want me to do about the ballers," Adrian asked, trying desperately to lighten the mood and change his thoughts.

"Ask them what they wanna do," Taea instructed him, giving him a look that said: you know what to do.

"All right then girl, I am on my way."

●●●

"Well damn, it's about time," Dirty growled, thoroughly pissed now, ready to really inflict bodily harm on Adrian. "Bring me some more fucking lemonade, and I want a strawberry shortcake."

"I would like a tea refill myself man, and what about the ladies," Devastator said pleasantly.

Adrian turned to him then, *God. Why couldn't the other one be like him? Hell, at least he's still civil.*

"They asked what y'all wanna do."

Adrian addressed Devastator, totally ignoring the still fuming Dirty. He didn't want to piss him off more by looking the wrong way.

Devastator flashed that million-dollar smile and Adrian wanted to melt into those pools in his cheeks. He replied without missing a beat.

"Tell them we want to go to The Industry."

The Industry was one of three clubs owned and run by The Clique. It was the most trendy and upscale of the three; with all the professional, celebrity, and athletic crowd making it their place to enjoy the party.

"Tell them to be there at 10:00. We'll leave their names at the door and they'll be escorted to VIP, where we'll be."

Devastator's mind already worked hours ahead.

Adrian nodded.

"I'll have your desserts to you in a few minutes."

He left to complete his mission.

"So what you want with this one," Dirty asked. "You usually just pick up one from the club, do your thing and move on. So what's up with this one?"

Devastator paused for a minute thinking to himself before responding to his friend. That was one helluva good question Dirty just asked. There was just something about her. He couldn't put his finger on it exactly, but it was there. He wanted to do more than just hit it. He actually wanted to get to know her.

"I'm not sure yet. Something's just different about her."

Dirty thought about that.

"Well, her friend is cute enough, and got a nice body. Hell, I would do her, so it won't be a total loss of the evening."

He laughed thinking of the fun he was going to have later that evening. It never occurred to him that he might not get lucky. He was Dirty. Either they gave it, or he took it, but either way, he got it.

●●●

Adrian returned to their table to talk to them about the plans for the evening.

"OK, here's the deal. They want to go to The Industry. They want y'all to meet them there at 10:00; they're going to leave your names at the door."

"And then what," Taea asked suspiciously.

She wasn't going to spend an evening at The Industry being stood up or left on the dance floor.

"They are having you escorted to VIP, where they'll meet you. But remember what I told you earlier and be careful."

Kayla wasn't really keen on this whole date thing, especially after Adrian filled them in on who these guys were. This was unfamiliar territory for her, and Kayla really didn't like being out of her element. She would go though because Taea would want to go; they were inseparable.

"Well, ain't much they can do to us at a public club," Taea countered, knowing Kayla was internalizing it. "We just wanna talk to them and see what's really up. So tell 'em it's all good."

She looked at Kayla.

"Hey, Adrian, why don't you come down to the club, too," Kayla asked. "We could actually hang out and get to know you outside of work."

Adrian thought about what his evening was undoubtedly going to be like after his earlier phone conversation.

"I'll keep it mind."

"That's cool," Kayla replied, a little disappointed.

"Yeah, we'll be looking out for you heffa," Taea giggled to him.

Adrian laughed himself. He took their checks and his tip, which was good as usual.

"Have a good day ladies and an even better night."

Laughing he went to the VIP table to let them know the evening was a go.

•••

Adrian looked directly at Devastator again, still not sure of Dirty's mood.

"Was everything all right?"

"Yeah, everything was straight," Devastator replied, flashing that million dollar smile.

He has got to be the most cultured killer I've ever seen. Everything about this man suggests class, finesse, even Wall Street; not the drugs, guns, prostitution, gambling and murder, which he knew was exactly what Devastator did.

"What was the verdict from the ladies," he asked, snapping Adrian out of his thoughts.

"They said it was all good and they would be there."

This again elicited a smile from Devastator as well as a hundred-dollar tip with his check. Devastator patted him on the back as he got up to leave.

"Thanks man."

Dirty simply growled.

"Speed your ass up next time."

He mashed the check and money into his hand.

Adrian was pleasantly surprised when he opened the folded mess to find Dirty had also left him a hundred-dollar tip. *Yes, it was a good lunch rush today.*

●●●

"So what's the plan for tonight," Dirty asked Devastator as they drove away from the restaurant.

They were flossing the Porsche 911 Turbo S today, black with the spoiler, 19-inch chrome wheels, black tint with the windows up, but they put the top down today. They enjoyed all the looks from women as they drove by or stopped at lights.

"Well let's see what they're about first, then we'll go from there. If they're just chicken heads or gold diggers, hell we know what to do."

Dirty joined him laughing, *Yeah. Fuck 'em and dump 'em.*

"I like the looks of the lil' chocolate one. What's her name again?"

"Taea, I think is what old boy said."

"That's a nice enough name. I'll just call her Tee though, that way I can't mess up," Dirty laughed again.

Normally he didn't care what their names were. They were just sex to him, but Devastator told him they were to be gentlemen tonight.

Dirty didn't really get it, but Devastator was his friend and he did a lot for him over the years. They were tight and he never wronged him. If he wanted this one thing from him, no problem. He would play this little game. *Hell it might even turn out to be fun.*

A Deadly 2 Encounter

Dirty and Dezi had some business to attend to before meeting up with the ladies later in the evening. They pulled into the parking lot of their private office plaza, entering the building headed up to the top floor. From the casual observer's point of view, this meeting would look just like any board meeting in any boardroom in America. Make no mistake; the men seated around this table were as deadly as they were intriguing. Devastator was almost ready to call the men to order to tackle the days agenda. Dirty sat to his immediate right. Monster, his top enforcer and bodyguard, sat to his left. The others were masters of various specialties: prostitution, drugs, money laundering, guns and gambling.

The cartel owned no real holdings, but the dummy corporations Devastator created and legally established to launder money from the illegal activities housed multimillion-dollar holdings and investments. Both Devastator and Dirty kept their own individual holdings in several offshore accounts making them both millionaires several times over. That was their money. They weren't going to reveal that to any of the Clique members.

The agenda included some house cleaning. There was a hole in the operation. Revenue was continually coming up short and locations were being raided. Devastator suspected a leak, telling Monster to check it out. The culprit, Bone, admittedly did a fairly decent job of covering himself until he made the fatal mistake of confiding in a woman. This particular woman, Honey, was one in his stable of hookers. She loved and worshipped Devastator, being faithful for years. She came to him laying out the whole plan. Monster was again sent to check it out, confirming it was Bone as Honey stated.

Bone held aspirations of grandeur; taking over The Clique. He believed himself better suited for the job than Devastator because he was in the game longer. He tipped off the police of locations to raid in exchange for protection of his growing investment. Bone was double dealing with Devastator's suppliers. Cutting side deals for himself, thus weakening the flow to the street. He even put his own stable of girls on the street to compete with the ones already established by The

Clique. Now, having received the report, Devastator knew what was necessary.

"Gentlemen, let's begin," Devastator stated as he called the men to order. "The first orders of business I want to address are the fluctuations in revenue we've been experiencing."

Dirty was just ready to do the deed, as patience was not his strong suit. He knew about Bone, and he knew what they were going to do. *Why do we always have to go around the maypole with this shit?* Dirty loved that Devastator made them money and got them respect, but he often wondered why everything was such a long drawn out process with him. Devastator loved the dramatic as much as he loved the bloodshed, unlike Dirty who simply gave it to his victim's straight, no chaser. Devastator enjoyed the thrill of tormenting his victims taking every opportunity to do just that. Devastator was still talking. *Sounding like the CEO of a Wall Street company.* Dirty chuckled lightly.

When he saw Monster begin to move slowly and methodically from his position at the door, Dirty knew it was almost show time. He could hardly contain his excitement.

"We have found the source of the problem and have come up with a viable solution to vastly improve it," Devastator concluded.

As soon as the words left his lips, a single gunshot rang out from Monster's gun. The .357 Magnum ripped through Bone's skull, spraying blood and tissue on the members sitting closest to him. Before even realizing he was shot, he was dead.

"And that, gentlemen, will end our revenue shortage."

Devastator calmly regarded the horrified men still remaining at the table.

The two unfortunate men, who were in the path of the spray were busy trying to clean themselves off.

Dirty clapped his hands gleefully, before speaking.

"Next order of business?"

The men were speechless. They all knew Devastator was nothing to play with. That he boasted a serious reputation; but there was truly no comprehension of the depth of evil he was capable of.

Devastator delegated this kill to Monster, leaving the body for the remainder of the meeting as a reminder to those who may have had aspirations they didn't share with him. He and Dirty were in charge. They weren't looking for any more partners. The meeting lasted another forty-five minutes, covering all the tasks they were undertaking for the month. After he was finished talking, Devastator asked for any questions.

Receiving none, he said simply, "Meeting adjourned," and told Monster to take out the trash lying on his boardroom table.

● ● ●

"Man that was excellent," Dirty laughed as they traveled on the expressway heading to see a dealer. "Did you see the looks on their fucking faces?"

Dirty was almost beside himself now, laughing so hard that tears were beginning to run down his cheeks. Devastator internally admitted he enjoyed the show. He always loved it when the plan was right and carried out correctly. That one was done to perfection.

Now, he was concentrating on the task he and Dirty were on their way to. One of the street-level distributors ripped off the Clique for five thousand dollars. Not a lot of money, actually pocket change for him and Dirty. Devastator supposed some would even wonder why they would personally handle the punishment, given the seeming insignificance of the amount.

He sighed lightly thinking these were the same people who would think nothing of killing someone over a color worn, or a city block they never did or would own. Devastator was a businessman, and for any form of mercy or weakness to be shown to someone who wronged him, would signal the beginning of the end of everything he ever built. It was the principle they were concerned with, and others trying to follow suit. For Devastator, principal was one thing worth killing over.

"What time is this fool supposed to be home," Devastator asked Dirty, whose laughter finally subsided to an occasional chuckle.

"Supposed to be there around 6:00," Dirty replied. "That's what Red told me."

Red was a crackhead, but he was generally accurate in the information he gave Dirty and Devastator about anyone they were inquiring about.

"All right good, that gives us time to get in and set up," Devastator replied, thinking ahead.

Here we go again, Dirty thought. They were going to kill this guy. Devastator wanted to kill not just him but his whole family, except the kids of course, which didn't bother Dirty at all. He just hated once again, the theatrics of it all. They arrived at the dealer's house. No one was home, just as Red told them. They eased around to the back door of the small, modest ranch home, picked the lock and entered the house.

It was a pleasant house for someone making minimum wage at a job. It was furnished nicely with high-end pieces. *Way more than this fucker could afford. Probably did it with the money he stole from us*, Devastator surmised as he looked around.

The house was neat and clean. Family photos lined the mantle above the fireplace. Devastator stepped up to look at them and saw there were three kids; two little ones and a teenage daughter. The mother was a fairly attractive woman, he thought. He chuckled, knowing that Dirty would do her.

Devastator made his way through each room. The master room was theirs he knew. It was neat, bed made and furnished in simple earth tones. The next room was the kids' room he surmised, finding lots of stuffed animals and Tonka trucks. The last room was the teenager's. Devastator found posters, CDs, and of course clothes thrown everywhere. This was the messiest room in the house. He chuckled again, thinking he would never allow his teenager to keep their room this messy. There he went again, thinking about shit that didn't exist. He couldn't help it, often wondering if he would ever have kids or a semi normal life doing what he did. Now, wasn't the time to think about that, Devastator chastised as he cleared his head and refocused on the task at hand.

After he made sure the house was empty, he began to set up for the evening's pleasure. He brought some of his favorite toys: the straight edge razor, 9 mm chrome pistol, .380 magnum pistol and his brass knuckles. Devastator sat down in the kitchen at the table, propped his feet on it and popped open one of the beers he found in the refrigerator and waited. Dirty hated this part; he hated waiting on them to come home, but Devastator loved that element of surprise thing. He loved the look on their faces when they walked in and found them waiting for them. Sometimes, Dirty admitted, he really liked it too. He just hated the waiting part.

This time he brought some chronic. He rolled a fat one and smoked. That would keep him mellow and the target should be home in a few minutes anyway. Then they would have some real fun. Dirty knew the wife and the teenage daughter were good looking. He was horny and he would have him a little fun before Devastator killed them.

Dirty already knew his role here was simply support and having his friend's back. He knew Devastator loved killing them in groups. It was his one hang up. *We all got our little quirks, so what the hell*, he shrugged.

Dirty heard the car pull up and looked at Devastator who had that little smile playing on his face. Dirty knew it was show time. They both kept quiet, listening intently. Devastator heard at least five voices that he could pick out, two of them kids. He would get rid of them first, Devastator plotted, pulling the mask down over his face. Dirty did the same. The lock clicked and the door opened, the kids running in first, as the adults followed.

As soon as he heard the door close and the lock click, Dirty stepped out of the shadows, glock drawn and hammer pulled back. The woman saw him first and screamed catching everyone else's attention and Dirty pointed the gun right at her. She stopped screaming. Devastator grabbed the first kid, who looked about six or seven, and held the chloroform to his nose. He struggled for a minute or two and was out. He repeated the same with the other kid who was about five. Devastator took the kids, one under each arm, and put them in a bedroom, closing the door behind him and propping a chair against it. He walked back into the living room where Dirty corralled all the victims, seated, and took off his mask.

The look on the dealers face was priceless. He gasped and immediately began to explain, plead, and beg. Devastator was genuinely amused and laughed. It never failed that they always did this when he showed up. He couldn't understand it. Why didn't they just do the right thing in the first place and avoid his visit? Didn't they know that once he came there was no more space to negotiate?

"What's shaking man," Devastator asked the dealer nonchalantly.

Dirty who removed his mask by this time, was smoking a cigarette, eyeing the wife and daughter of the dealer.

"N-N-N-Nothing," the dealer stammered "Man, I was gonna bring your money tonight, I swear it."

Devastator shot the dealer a no nonsense look. He fell silent for a minute, then began talking again.

"Man I know you gonna kill me, but please let my family go man," he was crying now. "They ain't do nothing. I did this man, me."

That's when Dirty saw it, and no matter how long he was with Devastator it still made him cringe. Devastator's eyes went flat and cold, his nostrils flared, his voice became low and hard.

He spoke directly to the dealer.

"I'm going to kill everybody in this fucking room, but I'ma save your thieving ass for last. I want you to live long enough to see me kill everything you love," Devastator told him matter of fact.

"I'ma let Dirty here do your wife in front of you. I'm going to make your daughter suck my dick. Then I'ma let Dirty do her too, while you see her cry and scream," he continued, feeling colder and meaner by the moment.

"Then I'ma beat on your woman for a while, fuck her up real good. Then I'ma kill them, one by one, slowly, and for me, enjoyably, while you watch. The last memory you have, will be of them looking into your cheating, stealing, lying eyes, asking you why you killed them," Devastator finished up, still looking him in the eye.

The dealer was inconsolable at this point.

"Man, please, please man," he cried almost screaming. "Let them go, they ain't steal your shit! I did it man! Punish me!"

Devastator looked at the dealer again, but Dirty knew he wasn't seeing him. Wherever his friend's mind was right now, it wasn't in this room.

A Deadly 3 Encounter

Dezi's mind was vividly recalling for him images of his first kill, and his mafia mentors Anthony Calucci and Dominic Trapoli.

"*Get yer ass ova there and sit down!*" Anthony told the quaking man and his family.

Anthony was Dezi's hero. He was the biggest guy he knew and tough as nails.

"*I'ma teach your ass to steal from the family,*" he bellowed to the man again.

Anthony was the enforcer for the D'Gassi family, one of the toughest mafia families in New York. He brought Dezi along on this hit to teach him to be a man and groom him for the business. Dezi was 14 years old. With horror and fascination, Dezi watched Anthony and his partner Dominic torture the man and his wife for at least an hour. There seemed no limit to the torment they would inflict. The couple were parents to a teenage daughter who held Dezi's attention the entire time Anthony and Domi were torturing her folks.

"*Hey kid, you ever been wit a girl before,*" Anthony said after noticing Dezi's fascination.

Embarrassed, Dezi shook his head no. Anthony laughed again and spoke.

"*Hey kid, don't be ashamed, we all hadda start somewheres,*" he said.

Anthony looked at the girl hard ordering her to strip and lay on the couch. Anthony looked at Dezi again.

"*Go ahead kid, give it to her,*" Anthony told him.

Domi laughed and joined in.

"*Yeah, do what comes natural, kid,*" and threw him a condom.

They both were laughing hard. Part of Dezi wanted to be nice to her, to stroke her hair and tell her he wouldn't hurt her, but he remembered this particular girl. She was one of the ones who teased him mercilessly about being a mutt because of his black heritage. She took great pleasure in humiliating him. Dezi would never forget that day or her. The more he thought about her taunting the angrier he became. Dezi put on the condom and plunged inside her, thrusting as hard as he could.

Dezi wanted her to hurt like he did that day on the street. He heard Anthony and Domi in the background egging him on.

Dezi didn't know how long it lasted, he just remembered feeling an incredible rush as he came. When he was finished, he got up and spit on her. She was nothing to him, and Dezi hated her for how she made him feel when she taunted him. She was crying almost hysterically and getting on his nerves.

Anthony and Domi handed him a gun, told him if he was done with the bitch, shoot her. Dezi knew this was the test. If he did this he would be in, but if he did this there was no turning back. He was a killer for the rest of his life. That pondering lasted maybe ten seconds before he shot her in the chest. There you go, you miserable full-blooded Italian bitch, Dezi thought when he shot her.

"Damn it, kid! You'se a natural," Anthony was patting him on the back and Domi was there, grinning at him like a proud parent.

"I like that, no hesitation. You gonna go places Dezi," Domi congratulated him.

He still didn't know why to this day, but Dezi turned around and killed both the mother and the father. Then again maybe he did. They were the parents of the bitch and allowed her to taunt and hurt him. They also reminded him of the absence of his own runaway parents with their existence.

"Now, that shit is worth you having a drink!" they both laughed and patted him on the back again.

"You is a fucking natural," they both exclaimed again, still laughing.

The dealers sobbing broke his thought and brought him rudely back to the present and the immediate task at hand.

"Stop fucking begging and crying like a bitch," Devastator said to the dealer.

The man managed to control himself to small quiet sobs. Devastator looked up at Dirty.

"Your dick hard yet or what," he asked laughing.

"Hell yeah! I thought you would never ask," Dirty replied laughing and reaching for the dealer's wife.

Terror filled her heart and she began to scream.

"Stop it! No! Leave me alone," the woman pleaded.

Dirty just laughed, slapped her a couple times and enjoyed ripping her clothes off more.

The teenager was looking at Devastator who was laughing and drinking a beer while his friend was attacking her mother. What scared her even more than the violence happening to her mother was this man's coldness. He had the most beautiful gray eyes but they were void of any emotion. This man was deadly. She wanted to make him like her enough to not kill her. She would do what he wanted, and do a good job, then maybe suggest he put her out on the street or something. Did she want to be a hooker? *Hell no*, she thought but she didn't want to be dead either.

Devastator felt the girl's eyes on him. He looked at her. She was cute for a little girl. He guessed she was about 16. She didn't flinch when he said something about her giving him head, confirming his assumption she wasn't a virgin. She was regarding him with an all too familiar look of fear. Devastator looked her over and decided that if she did a good enough job on him, maybe he wouldn't kill her. He could always use fresh meat on the street.

He turned his attention back to Dirty who stripped the woman's clothes off and was cruelly attacking her. Devastator laughed heartily as the woman screamed from Dirty's rough assault on her. He turned his attention to other pressing matters as he walked over to the dealer, eyes closed, crying again.

"Open your eyes bitch," Devastator barked at the man.

The dealer opened his eyes then, but only to look at Devastator.

"Don't look at me," he told him calmly. "Look at what you did to your wife."

The dealer looked over at his disconsolate wife whose questioning eyes pierced him to the core causing the dealer to cry harder.

"Man, stop all that fucking crying," Devastator yelled at him "You're beginning to really piss me the hell off!"

Dirty, who was finished with the woman at this point and pulling his pants back up, looked over at his friend because of the alarm this last sentence set off. Even the teenager jumped. He was angry and she got the feeling none of them wanted to see how angry this man could get.

Dirty walked over to the dealer and slapped him hard across the face.

"Shut your ass up man," Dirty growled at him in a no nonsense tone.

The dealer grew quiet again and Devastator began to relax and get in his rhythm once more, his mind returning from a vivid memory of his own abusive past. *That shit was too close*, Dirty thought.

"So man, you ready to get that head," Dirty asked, trying to bring Devastator all the way back to where they were now.

"Yeah I believe I may be ready at that," Devastator chuckled. "Come on girl; let's see what you're working with. Maybe you can save yours and your pitiful family's lives. Hey daddy," he yelled at the dealer still chuckling. "Keep your eye on the bobbing head!"

Devastator took a condom out of his pocket and put that on top of the plastic wrap he spread across his lap. He was always extra careful. He eyed the teenager calmly and evenly before speaking.

"Now, if anything in your mind is thinking about biting my dick, my friend will plant a slug in your skull before you can clamp your jaws good."

She was terrified and simply nodded. She harbored no intentions of biting him. She was trying to save her life, and she already saw enough to know he was indeed crazy. She came over to him and began.

She's actually pretty good at what she does. She wasn't a pro yet but she had potential, Devastator thought. He lasted a long time before finally cuming.

Afterward, Devastator showed no emotion. She was scared, even though she knew he came. He even made her clean him up afterward, but he didn't cry out or moaned when he came. He just pushed her away for a minute, later telling her to come clean him off. Now, he was looking at her like a bug under a glass, making her nervous as hell. She hoped she did a good enough job to save her life.

"How long you been fucking," Devastator asked her finally.

He's to the point isn't he, she thought.

"The last couple of years," she admitted.

She saw her father lower his head. He didn't know that, neither did her mother, who began to cry again softly. She saw him exchange a look with his partner, then turn his attention back to her.

"You like to fuck," Devastator asked her again flatly.

She bit her lip to keep from crying. She already saw his reaction to that emotion.

"Yes, I like it," she said with her eyes on the floor.

He and Dirty laughed.

"What would you do to save your life here today," Devastator asked, looking at her.

That's a no-brainer, she thought.

"Whatever you tell me to do," she said without hesitation.

Devastator smiled. He already knew that. They all say the same thing when he asks. He was still undecided and needed something to do while he thought more. Finally he got up, put on the brass knuckles and went to work on the dealer's wife.

•••

Dirty sat back, marveling at his friend's handiwork. Devastator loved beating on people and the muthafucker was good at it. The woman screamed a lot in the beginning, but now whimpered like a whipped dog. Devastator worked her over pretty well, closing one of her eyes and opening cuts on her face and arms. He hit her so hard in the kidneys she pissed herself. The dealer begged and pleaded with him to stop hurting her, which only made Devastator laugh and hit her even harder and longer. When he was finally spent beating the woman, he sat down, took another swig of his beer and looked at the weapons on the table. He would kill her now Dirty knew. That was his style. This time Devastator did something that surprised even Dirty.

"Yo man, hand me the salt outta the kitchen," Devastator told Dirty.

"What the --," Dirty said.

Still, he got up and went to get what Dezi asked for. He gave the salt to Devastator who poured a generous amount in his hand, walked over to the woman and began to rub it into the open wounds on her.

He was feeling extremely hateful this afternoon, the knowledge given by the teenager fueling his rage and triggering even more memories of his own pain sprinkled childhood. She began to scream again in agony from the burning of the salt on her open flesh. Devastator stood back and laughed. He was really enjoying the woman's pain as it helped mask some of his own.

Dirty, who was a little thrown at first, laughed too.

Devastator looked at the teenager who held tears in her eyes as she watched her mother but wouldn't let them fall. Devastator walked over to the kitchen table and retrieved the straight razor. He walked over to the dealer, who looked up at him, grateful, thinking he was going to put him out of this misery by killing him. Devastator read the man's look and smiled.

"No playa, this ain't for you," his tone colder than ice. "I made you a promise at the beginning of this and I fully intend to keep it."

The dealers face fell as he was close to crying again, but the look on Devastator's face made him hold back any water he may have wanted to release.

"Please man, I'm begging," the dealer pleaded as he watched Devastator slowly walk toward his now semiconscious wife.

"No man, please," he kept crying out. "I know I messed up, but it was my mess up man, please! She needs to take care of our kids! Please," the dealer tried appeal to Devastator's sense of family.

Dirty knew the man was wasting his breath. Devastator didn't kill little kids, but anyone else was fair game, and now that look was in his eye. It was time for the plan to come together.

Devastator looked at the semiconscious woman lying on the floor in front of him. *Another bitch*, he thought, angry at the woman for being with such a weak fucker as the dealer. Angry because she was such a terrible mother, unaware her daughter was getting dicked down for two years now. Angry because she reminded him of every other weak woman he ever knew, including his own mother. Devastator felt nothing but pure hate as he lifted her by her hair and slowly, methodically, slit her throat.

The dealer cried out, even the girl let out a small scream of horror, as the blood gushed from the open wound and the woman vainly tried to still the flow by putting her hands around her neck.

"There you go bitch," he said under his breath, walking away from the gurgling woman and satisfied with the judgment he meted out. "This is your reward for choosing the wrong fucker to lie down with."

Devastator walked back to the table and picked up the 9 mm, returned to the woman and fired two shots at point blank range into her. The teenager covered her mouth with her hand. Devastator wasn't sure if it was to keep from screaming or puking.

The dealer was beside himself at this point, all fear gone, seeing his wife brutally killed in front of him, jumped from the chair and tried to grab Devastator. Dirty was on him before he got halfway to Devastator. This made them both laugh heartily.

"Oh, so you a Billy Bad-ass now huh punk," Dirty asked as he hit the man hard in the midsection, knocking the air out of him.

The dealer collapsed back into the chair.

"Hey man, c'mon lets finish this shit. We gotta be at the club, remember," Dirty reminded his friend, looking at his watch.

It was already after 8:00 PM. They were at this damn house for the last two hours; and while he enjoyed fucking the dealer's wife, Dirty was ready to get his party on.

"You're right, I almost forgot about it, I was enjoying myself so much," Devastator replied, laughing softly as Dirty chuckled.

This fool does enjoy killing muthafuckers, Dirty thought again.

Finally Devastator looked at the dealer and said nothing, walked over to him, placed the gun in his mouth and blew his brains out the other side.

"So, what's the verdict on her," he asked Dirty, nodding toward the girl.

Dirty didn't think they needed anyone else on the stroll, and he honestly didn't want to be bothered with having to give her the horse, then take her over to Big D, the resident pimp for The Clique; way too much time and energy. He was ready to go get lit and have some fun. Still they could always use the money, so taking a deep breath, Dirty turned to the girl, and told her to get up. She hurriedly obeyed his command, going inside the room with her siblings, hearing Dirty secure the door once more.

They gathered their toys, checked on the kids in the room. They picked up their masks, took the kids from the room and laid them outside on the grass in the backyard.

The teenager they kept close at hand while they returned to the house taking the bottle of liquor from the cabinet, pouring it on the furniture and setting the place ablaze. Then they left.

●●●

"Man that was a good score," Dirty said as they drove down the expressway away from Big D and the house where the girls were kept.

They dropped the teenager off to Big D moments earlier with one final warning and gave him a look that explained everything he needed to know. Then they headed to Devastator's mansion where they would shower and change for the club.

"Yeah, truly satisfying," Devastator replied, his eyes closed enjoying the replay in his mind. "And since I've gotten off already, I can be good and patient with Miss Kayla this evening."

He smiled again when he thought about her. This one was going to be special. He could feel it.

"You remember to be a gentleman this evening," Devastator said, throwing a look in Dirty's direction.

"I told you man, church behavior," Dirty replied, his hand in the air as a solemn oath.

They both burst into laughter as they continued to speed down the interstate. It was 9:08 PM. They cut it close, but it was well worth it Devastator thought as Dirty pushed the Porsche to 95-mph and they headed toward the house.

A Deadly 4 Encounter

"I look good as hell," Dirty exclaimed, checking out his reflection in the full-length mirror.

He was wearing an Oleg Cassini suit, long coat of course, in his favorite color: black. He wore the matching accessories with a Rolex on one wrist and draped in ice on his fingers, neck and ears. He carried his pocket change, about five grand, in his money clip in his pocket.

Dirty's mind wandered as he looked into the mirror and he recalled the early days of his and Devastator's friendship.

They were running dope and numbers for Cobra, who was the top gang boss during that time and was known for not treating his people well. For many, he was the only source of employment, so they tolerated it.

Back then they went by different street names, Devastator was Italy and he was Ghetto. Cobra wasn't the most creative hustler, so these were the best names he could come up with.

Italy was complaining about working for Cobra one evening as they smoked weed. He cooked up a plan to liberate them from Cobra's tyranny and set them up on their own. Ghetto chuckled slightly asking Italy how they were going to pull it off, to which the man instantly supplied an answer.

Ghetto looked at his new friend like he was an alien. Italy must have been seriously high. He was talking about killing the top gang banger and he was calm and somber about it. Ghetto listened to Italy's plan and even though he didn't think it would work, he went along with it. There was something about Italy that made you take what he said seriously.

Three weeks to the day of their conversation, Ghetto and Italy rolled up on Cobra in the middle of a drug deal. Cobra of course was astounded by their brashness as they held him and the rest of his runners at gunpoint. Ghetto and Cobra began exchanging words, with Cobra reminding Ghetto how he rescued him from the streets after his mother threw him out. Cobra took great pleasure in telling all those listening how stupid he thought Ghetto was and how he was nothing and would always be nothing.

Just as Ghetto was getting ready to unload the AK's clip into Cobra, he heard a boom. He saw Cobra's head explode and his body crumple to the ground. Italy was standing there, calmly holding the still smoking 12-gauge.

From that day forward, they were partners and most of all friends. Italy never brought up that incident ever again and Ghetto tried to wipe it from his memory.

Six years later, things were still cool between him and Devastator. They picked up Monster right after Devastator took Cobra's punk ass out.

Devastator was a unique brutha, too, Dirty thought. He kept his promises and his word was actually as good as money. Dirty was done in by a lot of people in his life, but Devastator was the one who proved some people really are who they say they are.

Devastator was truly family to him and Dirty knew he felt the same way. He was worried about this new girl though. He could only recall seeing Devastator this interested in a girl once before and that didn't work out well at all, to put it mildly. *Just go out and enjoy the evening*, Dirty told himself. *Hell, he ain't even talked to the girl yet. He may not even like her.* As hard as he tried, Dirty couldn't shake the feeling that this evening and Devastator meeting Kayla was going to be the beginning of the end for him.

● ● ●

"So what are you wearing girl," Kayla was asking her best friend for the third time.

Taea changed outfits at least four times since Kayla arrived home from work.

"Girl, I gots to look good, cause if he straight, I might have to keep him for a minute," Taea responded laughing. "I know you got your own cash Miss Thang, but some of us still need that big baller."

Kayla wasn't offended because she knew Taea didn't mean any harm. It was how they communicated. There was no jealousy between them. She would give Taea the shirt off her back and Taea knew it.

"So are you wearing the blue number I told you to," Taea asked Kayla bringing her out of her deep thought.

"Yes, but I need to get to the mall," Kayla answered giving her friend the, I'm- waiting-on-you look. "I need shoes to go with it."

"Well, why didn't you say so? Let's go girl," Taea called out grabbing her purse. "I'll just buy me a new outfit," She laughed as they headed to the door.

●●●

They went through four stores and Taea still was yet to find anything she liked. It was already 8:30 and they needed to go home, shower, do hair and make-up, and be at the club no later than 10:15. Finally, Taea found something in 3-5-7 that she liked. They bought the skin tight, black leather, halter mini-dress and left. They swung through Sven's and picked up some fierce black pumps to go with it. Kayla already purchased her strappy blue sandals. Now they were finally ready to go. They made it to the house they shared by nine.

They didn't become roommates out of financial necessity. Each of them could easily afford their own place. They lived together because they genuinely enjoyed each other's company and loved each other like sisters.

Kayla still didn't know how they did it, but they were showered, dressed, made up and out the door by 9:45. They were speeding down the expressway in Kayla's silver Mercedes coupe. She loved this car. It was quick and Kayla secret loved speed.

It was totally customized, with 18" wheels and the body kit Kayla designed exclusively for it. The sound system boomed rather nicely and elicited stares and remarks everywhere they drove it.

Taea called it the man magnet. She liked that though because Taea loved guys. Kayla on the other hand was pretty content to just be left alone, although that seldom happened. She truly hoped this guy was not of the typical sleaze pool variety she was always being approached by. Kayla already knew he was dangerous, but according to Adrian, he was drop dead gorgeous.

"What are you so deeply in thought about Miss Thang," Taea asked snapping her fingers in front of Kayla.

She laughed a little.

"Sorry girl, just a little uptight about these guys and the stuff Adrian told us about them."

Taea looked at her squarely.

"Look, we are going to meet these guys in a very public place, we don't hafta ever see them again if we don't want to. I promise not to leave you alone, and I know you got my back, too. Maybe they are gangstas or whatever, but they may treat us like queens, and if that life don't spill over into the romance, it's just like any other job a brother may have. Besides, Adrian just wants him for himself," Taea said and started to laugh.

That was the one thing about Taea, she could always make you see the logic in any situation, whether it was there or not, Kayla laughed inside. She decided to relax and see exactly what this guy was about. She secretly hoped he was a yes instead of her usual no. Kayla was lonely and she wanted a man in her life.

They arrived at the club where the valet took her car giving her a VIP parking ticket. Placing the ticket in her evening bag Kayla proceeded with Taea to walk into the club.

•••

The Industry was jumping and seriously crowded. Kayla heard Cube and Mac 10 blaring from the speakers. Kayla was more a jazz fan herself, but she enjoyed the music nonetheless. They both knew they were looking good this evening as was confirmed by the both approving and lustful stares of the men and the disapproving, jealous glares of the females whose dates were looking at them.

"So where is our VIP guide," Taea asked, snapping her fingers, dancing a little and yelling to be heard over the music pumping from the sound system.

"I don't know, there's the podium over there," Kayla responded pointing. "Let's go give them our name and see what happens."

•••

"Damn, she is gorgeous," Devastator said under his breath, sipping his drink as he watched Kayla and Taea make their way to the podium from the skybox VIP section. He called Dirty over and pointed them out.

"Whooo shit, that dress is hot," he exclaimed looking Taea over from head to toe. "You sent Monster down to get them," Dirty asked, still eyeing Taea and the dress she was wearing.

"Yeah, he just got to them," Devastator replied, watching Monster escort the two ladies over to the private entrance.

"They just hit the elevator. Come on let's get ready to do this," he said looking at Dirty.

The ladies stepped off the elevator into one of the most beautifully decorated rooms they ever envisioned. There were beautiful works of art and sculptures, accentuated by a huge chandelier hanging in the middle of the room. Here, the music was a reasonable volume, making it easier to hold a conversation. There were separate dining and kitchen facilities strictly for the VIP area.

Kayla turned and took in Monster one last time. He was an attractive man with a smooth, dark chocolate complexion and straight white teeth. He looked around 5' 10" or so, but solidly built. Nice chest, arms and butt, she observed. He was extremely pleasant and polite as he introduced himself when he met them to bring them upstairs, but Kayla sensed an underlying darkness. Arriving at the VIP room put her more at ease. Everyone was having a good time, and there was absolutely nothing visible to suggest a violent cartel owned or operated it.

•••

Devastator stood there for a moment taking her in while finishing his drink. She was wearing a pale blue almost knee-length form fitting dress. He loved the color on her. The dress dipped dangerously low, revealing the small of her back. Devastator's imagination ran freely as he looked at the perfect butt attached to it. She showcased beautiful legs even though he knew she was no more than 5'5" or 5'6." Her toes were perfectly manicured, which he liked. A woman who took care of her feet, took care of other parts of her body as well, Devastator smiled at the thought. She turned around. Devastator freely took in the front view remaining slightly out of her line of sight.

Her hair was down tonight, displaying her true Hawaiian heritage. It was beautiful like the rest of her: thick, shiny and black. It framed her face and brought attention to her big, beautiful, light brown eyes that danced when she smiled. She had nice breasts. Firm, not saggy, like some he saw. Her jewelry was attractive, not gaudy. It accentuated her features. Her nails were beautifully manicured, with only one ring on each hand. This woman took good care of herself and he liked that. After watching her a few moments more, Devastator stepped out of the shadows to finally meet the woman who intrigued him so.

●●●

"Hello ladies," Devastator greeted them.

Kayla and Taea turned to find two of the sexiest men ever seen standing in front of them.

My God, Taea thought, *they do make them this sexy off the movie screen, too.*

"I'm Dezi," Devastator said. "This is my partner, Eric."

"Hi Dezi, Eric," Taea responded, taking charge as usual while sizing Eric up from head to toe. "I'm Taea and this is my sister Kayla."

Devastator was genuinely surprised. They looked nothing alike.

"Oh, you two are sisters?"

"Well, not biologically, but close enough," Taea responded again looking him over.

Yeah he's just what Kayla needs, Taea decided.

"Oh, I see," Devastator said smiling and thinking that made sense.

Kayla was speechless. She didn't trust her voice right now. She never saw a man this sexy in her life. She wanted to tell him to strip right now, so she could see the rest of his body, especially his walking stick. He was absolutely breathtaking, and those dimples were to die for. Kayla smiled a little at that thought, and Devastator, who was watching her intently the entire time, called her on it.

"Would you care to share," he softly asked.

She chuckled aloud. "Maybe later."

"Why don't we go sit down and get comfortable," Dirty suggested.

They went into the sky room. The room Devastator and Dirty built especially for them. Plush in amenities, it was furnished with oversized recliners, a couple of loveseats and a 68" big-screen TV, wet bar, and full-service fridge.

Taea and Dirty sat on one loveseat, and across the room Devastator and Kayla on another.

Kayla and Taea each knew the other was in the room, but couldn't see each other since they weren't facing. Devastator and Dirty designed the room this way, so they could each be in it, yet have privacy. Devastator managed to catch himself. He just couldn't stop looking at Kayla.

"What can I get you to drink," he asked.

"I would actually like some fruit juice, if you have it," Kayla responded.

She must be the designated driver for the evening, he chuckled silently.

"Sure, I can do that," Devastator said as he got up to walk to the mini bar.

Kayla watched him as he walked away, using the opportunity to take him in fully. He was fine in every aspect of the word. She saw from a glance the serious set of pecs on that beautiful chest of his. He held gorgeous dimples, with the most flawless set of teeth. His hands were manicured and he was very well built, which suggested he worked out at the gym, not to mention his perfect butt. It boasted a promise of power when combined with the walking stick in front.

The suit was Armani, confirming he spent well on his clothes and looked damned good in them. Kayla was glad she wore the blue, it matched his shirt. She wondered how it would feel having those huge arms wrapped around her, feeling herself getting turned on.

"Down girl," she laughed to herself. "Get to know the man first."

Moments later, Devastator returned with a glass of juice for her and some cognac for himself. He continued to look at her as he sipped his drink. Kayla was admiring a painting he purchased a week earlier.

"Do you like it," Devastator asked.

"Mmm? Yes, it's a wonderful piece," she responded.

He was looking at her very intently now.

"So, does your man know you're here with me this evening," Devastator asked calmly, sipped his drink and watched her reaction.

Where the hell did that come from, Kayla wondered.

It took her completely by surprise, but she didn't let it show.

"No, he doesn't know," she replied, just as calmly as he asked.

This time it was her turn to watch his reaction.

Devastator was careful to not let his face portray his feelings at the moment. He didn't like that answer one bit. It meant there was competition, and he didn't like competition, period, especially when it came to her. Damn, what was this woman doing to him? He barely knew her, and he was already jealous as hell. Devastator sipped his drink again and decided to size up the situation with another question.

"So why are you here with me, and not with your man," he asked, again watching her.

Boy, he is definitely to the point isn't he, Kayla thought. *Should I play with him some more,* she wondered, deciding against it. She actually liked him, and didn't want to risk turning him off.

"That's easy," Kayla said equally as calm. "I don't have a man, so he wouldn't know I was here with you, now would he?"

She looked Dezi directly in the eye.

Devastator liked her. She was cool with a wicked little sense of humor, he thought, seeing the smile playing at the corners of her mouth.

Devastator smiled, took another sip from his glass.

"Oh you like jokes do you?"

Devastator wanted to truly put her at ease and get close to this woman. He wanted her to be a part of his life. He knew more than anything else he wanted her around for a while. He put his glass down, leaned over and began to tickle her. It was just a guess on his part that she was ticklish, but it paid off well. Kayla giggled and laughed while she squirmed to get away from him.

That's what I'm talking about, Devastator smiled as he watched her beautiful face light up. He took the opportunity to hold her and pull her close. Damn, she felt good and smelled good. Devastator bet she tasted just as good.

"I'll let you go if you behave," he teased, very close to her ear.

He was actually enjoying holding her like this, feeling the warmth of her body.

Looking into those beautiful brown eyes, he knew he was gone already. Anything she wanted, he would give to her.

"OK, I'll be good, I promise," Kayla laughingly said.

She couldn't believe he did that to her, but she loved it. This one was okay with her so far. Maybe she would stick around a minute and see what was up. *Of course, the fringe benefits of these arms around me are a great incentive,* she giggled.

Devastator held her for a moment more, looking into those brown eyes, falling deeper every second that he did. He finally let her go. Kayla didn't move away from him. The ice was broken and now could really get to know each other. He wanted to kiss her, had to kiss her. He didn't act on that impulse though, not yet.

●●●

"You and your sister are total opposites," Dirty told Taea.

He liked her already. She didn't trip when he told her he wanted to call her just Tee like some sisters do about their name. She was sassy, upbeat, street, but classy with a body that didn't quit. Hell, he might think about paying a few bills for her and taking care of her for a minute if she acted right.

"Yeah we are, but that's what keeps us close," Taea responded. "If we were alike we probably couldn't stand each other."

This man is absolutely beautiful, Taea was thinking. *He is definitely creamy dark chocolate, nice abs, nice ass and very well endowed.* She giggled at that last thought, and Dirty gave her a look, but didn't say anything. He noticed her checking out the family jewels. He guessed she liked what she saw.

"So where your man at," Dirty asked again, playing with her hair.

She ignored his question the first time and this time he wanted an answer.

"I'm not seeing anyone right now," Taea answered.

That was a good thing in Dirty's book. He hated competition. He and Devastator were definitely alike on that. Dirty actually was beginning to think he found someone he wanted to make that number one woman.

"Where is your woman," Taea fired back interrupting his thoughts.

She wasn't going to be one in a harem of women. She wanted this one all to herself.

Damn, he liked her! She was fiery. *Bet she is a demon in bed too*, Dirty thought smiling.

"I'm living the single life right now baby girl," he answered.

Taea seemed to be satisfied with that for now.

"You wanna play pool? We got a table in the room next door," Dirty asked Taea, wanting to get her completely alone.

Maybe he would get some sugar from her or touch that beautiful body he spent most of the evening looking at.

I want to play a lot more than pool, Taea was thinking. *I'm going to hafta sample some of this tonight*, she thought. *He is too damned fine to let go home and not even have a taste.*

Taea never met a man who intrigued her the way Eric did. It wasn't just looks, it was the total package. She loved the way he talked to her and the way he made her feel special without even trying. She promised not to leave Kayla alone though, knowing how she felt being in a strange place out of her element.

Taea looked over where Kayla and Dezi sat, noticing them sitting closer. Of course, with their backs to her, she couldn't see Kayla's face. *If she's sitting that close she must be OK*, Taea was thinking, *but still*.

Dirty saw her face and read her mind.

"Look, your girl is in good hands. Dezi is good people. He ain't gonna hurt her or do anything to her she don't want done," Dirty looked her in the eye.

Taea got a good feeling about what Eric said and she believed him. She noticed that Dezi was mesmerized by Kayla since he walked up to her. Taea decided it would be fine.

"OK, let's go play. Don't be crying and stuff when I beat you," she teased Dirty, already thinking way ahead to some of the wagers she would get him to make once they started playing.

Yeah, Taea liked this baller, and she wasn't gonna let him get away too easily.

"Girl come on, let me show you how it's done," Dirty laughed as he got up and took her hand to go to the pool room. *Yeah*, he thought, *this one might be all right.*

A Deadly 5 Encounter

They were all in the poolroom now. Kayla admitted to herself she was having the time of her life. Dezi was unlike any man she ever met. They talked for a while after Taea and Eric left to play. She found him to be charming, intelligent, caring and extremely gentle for someone with his reputation. Kayla guessed this was a side he didn't share often, since it would definitely not serve to make him the revered demigod he was.

She and Taea excused themselves to go to the ladies room, so they could talk of course.

"We'll be right back and don't be trying to stack the table either," Taea playfully told Eric, who lost the last three games to her.

Which, Kayla figured was on purpose. She could tell Eric really liked Taea.

"Whatever," Eric laughed.

They headed down the hallway to the ladies room, which was just as decadently decorated as the entire VIP area. They obviously spared no expense on the amenities.

"OK girl, dish it," Taea jumped on her as soon as they were alone in the ladies room.

"He's great," Kayla giggled. "Fine to death, smart, sensitive and from what I can see, well equipped for the task!"

Taea laughed too, thinking how she too already sized up Dirty's manly assets.

"Yeah I think Eric is great, too. I mean surprisingly, neither of them are stuck on themselves."

"You're right," Kayla again responded. "They're both pretty down to earth."

"I did not know men looking like that were number one: still straight and number two: walking free and unattached," Taea said and they cracked up.

"OK, so on the scale, and you know the deal, what's the number," Taea asked looking at Kayla levelly and waiting for her response.

It didn't take Kayla long to answer that one.

"Girl please, definitely a 10!"

They both laughed again.

"And you," she asked Taea when they stopped laughing.

"OK what's higher than 10!" Taea replied, again peeling into laughter.

They couldn't believe these guys, and how great they seemed to be. They became quiet, exchanging looks of both caution and warning. The scale was what they used to tell each other what they thought of the men they just met. It wasn't just looks, but personality, finances, and of course whether they would sleep with them. Both Dezi and Eric passed with flying colors.

As they walked back to the poolroom, Kayla glanced onto the dance floor and saw someone she thought was vaguely familiar.

"Taea, isn't that Adrian," Kayla asked pointing.

"Where girl," Taea answered trying to see through the sea of people on the floor beneath them.

"Right there in the blue shirt," Kayla responded again, still pointing.

Following her friend's finger, she finally saw him.

"Girl no, he just looks like Miss Thang," Taea continued. "Come on, let's get back to our game."

They entered the room as the guys were obviously in deep conversation, stopping once they arrived.

"You two musta been talking about us," Taea teased.

"We could say the same for you two and your bathroom trip," Dirty threw back as Taea playfully rolled her eyes at him.

"Aww, don't be like that baby girl," Dirty told Taea, hugging her.

She kissed him on the cheek in response. *Perfect*, Dirty thought. *Here's the chance I been waiting on.* Dirty smiled and kissed Taea on the mouth.

She didn't pull away; he was glad of that. Taea gave him yet another surprise. She put her arms around him and kissed him back.

Devastator smiled and turned away. He wanted so much to do the same thing to Kayla, but he would be patient. He wanted it to be the perfect moment. He wouldn't rush it and lose this one. She was everything he wanted in a woman and Devastator was determined to have her.

Kayla walked over to the window to watch the people continue to dance below. She saw Monster wading through the throngs of people and wondered where he was going. She also wondered if Dezi would try to kiss her, equally wondering if she would let him. Things were moving a little too fast for her. She was hurt before, badly. She was in no hurry to repeat that drama. She decided to not worry about it, just react when or if it should happen. Coming back to the moment, Kayla saw Monster make his way through the crowd and tap the DJ on the shoulder. He leaned over, saying something in the man's ear. She saw him give Monster thumbs up and smile.

They all started playing pool again once Taea and Eric ended their kiss. Kayla beat Dezi two out of the five games they played. She teased him for a while until he threatened to tickle her again.

"Sore loser," she laughingly replied as Dezi agreed and continued to play.

"Do you have a curfew or can I keep you out a little longer," Devastator playfully asked Kayla after they finished the last game.

"I think I might be able to hang out with you a little while longer," she said laughing.

Devastator didn't ever want her to go home. He wanted to be with Kayla all night. He just met this woman, but she already captured his heart in a way no other woman touched him in a long time.

"Let's go to the house and chill," Taea suggested. "We have mad DVDs," she added.

Kayla knew her friend well enough to know that Taea was plotting. She almost laughed out loud at Taea trying to sound innocent and sincere. Taea wanted a piece of Eric and she wanted it on her own home turf.

Devastator jumped at the idea. He wanted to be around Kayla as long as possible, and if she were already home he didn't have to worry about time. Devastator could stay with her as long as she would allow him.

"Sounds like a plan to me," he answered.

Dirty was all for it too, having his own plan for Taea tonight. He wanted to see just what a demon in bed she really was and she already let him know it was on and popping.

"I'll have your car brought around and we'll follow you," Devastator told Kayla while they were on their way downstairs.

"That's fine," Kayla replied.

Her head was spinning. She was thrilled at the fact Dezi was coming home with her, yet terrified at the same time. She wasn't ready to go there with him yet. Kayla wasn't like Taea on that end of the spectrum. She was slow and deliberately cautious when it came to sex. She didn't want another Chris episode on her hands. She gave that bastard her virginity, and he cheated on her.

Kayla felt Dezi looking at her, and snapped out of her memories of her sordid past. She turned and looked into his eyes. Dezi was staring at her and smiling. *What the hell is he thinking,* Kayla wondered. *Damn those dimples,* she thought again, knowing she was no match for the power they held over her. Kayla kept wondering what those perfect lips would feel like on hers. Dezi interrupted her thoughts.

"Do we need to stop and pick up anything on the way?"

"We have plenty of snacks and such, but it want something special to drink, you can stop and get that," Kayla answered.

●●●

"OK heffa," Kayla laughed when she and Taea were alone in the car speeding down the interstate on the way home. "You do have condoms right," she laughed again.

"Girl, you know I gots plenty of condoms," Taea giggled.

Kayla didn't think Taea should sleep with Eric so soon, but Taea was a big girl and made her own decisions.

"Girl, I hope it's all I think it is," Taea said. "When we were kissing, whew, I was wet and ready right there girl!"

They both laughed.

"Well try not to be too loud, because I'm not going there with Dezi right now." Kayla playfully chided her best friend.

"You better not heffa," Taea admonished her.

"OK, but you're going there," Kayla countered laughing.

"That's right, 'cause I'm grown, you is still a young one," Taea laughed.

"Seriously though, I know you aren't ready for that yet, and I want to make sure this buster doesn't hurt you," Taea said, holding Kayla's hand. "You my girl, my sister, and I'm not gonna see anybody hurt you again."

Taea was fiercely protective of her best friend and she would literally kill the next joker that hurt Kayla like that moron Chris. Kayla still didn't know to this day how Taea paid the two guys from the hood to go whip his ass. They messed Chris up good too. Taea thought about the lame lie he told Kayla when she saw him the next day. That he was mugged. *Yeah right. Trifling dog!* Taea smiled in secret.

"I wouldn't mind if he kissed me though," Kayla interjected, bringing Taea back to now.

Taea was glad to see her friend happy and interested in someone again, praying Dezi didn't hurt her. They both broke into laughter again.

"Oh, trust me sistah girl, he will. He's been waiting for that chance all night," Taea said. "I saw it all over him."

Then Taea cautioned Kayla. "Be careful with this one. He gives me the impression he can hold on pretty tight, and not know when to let go. Feel me?"

Taea was actually telling Kayla something Eric said to her about Dezi that bothered her. Taea didn't want her friend in any danger. Although Eric assured her Dezi would never hurt Kayla, Taea wasn't completely sold on that yet. Kayla nodded that she understood. Kayla thought about what her friend said, and wondered what exactly Taea wasn't telling her. She let it pass and concentrated on making sure Dezi didn't charm the clothes off her this evening.

•••

"Here we are," Taea announced. "Home sweet home," as they entered the house.

Devastator and Dirty talked on the way, laughing about how fast Kayla drove. They both were impressed with the house when they drove up. Taea told Dirty earlier that Kayla bought the house and they lived there together.

She told him a lot about Kayla's investments and her financial stability, as well as her own, reiterating that neither she nor Kayla were anybody's gold diggers.

The house was in an exclusive subdivision outside the city with huge private wooded lots. It boasted 7 bedrooms, 5 ½ baths, great room, workout room, formal dining, den w/fireplace and a wraparound deck with a wonderful view. It also had another unique feature of hosting three master bedrooms. Kayla and Taea's bedrooms were on opposite sides of the house. Taea told Dirty that earlier when he asked whether the noise they would surely make would disturb Kayla and Dezi.

"Can I get the grand tour," Devastator asked, looking directly at Kayla.

"Sure come on," she replied taking his hand.

Kayla hoped he didn't feel her trembling, she was so nervous. She started with the downstairs where the den was and where they would be later. It was very nicely furnished with a comfortable couch and two recliners directly in front of the 52-inch big screen television with home theater attached. They made their way through the living room, dining room and kitchen before heading upstairs. Devastator loved every room of her home. It was warm and comfortable. Kayla had great taste in everything it seemed; art, books, furnishings and colors. Taea told Dirty that she wasn't into decorating. Kayla did the entire house except for Taea's room.

As they toured the house, Devastator thought about how nice it would be to have Kayla at home every night when he got there. Damn, he was tripping again, but Devastator couldn't help thinking that he wanted a future with this woman. They were coming up to her bedroom, which he was definitely interested in seeing and spending some time in. You could tell a lot about a woman from her room. Kayla opened the door and invited Dezi in. The room was beautifully alive with color.

There was a chaise lounge by the window with a book resting on it. The queen-sized bed was adorned with a vibrant multicolor comforter and equally vibrant decorative pillows. Devastator could see himself waking up there with her. Kayla took Dezi over to the window to show him the view, which was beautifully accented with endless trees that danced along the skyline, certainly a sight to behold at both sunrise and sunset.

"I would rather have purchased one by the ocean, but Taea is deathly afraid of water," Kayla admitted.

Devastator watched Kayla as she talked, deciding the time was finally right for that kiss he wanted. He stepped behind her as she talked. Kayla would be right in his arms when she turned around.

"There aren't any pool restrictions," Kayla said. "So I'm thinking about putting one over there, in the corner area, under those trees. What do you think," she asked, turning to get his answer.

It put her in exactly the position Devastator was waiting for.

OK, show time. he thought, reaching down, gently stroking her face, and tilting her head up to him, Devastator kissed her lightly on the lips. Kayla held her breath. He looked into her eyes, saw that she was willing, and kissed her again, this time deeply and passionately.

When Devastator finally pulled away, Kayla knew if he wanted her right now, she lost the fight. She was completely consumed with the kiss he had just given her. She never enjoyed a man that kissed her like that. Now, there are men that can kiss, then there are men that can really kiss. Dezi was definitely the latter.

Devastator couldn't believe how right that felt. He wanted to take Kayla right then and there, but promised he would be patient. Devastator wanted it to be right for both of them when it happened. He wanted to make sure she didn't regret it when they did finally make love. However, he did kiss Kayla again, long and passionately. He didn't see the need to deny himself that pleasure.

They were back in the den watching a movie and Kayla's mind was still reeling from the kisses shared upstairs. *Oh my God*, she thought, *if he kisses me like that again, I'm gonna be the one ripping his clothes off.* Kayla smiled at the thought. She changed into a tank top and shorts. Devastator thought she looked great. He got more comfortable himself, taking off his shoes, tie and cufflinks. He kept an overnight bag in the car, but he wouldn't bring that up unless Kayla asked him to stay, and he hoped with everything in him, she would.

"You're awfully quiet," Kayla said softly, stroking his hair, breaking his thought. Devastator was lying with his head in her lap.

"I'm cool, just enjoying the movie," he responded, thinking *if she only knew how much I really want to be upstairs with her*, and wondering what it would be like to wake up next to her later in the morning. At that moment, his cell went off. Devastator looked at the number. It was Monster. Monster didn't call unless things went very, very bad. *Fuck!* He thought, *Trouble*.

Devastator got up and spoke. "I gotta go handle this business right quick."

Kayla was taken aback but recovered quickly. Dezi asked her to go get Eric. There was an emergency to take care of.

"OK, I'll go get him" Kayla said, sensing the urgency in Dezi's voice.

Devastator wasn't upset about the thing they were about to handle. He could deal with any of the standard bullshit that came up from the business. It was having it tear him away from Kayla when he was so close to staying the night with her.

Devastator didn't want her to think this was habit. He ran his business well enough that he could lead a semi normal existence most times, and he wanted that very much with her now.

Dirty came around the corner dressed and alert. He knew things must be heavy for Devastator to bail when he was where he obviously wanted to be.

"Let's roll man," Dirty said. "I told Tee I would be back later after we handle this business."

Devastator needed to handle that end, too. "Cool, go ahead to the car; I need to tell Kayla something. I'll be right out,"

Dirty nodded and headed out to the car. Devastator went to get Kayla. He found her in the kitchen with Taea making some herbal tea. He walked in, pulling Kayla to him, spoke softly as he stroked her hair.

"I'll be back, if that's okay with you."

Kayla smiled that smile he already loved.

"Yeah, that's fine."

Devastator kissed her again, passionately, hugged her and told her softly in her ear, "I'm falling hard for you."

Then as quickly as he said it, he was gone. Kayla was stunned. Taea was looking at her quizzically.

"Well," she demanded. "What the hell did he say to you? You look like you just saw a ghost."

Taea hoped Dezi wasn't starting already. Taea told Eric she got a bad feeling about him. Eric told her she was way off on this one. Dezi was cool peeps and Taea would see that in time. Now, watching her friend, she wasn't so sure.

Kayla needed a moment to gather her thoughts, what did Dezi mean falling hard? Kayla knew she was already far more caught up than she should be, but was he in the same place, too? You're not supposed to feel this way about someone only hours after meeting are you, Kayla asked herself. She didn't know, but she felt it.

"He told me he was falling hard for me," Kayla answered as she went to sit at the kitchen table.

Taea came over and began to smooth her friend's hair. She was wondering how much of her conversation with Eric she should repeat. She promised herself she would watch Kayla's back for her, but now, Taea wondered if she should tell Kayla everything. Taea decided against it, only to tell Kayla what she felt she needed to know right now.

"Kayla," Taea began. "From what Eric tells me, Dezi doesn't love easily. He's very leery of women, and doesn't trust them, but when he does fall, he falls hard, and I would say Dezi has fallen real hard for you."

Taea was quiet for a moment before she continued, choosing her words carefully. "So what are you gonna do about it," she asked softly.

Kayla didn't know what to say. She was really attracted to this man. She could easily fall for Dezi, but should she? There were warning signs. She thought about what he really did for a living. Could she be with someone she knew was doing illegal stuff? Maybe even killing people? Kayla thought about her businesses and reputation. She needed to consider all of that if Dezi were ever busted and linked to her. She thought about what Taea told her earlier about it being their job, but Kayla wasn't so sure she could deal with it.

Dezi was so damned perfect though. He was everything Kayla wanted in a man. He made her feel emotions she hadn't felt since, well hell, since never. Kayla wanted Dezi and she wanted to be with him, that much was true. She really needed to search within for the answers to those other nagging questions and doubts though, and the time was now. Kayla got the impression Dezi was not a man who took rejection well at all, and if she wanted to bail, she better do it now.

A Deadly 6 Encounter

They were heading down the interstate toward MLK, Jr. Blvd and Haynes Avenue, better known as the lowers. This was the section of town where the poorer working class families lived out their existence. They owned a club there named Whispers that catered to their type of party and it always did banner business.

"What the fuck could be going on at this damn club tonight that Monster needed to call our ass," Dirty growled.

He was right in the middle of what promised to be some of the best sex of his life. Thankfully, they were still working on the foreplay when Kayla knocked.

"He said the cops were involved in the shit," Devastator replied, in his own angry state.

Whoever or whatever called him out to this place was going to pay the price for making him leave Kayla before he was ready to.

"Try to call Monster's ass back," he told Dirty. "We need to know what the fuck we're walking into."

They were almost to the club when Dirty hung up with monster.

"He said some muthafucker's came in and torched shit. Said they was rolling with Bone and didn't 'preciate the shit that went down today," Dirty told Devastator.

"Monster caught the one with the biggest mouth. He's holding that son of a bitch at the spot for us," Dirty said, knowing they both were thinking the same thing about that loser.

"Well, let's go see what the damage is to the club first. That muthafucker ain't going anywhere," Devastator spat, seeing blood already.

They arrived at Whispers ten minutes later. The club was totaled. The roof collapsed and it was basically a shell.

"Look at all our fucking money up in smoke," Devastator said to Dirty, who nodded in agreement.

The fire crew was putting out the last few hot spots when they drove up. Devastator called Todd en route, his business manager, to come handle things. Devastator kept a low profile for the most part when dealing with the police. He didn't like them, and they sure as hell didn't like him. Except for the few Devastator kept employed to keep him aware of what was going on in the city, he didn't bother with them at all.

He and Dirty watched Todd deal with the fire chief and police, so they knew that was being taken care of. They turned their attention to the guest Monster held waiting for them; leaving the parking lot and heading for the spot. They made a quick stop at the house and changed their clothes. They didn't dress this nice to get blood on their shit.

"Where this asshole at," Dirty asked as soon as he walked in and spoke to Monster.

"I'm sorry for interrupting you evenings, but I knew you would want to deal with this asshole yourselves," Monster apologized.

"Well, let's do this shit. I have other things I would much rather be doing," Devastator said.

Dirty couldn't believe his ears, but he was happy to hear it. That meant there wouldn't be the usual long drawn out drama before they killed this fool. Hell, he wanted to get back to Taea his damn self. Dirty started getting aroused thinking about her and consciously reigned his thoughts in. Monster took them to the room he put the loudmouth in. They walked in and he turned around.

"Damn," Dirty swore under his breath.

Devastator knew exactly what he meant. He was just a kid, couldn't be more than 15 at the most. There was something else about him, too. The kid was the spitting image of his father, Cobra. The sonofabitch Devastator killed when The Clique started.

"What's your name kid," Devastator asked taking a seat.

"What the fuck is it to you," the kid spat back full of foolish adolescent bravado.

Devastator, normally patient and amused by banter like this, really wasn't in the mood tonight. He had half a mind to pull his .9mm out and do the little bastard right now. *Hell, like father like son* he thought, but continued.

"Look, you just torched a hundred thousand dollars' worth of our property. Your shit is hanging by a thread. So if I were you, I would chill on all that macho bullshit you're trying to sell," Devastator warned the kid, the familiar dead monotone in his voice he got when he was ready to kill.

Wanting to hurry and get this done and back to Taea, Dirty added, "Yeah, cause it ain't gone get your ass nothing but killed up in this piece."

The kid, looking at Devastator and Dirty, finally realized the magnitude of the situation and decided to cooperate.

"They call me Lil' Cobra," the kid answered finally.

Figures, Dirty thought.

"Well Lil' Cobra I want to know who sent you to our club and why," Devastator asked.

His eyes changed and the kid noticed the emotion gone from them. They were flat and lifeless. He actually began to be afraid he was going to die for the first time since the two of them walked in the door.

"A couple guys gave me and my crew a grand to go do it," the kid continued in a small, frightened voice. "Said all we had to do was walk in, say we was Bone's crew, break a couple liquor bottles and torch the place."

Devastator sighed heavily, growing more impatient. "Who were the guys," he asked evenly, not betraying the smoldering anger he felt at the moment.

"And don't lie fucker," Dirty interrupted before the kid could say anything stupid. "Your ass is already in enough trouble."

He, too, was growing impatient. The longer this little bastard took to give them the info they wanted, the longer Dirty had to wait to get back to Taea.

"It was Slick and Beanie," the kid blurted, trying to save his life now, hoping this information had done just that.

Well, I'll just be damned, Devastator thought. *What the fuck was wrong with all these people? Why was everyone intent on trying him today?*

"OK kid, thanks for the info," Devastator said to him casually, turning around to leave.

They walked toward the door without looking back.

Dirty yelled over his shoulder, "Monster, let him loose, we're finished with him."

So Slick and Beanie were trying to flex were they, Devastator thought. They were small time hoods who also shared visions of grandeur like Bone. He guessed they all gathered together and worked out a plan for the takeover. So with Bone dead, these two jackasses figured they would pick up where he left off? Wrong answer. Well, if they wanted to play, he would play with them.

Dirty was watching Devastator intently since they got in the car. He remained silent. That was a very bad sign things were going to get real ugly. Finally, Devastator broke his silence.

"Call Monster, have him get the Front 5, and bring them to that hole in wall club Slick and Beanie hang out in, " Devastator said calmly and coldly.

Shit! Dirty thought, now he knew it was going to be bad. The Front 5 was what Devastator called the hired guns they employed when they wanted to shoot up everything and everyone in a place they were going to visit. Devastator wanted a bloodbath tonight and he was definitely about to get one. Dirty called Monster who answered on the first ring.

"I'm on my way."

●●●

They arrived at the sleazy, rundown dive about 15 minutes later. It was nestled between a laundry mat and a custom frame store. The neighborhood was mostly abandoned shops along the strip they stood in front of, but a few of the businesses managed to survive the great urban flight.

The Front 5 were already there waiting for them. Devastator got out of the car, went into the trunk and pulled out one of the two AK-47s they brought. Dirty took the other. They met Monster and the Front 5 at the Hummer and, together, walked into the front door of The Half Moon club.

Slick was sitting at a table in the corner with his back to them and a half drunken woman sitting next to him. There were about eight other people in the club.

Too bad, Dirty thought, *All you fuckers fixing to die,* he mused. Beanie was facing the door and saw them come in. He jumped up and tried to run. Dirty cut him down before he could take three steps. Everyone started to scream and panic. One of the Front 5 fired several warning shots in the air.

"Shut the fuck up," Devastator raised his voice.

Once they quieted down, Dirty heard lots of moans, prayers and crying.

"You," Devastator spoke. "Get the fuck out," he ordered the bartender.

He would be the one witness to give the warning to any other aspirers with visions of taking on The Clique to be wary because they were nothing to play around with. The bartender didn't need to be asked twice. He ran out of the door and didn't stop running until he was as far away from the club as his legs would carry him.

As soon as the door swung closed, the mayhem began. Devastator, Dirty, Monster and the Front 5 opened fire on every living thing in the club. Men and women alike were killed. They shot up everything, including the bar, the liquor bottles, the tables, chairs and jukebox. The carnage seemed to go for hours, when in reality only a few scant minutes. After the smoke cleared, there was no one left alive or moving in the club.

The Front 5 admired their handiwork. They took all the jewelry, money, wallets and purses. Devastator didn't mind. It was their trophy and he didn't need it. They left. Dirty knew they would meet up later and settle the debt. After admiring the handiwork one last time, Dirty lit his cigarette and flicked the match into the spilled liquor. The place went up like a torch. They calmly exited the club and went their separate ways.

After tonight's message anyone with any doubt will know The Clique will still kill that ass! Dirty closed his eyes and turned his thoughts back to Taea, and what he was going to do to her when he got back to her house. It brought a huge smile to his face.

● ● ●

The phone was ringing. Kayla looked over at the clock on her nightstand; it was 5:30 a.m.

"Hello," she answered sleepily.

Devastator smiled into the receiver. She even sounded sexy half awake.

"Hi," he said softly. "I'm back. Can I come in?"

It took Kayla a couple of seconds to clear the cobwebs and realize she was talking to Dezi.

"Yeah, I'll be down in a couple minutes," she replied still trying to gather herself.

"Well, actually," Devastator told her chuckling lightly. "I'm right outside your bedroom door."

What the hell, Kayla thought. *Damn, Taea must have let them in.* She was completely naked. She liked to sleep that way, but she couldn't let him see her like that, not yet anyway.

"OK, give me a sec, then come on in," Kayla told Dezi and hung up.

She jumped out of bed to find a reasonable nightie, brush her teeth and wash her face. Devastator smiled again, thinking she wanted to run brush her teeth or something.

He waited exactly three minutes and came in, hoping to catch her naked. God she looked good, Devastator thought as he watched her. She was dressed in a cute pink nightie, not grandma, but not hooker either, perfect middle ground. He loved it, liked the way it moved with her. Kayla was walking back to the bed when he came in.

Devastator drank her in from head to toe. The nightie was sheer enough that he could tell she was braless. Her breasts were beautiful with full round nipples and they were hard. Was she aroused, Devastator wondered, aroused himself by the thought.

She was also wearing a thong, pink like her nightie. *Very nice*, Devastator smiled and turned his head away, allowing Kayla to get into bed and himself to cool off. She pulled her hair back in a ponytail, which was cute on her and she smelled divine. He saw the Victoria's Secrets earlier. Devastator wanted this woman in the worst way. This was going to be a long morning.

"Everything OK," Kayla asked softly looking at Dezi intently.

"Yeah, everything is cool now," he told her, which was true.

Devastator was sure they squashed any more drama that might come up behind Bone. He sat on the bed and leaned over to kiss her. He needed that right now more than anything.

"So do you wanna lay down," she asked. "You look exhausted."

Kayla couldn't believe she was saying the stuff coming out of her mouth. How the hell was she going to succeed in keeping her legs closed with this man lying right next to her? Especially with the way Dezi loved to kiss her.

"Yeah, I'm beat," he replied as he lay on the comforter.

Devastator kicked his shoes off and got fully on the bed. He was still dressed. He decided before they got here that he wouldn't get under the covers with her. He wasn't made of steel, and he didn't want to rush her. Devastator didn't realize how tired he was until he laid his head on her pillow or maybe it was how good Kayla felt in his arms as he held her. Either way, Devastator was asleep in no time.

●●●

"Oh shit baby, yeah," Dirty was saying. "Ride it girl, damn!"

Dirty's eyes were closed and he was obviously enjoying every sensation, Taea smiled. She too was enjoying this bucking bronco. He was everything she hoped. They enjoyed wonderful foreplay when he came back. Dirty licked her everywhere and knew just what he was doing at the buffet table. Now, Taea was enjoying all nine inches Dirty offered. She felt him getting faster in his rhythm and knew he was getting ready to cum. She was damn near there herself.

"Hellllllll yes!" Taea heard Dirty cry out as he released. She reached her orgasm at exactly the same time he did and they both collapsed.

Wow! This one was definitely a keeper, Taea thought. They smoked a joint afterward and relaxed. Dirty was quiet and thoughtful for quite a while. Taea wondered what the hell he was so preoccupied with.

"So what's the verdict baby girl," Dirty finally asked her.

What the hell was he talking about? The sex or them, Taea was trying to figure out.

"This some good ass chronic," Taea answered, deliberately avoiding the question she wasn't sure of.

Dirty laughed. "No girl, I'm talking about tonight, us, this whole thing."

Now she had a handle on what the hell was going on. Taea could actually field this one.

"Tonight was great, and you were spectacular!"

That brought another smile to his face.

"So you want it to be a one-time thing or you wanna hang out for a while," Dirty asked again.

Taea guessed this was his way of establishing a relationship with her, and hell yes, she definitely wanted one with this man. Taea got him back though. She was quiet for a long time until she felt his eyes piercing her then she answered.

"I think I would like to hang out for a while, sounds like a plan," Taea answered a lot cooler than she felt.

She was very excited and happy to have finally met someone she felt was worth her time and energy.

Dirty was pleased. He knew Taea was messing with him taking her time to answer his question. It was cool though. He loved that sassiness about her.

"OK, so we're on then," Dirty replied and that was that.

They began to kiss and made love again before drifting off into fitful, contented sleep.

● ● ●

She knew he was tired. Dezi was breathing deeply now, snoring lightly. Kayla smiled inwardly as she lay there looking at him. She was actually awake now. She couldn't go right back to sleep after he awakened her, but she didn't want to move too much and disturb his rest. Kayla carefully turned over on her side, so her back was to him. Dezi pulled her closer, one of his hands brushing her breast and began to mumble in her ear.

Kayla thought he was awake but realized he was still sleeping. Dezi was speaking softly, almost inaudibly, but distinctly in Italian. Kayla would try and remember the words so she could ask Isabella, her Italian housekeeper, what they meant. She looked at the clock again. It was 6:45. She was suddenly sleepy as she closed her eyes and drifted off.

A Deadly 7 Encounter

Taea was thinking about her life again as she dressed heading out with Kayla to do a little shopping. She smiled slightly thinking of her childhood. She was always a willful and outspoken child and that didn't change into adulthood. She always did what she wanted to do when she wanted to do it.

Taea held a wonderful job with a retail leasing company and was doing well for herself. She was glad to have gone on to school and getting her degree.

She thought about her siblings periodically, and wondered how they were doing. Once she left South Carolina to go college with Kayla, she never looked back. Kayla always kept Taea grounded and levelheaded, and Taea always protected Kayla, who trusted everybody.

Taea liked Eric. He was different and special to her. He reminded her of some of the guys she used to know back home. He was kind of slow, but she didn't care. He was genuine and real. Something most of the guys she met here definitely were not. Taea hoped they would be together for a long time. She really did want to settle down.

She remained realistic however about Eric being a gangster, a very dangerous one at that. She didn't think he would ever hurt her though. Taea could tell Eric really cared for her in his own rough, but sweet way. She cared for him, too. Besides, she needed him around to keep her updated on what Dezi was up to. That brother was going to take watching. Kayla was her girl and Taea loved her, but even best friends have to keep secrets sometimes.

•••

Adrian arrived at work by 9:55 after having one seriously bad night. Joe yelled a good morning at him when he walked in. Adrian managed to sound like his normal self when he yelled it back. He hoped no one would ask about his eye. It was a trophy from last night's breakup and confrontation. He thought he did a good job covering it with the concealer and foundation. They knew Adrian was gay, so he hoped they would just think he was being extra gay today with the makeup.

He began setting up for the brunch and lunch crowd that they would surely get on a Saturday.

Adrian wanted to think of something other than his messed up life right now. He wondered how the girls made out last night. He wondered if Kayla got to see Devastator naked yet. Adrian laughed quietly, despite the pain he still felt in his ribs. He surely would have had Devastator stripped and ready if it were him. Adrian chuckled again and looked at the clock. It was 10:55.

"Open the doors man," Joe yelled at Adrian from the kitchen.

He went and unlocked the doors as Le Bistro opened for business.

Business was brisk, even for 11:45 in the morning. Adrian was waiting on his fourth table when unknown to him, Kayla's ex-boyfriend Chris walked in. He sat at another table out of Adrian's section, but he definitely would not have minded waiting on the man. Chris was about 6'2" and built very nicely. Almost put Adrian in the mind of Devastator, but not as defined and no dimples.

Hmm, gonna hafta get the 411 from Barb, he made a mental note, the other server who was waiting on the man.

●●●

Chris heard Kayla ate here all the time. He would stay here all day if necessary. He wanted to see her, had to see her. A little more than a year passed since she broke up with him and stormed out of his apartment. It was his fault. He was a complete asshole.

Chris didn't even go after her. He was really stupid then. He loved Kayla, but he wanted to be a dog. He thought he could keep her and have his side fun, too. He knew now that he was wrong and that he lost a really good woman.

Now, Chris was determined to get her back no matter what it took. He figured he wouldn't need to be here that long. Chris knew her well and Kayla was a creature of habit. She loved to shop on Saturday. So more than likely she and Taea, whom Chris couldn't stand, would be here around noon to eat, and then hit the stores for the day. *If Kayla wasn't here by 2:00, then he would leave*, Chris thought. It meant she wasn't coming today.

"Hi, what can I get for you today," the server asked Chris.

"I'll have some coffee for now please," Chris smoothly replied, giving her his best smile and looking her over.

She wasn't half bad he thought. She smiled back and left to get his coffee. His cell rang.

"Yeah," he answered.

"Don't forget our little arrangement," Monster said, immediately striking fear in Chris's heart.

"Yeah, I haven't forgotten, I'll have it for you," Chris said smoother than he felt.

"You better, cause if not, I'll be paying you a little visit, and you ain't gonna like that at all," Monster added before disconnecting the call.

"Damn," Chris swore under his breath.

He needed to get this debt taken care of. Gambling cost him big and now he was in a serious jam. Where was he going to get five grand? Chris was broke and pretty much borrowed out. He thought for a minute and then it hit him. Smiling slyly, he began to dial.

"Here's your coffee sir," the server returned. "Would you like anything to eat?"

This time she was the one doing the looking.

"As a matter of fact," Chris began. "Please bring me a steak, medium, with a baked potato and salad."

"Sour cream and butter for your potato," she asked

"Yes, that'll be fine, and make the dressing ranch for the salad," Chris added.

"I'll get it right out to you sir," she replied and was gone to get his food.

Chris didn't get an answer from the call. He didn't leave a message. The server returned moments later with his food. Feeling ravenous, Chris ate heartily while keeping a watchful eye out for Kayla.

●●●

As predicted, they walked in around 12:30. Chris saw Kayla as soon as she walked in. She was wearing low cut jeans and a pink tank. She wore her hair pulled up into a ponytail with a pink ribbon and pink stack sandals. She was smiling and talking. She was a vision. Taea was with her of course, which he hated because it meant he would have to wait for the chance to talk to her alone.

Chris hated Taea. She was always in the middle. Always messing things up when he could have worked it out with Kayla, giving her bad advice and always bringing up things to upset Kayla with him. Taea was the one who sent those two gorillas to his place. Chris missed a week of work behind that shit because they messed him up pretty good. Kayla still didn't know about that until this day. Well, he planned a little something for that bitch though, just wait. Chris wanted so much to go over and say hello to Kayla, but he continued to bide his time.

•••

"Girl it was great waking up with him this morning," Taea was telling Kayla.

They actually left the guys at home in bed. They told them they were going shopping. Kayla gave Dezi a key and the alarm code, asking him to lock the house when they left. They both possessed plenty of money, so she wasn't worried about them taking anything. He kissed her and told her he would be there when she got back. Kayla liked the way that made her feel. She liked having Dezi around.

"So, have you given any more thought to what you're gonna do about Dezi," Taea asked.

"Honestly, Taea I'm really into this guy. He makes me feel like a princess, and I like it," Kayla answered frankly, thinking of the night before.

"I would like to give it a try and see what happens. I just don't let myself think about his other life," Kayla continued. "He hasn't let it interfere so far, so I'm just gonna go with the flow."

Taea was thoughtful for a minute. She thought about what Eric told her and she was torn over what to do or say to her friend right now. Eric assured her repeatedly that Dezi would not hurt Kayla ever. Taea looked at her friend looking so happy and content and decided she would never tell Kayla. Not unless it was life or death, and Taea would make sure that never happened.

"Well, I'm happy for you girl. You deserve a Mister Right, especially after mister hell no," she said and broke into laughter.

Kayla laughed with her, feeling she was finally over Chris; excited about that. She remained in that prison far too long. Now, she was free and loving it.

Taea's cell buzzed on her hip. Kayla was talking to Adrian and didn't notice. She looked down and saw the text message. 'Meet me now, no attitude, no BS or Kayla will find out right now, signed C'.

Muthafucker! Taea thought. *What hole did he come out of? He wasn't even supposed to live in the city anymore last time she checked. Where was the dog?*

Taea looked around the restaurant. She spotted him sitting in a corner on the other side of the Bistro. Chris waved cheerfully, then pointed to the restroom, got up and headed there. Taea told Kayla she would be right back and headed to the restroom herself.

• • •

"What the fuck do you want," she asked Chris acidly.

Since there was definitely no love lost between the two, Chris didn't try hard to be civil either.

"I want five grand bitch, and don't lie and say you ain't got it," he told her.

Chris knew she did. He knew Kayla saw to it that Taea amassed plenty of money. She handled her finances for her, so there wasn't going to be any lying today. Taea thought about it for a minute and almost called his bluff, but she knew Kayla would never understand. It wasn't her nature to understand stuff like revenge. So Taea agreed to pay this slime.

"When, and where?"

"Monday, here, 3:00," Chris replied.

He knew Kayla would have come and gone by then and wouldn't see them conducting their business.

"Fine," Taea said looking at him distastefully. "Why are you back Chris? Just to blackmail me or what?"

Chris smiled. *This trick really is conceited.*

"No not really," he replied smoothly. "I'm here to get my woman and my life back."

Taea nearly laughed aloud at that statement. *Dezi is gonna kill this fool and I won't hafta ever worry about him again.*

"I'll be here Monday, don't be late," Taea told him as she gathered herself and walked away.

She hated Chris. She couldn't wait until Dezi got wind that he was trying to get back with Kayla. Taea already knew the end of that story. She actually did chuckle this time. She couldn't mention it yet though, not even to Eric. Not until he actually made contact with Kayla, but knowing Chris that would be soon. He was a snake and he would mess up. He always did.

Taea wondered what kind of trap he got himself into that he needed five grand. She didn't dwell on it too long.

●●●

With that small bit of business taken care of, Chris paid his check, took one last look at Kayla and quietly slipped out of the restaurant.

●●●

"Hey girl," Kayla said when she got back to the table. "Adrian was telling me about a cute guy he was checking out in here and wanted our opinion," she laughed.

Adrian returned with their desert.

"Who is this joker you looking at," Taea teased him.

"He was over there, but he musta dipped girl," he told them.

"What did he look like," Taea asked.

"Tall and chocolate, built up kinda like Dezi, but no dimples," Adrian told them.

Taea knew he was talking about Chris and fought hard to keep from frowning and giving herself away.

"Sorry we missed him," Kayla said still smiling.

Taea sipped her drink and said nothing.

"So, heffas," Adrian began, changing the subject. "What happened last night?"

They exchanged looks and both burst into laughter. That was all he needed to hear.

"You two heffas is grounded," Adrian told them laughing and walked away.

●●●

"Yo man, what time is the meeting tonight," Dirty asked Devastator.

They were in the den watching a game on ESPN.

"11:00, down at the lowers," he answered.

"That fucker better have all my shit this time," Devastator growled.

Dirty knew Devastator was pissed about Tony not having all the drugs. He was coming up short for the last two shipments and Devastator promised to slab him if he came up short again. Dirty knew he endured a bad night last night. He was wearing that look. Devastator had this recurring dream that always left him mean and hateful the next day. Dirty also noticed that he did a good job with Kayla this morning; she didn't suspect anything at all was wrong.

"Man, I gotta do something to shake this mood before my girl gets back," Devastator said. "You got some more chronic?"

Dirty told him he did and went to get it for him from Taea's room. After they smoked a few joints and popped a couple beers, he saw Devastator begin to mellow out. Dirty was relieved. Devastator was a mean sonofabitch when he was like that, although, Dirty still believed that Tony was going to find himself on a slab if the shit came up short tonight. Devastator was still a man of his word.

●●●

Devastator dreamed about his mother again last night. He hated that. Why couldn't he just forget her? Hell, she certainly forgot all about him. He was glad he was able to control that this morning when he was dealing with Kayla. He didn't want anything to cast a dark shadow on something that was coming along so wonderfully.

Devastator thought about how nice it was sleeping with her last night. He wanted to make love to her, but holding her was nice enough, too. It was already 6:48, and he knew they would be back soon. He told her he wanted to go out to dinner at 7:30. As soon as he completed his thought, Devastator heard the garage door lift.

"Hey baby," he greeted her with a long kiss.

This is really nice, Kayla thought. *I could get very used to this.*

"Hey there," she said back. "What have you two been doing," as she walked into the kitchen.

"Watched the game, chilled, just relaxed," he told her. "Something we don't get a chance to do often."

"Can I talk to you for a minute," Devastator asked now.

He was looking at Kayla levelly. He looked serious. Kayla was a little unsettled. *I wonder what's on his mind?*

"Sure, you wanna talk here," she asked still standing in the kitchen.

"No, let's go up to your room, if that's OK," he said still not betraying any particular emotion.

He is really starting to spook me now, Kayla thought.

"All right, let's go," she replied as they climbed the stairs to her room.

They walked in and he led her to the chaise lounge. Devastator asked her to sit down.

OK, this can't be good, Kayla fretted. He sat down beside her. He made up his mind before she got back that he wanted to know exactly where they were in this thing. If Kayla didn't want to be with him, Devastator needed to know that now. He was already in too deep but he needed an answer.

"I wanted you to know that I had a wonderful time with you last night. I've never met anyone quite like you," he paused. "And I need to know if you think we may be able to have something more than just a casual friendship."

Devastator stopped talking to look at Kayla and see if he could read her thoughts. She was deliberately keeping her face as neutral as possible. Kayla didn't want Dezi to see how damned excited she was about being with him.

"I really enjoyed being with you last night, too," Kayla responded.

Devastator's heart sank. He wasn't prepared for that. He thought they connected and that they could be together.

After what seemed like an eternity, Kayla looked him in the eye and spoke again.

"I would love to spend time with you. And yes, I think we can have more than a casual friendship."

This woman was gonna give him a heart attack, Devastator thought. He smiled and pulled Kayla to him, kissing her again. He was glad that was settled.

●●●

The four of them went to dinner at one of the new celebrity joints that just opened up. They had a great time teasing Taea, who wouldn't eat the calamari, once she found out what it was.

Dirty and Devastator had work to do tonight, so they sent the girls home in Dirty's Range Rover after dinner, and took the Porsche to go do the meet.

A Deadly 8 *Encounter*

They got to the lowers, or the Industrial district, as it was correctly supposed to be known, at 10:30. The huge yard was filled with warehouses, which were all closed this time of night. The vast maze kept the police from venturing too far during their nightly patrols and of course Devastator always got inside information on the nights they would visit from the officers on his payroll. The Front 5 were already in position. Devastator didn't leave anything to chance. He didn't trust Tony, and he surely wasn't about to leave himself, and Dirty, out in the open. It was 11:10. He was late again. Dirty knew Devastator was pissed and ready to draw blood. Tony arrived at 11:13.

"You late muthafucker," Dirty told him.

Devastator just looked at him.

"Look man, something came up, but I'm here now," Tony said being a wiseass.

"Where is the stuff," Devastator asked, finally speaking, ignoring the attitude from Tony.

"It's over here in the trunk," he replied.

Dirty sent Monster to the car's trunk to check out the contents. The Front 5 held Tony in their scopes from five different vantage points, each one ready to kill him as soon as the signal was given.

Monster checked the trunk finding the product. No shortages this time. He told Devastator as much, who directed him to cut and taste it. He had a feeling about the stuff. Monster took the next fifteen minutes doing as Devastator directed, finding that some of it was fake.

"The shit is wrong," Monster told Devastator who turned to Tony and spoke.

"So, you're trying to get over on The Clique with this bullshit?"

Tony saw the look on Devastator's face and knew he made a fatal error.

"Wait," Monster said. "Five of the blocks are fake. The rest is straight."

So he was short again, Dirty thought. *This muthafucker got a death wish, and that shit gonna get answered tonight.*

"Tony," Devastator began calmly. "Who are you giving the rest of my stuff, too?"

Tony thought for a minute. He wasn't selling it to anyone. He was trying to build his own supply and start his own dealings. Being the middleman for the sellers to bring the stuff to Devastator didn't give him the kind of money or lifestyle he wanted to live. So he started taking a few here and there. No harm no foul. Now, it caught up with him and he needed to think of something good, fast!

"Man look, these guys, they shake me down," Tony began. "I just give them enough that they leave me alone and don't kill me."

Devastator walked up to Tony. Looked him squarely in the eye and spoke again. "Do I fucking look like I just got off the damned turnip truck today?"

Tony nearly pissed himself. This guy was crazy, with a look that would refreeze ice.

"Here's what you're going to do Tony," Devastator began again. "You're gonna get my stuff, and you're gonna have it here for me tomorrow night at 11:00, not 11:01, not 11:13. And if you don't show up, I'm coming to your house, and I will kill every living, breathing thing in there. Do you understand what the fuck I am saying to you?"

Tony was terrified. He believed Devastator, without doubt, would carry out his threat. He shook his head yes, trying to not pee in his pants.

Devastator instructed Monster to get the stuff out of the trunk, minus the bad blocks. He then turned to Tony again and told him to get out of there.

Tony didn't need a second invitation.

Devastator wasn't done however. He told Dirty they were going to pay Tony's family a little visit. Dirty knew it was on now for real.

After their visit they smoked on the way back to the house. Devastator wanted to be with Kayla tonight, but he was still too out of it to trust himself around her. He enjoyed killing Tony and his family, minus the kids of course. He reflected on it and smiled again. They were particularly bloody and vicious this time, wanting to send a clear message to the next supplier they got. Devastator never wanted to let Kayla to see that side of him.

•••

The phone rang. Kayla looked at the clock, 2:00 a.m. She figured it must be Dezi.

"Hello," she said into the receiver.

Nothing.

"Hello?"

Again silence.

Kayla was getting a little rattled. She could hear them breathing, so she knew there was someone there, but this wasn't Dezi. He would have said something by now. She heard the click of the line disconnecting. Kayla looked at the caller I.D., but the number was private. She chalked it up to the wrong number, lay back down and closed her eyes.

•••

"Man, it was good to hear her voice," Chris said aloud, still holding the receiver.

He finally worked up the nerve to call her, but couldn't bring himself to say anything when she answered.

He was trying to figure out how he was going to approach her. He wondered if she was still as angry and hurt as before. He looked at the picture he kept of them together, holding each other, smiling, realizing he messed up royally. He hoped there was no one in her life. He didn't care if there was. He wasn't going to let anything stop him from having her again. He was her first, and he knew that would always make him special to her. He was counting on that to get her back.

•••

The phone was ringing again. It was 3:30.

"Hello," Kayla answered.

"Hey baby," Devastator said softly. "I'm sorry to wake you. I just wanted to hear your voice"

She smiled. This was Dezi.

"It's okay," she told him. "I was hoping you would call. I was thinking about you earlier."

Devastator smiled, liking the sound of that.

"It's all good baby, just hanging with the fellas tonight," he told her. "How about we get together tomorrow afternoon and I'll take you sailing?"

"That sounds like a plan," Kayla answered. "I have to go to the office for a little while in the morning, but after noon, I'm all yours."

"Why are you working on Sunday," Devastator questioned.

"There are some loose ends I need to tie up for a major buy, Monday," Kayla explained.

"Can I have your office number," Devastator asked, which she supplied.

"I'll call and check on you tomorrow," Devastator now spoke.

"Sure, that's fine," Kayla replied.

They said good night and hung up. Devastator handed the number to Monster.

"You know what do."

Monster nodded and took the paper from his hand.

A Deadly 9 *Encounter*

Damn, it was Monday again, Taea thought as she dressed for work. At least this was her half-day, so that made her a little happier. She didn't hate her job. It was actually cool. She just hated not being able to do what she wanted to do, when she wanted to do it. That would soon change. She managed a pretty decent nest egg, and now she was with Eric, with much capital of his own. Taea thought about her errand today, and whom she was meeting. It almost ruined her entire mood.

"I hate that fucker," Taea swore aloud.

She would swing by the bank after she got off at 1:00, and then meet his sorry ass at 3:00. She wished Chris would go ahead and make his move so she could clue Eric in on who he was and what he was up to. She really wanted Dezi to go ahead and kill him.

"Hey girl," Taea greeted Kayla in the kitchen. "I thought you would be gone by now."

Kayla smiled at her. "I'm on my way out the door now," she replied.

"Be careful and break the bank girl," Taea yelled after her as she left, grabbing her keys and heading for her own car.

She suddenly remembered Eric's truck in the driveway, so she drove that instead. It smelled like him and she liked that. She missed Eric and wanted some more of him. *She would definitely remedy that tonight when he came over*, Taea giggled.

• • •

Kayla looked at the speedometer. She was doing 85 miles per hour. *Not too bad*, she thought. She would get one helluva ticket if she got pulled over, but she loved the way this car drove. She put in a jazz CD and turned up the sound, replaying the weekend. Kayla couldn't believe how happy she was, or how quickly everything fell into place.

She saw her exit and worked her way over. She held a reserved parking space that came with the office she leased. Kayla got out and headed for the elevator. She was deep in thought about Dezi's sexy dimples, smiling inwardly.

Kayla saw the flowers as soon as she rounded the corner from the elevator.

"Wow, these are gorgeous," she said as she picked up the vase containing the two-dozen long stem red roses.

The card read simply, 'thinking of you.' Kayla smiled. *So this is why Dezi really wanted my office number*, she happily mused, picking up the flowers and heading inside to start her day. She would call Dezi in a couple hours and tell him thanks. He was in New York on business. She turned on her computer, made some coffee, and hit the speed dial on her phone to get the show on the road.

●●●

K. DeWitt, 519, the directory read. She did well for herself in the year they spent apart. Chris knew she would. She was always a great businesswoman.

He remained in the building since 9:30, ate breakfast and read the papers and magazines available. It was after 11:00. Chris longed to go up to her office and say hi, ask her if she liked the roses. He was yet to gather enough courage actually to go. *What if she calls security and throws me out*, Chris feared. *What if she tells me to go the hell or something?*

He wanted to believe Kayla would welcome him with open arms and tell him she still loved him, but Chris knew he was reaching. This was going to be a battle and he better be ready. He hurt Kayla deeply and it was going to be hard, if not impossible, to get her to trust him again.

Chris looked at his watch, 11:45. *OK, if I'm going to do this, I need to do it now*, he surmised, taking a deep breath, turning to the elevator and pressing the up button.

●●●

Devastator felt his cell going off. He checked the display. "Hey girl," he said cheerfully.

"Hey you," Kayla happily replied. "I absolutely love the flowers baby, thank you so much."

Devastator was completely caught off guard but recovered quickly.

"You're very welcome baby," he told her. "You know how much I love spoiling you."

Devastator heard her giggle, his mind going in different directions. *Who the hell sent her roses? What the hell was going on? Was someone trying to put the moves on his woman?* His blood was beginning to boil. Devastator was going to look into this shit as soon as he got Kayla off the phone.

He remained quiet for a moment before Kayla spoke again.

"I know you're busy honey, but I wanted to at least say thanks," she said.

"Never a problem when you call baby," Devastator told Kayla. "I'll call you later tonight."

"OK, baby, have a great day," Kayla told him and disconnected.

Devastator called Monster into the room, telling him what he needed and that he needed it yesterday.

"You got it boss," Monster told him, leaving to get the ball rolling.

Devastator was still brooding when Dirty came back from the store. Dirty was flying back tonight.

"Wassup man," he asked when he saw his friends expression.

"Somebody's got a death wish," Devastator replied coldly.

Dirty wondered what the hell happened to put his friend in such a foul mood. Everything was going smoothly with the deal they came to do, so what gave?

"So give me the details man," Dirty told him.

Devastator told him about his earlier conversation with Kayla, and the mysterious two-dozen red roses that were at her office.

Oh shit, Dirty thought, *he didn't know who this fool was, but he knew he was going to soon be deceased.*

He knew his friend well enough to know, this was one thing you didn't mess around with him about. It took Devastator years, at least four, to get over Sasha and find Kayla. He wouldn't let anything, or anyone, get in the way of that now.

This fool is walking around with a target on him, and his dumb ass doesn't even know it yet, Dirty thought.

Chris stepped off the elevator. Her office was around the corner.

OK, he primed himself, *here we go*. He took another deep breath and walked through her door.

"No, I don't want to hear about what you can't do," Kayla was angrily telling one of her vendors. "Tell me how you are going to fix it, and how fast you can do it."

Chris waited until he heard her hang up. *Maybe now is not a good time*, he thought. *She's already angry*.

"Don't punk out now man," he told himself. "You been waiting all this time to see her, go ahead and see her."

He already walked through the door into the reception area. Although Kayla worked for herself, she did have a small staff. There was Anne her receptionist, who didn't let much get by her. She was there for the last three years, along with a couple of runners that being the extent of her staff.

"May I help you," Anne asked the handsome, well-dressed man in front of her.

"I would like to see Ms. DeWitt please," Chris replied.

"Is she expecting you?"

"No, but I'm an old friend and I'm only in town for today," he lied.

"Hmmm, well let me see if she'll see you," Anne told him dialing Kayla, who told her yes, it was fine.

Kayla had no idea who could be coming to see her, but she had a few minutes to kill, and after her last phone call, it might be a nice diversion.

"You can go back to her office now sir, last door on your left," she told him.

"Thank you," Chris replied with a smile and began the longest walk of his life.

Chris knocked lightly on her closed door.

"Come in," Kayla called out pleasantly.

He opened the door and walked in. Kayla was sitting at her desk facing the window. After hearing the door open, she turned around and her mouth froze before she could say hello.

"Hi Kayla," Chris spoke softly, looking directly at her. "You look great."

Kayla was absolutely speechless. So many different emotions were running through her right now. She needed to pick one and get a handle on this situation, quick. She went for nonchalance.

"Well, hello Chris," Kayla replied coolly. "What brings you by today," she asked sitting back in her chair and folding her hands in her lap.

Chris recognized her tone and attitude. She was angry but trying hard to be civil.

"I wanted to see you," he replied "I needed to apologize to you for a lot of things and I needed to do it in person."

Chris was telling the truth about this much. He very much wanted to apologize, among other things he wanted to do to her.

"Well, that was very big of you," Kayla said frostily, still sitting and looking at Chris like he shouldered two heads. "But we are way past over with that situation, and I, for one, have moved on with my life."

Chris was sinking fast. "I know you're still angry with me, and I deserve that," he said. "I did some really hurtful things to you, and God knows you didn't deserve any of them. I realize now, what a wonderful, beautiful, person I lost back then. I just want a chance to at least have a friendship with you now."

Kayla was looking at him like she could see right through him. Chris wasn't sure if she was going to yell at him or throw something at him.

"Christopher," Kayla began.

Damn, he thought. *Not a good sign. She's using my full name.*

"We shared a relationship a long time ago. I gave you something I can never take back. You gave me a resounding screw you in return. It took me a long time to move on, to trust again, to even care again, but I'm over that now and I'm over you. I have someone in my life, and he is more man than you could ever hope to be. We are not now, nor will we ever be, friends. Is that clear enough for you," Kayla finished coldly.

Chris's heart sunk. *Damn, not only was she still angry, there was someone else. Didn't he already have enough work to do with just her? Now, he added getting rid of this buster she was dating too, just damn!*

"OK Kayla, I understand," Chris told her, watching and observing her.

He looked directly into her eyes before speaking.

"I know it's asking a lot, but, can I please have just one hug before I go, considering I'll never see you again."

Chris knew it was a long shot.

Kayla was quiet for a long time, thinking, he knew. Finally, she let out a deep sigh and spoke.

"Sure, why not," she told him, shrugging.

He breathed, feeling like he won the trifecta at the track and walked toward her desk. Kayla rose and met Chris halfway. He reached out for her, and she stepped into his arms. They embraced, his mind going a million different places. He waited a year for this hug. God, she felt good; soft and warm. She smelled so damned good. Chris couldn't let it end like this. He took a chance. He knew Kayla must have something still inside her for him. Why else would she be this angry still? As they were releasing each other, Chris kissed her full on the mouth.

"I'm sorry Kayla," he said as he looked at her face.

Kayla was furious.

"Please baby, it was just a reaction. I'm still in love with you, and it was just reflex," Chris finished.

Kayla slapped him hard and ordered him out of her office. Realizing there was nothing else he could do at the moment, Chris left. There was a small glimmer of hope though. He felt Kayla respond a little when he hugged her. That was enough to let Chris know there was a chance, albeit a slim one, but he was going to take it.

After Chris left, Kayla was still in shock over his even being there. She was angry with herself for letting him hug her and even angrier because a part of her responded and enjoyed it. Kayla was genuinely angry about the kiss though.

Why the hell did he come back now of all times? What did he want? She heard Chris wasn't doing well in the business anymore. Money maybe, she decided.

Kayla knew one thing for sure, if Dezi ever found out about today, it wouldn't be a good thing for Chris's health. Kayla decided this was one secret she must keep, even from Taea.

● ● ●

"Hmph, I knew the slimy dog would make a move soon," Taea grumbled, as she watched Chris leave Kayla's office.

She ducked into an open office just as he was coming out of the front door. Chris didn't look happy, and he was rubbing his jaw. Taea guessed what happened, and was proud of Kayla for smacking him. Now, she could tell Eric and let him pass it on. Taea snapped her fingers.

"No more Chris," she laughed as she breezed into the office now, spoke to Anne and headed for Kayla's office.

"Hey girlie girl," Taea called out cheerily.

"Hey, wassup," Kayla replied.

Taea knew her friend like a book. Kayla was trying to sound normal, but was nowhere near it. They were having lunch. Since it was her short day, she suggested they get together at Kayla's office, knowing Monday's were her worst days, and she would surely skip eating, to complete a deal.

They ordered Chinese, and were enjoying the food, making small talk, when Taea, who was tired of Kayla trying to fool her, called her out.

"So, what did Chris want?"

Kayla stopped chewing and swallowed the food in her mouth. She looked at her friend. *Dang, couldn't she keep anything a secret from Taea?*

"Nothing in particular," Kayla replied.

Taea could see there was something she wasn't telling her.

"What happened? And remember who you're talking to before you answer," she said, pointing her chopsticks at her.

Kayla chuckled, closed her eyes and took a deep breath. She knew she couldn't lie to Taea. She always saw right through her, not to mention, Kayla was the world's worst liar.

"Nothing Taea," she said softly.

"Why are you lying to me Kayla," Taea countered. "Did he hurt you? Did he touch you or something," she asked, getting angry at the thought of him doing anything to Kayla.

Taea didn't put it past the slimy bastard.

"No," Kayla said again softly. "He wanted a hug, so I hugged him."

Taea thought for a moment.

"Well that's not so bad," she responded. "But you're still not telling me something. Out with it."

Kayla looked at her for a minute, exhaled deeply and told her.

"He kissed me," she said, almost whispering.

"He what," Taea yelled.

Kayla jumped like she was struck.

"I'm sorry Kayla, I didn't mean to yell," Taea said, her voice full of concern. "Did he hurt you?"

Kayla frowned.

"No, he did piss me off though," she said, recalling the incident in her mind. "I slapped him."

"Good for you girl, good for you," Taea told her laughing.

"You can't tell Eric or Dezi, Taea," Kayla was pleading with her.

This was not what Taea wanted to hear. She wanted to get rid of this puss bucket, once and for all.

"Why do you care Kayla? This asshole has done nothing but hurt you to your heart," she said.

Kayla looked at her, pleading her understanding.

"I know that, but I could never forgive myself if it was my fault Chris got hurt or worse," she said softly.

Classic Kayla, Taea thought. *Always worried about everyone else.*

Did Kayla still have some feelings for Chris? Taea called her on it again.

"Do you still love him," she asked her point blank.

Kayla was silent. A single tear rolled down her cheek.

"I honestly don't know," Kayla replied quietly.

This was bad news of the worst kind, Taea instantly concluded. She kept remembering what Eric told her about Dezi, and the last woman he was in love with. Taea couldn't let Kayla get hurt, but she couldn't tell her yet either. Kayla said she didn't know, so maybe she was just feeling sentimental. Taea needed to help Kayla out real quick, so that she wouldn't forget what Chris did to her.

"Do you remember the pain you felt when you walked in that room and found him screwing little miss Sabrina Malek, the office assistant," Taea asked.

Kayla's face clouded.

"Of course," she replied. "I could never ever forget that."

Kayla still saw it in some of her nightmares, but she didn't share that with Taea.

"Do you remember what he said to you," Taea asked again.

Kayla burst into tears at that point. Taea walked over and held her friend. She hated doing that, but knew it was necessary. Taea held Kayla up, looked at her and spoke again.

"Be with Dezi, Kayla. Chris will never change, and he will only end up hurting you again," she admonished her friend.

Kayla shook her head yes and thanked Taea for being there for her. Taea closed her eyes and breathed a sigh of relief.

A Deadly 10 Encounter

Taea was glad to be home. The rest of the day was pretty decent after her meeting with Chris. She gave him the money and told him that was the end of it. Chris, of course, threatened her again, and told her it was over when he said it was. Taea grabbed her purse and jetted.

Hmph, she thought now, *once I drop that little bug in Eric's about you, and Dezi pays your ass a visit, we'll see who has the last laugh.*

Taea needed to be careful though. This was a dangerous game and she stood to lose a lot, too.

"Hey, Isabella," Taea said to the housekeeper.

Isabella worked for them going on two years. She was great. She cooked them nice Italian meals and teased them about being skinny all the time. She did a great job on the house and taking care of them. She would often give them advice about guys they were dating when they brought them home. Taea laughed, thinking that each one Isabella met, she hated. She was beginning to think Isabella wanted to keep them single.

"What's for dinner," Taea asked.

The kitchen smelled divine.

"Stuffed shells," Isabella replied with her thick Italian accent. "Garlic rolls, salad and I make strawberry cheesecake for dessert."

Taea's mouth was watering. If she couldn't do anything else, Isabella was a serious cook.

"Well, I'm having company tonight, so set three plates please," Taea told her.

"OK, I'll do that," Isabella replied. "Miss Kayla, she no have a date?"

"Oh, hers is out of town, so you get to inspect mine tonight, and see hers this weekend, maybe," Taea giggled.

Isabella laughed, too.

"OK, I can't wait to meet this one," she said. "I hope he's better than the skinny one you bring last time."

They both laughed together and Taea went to shower and get herself together for Eric.

"I'm home," Kayla yelled. "If anyone cares that is," she laughed.

Isabella greeted her. Kayla loved Isabella. She showed her all sorts of things in the kitchen and throughout the house that helped her out a lot. Isabella also taught her a little bit of Italian.

"Isabella can you tell me what this means," Kayla asked and began to repeat the things Dezi said in her ear the first night they spent together.

Isabella listened intently. Kayla hoped she repeated them correctly. Isabella looked at her for a long time.

"Where did you hear these words," Isabella asked.

"A friend," Kayla told her.

Isabella looked at her again and smiled.

"The friend is a man, yes?"

Kayla blushed. She hoped they weren't dirty words. She instantly regretted asking. Isabella saw her embarrassment.

"It means, please don't leave me," she replied.

Kayla was relieved. She was glad it was nothing worse. It never occurred to her that he could have said something dirty. Kayla was just glad this wasn't one of those occasions.

"I'll get ready to serve dinner now," Isabella inquired, still smiling.

"Yes, that'll be great," Kayla replied and went upstairs to wash up.

Isabella was still amused by what just happened. She wondered why the man spoke his plea to Kayla in Italian. *Probably trying to impress her with a few words he knew*, Isabella thought. Such men are not worthy of her time. Isabella made a mental note to tell Kayla when she asked her opinion, as she always did, about her male friends.

Isabella was glad Kayla had a friend now. She knew Kayla was lonely for a long time since that other one.

●●●

"Come and eat now everyone," Isabella announced.

She served dinner and went back to kitchen to finish dessert. Taea and Eric were busy chattering at dinner. Kayla was deep in thought about what Isabella told her the words meant.

She wondered was he talking about me or was he dreaming about someone else? Dezi obviously didn't know he talked in his sleep, and she didn't want to come out and ask him. It didn't happen since, so Kayla decided to let it go; dismissing it as fluke.

Feeling stuffed, they all complimented Isabella on how wonderful the meal was. She thanked them and excused herself to finish her work. Taea and Eric announced they were going to go work off some of the food they just ate.

Kayla laughed. "I'm going out for a little while."

"Okay, but be careful," Taea told her.

However, Eric asked her a few questions.

"Where are you going? Are you going alone? When will you be back?"

Kayla thought it was a bit odd, but she assumed Eric was being protective of her. She was, after all, Taea's best friend, and Eric knew how close they were. So Kayla answered his questions and he seemed satisfied, even telling her to have a good time.

Neither one of them saw Dirty hit the speed dial on his cell nor heard it connect. Devastator listened intently as Kayla answered Dirty's questions.

●●●

Kayla arrived at Impressions, the cozy jazz club she loved, around 9:00. It was a Monday night and the crowd was thin. She got her usual table in the corner, away from the stage. Kayla could still enjoy the music and some privacy. She wouldn't be disturbed by various offers of drinks and pick-up lines.

The waitress took her order. Kayla ordered a cranberry spritzer. She didn't drink when she was out alone and driving. She loved going fast too much to be impaired, Kayla chuckled at the thought.

The waitress returned with her drink just as the musicians took the stage and began to play. Kayla sipped her drink, sat back and closed her eyes, letting the music engulf her.

Across the room, Chris was thinking that he couldn't believe his luck. There she was looking great as usual and alone for a change. Chris thanked whatever invisible gods were doing his bidding and prepared to go say hello. He hoped she wasn't still as angry as she was earlier. He needed to get close to her again. He had a month to accomplish it. Chris thought about his meeting earlier.

"Well, you got what I came for," Monster asked Chris in a no nonsense tone.

"Yeah, here, I told you I would have it," he replied.

"Good thing for you," Monster said again. *"Remember, next payment's due in two weeks."*

"Yeah, I know, I'll have that too," Chris replied.

He actually did have that payment. That's why he hit Taea up for five G's, instead of two. Chris actually kept a few bucks to play with and go a few places like the club.

Chris knew he needed to find a consistent stream of money to get this monkey off his back. Kayla was the one person who could supply that. He wasn't trying to use her. Chris honestly did love her and wanted to be with her. Kayla having money was just a bonus. Chris was into the gambling houses big. He owed them over twenty grand, and these payments were killing him.

Chris knew Kayla would give him the money without even asking what it was for. The problem was she wasn't in love with him anymore. There was some new joker that held her attention. Chris would squash all that drama though. He had to get her back. His life depended on it. He got up. His confidence boosted by the thought of his own mortality and walked over to her table.

●●●

Kayla was enjoying the music, swaying back and forth in her seat. They were playing one of her favorite tunes.

"Hello again," she heard the familiar voice.

That immediately broke her mellow mood. She opened her eyes to find Chris standing in front of her. *Not again*, Kayla thought.

"Hello, Christopher," she replied curtly.

He pretty much expected this reaction but charged ahead anyway.

"I don't want to upset you again, Kayla," Chris said. "I just wanted to say hi when I saw you sitting here."

Kayla looked at him for a long moment before she sighed and spoke again.

"I'm not upset; I just don't see that we have anything more to talk about," she said blandly.

Chris searched her face for any hint that she may not be as unwilling to talk to him as she said. He found it in her eyes. They held a faraway look in them, like she was reminiscing, hopefully remembering something good.

"Kayla," Chris said softly. "I don't want to be your enemy. I know how much I hurt you, believe me when I tell you that, but I know you're not capable of hating me."

Kayla looked up at him. He was taken aback at the coldness reflected in her eyes.

"Yes, Christopher, I am very capable of hating you," Kayla said matter-of-fact. "I simply choose not to."

Kayla ended the conversation as she got up and paid her tab. Have a great evening was the last thing she said as she walked out of the club and left Chris standing there, speechless.

●●●

Kayla was speeding down the freeway again. Her thoughts were traveling almost as fast as the 90 mph she was doing. What the hell did he want from her? Why come back now? Why couldn't Chris just leave her alone, stirring up feelings she thought were long dead, and that she desperately needed to be.

"Damn him," she swore out loud.

Kayla hated how he kept throwing her off balance. She was seeing Dezi now, and he was wonderful. She knew he cared deeply for her, and she wanted to pursue this course chosen. Why couldn't she shake those feelings for Chris that were threatening her happiness? Was it sexual? Maybe she was just in need, and he was familiar.

That had to be it. Her radar detector went off and Kayla broke the Benz down to a reasonable speed. She passed the officer about half a mile later. Kayla looked at her detector and blew it a kiss.

"I gotta stop thinking about that dog," she chided herself.

Concentrate on that sexy Italian you have at your beck and call, her mind advised. Kayla smiled thinking how good it would be when they finally made love to each other.

●●●

Kayla's mind shifted from to Chris to another good situation that turned bad, her childhood.

Kayla's father was in the military when he met her mother. They fell in love and she was born. Her mother died when Kayla was two, so she only knew her from photographs. Her father took care of her for a while as they traveled to other countries he was stationed in. She experienced her share of 'aunties' who were dating her father. None of them ever treated her very well. She was thrilled to go live with Nana. She was 13 years old by then.

One month before graduation and her eighteenth birthday, Nana talked with her about life, and her future.

"Kayla," Nana began. "You are a good girl. I know you don't run around with boys and you do good in school," she was looking at her closely now. "Yo mama left you some money when she died, and yo daddy have some put aside for you, too. It's in an account in the bank downtown."

Nana handed Kayla a bankbook. "When you turn 18, that money is yours. I want you to promise me something though."

Kayla was clueless what Nana could have wanted from her, but whatever it was, she would definitely give it to her. There was nothing Kayla wouldn't have done for Nana. She was looking at her intensely now. She told Kayla she wanted her to leave South Carolina.

Kayla was mortified. Leave Nana?! No, she could never do that. She wouldn't do that. She told Nana as much, but the older woman was adamant; making her swear before God that she would indeed leave and make something of herself.

Kayla was devastated. Why would Nana want her gone? Did she do something wrong? Kayla looked at Nana, who was waiting for her to do what she asked. She took a deep breath, slowly exhaled and made the promise.

Nana seemed relieved as she smiled at her. She hugged Kayla tightly and told her how much she loved her.

Three days after Kayla graduated high school, and two days after her birthday, Nana died peacefully in her sleep as Kayla finally understood the promise.

She couldn't complain about her life after Nana's death though. It so far was a relatively good one. Taea moved to the coast with her and became her new family. Kayla started a successful business and was doing well with her investments. She owned a wonderful home and enjoyed life.

There was only one part of her that still felt empty and she thought she found someone to fill it in Chris. They met at school and instantly hit it off. He was charming to a fault and even though Taea warned her he probably wasn't any good, Kayla dated him.

They were together for nearly a year, before she decided to sleep with him. Kayla was still a virgin, and she wanted to be very sure before she gave herself to Chris or any man. The first time they were together was wonderful. Chris was a wonderful lover. He was patient and gentle making sure Kayla was satisfied as well as himself. He told her he loved her. Kayla was at peace and secure for the first time since Nana died; but that wouldn't last.

A few months later, Chris started standing her up for dates and coming up with excuses for why they couldn't see each other on certain days. Kayla talked to Taea about it. Taea told her they were going to get to bottom of the BS. So they went to his house that he gave Kayla a key to. Taea heard them first and looked at Kayla. They walked to the bedroom and Kayla opened the door. There they were in all their glory, going at it hot and heavy like two dogs in heat. Kayla couldn't believe this. Chris didn't even try to pretend. He looked at her standing there crying and said the words she would never forget.

"Hey, stick around and see how a real woman makes love to a man," Chris *laughed and went right back to Sabrina like it was nothing.* Kayla's heart was broken that day and she didn't think she would ever make it back from that place of pain. She survived though.

Taea was there for her every step of the way and Kayla could never thank her enough for that. Now, there was Dezi. He was wonderful. Kayla hoped he wouldn't hurt her like Chris did. She wanted Dezi to fill that empty place inside her that wanted someone to love, and someone to love her. Kayla wanted a life. She wanted kids, the total package.

Well only time will tell, she thought. She reflected on something Nana told her a long time ago. Life is a chance. You simply have to take it. So she was going to take a chance on Mr. Dezi Gianni. Kayla just hoped she didn't come up bankrupt again.

KR Bankston

A Deadly 11 Encounter

It was hard to believe a month was gone by already, Adrian mused to himself of the turbulent breakup between himself and his lover. Now, he was actually enjoying being single. Adrian managed to get more furniture after the split. Although nowhere near as elaborate as the place once was before the breakup, the apartment was coming along.

He went out a couple more times with the girls and they all had a blast. He took them to Caribbean, the local gay hotspot, and of course everyone thought they were a couple. Taea and Kayla were quite amused by that still enjoying a great time. Adrian was shopping today, armed with a little extra money wanting to get himself something nice. He planned to go out again tonight. Maybe back to The Industry. He was walking out of Carl's, an independently owned tailor shop in the mall, when he saw Monster.

"Hmph," Adrian said aloud. "There's Mr. Homophobe. I ought to go walk up to him and say hi. That would really get his shorts in a bunch," he laughed devilishly, recalling seeing him at the Industry on a couple of occasions.

He always found the man watching him intently as if he were disturbed by his presence.

Adrian was feeling pretty devious today. *So hey, why not,* he thought. He walked over to Monster just as he was buying a drink from the food court. Adrian tapped him on the shoulder. As soon as Monster turned around, Adrian put on his best smile.

"Hi, remember me from The Industry," Adrian asked casually.

Monster couldn't believe Adrian was standing right here in front of him. He continually thought about him since the night he saw him. He wondered if they would ever cross paths again outside of work and his boss's presence. Now, Adrian was here in the flesh. Monster wasn't going to let him walk away again without at least a number.

Adrian couldn't quite tell what Monster was thinking because it took him a minute to answer.

"Yeah, I remember you," Monster said without much expression.

"Well, I just wanted to come over and say hi since I saw you here," Adrian said already thinking this was a bad idea after all.

"I'm glad you did," Monster replied calmly, "I've been thinking about you."

Adrian was speechless. There was no mistaking what this man was saying to him, but was he hearing him right? It never entered his mind that Monster was the least bit interested in him. Usually, Adrian could pick them out wherever he went, even if they were down low brothers, but this one completely escaped him.

Monster was studying Adrian now. He knew he rattled him. Monster almost smiled, but he wanted to see Adrian squirm a little more.

"Why would you be thinking about me," Adrian asked, knowing the answer, but wanting to hear it nonetheless.

"Why do you think," Monster asked without giving away anything.

Before Adrian could say anything else, Monster asked if they could go somewhere and continue this conversation, perhaps over lunch. Adrian was still reeling from the surprise encounter but accepted his lunch invitation.

●●●

Devastator was awake. He just didn't feel like getting out of bed yet. He loved being in her bed. It was cozy and it always smelled like her. He reflected over the past month being with her. Kayla was everything Devastator knew she would be. She was always honest with him. Wherever she said she was going, she did. Whatever she said was going on, was. She never told him a lie, not even a little white lie and he liked that.

There was the absence of lovemaking however, and Devastator really wanted to. He knew Kayla wanted it, too. They came really close a couple of times but she always stopped herself. Not tonight. He made plans for them. Devastator held a lot of plans when it came to Kayla, she just didn't know about them yet. He laughed internally at that.

He bought wine, even though Kayla didn't drink much, she agreed. She told Devastator their housekeeper was a great Italian cook. He wanted something special for tonight, so he was going downstairs to talk to the housekeeper in a few. Devastator heard her come in a while ago.

Yes, tonight was going to be special. He gathered scented candles, flowers, music, and a few other surprises. Devastator wanted everything to be perfect for her. Kayla deserved that. His cell rang and brought him out of his thoughts. It was Dirty.

"What's up man?"

Dirty told him about the town he accompanied Taea to see about her sick mother. Devastator and Dirty talked about expanding their operation, and little towns were perfect breeding grounds to start. They didn't have anything else to do, they laughed to themselves.

"Everything looks good," Dirty told him. "I'm finding some guys we can trust so they can run things for us."

"That's cool," Devastator replied. "Just let me know where everything is in place."

"You got everything set up for tonight," Dirty asked .

"Yeah," Devastator replied. "By the time you head back, you should be well on your way to being Uncle Dirty," he added as they laughed and he disconnected.

Devastator reflected on his plans. He was in love with her. There was no doubt about that in his mind. He wanted Kayla around for a long time, and he wanted something permanent between them. Devastator wanted a child. He desired one for a long time, but never met anyone worthy of having one with in his mind. Even when he was with Sasha, four years ago, she wasn't good enough, but Kayla was. She was perfect and Devastator knew she would be a perfect mother, unlike some women he knew.

He never in his life was inside a woman without a condom, but tonight he was planning to be with Kayla, and a condom was the farthest thing from his mind. Devastator smiled, and decided he better get up and go get the menu planned. He wanted everything ready and perfect when Kayla got home.

●●●

Isabella heard him coming down the stairs. She knew he was there, Miss Kayla told her. She hoped he wouldn't come down. She was cursed with a bad dream last night and wasn't feeling exactly social. She would nonetheless be nice to him. He was still Miss Kayla's friend and she would show him respect. Isabella heard him enter the kitchen and speak to her in Italian.

"Ciao," Devastator greeted the woman.

"Ciao," she returned, placing something in the cabinet before turning around. The smile on her face froze as Isabella looked at the man standing on the other side of the island.

He could not believe his eyes.

This can't be happening, Devastator thought. He looked at her for a long time, and she at him. Neither of them spoke. Finally, he did.

"I thought you were dead," Devastator said to her in Italian.

Isabella was impressed that he still used it after all these years.

"No, I am not dead," she said softly still looking at him.

He was handsome and grown as tall as his father. He inherited the same gray eyes, and they were trained on her at the moment, cold and lifeless.

"It's good to see you again," Isabella spoke, still drinking him in from head to toe.

"Is it really," he asked, this time in English.

Of all the housekeepers in the world, Kayla hired this one, Devastator thought.

"How have you been? How has your life been," Isabella asked him.

"Why are you worried now? You weren't worried when you left me," Devastator spoke again in Italian.

The words stung Isabella and she recoiled as if slapped.

"You left me like garbage, and now I should be happy to see you," Devastator threw at her coldly. "You died to me a long time ago," he added pleased at the pain he saw in her face.

She couldn't believe he considered her dead, felt nothing at all for her.

"I've always loved you Dezi, always," Isabella tried, begging him to listen and to understand.

"I left to try and make a better life for you, for us," she tried to explain.

"Yeah," Devastator asked angrily. "So when the hell were you coming back to get me," he finished breathing hard trying to contain the coldness that was threatening to overtake him.

"Where is that bastard of a father of mine," Dezi asked Isabella frostily as he continued to regard her.

Isabella sighed deeply, hurt by the depth of hatred still etched on his face.

"He died practically four years ago," she replied quietly.

Dezi grunted shortly before speaking.

"Well no great loss to humanity there," he replied evenly.

"Please Dezi, show some respect," she replied as sternly as she dared. "He was still your father," she finished as Dezi sucked his teeth in disgust.

"He was the bastard that impregnated you," he returned angrily. "He's never been a father."

"Dezi please listen, please," Isabella tried once more.

"Shut up," Devastator growled at her. "I don't want to hear any more damned lies or too late apologies from you," he finished dismissing any response from her.

Devastator told Isabella what he wanted for dinner and what time he wanted her gone, then prepared to leave the kitchen. Isabella was crying softly now, but Devastator didn't care. It secretly pleased him to see her in so much pain. It matched the hole in his own heart since the time she deserted him. Devastator was almost out the door of the kitchen, when he turned and spoke to her one last time.

"You are never to tell Kayla who you really are to me! Understand," he said again in Italian with a tone of finality.

Fearfully, Isabella hurriedly agreed. She cried even harder now. She loved Miss Kayla. How could she be dishonest with her? How could she pretend she didn't know Dezi when they were in the same room? Isabella was confused. She was happy to see him. Happy he found Miss Kayla because she was such a good girl, but sad because she would have to leave now. What would she tell Miss Kayla who would surely question her? Isabella could never tell her, never let her know, the woman she respects, loves and asks for advice is the same woman who left her son, the man Kayla was in love with, 14 years ago.

KR Bankston

A Deadly 12 Encounter

Seeing his mother again after all these years brought the horrid memories of his childhood crashing back. Devastator closed his eyes, breathing deeply trying to keep the raw hurt and anger he still felt at bay.

"Non vada prego! Non vada prego!" he screamed, tears streaming down his cheeks.

Devastator was begging Isabella, his mother, not to leave him. He would be a good boy, he could help her, please take him with her. He was only 13 years old. Even though his childhood was peppered with beatings and abuse, Devastator loved his mother with all his heart. Yet here she was once again taking sides with his no good father.

Eddie Rollins was a deadbeat, a drunk, and a womanizer, yet Isabella wouldn't leave him alone. Eddie terrorized his son daily, calling him a punk, a mutt, a half-breed or any other insulting term he felt would bring hurt to the boy. His abuse seemed to know no end as he held loaded guns to Devastator's head, and burned him with hot knife tips or wire hangers. Devastator hated him. The only thing they shared was the color of their eyes. Eddie never even bothered to give his son his last name. Isabella always believed Eddie when he told her that. he didn't hurt Devastator or cause the nosebleeds, bruises, and scratches present on the child's body.

How could she be so blind, Devastator thought often as he cried himself to sleep in the small closet his father would lock him in. Being too young to get the revenge he wanted, Devastator took to hurting smaller children, bullying and threatening them into secrecy of his torment. When even that didn't ease the pain he carried, he began torturing and killing things; stray cats, small dogs, birds, and the like. By the time Isabella finally left him, Devastator was permanently twisted and his sense of right and wrong, acceptable and unacceptable, severely skewed.

Isabella left him with her sister Sophia who was kind enough, not having any children of her own, to care for him. Sophia did the best she could with Devastator, but he was wild by this time. He hated his mother for leaving him, yet he was scared and lonely without her.

He met Anthony and Dominic at the corner store where he stole candy, or whatever he wanted. Devastator knew they worked for the mob. He thought that was cool and wanted to be a part of it, to belong to a family. Devastator heard them call themselves that and liked it.

Anthony liked him. He would show Devastator around, and he didn't talk about his mixed heritage the way some of the others would. Later, he would find out that Anthony possessed a separate family of his own, with a black woman name Sharon, who lived in Harlem.

Domi took a little longer to warm up to him, but they too, soon became fast friends. They took Devastator everywhere with them, showed him the ropes. Things like how to make deals, how to run books and run numbers. They took Devastator to collect protection payments. He was seasoned by his fourteenth birthday so they took him to his first hit.

He caught on quickly, even managed to lose his virginity. Devastator loved the life, and after that, couldn't get enough of it. Anthony kept Devastator under his wing and kept him protected.

Domi was killed right after Devastator's sixteenth birthday, a buy gone wrong. The guy double crossed the family and brought an execution squad. Anthony didn't go with Domi on that run. He was in Harlem with Sharon that day. They kept working and running together until a few months after his nineteenth birthday. He and Anthony were coming home from Harlem after visiting Sharon and the kids. They were laughing and talking, having a great time. Anthony wanted to stop at the liquor store to get something to drink. It was familiar territory. They were near home, so Devastator said OK.

Anthony made him wait in the car, going into the store alone. Devastator heard gunshots ring out a moment later and saw two guys running out to a waiting car. Devastator ran in the store and found Anthony on the floor. He was shot while they were robbing the store. As he lay dying, he managed to talk to Devastator.

Anthony told him to tell Sharon to take the money and the kids and leave town. He told Devastator to take the keys to his car and go to his place, get the money he stashed and get the hell out of New York. Anthony died while they were waiting for the ambulance.

Devastator did what he was asked. He left the next morning. He worked for Cobra for two years after arriving in his new home.

Scraping by with next to nothing, Devastator met Dirty and talked him into partnership. That was the beginning of something good for both of them. Then he met Sasha. She was beautiful, cultured, sophisticated and five years older than him.

Dirty tried to warn him. He told Devastator he heard she was all about money. That she got around and would sleep with whoever the highest bidder was for her affections. Devastator didn't care about any of that. He was Devastator; head of The Clique. Even though they were nowhere near as powerful and rich as they were now, Devastator figured he possessed enough money and charm to keep her happy.

Devastator courted Sasha hard wining and dining her. She stayed with him at his apartment, and he thought they were straight. A few months into the relationship, Devastator started hearing the rumors. Sasha started staying out later. Sometimes she wouldn't come home at all. Devastator confronted her and Sasha told him she had her own life and she didn't want him smothering her.

Devastator backed off because he didn't want to lose her. He believed her lies to very end. That end came for them the night Dirty called him and said he had something to show him. He picked Devastator up and they headed for Sunscape Hills, and exclusive tree lined subdivision where the extremely wealthy played house.

What the hell are we doing here? Devastator remembered thinking.

Dirty parked the car down the street from one of the biggest houses Devastator ever saw and told him to come on. They walked up the hill to the house and Dirty motioned him to come around back with him.

They crept inside. The people that lived there were obviously too self-absorbed to remember to lock the door.

They heard laughter from the living room and made their way to see what was going on. Devastator heard Sasha's voice. He didn't want to believe it. They were talking about him, laughing about him. Sasha told him how she had this 'little boy' she was trying to train. That she was only hanging around another couple weeks because she received a better offer. They laughed again, then the man asked her if they could get down to what she came there for. She laughed again.

"Hell yes, because I'm certainly not getting it at home," she told the man.

Devastator was crushed, hurt and angry, all at the same time. He got up and strode into the room with Dirty right beside him and yanked her up by her hair. Sasha screamed. Devastator looked her into her eyes and told her she was a bitch. Her companion never moved. Dirty held a .357 trained right on him and the companion intelligently figured she wasn't worth dying for. Devastator dragged her out of the house back to the car. Sasha tried to explain and reason with him, but Devastator was already well beyond that point. He took her back to his apartment where he beat the hell out of her, but Devastator wasn't done with her yet.

He went to the kitchen, took some crystal drain cleaner from under the sink, added water and brought it back to the bedroom. Sasha was struggling to get up and get out of the apartment. Devastator pushed her back inside the room, taunting her with the caustic cleaner, telling her she would never forget this night.

Sasha screamed when she saw what he was going to do. Devastator held her down as he slowly and deliberately poured the cleaner on the right side of her face. She screamed as it burned her skin. Sasha felt it in her eye and running down her cheek.

Devastator watched for a minute, then dragged her to the bathroom and rinsed her face. The damage was done. She was seriously scarred and the right eye was blinded. He showed her reflection in the mirror. Sasha screamed again. Devastator laughed as he pulled out the black bag he kept. He fixed up the hit of heroin and injected her. She calmed way down after that.

Devastator called Dirty and told him there was a new whore for them to put on the stroll. She's been working for them ever since. They market her as the exotic one because of the eye patch. Sasha was the woman who made the mistake of breaking Dezi's heart.

A Deadly 13 Encounter

"You got my money," Monster asked Chris on the other end of the phone.

He didn't have it and he knew what that meant. He better stall and buy some time.

"Yeah man, I'm having it wired in today, it won't be here till after 5:00 though," Chris lied.

"Mmm," Monster replied.

"I'll have it after 5:00 today man, as soon as the bank opens at 9:00 tomorrow I can get it," Chris said. "Just one day man, just a few hours. It's not my fault, I can't control bank hours."

"At 9:45 AM, I want my money in my hand, or I'm coming to visit you. You don't want that," Monster replied.

Chris was sweating bullets as he listened to a dial tone. Where the hell was he going to get another two grand? A month was gone by already, and Kayla was still cold to him. Damn, he was going to get killed before he could ever get her back.

He could possibly hit Taea up again. Chris needed to do something, quick. He was desperate to buy more time; but two grand would only buy him two more weeks.

OK, he thought, *Go to the well one more time. Buy yourself another month and kick it into high gear getting your woman back.* Chris picked up his cell and dialed Taea's number. She answered on the second ring.

"What," Taea asked him curtly.

"You know what bitch! Don't get cute now," Chris warned.

Taea sighed, *Damn, I knew he was gonna hit me up again. He was broke. She had to find out who, and what, he owed. She couldn't keep giving him this kind of money.*

"I'm outta town Chris," she said dryly.

Shit, he didn't need to hear that. He needed that money and he needed it now.

"Well," Chris replied. "They have banks where you are, go get it and overnight it to me."

Taea sighed again.

"Yeah, OK, give me the address asshole," she countered.

Chris gave her the address.

"If I don't have the money by 9:00, I'll be on my way to see Kayla at 9:01."

"Yeah, whatever," Taea replied, then disconnected.

Chris knew she would send it. The only thing Taea loved more in the world than herself was Kayla, and he was counting on that more than ever now.

•••

Taea was absolutely livid after her conversation with Chris.

"Slimy bastard," she fumed.

She wanted so much to tell Kayla the truth, but she couldn't bring herself to do it. Taea sighed inwardly, *I've got to find out what he's using this money for and why Mr. Successful Broker is actually broke.*

Taea picked up her cell. She needed to make a few calls. While she was waiting on one of her calls to connect, Dirty walked in.

"Wassup baby," he asked. "Everything all right?"

Taea recovered quickly. "Just some crap at work I'm checking on."

He seemed satisfied with the answer and didn't question her any further.

"You ready to go," Dirty asked.

They were on their way to the hospital to see her mother who was diagnosed with cancer about six months ago. Since then, the disease ravaged her. The doctors didn't expect her to live beyond the month, so Taea came home to see her one last time while she was alive.

"Yeah, I'm ready," she told him, grabbing her purse as they headed out to the car.

She hated hospitals, sickness and death. Eric was her rock since they arrived. She felt so much love for him. He was truly there for her.

Taea managed to slip off unnoticed at the hospital and went to the bank. She sent the money overnight with a guaranteed 8:00 a.m. delivery time.

She hated Chris and wanted him out of her and Kayla's lives. Damn, why did she promise Kayla that she wouldn't tell Eric or Dezi?

Well, Taea thought. *There's more than one way to skin a cat.* She smiled at the thought as she made her way back to the hospital.

• • •

Dirty heard her slip out. He was napping lightly. He heard her when she came back into the room. She wasn't gone long. Dirty figured she tried to call Kayla and knew that she didn't get an answer. He was pretty sure Kayla had her hands full with Devastator right about now, he smiled at the thought.

• • •

The drive home was absolutely horrible. Kayla arrived home cranky and late. She called Dezi to let him know she was stuck. He was sweet and understanding. She didn't want to take this funky mood inside with her, so Kayla took a deep breath, about ten of them, before she went in.

The smell from the kitchen hit her as soon as she walked in the door and put her things down. She began to relax. Devastator met her at the kitchen entrance with a glass of wine and a kiss. Kayla assumed he sent Isabella home early. He told her he wanted to be alone with her this evening.

"Mmmm, it smells absolutely delicious in here," Kayla murmured as Devastator held her, stroking her hair.

"Glad you approve," he chuckled. "Come on and sit down, and I will serve you," Devastator said in a very bad English butler imitation.

They both laughed.

Devastator brought her plate and more wine. He lit the candles as they enjoyed a wonderful intimate dinner. Afterward, he cleared the table and told Kayla to come upstairs with him, so he could help her relax.

She was breathless when she entered the room. He placed candles and pink, white, yellow, and red, rose petals everywhere. It was absolutely beautiful.

While Kayla absorbed the breathtaking sight, Devastator led her to the bathroom. The oversized garden tub was filled with bubbles and more rose petals. There was soft jazz playing in the background and candles lined the rim of the tub. Kayla was blown away. He went to a lot of trouble and she was thoroughly impressed.

Devastator looked into her eyes and began to slowly undress her. Kayla didn't stop him. Soon he was down to her bra and thong. Kayla knew where this was going to lead, but she wanted it.

He kissed her softly then pulled back and looked into her eyes again. Kayla didn't protest when Dezi reached for the hook on her bra. It fell to the floor and he looked at her again. She didn't move. Devastator kissed her, his hand gently cupping one of her breasts. She didn't pull away. Kayla didn't want him to ever stop, but he did. Devastator pulled away and looked at her again. He began to remove her thong, kissing her down her body as he did. Kayla was really turned on and about ready to lose it.

Devastator took the time to drink her in again. She was beautiful, in every sense of the word. Her skin was flawless and smooth, her breasts firm and inviting. It was taking all his internal will not to take her right now. He would be patient. He planned this evening for them, and he wouldn't spoil it by being overzealous.

Devastator gently lifted her and placed her in the tub. He kissed her again, gently on the lips.

"I'll be waiting for you when you get out," he whispered, leaving her alone. Kayla sat back in the tub and marveled at what just happened.

Oh my God, she thought, *this man is wonderful. I can't wait for him to touch me and really make love to me.* She panicked for a quick moment. *What if he doesn't like making love with me? What if he thinks the same thing Chris did and finds someone else.*

She began to think she shouldn't do this. She obviously wasn't good at it. That's what the experience with Chris taught her. Kayla began to get scared.

She sat in the tub still thinking. Then she thought of Taea. That brought a smile and new confidence. They talked about this. About when she and Dezi would ultimately make love. She told her how she felt.

"Forget that bullshit Chris said. He was a bastard," Taea told her.

That remark made Kayla laugh out loud.

"Kayla look," she'd told her. "There is no art to making love to a man, you do what you feel, and you allow yourself to feel what he's doing to you. When you and Dezi get to that point, just relax, let him feel you, and you relax and feel him."

Kayla smiled and pushed any thoughts of hurtful words from Chris out of her mind. The man waiting for her on the other side of that door was nowhere near the jerk that Chris was. If the undressing preview Dezi just gave her was any indication, she was in for the most wonderful lovemaking ever experienced.

●●●

Devastator retrieved the strawberries, warm chocolate and whipped cream from the kitchen while Kayla was in the tub. He was thinking about how good it felt to touch her. How she responded to his kisses. There was a lot more in store for her. He would make her forget the man she was with before him. She would only want him, and her body would only respond to his touch. Devastator heard her getting out of the tub. He set up the fruit for them, took off the rest of his clothes, and climbed into bed. Kayla came into the room and slid into the bed beside Dezi. She smelled great he thought, as he leaned over to kiss her again. He moved the tray onto the bed. Kayla smiled when she saw it.

"Are we making a sundae," she giggled.

Devastator loved the way her eyes sparkled when she was happy.

"Could be," he replied, smiling as he fed her a chocolate covered berry.

Some of the chocolate dripped onto her chest, near her breast. He leaned down and gently licked it off, purposely managing to graze her nipple in the process. Kayla gasped lightly. Devastator smiled silently. He removed the tray, leaned over and began kissing her again, laying her down as he did. His hands began to move over her body and he touched her breasts again. He began kissing her neck and chest, licking her nipples and moving down her body with his tongue. Kayla was moaning lightly, and Devastator knew she was turned on.

He kissed her all the way to her toes, and then began working his way back up to her most sensitive spot. He began to lick her there. Kayla was completely aroused now. Devastator stayed until he felt her body begin to spasm and heard her cry out softly. He knew she reached orgasm.

That's a good start, he thought. He continued to taste her until she was aroused again. Then he began licking his way back up to her perfect lips. He stopped at her breasts and gave them extra attention, eliciting more moans of pleasure from her.

Devastator knew Kayla was ready now. He slowly entered her and they began to move in rhythm together. God, she felt incredible, like she was made for him, Devastator thought as they made love. Kayla was moaning and kissing his neck. He liked that, so he gave her more of him. She moaned even louder. Her rhythm got quicker and Devastator knew she was nearing orgasm again. Kayla dug her nails into his back and that turned him on. Devastator felt himself growing closer. They clung to each other as their pace grew frenzied. Kayla cried out and he shuddered as they both reached orgasms together.

Devastator kissed her neck as he looked into her eyes. He could see that Kayla was satisfied. He saw something else, too. She loved him. She didn't have to say it, but right in that moment Devastator saw it.

They began to kiss passionately and he felt himself growing hard again inside her. Kayla responded and they made love again.

She was breathing evenly and sleeping peacefully as Devastator eased out of bed and slipped into the bathroom. His cell went off and awakened him. He flipped on the light once he closed the door and looked at the ID. It was Dirty.

"Yeah man, what's up," Devastator asked as soon as Dirty answered the phone.

"Hey, hope I ain't break up nothing man," Dirty replied. "Got everything set up and on my way to the spot for that trial run today."

"That's cool. Let me know how it goes. If they act right, could be some very well off brothers there in good old South Carolina," Devastator told him.

"Sooo," Dirty said chuckling. "Am I an uncle yet?"

Devastator smiled.

"I certainly hope so, but just in case we will keep trying."

They both broke into laughter.

"You sure about his man," Dirty asked. "Because once Kayla gets pregnant there's no going back."

"Yeah, I'm sure," Devastator said.

He inwardly thought that any doubts he had were gone after being with her tonight.

"Okay, good luck then," Dirty told him. "See you in a few days."

Devastator closed his eyes for a moment and reflected again on what Dirty asked him about being sure. He didn't waiver. Yes, he was sure. He wanted this and he was excited about it. He came back to bed and slipped in beside Kayla. She only stirred a moment and then drifted back into a fitful sleep.

Devastator was propped on his elbow looking at Kayla, thinking how much he loved her. He thought about what he would do to keep her, and how quickly he would kill anyone who tried to take her from him. He lay down, put his arms around Kayla, pulled her close and closed his eyes to go back to sleep. Devastator was content. He was, for the first time in a long time, at peace.

•••

Kayla heard the shower running when she awoke. She smiled and looked out the window. Dezi obviously opened the drapes for her. She began thinking about the night before.

I have never felt like that in my entire life, Kayla thought. *Well, I wasn't wrong about the package he was carrying,* she chuckled inaudibly. She thought about what Taea told her about Eric.

"They ought to call them the anaconda twins," Kayla said softly and laughed as she stretched, getting ready to get out of bed, content that she made the right choice.

She almost wavered and gave Chris a second chance. Now, she was glad she didn't. He never touched her the way Dezi did. He never made her feel the emotions Dezi did. Kayla couldn't imagine letting another man touch her now. She was his and her body loved him. Kayla giggled at the thought.

He felt so good inside her last night. She got caught up. They both did and forgot to use a condom. Not once, but twice. She thought about going to the clinic and getting a morning after pill, but then remembered Taea was on birth control pills. She could take a few of those.

She picked up the phone to call Taea to ask her about her mom and where she could find her birth-control pills. She already knew Taea was going to want to know all about last night. Kayla laughed out loud and rolled her eyes.

"Hey girlie," Taea answered.

She sounded like she was in a really good mood, Kayla thought.

"Hey yourself," Kayla said "You're in an awfully good mood."

Taea giggled at that.

"Yeah girl, you know I got me some last night, so I'm all right today," she laughed.

"Hmm," Kayla said slyly. "I got me some last night too as a matter of fact."

Taea screamed in her ear, then laughed.

"You is too hot for your own good," Taea told her still laughing. "Didn't I tell you not to give him none yet?!"

She was beside herself and Kayla knew there were tears rolling down her cheeks from laughing so hard.

"How was it," Taea asked after pulling herself together.

Kayla thought a moment.

"I'm not sure I have the vocabulary to put something that good into words," she replied.

"Well, just damn then, Miss Thang," Taea roared again. "I am so happy for you girl and I know Mr. Dezi is on top of the world."

They both giggled.

"Listen, we been talking and I haven't even asked how your mom is," she said seriously.

Taea was quiet for a minute before she answered.

"She's as well as can be expected. They don't think she'll be with us for much longer, but Eric has been so great through all this Kayla, he really has," she said.

Kayla was glad to hear that her friend had someone there for her. She knew how much Taea actually loved this man. She admitted it to Kayla during their talk about her, Dezi, and sex. Kayla told Taea she missed her and Taea told her that went without saying on her end, too.

"Oh yeah, I need some of your birth-control pills," Kayla said. "We got caught up in the moment and didn't use a condom."

Taea was quiet and Kayla thought she was angry. Taea was always on her about not letting some joker mess up her life.

"Taea please don't be mad at me," Kayla said softly.

Taea snapped out of her thoughts to answer her.

"No, Kayla, I'm not mad. I promise," she said.

Taea told her where she kept the pills and how many to take.

"Make me a promise though," Taea said to her afterward.

Kayla didn't like to make promises before hearing what they were first, but she reluctantly agreed.

"Don't let him make love to you again without a condom, OK," Taea said.

"I promise," Kayla told Taea, knowing better and internally promising she wouldn't let herself get caught up like that again, as they disconnected and Kayla headed over to her best friends room.

●●●

Devastator heard most of the conversation. He never intended to eavesdrop, but she was so engrossed in discussion that he didn't want to interrupt by walking in the room. He didn't care that she told Taea about last night. He was disturbed though that she wanted the birth control. That wasn't part of his plan. He wasn't too upset though, he loved Kayla, and he knew now she loved him back. Devastator would get past that issue, but he had to get that damned birth control away from her.

Devastator heard the phone click. It was a defect hers embodied. If someone picked up the phone in any other room, this one clicked. He carefully lifted the receiver and listened.

"I can't find them," he heard Kayla telling Taea.

"Did you look where I told you?"

"Yes, of course I did," Kayla answered back. "They're not there."

"Hang on, let me think," she said.

Taea couldn't understand. She was the only person who knew where her stuff was. Then she remembered. Eric saw them one night when she asked him to get her some panties out of the drawer and asked her about them. *But why would he take them?*

"I'm sorry Kayla, I have my last pack with me," she said lying. "I totally forgot I needed to get my prescription filled."

"It's okay," Kayla sighed. "I just hope I don't get pregnant because I'm not too sure how Dezi would take that right now."

"Don't stress, you should be fine," Taea told her. "Just make sure you use protection from now on."

"You already know I will," Kayla promised again and they hung up again.

Devastator smiled as he put the receiver back in its cradle. *Thanks Dirty,* he thought and walked back into the bathroom.

•••

"What the hell is going on," Taea said aloud to no one in particular.

Her mind was racing. Why would Eric take her pills? When did he take them? She didn't have a reason to look for them. She was still taking the current pack, which reminded her she didn't take one last night. Taea looked for her pack and it was gone.

"OK, this is not happening," she said to herself.

I am not crazy and losing my stuff, Taea thought. Was Eric trying to get her pregnant? If that's what he wanted, why didn't he just ask her?

Taea immediately thought of Dezi and Kayla. Was he trying to do the same thing? She knew that forgetting the condom stuff was probably true on Kayla's part, but not Dezi. Eric told her they were both extremely careful and meticulous when it came to that.

She knew Dezi was really into Kayla and struck her as extremely possessive. She wondered if he and Eric were on the same playing field. They didn't use condoms for a while now, but that was because she was on the pill. Now, her pills were missing.

A Deadly 14 Encounter

For Adrian, the last couple of months flew by in a blur. He couldn't recall being this happy in a very long time. Monster, his real name was Kevin he found out, was true to his word from day one, never letting him regret the decision he made to be with him. Adrian traveled extensively with Kevin. They went on cruises and to casinos. He was having the time of his life.

Kevin wanted him to stop working at Le Bistro, so he could be home spending more time with him. Kevin also hated when Adrian went clubbing, one of three things that Adrian loved. He also loved his job and meeting people. Anyway, it wasn't like he went every weekend. Well OK, maybe he did. Adrian was thinking about stopping because he really loved Kevin and he gave him so much. Was that really a lot to ask from him?

Since Adrian connected with Kevin, he saw Devastator and Dirty. He was over Devastator now. Adrian did learn that he and Kayla were a serious couple now. He could also tell they were sleeping together. Devastator wouldn't let anyone get within 10 feet of Kayla, mostly males, except him of course. Adrian laughed out loud at that thought.

He thought Kayla suspected he and Kevin were together, but she never said anything or asked him about it either. That was a good thing. It was just the way she watched them when they were around each other. Adrian loved them both dearly. They grew close over the months, but he knew he needed to protect Kevin's privacy. Even evil Dirty and Taea were serious. *It's amazing what the right person coming into your life can do*, he mused. Everyone seemed happy. Adrian was hoping it stayed that way.

He wanted to stay with Kevin and love him forever, but Adrian was realistic. In the business they were in, he was always waiting to get that call that something happened to Kevin. That he was either hurt, or God forbid, dead. Adrian shuddered at that thought as he got up to go into the kitchen. It was bright and sunny in here. He loved how the sunlight made the room alive with warmth.

"No more bad thoughts," Adrian mused aloud. "Kevin is here, and he is all mine."

He made himself a drink and went outside to sit by the pool.

•••

Chris couldn't believe his good fortune. He did very well at the track and a couple of the casinos in the last month or so. He managed to pay off his debt. He was rather cocky when he gave the guy his last payment. Chris laughed to himself, but he was thankful he didn't get himself killed that day. The guy didn't appreciate his flippant attitude much.

He managed to win enough to buy himself some nice new clothes, shoes, and get a much nicer apartment. Somewhere he wouldn't be ashamed to bring Kayla when they got together.

Damn, he thought, *he was still fantasizing about her.* Reality was a far harsher picture. Kayla was still extremely cold to him, barely speaking the few times Chris saw her out alone. He never actually saw this guy she was supposedly seeing. He was beginning to think she made the story up to get him to back off.

Well, that wasn't happening. Chris wanted her back and felt that he was in the position now to do something about it. He picked up his cell and dialed her office. He was feeling lucky today. Kayla was out of the office, the receptionist told him. He didn't let it discourage him or ruin his mood. Chris politely declined when she asked him if he wanted to leave her a message.

After he hung up, Chris looked at the clock and saw that it was lunchtime. He smiled. He knew exactly where she would be. Chris grabbed his wallet and headed out to Le Bistro.

"Yep, today is going to be a good day," he chuckled as he locked the door.

•••

Devastator and Dirty were getting ready for the road trip. Their operation in South Carolina was doing well, but now there was trouble. It appeared as though some of the boys from Florida didn't appreciate them moving into their territory, so they sent some hardware to disrupt things.

Devastator wasn't in the mood for this drama. He wasn't thrilled about going to South Carolina. He had things here he would rather be doing. Devastator didn't like being away from Kayla. He was better about trusting her. She still never lied to him once since they were together.

Devastator didn't like leaving her because he knew there was someone else out there; someone who was trying to muscle their way in and take Kayla from him. He still wasn't able to find out who this clown was. He paid for the flowers he sent with cash. He would mess up soon enough though and when he did, that was his ass.

Devastator turned his focus back to the boys in South Carolina. He and Dirty were taking Monster and the Front 5 with them. They were going down to show them a little competitive firepower. They were going to let them know they weren't playing about their business. That would settle things down and Devastator could get back home to Kayla.

He thought about last night when he told her he would be gone for about a week or so. As always, she understood. Devastator loved that about her. She just told him to make it back to her safely. He made love to her then. Devastator smiled again thinking about her. He wouldn't see her before he left. He needed to get his mind set for this storm they were getting ready to rain down on these fools.

●●●

Chris returned to his apartment a little disappointed, but still upbeat. He went to Le Bistro, but apparently missed Kayla today. He stayed and enjoyed a nice lunch anyway. He managed to talk the pretty waitress who served him today into coming over this evening and spending some time. Chris loved Kayla, but he was still a man. He was horny as hell. He hadn't been with anyone since arriving here and he was way overdue. He stopped at the grocery store after a few other stops during his day and bought a nice bottle of wine and some cheese for tonight.

Chris also scored some weed in case she wanted to get her smoke on. He sure hoped she was down for whatever because he wasn't looking for a relationship.

He wanted that with Kayla. Chris only wanted sex from this girl and wanted to make sure she knew that before they did anything. He didn't need any crazy stalker attachments while he was trying to get his woman back into his bed.

Chris put the wine on ice. Made a mental note to come back and deal with the cheese after his shower and headed off toward his bathroom. He was in the shower when the phone rang. He hopped out to answer it.

"Hello," Chris answered, dripping on the carpet.

"Hi, it's me," the female voice said.

"What's up?"

Damn, he hoped she wasn't calling to cancel.

"I just wanted to tell you I was gonna be there a little later. My shift ran over," she said.

"That's cool baby," he replied smoothly. "Just take your time, come on over when you're ready. I'll be here."

"OK, I'll see you in a bit," she giggled.

Chris hung up and went back to his shower, whistling while he washed his hair.

●●●

"Yo man, everything straight and ready to go," Dirty asked, walking into the room.

"Yeah, everybody is in place," Devastator replied.

Dirty was ready for this trip too. He set up this operation. He took it very personally when these morons came in and disrupted things.

"You talk to Tee since yesterday," Devastator asked him.

Dirty thought about Taea and smiled.

"Naw man, you know how we do," Dirty replied. "I took care of that business the other night."

He laughed. Devastator laughed too. He knew exactly what his friend was saying.

"So what's the plan," Dirty asked.

They sat down and began to go over the details of everything that was going to happen once they got there. That small town would never be the same after this visit from The Clique. They talked for about two hours, finally deciding they liked the setup of everything. Devastator and Dirty grabbed their bags. The weapons were already loaded in the Hummers and gone with Monster, and the Front 5. Three different vehicles were taking three different routes to South Carolina. They liked it this way. It kept everyone off balance in case word leaked they were coming.

Devastator and Dirty never traveled with weapons. There were too many overzealous police and state troopers who wanted to pull over two brothers in a Porsche. They looked at each other and sighed deeply. They turned the Porsche toward the interstate and took off, spinning dirt and rocks into the air as they went.

●●●

Chris finished his shower, cut up the cheese, added some strawberries and grapes to the platter and put it in the fridge to chill. The wine was still on ice. He went to see what kind of music he wanted for the evening. He ran across his Best of Jodeci CD. *Now that was definitely lovemaking music*, Chris chuckled to himself. *Maybe I should save this for Kayla.*

"Whoa, Chris," he told himself. "One step at a time, you gotta get her to even talk to you again first."

He chuckled and finished picking out music for the night. He decided on Carl Thomas and a couple other jazz CDs. He put them in the CD player so that it was ready to play once she got there.

Chris sat down and rolled himself a joint, leaned back in his chair and smoked. He wanted to be nice and mellow when she came over. Chris hated all the games you had to play just to get sex, but he wasn't ready to go out and get a hooker just yet. So he would roll the dice tonight, and hopefully not crap out.

A Deadly 15 Encounter

"Man, there ain't shit in this little ass town," Devastator remarked after they arrived.

They passed a total of two food joints, a Mom and Pop general store, liquor store, and funeral home. That was about the extent of this place from what he could see.

It took two days to get here and they were ready to do some damage. They met up with Monster and the rest of the entourage. Everyone was at the assigned place. They didn't stay at hotels because it was too easy to target. They were staying with members of the operation that lived here. Devastator and Dirty were staying with Taea's older brother Stan.

"When's the last time you talked to your sister," Dirty asked him.

"I called her the other day man," Stan replied.

Dirty just grunted and nodded.

"OK, so where them boys at we need to visit," Dirty asked now.

"They're at the Desert Inn. It's on the outside of town," Stan replied.

Devastator asked him to show them. They all got into his suburban and headed for the inn.

"This shit is perfect," Dirty laughed when he saw the small motel right off the interstate.

Devastator agreed. *These guys were fucking amateurs,* he dismissed. There was absolutely nothing out here. The nearest restaurant was at least five miles away. It was totally secluded, perfect for the kind of festivities they were planning.

"OK, here's the set up," Devastator began.

After they made the few revisions necessary to their former plans, he told them to call it a night. Devastator wanted to make one more run out here in the morning. He wanted to see the layout during the daytime.

They would take care of this tomorrow night. It would be Friday. Devastator knew they would make a move and that's exactly what he wanted. They all left and went back to the house. He wanted to call Kayla and check on her but decided to wait and call her later.

"Hey, where the smoke at," Devastator asked instead.

He called Monster and the rest of the group. They were starting to arrive now. They all sat down and went over the plan again.

While they were talking, Dirty noticed Taea's brother watching one of the guys intently. He wondered what that was about. Stan seemed to be irritated with the guy. Dirty hoped there wasn't any internal bickering and struggling going on, because he would have to nip that real quickly. He learned that from Devastator. You can't have your members bumping heads with each other. It didn't make for good business. Dirty made a mental note to check it out later.

•••

"I hear you been having a lot to say lately," Stan, asked the slim, dark complexioned man he was looking at.

"I don't know what you're talking about man," he replied.

Stan didn't like Gavin Freeley one bit. He held the reputation for being trouble and he heard rumors.

"Oh, fool, you know exactly what the hell I'm talking about," Stan replied getting irritated, but trying hard to control it.

He didn't want Dirty to hear any of this. Stan needed this operation to continue here. It was good to him and his family. They were doing a lot better lately and he wasn't going to let this fool mess it up. Gavin looked at him long and hard, then answered him coolly.

"I told you, I don't know what you're talking about. So if you'll excuse me," he said, walking away before Stan could say anything else.

Stan stared at his back.

"That bastard is lying," he fumed, letting it go for now, but determined to get to the bottom of it later.

•••

Several girls came over to the party. Most of the guys were indulging themselves. *The sistas are tight, no doubt about that,* Devastator thought, looking at one of the girls. He wouldn't do anything though. Devastator looked over to see where Dirty was. He and Stan were smoking and shooting the breeze with each other. Monster was double-checking the supply and the weapons. *That's cool* Devastator thought, as he closed his eyes and his mind began to drift. He started thinking about Isabella. He didn't know why she crossed his mind. Well, maybe he did. They were talking about Stan and Taea's mom earlier and how they wished they did more for her during her life.

Devastator didn't like thinking about Isabella. It made him cold inside, but he guessed that was okay, considering the task they were going to undertake tomorrow night. He thought about their meeting in Kayla's kitchen. It really pissed him off that she had turned up at all, especially at the home of the woman he loved. He was going to make her quit. He made her tell Kayla she was leaving. Even gave her the excuse she would use when she told her, but he ended up having to let her stay in spite of his feelings about her.

Kayla came to him in tears and he hated to see her cry. She loved Isabella and couldn't understand why she would want to leave after being with them for the past two years. Devastator couldn't take seeing Kayla hurting like that and he couldn't risk her finding out the truth by some last minute confession Isabella might make, so Devastator told Isabella she could stay.

"Hey man," Dirty was tapping him. "What, or should I say who, got your mind that tied up?"

Devastator laughed. "I'm just buzzed."

"Well," Dirty replied again. "Ain't nothing like some more chronic to help that right out."

They both broke into laughter. *Yeah,* Devastator thought, *anything to get my mind off her.* He took the blunt and inhaled a deep drag from it. It was close to 4 a.m. now and everyone was either asleep or passed out. He and Dirty talked for a while about the business, themselves and of course their women. They both went to sleep around 6 a.m.

● ● ●

Stan was up early even though he passed out around 3 a.m. He couldn't help it. His body was accustomed to getting up early. He looked at the clock, 9 a.m. *These jokers won't be up for a while*, he thought looking at his crew passed out in his living room. He didn't see Dirty or Devastator. He wondered where they ventured off to. Stan liked Devastator. He was cool people, but he could feel that underlying coldness Devastator summoned when he needed too.

Stan never wanted to be on the receiving end of it, that much he knew. He thought he remembered that they were still up when he passed out. He walked through the house and found them in the den. They were both still asleep, so he didn't disturb them.

Stan was looking for someone else anyway. He wanted to find Gavin. He walked away from him last night, but not today. He wanted some answers and he wanted them right now. Stan was disappointed to learn Gavin left with a girl last night and wasn't at the house. *That's OK,* Stan thought, *the fucker can't hide from me forever.* He went back to the kitchen, got him some OJ and rolled himself a blunt. He sat down and enjoyed his breakfast.

● ● ●

Monster, the Front 5 and the rest made it back to the house around 1:00 p.m. Devastator wanted them to go over the plan and go out to the spot. The watchers called and told them the Florida muscle had left the motel, headed for he was sure, one of their spots.

Devastator and Dirty had already discussed what they wanted to do, agreeing to let them hit one their spots. They needed them distracted long enough for them to set up tonight's party.

They got in the trucks and headed back out to the motel. Monster and the Front 5 shared Devastator's initial impression when they saw the spot too. They were shown the locations, and given instructions on how it was going to go down.

"Where is the fire department," Dirty asked Stan.

Stan thought it was an odd question.

"About 10 miles in the opposite direction," he responded.

He saw Dirty and Devastator exchange a look. Stan knew then this was going to be really bad.

"OK, let's get up outta here," Dirty told them after they were finished.

"Everybody go do what you need to do to get yourself set for this shit. We can't afford any fuck ups tonight or your ass may be going back home in a body bag," he said.

Everyone nodded in agreement.

They headed back to the houses. As they were riding, Devastator called Kayla.

"Hey baby," he said when she answered.

"Hey you, when are you coming home," Kayla was whining now, which Devastator thought was cute.

"Soon baby. You miss big daddy?"

She giggled.

"Of course I do. I need some of you badly."

He laughed out loud.

"Well in that case, I'ma hurry up and wrap this up and be on my way."

Kayla laughed.

"OK," she replied before growing quiet.

"Baby, please be careful," she added softly.

Devastator knew she was worried. He wanted to put her at ease.

"It's going to be a simple in and out, piece of cake," he told her. "Don't worry. I promise, I'll be back home soon."

"OK, love you, see you soon," Kayla responded as a final point.

Devastator needed to make sure he kept his promise to her. This stunt better go down right, and that was just that.

●●●

Dirty waited until they were back at the house to call Taea. He went into the den to have some privacy, so he could talk nasty to her. He laughed at that thought.

"Wassup baby girl," Dirty asked when she answered her cell.

"My damn pressure," Taea told him laughing.

He knew exactly what she was talking about.

"I can help you with that you know," Dirty teased.

"Oh really? How you gonna do that and you're two days away," Taea threw back.

"We can have some phone sex," he teased.

"I don't want phone sex," Taea purred. "I want Eric sex."

Damn, he loved this woman.

"I'll be home soon," Dirty laughed.

"Well, OK, I guess," Taea said.

Dirty knew she was pouting.

"Eric," she started, her tone serious. "Be careful."

"I will be baby, I promise," Dirty told her. "And I'll be home before you know it, then we can take care of that pressure problem you got," he laughed again.

Taea giggled.

"OK, I'm holding you to that."

● ● ●

It was 7:00 pm. They received the report that the second spot was hit. They took 10K in supply and 50K in cash. That was fine. They would get that back tonight at the party. Dirty and Devastator were smoking. It was what they did to get ready, but they didn't get high. They smoked the one blunt, only to take the edge off. They made sure they were always alert. Things could go wrong real quick if they went in half off their ass. This was the sort of thing they wouldn't get a second chance at.

Monster was on his cell. He ventured out into the yard to get some air and to have privacy. He called Adrian, whom he missed greatly.

"Whatcha wearing," he asked slyly when Adrian answered the phone.

"Nothing," Adrian replied smoothly.

"Boy, you're gonna make me get in the damn truck and drive home right now," Monster told him laughing softly.

It was good to hear his voice. This scene was getting ready to get tight and Monster needed to unwind just a little.

"When are you coming home," Adrian asked.

"We're hitting the road as soon as the transaction is done," Monster told him. "OK, well I'm looking forward to you. I'm headed to the club."

Monster sighed gently.

"I love you," Adrian told him.

"Love you too, boy," Monster returned the two disconnected.

Monster looked at his watch, 10:00. *OK*, he thought, *time to load up and get this show on the road.*

•••

Dirty, Devastator and Stan were all heading out the door to the truck. They enlisted a runner that would bring the Porsche and their clothes. They already confirmed everyone else was heading out, too. It was almost show time. Dirty looked at Stan and spoke, noticing how tense Stan was.

"This your first show?"

"Yeah, but I'm cool man," he replied.

Devastator shot Dirty a look.

"Here," Dirty told Stan holding out a pill.

Stan looked at the pill, then at Dirty.

"What's this?"

"Valium," Dirty told him. "It'll take the edge off."

"I already smoked some chronic man, I'm all right," Stan told him again.

Dirty looked at Stan hard now.

"Look man," he began. "You're basically family and I'm looking out for you. You're gonna see some shit tonight you only thought happened in movies. You're gonna need this, trust me on that."

Dirty didn't take his eyes off Stan. Stan thought about it for a moment, and realized Dirty was probably right. He was way out of his league on this one. He took the pill from Dirty and swallowed it down.

"That's it man," Dirty said, smiling now. "You're gonna be all right. Yes sir, all right," he chortled.

They arrived at the spot; parked the trucks and fanned out. They headed for the rooms on the backside of the inn.

The motel was single level, old, with back doors as well as front doors. The rooms were adjoining, so that made it even better for their plans. They were in position and Dirty gave the signal. Devastator was simply here for the kill. He was letting Dirty call the shots. This was his set up and Devastator knew Dirty took the intrusion personally.

The six shooters and two of the Front 5 came in the front and back doors of both rooms simultaneously. They exchanged gunfire with two of the men in the room, who already held their guns in hand, killing them.

Once the smoke cleared and the rooms secured, Dirty, Devastator, Monster, and Stan walked in. The men recognized Stan from the spot they hit but were clueless who the other three were. Dirty gave Devastator a look. Devastator smiled and Dirty laughed. The party was on. The other three members of the Front 5 came in and took down the ceiling tiles to reveal the bindings they put up earlier when they first came. The men were astonished.

"So, which one of you muthafuckers is in charge," Dirty asked, looking at each of them hard.

None of the men spoke, staring back at him just as hard.

"Oh, y'all some tough hard asses huh," Dirty said again, chuckling.

Still the men said nothing. Devastator sighed and sat down in a chair. He pulled out his .9mm and laid it on the table. He looked at Dirty and they exchanged another look.

"OK then," Dirty said. "You, you, and you," he said pointing at three of the seven men they held in the room.

The shooters grabbed them and strung them each up leaving them hanging by their arms. They stripped them down to their shorts and waited for Dirty to give direction.

Devastator was watching the four that remained intently. He noticed the men giving one of their colleagues more sideways glances than the others.

Gotcha, Devastator thought. Monster watched his boss and knew he found the leader.

Devastator looked at Monster and that was all that needed to be said. The man heard the .357 cock and felt the cold muzzle against the back of his head.

"If y'all here to rob our ass, take the shit and get the fuck out," he said calmly, the total opposite of what he actually felt right now with the gun at his head.

Dirty laughed.

"Muthafucker, do we look like we need to be robbing your broke ass?"

"Actually, we came to get our shit back that you took earlier and to give your ass a little message," he cryptically answered.

Shit, the man thought, *these them fools from the coast*.

"So take the shit, and get the fuck on then," the man repeated.

Devastator was genuinely amused. Here was this fool talking boldly and they were the ones with the guns. He did admire his courage. He grew a little restless. Devastator walked over to one of the men hanging and cut him with the razor. The man screamed.

"Oh, stop being a bitch," Devastator told him. "I didn't cut you that deep, not yet anyway."

Dirty smiled again. He liked it when Devastator did things like that. It threw everybody off and they never knew what was going to happen next.

Dirty walked over to the guy with the mouth and hit him as hard as he could. The guy spit out a couple of teeth and both his lip and nose were bleeding.

"I'm not happy at all about you messing with our shit here," Dirty said as he hit him again.

He fell out of the chair this time and Dirty kicked him in the gut. The man was gasping for air now. Dirty snatched him up and threw him back in the chair.

"So my partner and I are gonna show you how much we don't like it. Then we're gonna send you home with the message to share with all your friends about how much we don't like it," Dirty said hitting the man again.

He stayed in the chair this time.

They agreed they wanted to make a serious impression on the witness they left alive. They didn't want to have to come back here again for this nonsense.

Dirty gave the nod and the six shooters began to beat the other three men, leaving the leader and the ones hanging to watch.

They beat them until they were unrecognizable, killing two of them with a blow from the tire iron. The other they simply shot.

Devastator clapped and whistled. He enjoyed the show. Stan was staring like he was dreaming. He probably would have passed out by now if he didn't take the drug Dirty gave him.

These guys are serious, Stan thought. *I better never fuck up, cause it would be my ass, sister or no sister.*

The leader looked at Devastator like he was crazy when he applauded. Devastator felt the man's gaze and turned to look at him. The leader, who didn't spook easily, was chilled to his bones. He never saw anyone look like pure evil before until he looked into this crazy man's cold, gray eyes.

Devastator got up, walked over to the cooler the men kept beer in and grabbed himself one. He popped it open, walked over to the leader, leaned down in his ear and spoke.

"My dick is hard from enjoying this shit. Watch me get off," Devastator whispered softly.

The man was terrified. He was sure he didn't want to see this.

Devastator walked in front of the men and looked each of them over. The one in the middle must be the newest one, he figured. He looked the most scared and he was about ready to shed tears. Devastator flipped out the hunting knife he brought for this occasion. The man's eyes grew big as he watched Devastator handle the knife. He started at the right hip and came around slowly to the left one. The man screamed during the incision, trying to flail and kick at Devastator who simply deflected him and continued.

"There," he said, stepping back to admire his handiwork.

As soon as Devastator stepped back, the man's intestines spilled out of his body onto the floor below.

The room was engulfed in the stench of human feces, bile and blood. His two hang mates began screaming and trying to get down. Two of the Front 5 hit them with the gun butts and made them quiet down.

The leader was growing sicker by the minute. He thought, *this guy was Satan's son*. Stan was throwing up in the corner, not believing what he had just seen. Monster and Dirty were laughing and congratulating Devastator on his medical skills. The Front 5 were exchanging money with the shooters. They bet on how he was going to kill the man.

Devastator walked over to the table, picked up his beer, took a long drink and returned to the next man. He stabbed him hard, right in the center of the chest. The blow alone didn't kill him. It was what followed that finally did the deed.

Devastator took both hands and pulled the knife straight down the man's torso, effectively opening his chest and stomach cavity. The room once again reeked with a metallic scent and taste of blood.

The leader began to wretch in earnest. The room burst into full applause at that kill. Devastator smiled and took a small bow. He was down to the final man and looking directly at the leader.

"I want you to make sure you tell the boys in Florida that this shit belongs to The Clique. We don't need any help and we aren't looking for any fucking partners," Devastator said matter of fact.

The man was nodding his head profusely that he understood. Maybe if he gave in quick, he wouldn't kill the other guy and just let them both go. He watched too many of his partners die tonight already.

"Now," Devastator said again stepping up to the last hanging man and looking at him.

"What shall we do to you," he smiled at him.

The man never felt such coldness from a smile before.

"Cut his balls off," came one suggestion from the Front 5.

They all laughed at that one.

Devastator smiled again.

"Yes that is an option."

The man's eyes grew big. Devastator looked at him again and asked him how he wanted to die.

"Of old age," the man replied quietly.

They all roared with laughter. Even Devastator admitted that was a good one, so he questioned the man.

"So what do you propose I do," he asked. "Save you and kill him? Kill you both? Or save you both and let you go?"

The man answered with no hesitation or loyalty.

"Save me," he said simply.

Devastator liked his honesty.

"Cut him down," he told Stan, as he walked over to the leader.

"Looks like your luck has run out tonight loser," Devastator told him.

The man didn't hear the whole sentence before Devastator put 8 inches of steel into his left temple as he was speaking into his right ear. The man convulsed a couple times and dropped from the chair onto the floor dead. Devastator then turned his attention to the lone survivor and spoke.

"Where is our shit?"

The man didn't hesitate giving them the information. They gathered up all the weapons and money. The shooters and the Front 5 took their usual trophies.

Devastator and Dirty gave the survivor one last warning and sent him into the night, still clad only in his shorts with keys to drive himself back to Florida. They surveyed the room one last time and left the Front 5 to soak and torch it.

•••

Once they were back at the trucks and the Porsche, everyone settled their scores, talked about the hit and how great the plan came together. They changed their clothes, burned the others and loaded up to head out. Dirty gave Stan the stuff back and some of the money.

"You did good," Dirty amiably complimented.

"Thanks man," Stan told Dirty. "I'll keep it straight here. You won't have come back, not for that anyway."

They gave him some weapons telling Stan to find himself some shooters. Stan shook hands and gave dap to everyone there as they told him they were out.

Everyone got into their vehicles and spun out, each to their own route, and headed home. Dirty and Devastator were content. The plan went well. They were both looking forward to getting home and just plain getting some.

A Deadly 16 *Encounter*

They were glad to be back. They needed to go to the spot and have a quick meeting with the rest of The Clique to make sure everything was still operating correctly. Then they were going to see their ladies.

"Gentlemen," Devastator began.

The men at the table quickly came to order, remembering what happened at their last gathering. He went down the table asking each of them about their area of responsibility. Devastator was pleased to hear that all was well. They was a new supplier and he was never short. Word of Tony's demise spread as did the horror of what happened to his family.

"Good to hear all the reports, so if there is nothing else, I will let you gentlemen get back to work," Devastator said, finishing up.

He told them goodnight after the men introduced no further business.

Big D hung around for a minute.

"Can I speak to you alone, Devastator," Big D queried.

Devastator looked at him long and hard for a while before speaking.

"I don't keep secrets from my partner," he replied. "Whatever you have to say, you can say in front of Dirty."

"I'm sorry, no disrespect," Big D apologized.

"Sasha is dead," Big D said simply.

Dirty thought he heard him wrong.

"She's what?"

"She's dead," Big D repeated. "Overdose."

"Cops involved," Devastator asked.

"No. She did herself at some john's hotel. Maid found her," Big D told them.

"OK," Devastator said and was quiet for a moment.

Big D thought he was finished and was about to leave when he looked at him and spoke.

"Ship her home to her parents. They live in Alabama. Monster will give you the information," Devastator said. "Make sure she looks as nice as possible."

Dirty was proud of him. He knew this woman hurt Devastator badly, but he was still being decent. He could have let the state stick her in a hole somewhere and her parents never know.

"OK, I'll take care of it," Big D replied and then left.

Devastator sat down. He thought about what Big D just told him and he needed a drink. He wanted her to suffer like he suffered.

"Guess she just got tired," Devastator said out loud.

Dirty didn't say anything. He knew his friend was just thinking aloud.

Well that's the price of the street, Devastator thought before getting up to go see Kayla.

The news Big D gave put a damper on their otherwise good mood, but after smoking a of couple blunts they were good as new again.

"Man, I can't wait to get my hands on that girl," Dirty was chuckling, thinking about Taea.

"Shit, my hands ain't what I'm trying to put on Kayla," Devastator said and they both broke into laughter.

They arrived at the house 10 minutes later. After letting themselves in, they each headed in separate directions to the rooms they waited almost two weeks to enter.

Devastator heard the shower when he walked in the room. *Perfect*, he thought. Kayla had the music playing and her face under the spray, enjoying the water. She never heard Devastator come in. Never heard him gently pull the shower door open and step in. When Kayla turned to get her body wash the most magnificent set of pecs she ever beheld were staring at her.

"Hey baby, Big Daddy's home," Devastator said huskily, kissing her before she could even greet him.

He startled her, but she recovered quickly. Kayla was glad he was here. She wanted him so much. She thought about him getting back all day. Now, here he was, touching, kissing and turning her on like hell.

"I sure am glad to see you Big Daddy," Kayla said softly between kisses.

Devastator wanted her. He lifted her up against the shower wall and Kayla wrapped her legs around him. He entered her and she moaned in pleasure. They made love at a frenzied pace, both of their heat and passion exploding.

Afterward, they washed each other, giggling like high-schoolers, before getting out drying each other. Her touch began to arouse him again. Devastator picked her up, carried her out of the bathroom to the bed, and made love to her once again.

•••

"The doctor is in, baby," Dirty was telling Taea.

They were talking about her pressure problem again.

"Not yet, but he soon will be," Taea laughed and straddled him.

God, he felt good. She missed him so much. She was hot and needed cooling badly.

"I sure missed you too baby girl," Dirty was saying as he thrust deep inside her.

Taea felt herself nearing her peak. She needed an orgasm, needed several. It was a minute because Eric was out of town. She came hard, screaming his name and he came right behind her, screaming hell yes!

He smoked afterward. She didn't feel like it.

"So everything went good," Taea asked.

"Yeah baby, straight," Dirty told her. "Your brother handled his shit good."

Taea wasn't all that happy about Stan getting into the life, but she knew he needed to be able to take care of his family. Not to mention, helping out their two other sisters and all those damn kids they had. Taea almost laughed out loud.

"Well, I'm glad to hear that," Taea told Dirty. "But I think I have a fever. Could you check me out?"

She looked seductively at him.

"Hell yes and I got just the thermometer you need too," he told her, kissing her and rolling over to make love to her again.

●●●

"I won't be long, I promise," Kayla said to Devastator.

Devastator didn't want her going to the office today. He just returned and he wanted to spend time with her.

"Baby, please don't be mad," Kayla was pleading. "I promise I'll be done by noon."

He looked her in the eye. Devastator wanted to be angry, but he couldn't. He kissed her.

"OK, but after 12:00, you're all mine,"

Kayla laughed.

"That's cool."

"Why don't we all go to the yacht club and have lunch," Devastator suggested.

"Sounds good, come by the office with Eric and Taea. We can take my car."

"OK," he replied.

Kayla went to get dressed and Devastator flipped on the television, found a movie and started watching it.

She came out and was getting ready to leave, wearing a cute little blue tank and a jean mini. It was very tasteful. .

"So what color is your bra," Devastator asked Kayla.

She looked at him curiously.

"Blue, like my shirt," she returned, still confused.

"Hmm, so does the thong match," he mischievously asked.

Kayla laughed and threw a pillow at him.

"Bye baby, I'll see you at noon, sharp," she told Dezi as she kissed him and headed out the door.

● ● ●

Chris was up most of the night, brooding. He was continually thinking about Kayla again last night. He was supposed to get together with the waitress, but he didn't feel like it.

He skimmed through the photos he kept, reminiscing on the fun they used to have together. *Why did I hafta go and mess all that up,* Chris asked himself, for what seemed like the millionth time. It didn't help that he smoked weed most of the night, too. He was starting to come down off his high and feeling melancholy.

"I gotta get outta here for a while," Chris spoke to the empty room.

He jumped into the shower, got dressed and headed for the office. He ran into his old friend Brendan who was also a broker. He rented an office in the same building as Kayla located on the 7th floor. He asked Chris what he was doing now. Once he found out that he was back and looking for a place to set up, he suggested they share the office and the cost.

Chris readily accepted, not only because he needed to get back into the business full steam, but because he would be near Kayla and could see her more often.

He put on his sweats and a T-shirt, stuffed a condom in his pocket, *just in case* he chuckled privately, picked up his keys and headed out the door.

● ● ●

Devastator walked downstairs to grab himself a glass of juice. Dirty was sitting at the table having cereal when he arrived.

"What's up man," Devastator asked him, grabbing a bowl for himself.

"Nothing," Dirty replied. "We going to get Kayla's present now or later?"

Devastator bought Kayla some things for her birthday next week. He was going to pick them all up at the same time, but this one came early and he figured he would go ahead and give it to her.

"We can go pick it up before we stop and scoop her up from work," he told Dirty.

"She is gonna flip man," Dirty told him, laughing.

Devastator smiled. He sure hoped so. He took a lot of time, and care, trying to find just the right thing for her. Kayla wasn't picky; he was.

Devastator wanted something as perfect as she was to him. He found it at the last store they went to. It was beautiful. Five carats and it was flawless. Devastator couldn't wait to see the look on her face when he gave it to her.

"C'mon man, we need to get up outta here if we gonna be on time to get Kayla," Dirty said breaking his thought.

Devastator looked at the clock. It was already 10:00.

"Hey, lemme run upstairs. I'll be ready in 30," he said.

"Cool," Dirty replied. "Now, let me go in here and light a fire under baby girl and we can be out," he laughed as he left the kitchen.

●●●

Chris rounded the corner toward the elevator when he saw Kayla. *What is she doing here*, he questioned and then remembered Brendan mentioning two companies hitting the market Monday. Chris knew she was probably setting up some deals, to make a move on one or both of them.

God she looks good, he held. He missed her so much. He wanted to run and catch up to her and say hello. Maybe get a hug. Instead, he stood behind the pillar and waited for Kayla to board the elevator and go up.

Now, Chris was waiting on it to come down. He still wanted to see her, just to talk to her. Maybe he should stop by her office. There would be no one there today and he could really make her see how much he still loved her. Chris boarded the elevator and stood looking at the buttons for a long time until he finally hit one. The doors closed and he was on his way up.

●●●

"Well this just makes my gift look like crap now doesn't it," Taea teased Devastator, when they picked up Kayla's gift.

Devastator smiled.

"Now, now, you know she'll love them both. She'll just love mine better," he laughed.

Taea rolled her eyes and stuck out her tongue at him. They all laughed.

"Seriously though," she began. "She will absolutely love it Dezi."

He really hoped so.

"Let's head on out. I need to stop by the store and grab a couple things before we get to Kayla," Devastator said.

They all left the jewelers headed for the store.

●●●

"Look, I understand what you're telling me," Kayla was going on to the person on the other end of the phone. "But I need those figures now, not Monday. That will be entirely too late. Yes, I'll hold while you do them."

She was totally engrossed in her conversation. She never heard the front door close. She never heard him come into her office or close the door and lock it. Chris was standing there looking at her.

He intended to go on to his own office on the 7th floor, he really did, but he got off at the 5th floor instead. He wasn't sure how Kayla would react, seeing him again, but he missed her so much. Now, standing here in her office, looking at her, Chris wanted nothing else at that moment, but to be with her.

"OK, look," Kayla was talking again, bringing Chris out of his thoughts. "You call me back when you get them, but you call me back today. OK?!"

She sounded angry. He hoped his being here would help calm her down.

Kayla was shocked to find Chris standing there when she turned around to hang up the phone.

"Hi Kayla," Chris said gently as he stared at her.

Recovering from the initial shock of finding him there, "Hi Chris," Kayla said guardedly. "How did you know I was here?"

Looking her over lustily, he continued.

"I saw you downstairs, when I was heading for the elevator," Chris told her. "I have an office in this building a couple floors up."

He was making her nervous. Why did he come to see her? Why did he close her door? Kayla didn't like the way he was looking at her either.

"Well, I'm happy for you getting yourself back on track Chris. I really am," Kayla told him.

He was still looking at her like there was something he wanted her to say, but she hadn't said it yet.

"Kayla," he questioned, looking at her quizzically. "Why have you been lying to me all this time?"

OK, here we go, Kayla thought, trying to gauge his mood. *What is he up to? What is he talking about?* She wondered. *Lying about what?*

"I'm sorry Chris; I don't understand what you're asking me?" Kayla replied carefully.

"Why do you keep lying to me about having a boyfriend?" Chris went on. "I've never seen you with anyone."

He paused for a moment and took a deep breath.

"What are you afraid of? Are you afraid I'll hurt you again? Is that why you keep lying to me?"

Chris was looking at her evenly now, waiting for an answer. *I have to get outta here*, Kayla thought. She didn't like where this was going.

"Chris, I haven't been lying to you," she told him. "It's just been a coincidence that you always see me by myself. I honestly do have a boyfriend."

Chris looked at Kayla long and hard before he spoke. He thought she was still lying to him.

"Stop it," he yelled at her. "You don't hafta do this Kayla. I know I hurt you, but haven't you punished me enough?"

Chris was angry now and Kayla definitely wanted out of this room.

She didn't say anything. Chris began to walk toward her. She was behind her desk with only one way out, and he was blocking that. Kayla was starting to panic, but told herself to calm down. She needed to think her way out of here.

"What do you want me to do Chris," Kayla asked softly.

Chris seemed to be taken aback by her question and stopped walking.

"I want you to tell me the truth that you don't have a boyfriend and you were only doing it to get back at me for hurting you," he seemed to be pleading with her now.

She would tell him whatever he wanted to hear if it would get her to that door and out of here, Kayla thought. She took a deep breath for dramatic effect and told him what he wanted to hear.

Chris seemed to relax and held out his hand for Kayla to come to him. She didn't want to do that. Kayla knew Chris was too big for her to fight and she didn't want him close enough to grab her, but what choice did she have at the moment. Kayla walked to Chris and took his hand.

"See," he said, gently stroking her hair. "That wasn't so bad was it?"

Chris leaned down and began to kiss her.

• • •

"Will you two hurry up?!"

Taea was impatiently telling Devastator and Dirty, who were picking up odds and ends in the store and now shooting the breeze with the clerk.

"We're coming girl, hold your horses," Dirty shot back, laughing with Devastator.

"Did you get the skittles Mr. Man," she asked Devastator, giving him a look.

"Oh shit, no I forgot," he replied laughing.

He had to get those. Kayla loved them. She would eat them by the bag full, separating them by color first. Devastator laughed to himself at the thought.

Taea was just about to yell at them to come on again when she heard her cell go off. She began searching in her bag for it.

● ● ●

She pushed Chris away. He looked at her again,

"Why did you do that," he asked genuinely hurt now.

"Chris please, this is all too much for me right now," Kayla said, trying to sound reasonable.

She pushed him away because she couldn't stand him kissing her or even touching her for that matter.

"Baby listen," Chris began. "Just relax, it's OK. I'm not upset with you, I love you."

What the hell was she supposed to say? She told one lie and got away with it, would he believe her again?

"I know you're not angry anymore. I'm just feeling a little overwhelmed right now, that's all," Kayla replied.

Chris smiled.

"Well, I know what will relax you," he said looking Kayla over.

Oh hell no, she thought. *He wants to have sex. OK girl, it's time to get your butt up outta here.* Kayla moved toward the door. Chris blocked her.

"Where are you going," he asked, trying to touch her breasts.

Kayla gently deflected his hand.

"I need to use the restroom, Chris," she replied trying to sound calm and normal, even though she was anything but.

"You can do that afterward," Chris told her as he grabbed her and pulled her to him.

He began trying to kiss Kayla again, pulling at her clothes.

"Stop it! I don't want to do this," Kayla continued to scream, as she fought him.

She pushed Chris as hard as she could and he fell off balance.

Kayla tried to run for the door, but Chris was too quick. He grabbed her as she reached for the handle and threw her against the wall. Chris was out of control now. He grabbed Kayla by both arms and banged her head against the wall screaming at her that he loved her and why the hell was she being so damned cruel to him.

Kayla tried to fight back, biting Chris on his arm and drawing blood. He hit her then, closed fist. All she remembered was blackness.

•••

Taea's cell was still going off, D*amn it*, she thought as she searched.

"They will have hung up by the time I find this thing," she muttered, finally reaching the instrument.

"Hey girl, wassup," she quipped into the phone knowing it was Kayla.

Her name spoken was all she heard and crying. Taea dropped her drink on the floor, and it shattered.

Both Dirty and Devastator gave her their full attention. The look on her face said it all. Taea was pleading with Kayla to talk to her and evidently wasn't getting an answer. Something had gone horribly wrong. She needed to get to Kayla right away. Dirty and Devastator were standing right beside Taea now.

"It's OK Kayla. I'm on my way," Taea told her again.

The phone went dead. Taea was beside herself and Dirty knew Devastator was too. Hell, he was worried himself. They ran to the truck. They were still 15 minutes away from her. Taea was trying hard not to cry. God please, she prayed silently, let Kayla be all right.

•••

They turned into the parking garage. Dirty watched Devastator the whole trip. He never said a word, but the look on his face told Dirty everything he needed to know.

Devastator was trying not to get upset yet. Maybe Kayla was just having a girl moment and being hysterical. Devastator knew in his heart that was a long shot. Kayla was extremely stable and she didn't go off the deep end often. The feeling in his gut was that something really bad happened to his baby and he wasn't there to protect her. Dirty parked the truck in the first space closest to the garage elevator and they jumped out, heading up to the 5th floor to find out what the hell was going on.

"This damned elevator is taking forever," Taea cursed out loud.

She was worried and anxious. Dirty put his arms around her.

"Calm down baby, it's going to be alright," he tried.

"Thanks," Taea told him with a marginal smile.

She knew he was trying to help, but Eric didn't understand. He didn't hear Kayla's voice or the pain in it. Something was very wrong.

• • •

She thought she heard someone calling her, but she was probably dreaming again, Kayla thought not remembering if she actually called Taea or not. Then she felt them touching her and opened her eyes.

They arrived at her office.

Taea ran in screaming her name, but Kayla didn't answer. Dirty and Devastator made sure no one was in any of the other offices inside her suite. They were on their way down the hall to her office when they heard Taea scream. Devastator arrived first, and saw Kayla lying there, naked. The room looked like a war zone. He saw the condom wrapper next to her underwear lying beside her and Devastator knew exactly what happened.

"Taea," she said weakly trying to focus.

"Yes Kayla, it's me. I'm here," Taea said, rocking her best friend in her arms.

Who would do this to her, she was thinking. *Why would anyone hurt her like this?*

Taea looked at Eric and told him to hand her the blanket on the shelf. Before he could move, Devastator grabbed the blanket and brought it to her. He unfolded it and put it around Kayla's shivering body.

"I'm sorry," Kayla told Dezi softly, ashamed for letting this happen to her.

"This isn't your fault baby," Devastator told Kayla gently as he took her from Taea and held her in his arms.

Devastator finished wrapping her in the blanket, picked her up, and told her they were going to take her home. Devastator laid Kayla carefully on the backseat. Taea got in with her and put Kayla's head on her lap, stroking her hair, and telling her it was OK. Kayla cried quietly most of the way home.

Taea was livid. She wanted to know who and she wanted to know why, but Taea knew Kayla was in no condition to talk to them right now.

●●●

Devastator needed a drink and a smoke. Dirty provided him with both.

"When I find the muthafucker that did this shit to her, he is gonna be praying for death to come," Devastator said calmly.

"Oh we're going to find his ass, and we're going to enjoy ending his lousy ass life," Dirty told him.

He handed Devastator a manila envelope.

"What's this," he asked crossly.

"Probably the son of a bitch that did that foul shit to Kayla," Dirty replied.

Devastator looked at him long and hard. Dirty wasn't bothered. He knew his friend well enough to know he wasn't even seeing him at that point.

"I know this muthafucker," Devastator said, looking at the photos.

The eyes they hired finally came through with her stalker.

"You should. That fool was into us for 20 G's," Dirty replied, "He's also Kayla's ex-boyfriend."

Devastator dropped the photos. He looked at Dirty, and Dirty saw him get that look.

"I need confirmation first," Devastator told him. "Do you think Taea can get her to tell who did this to her?"

Dirty gave him a look.

"You know she'll tell her," he replied.

Dirty went upstairs to talk to Taea and let her know what he needed. Devastator closed his eyes, replaying the scene he walked into.

"If this is the son of a bitch," he growled, turning the pictures over in his hands again. "He is so fucking dead."

Dirty returned a few minutes later telling him everything was a go. Taea was helping Kayla take a bath and would question her then.

A Deadly 17 Encounter

The water felt good. It was good to be home and away from what happened. Kayla closed her eyes. She was trying not to cry again. How could Chris have done that to her? He said he loved her, but he hit her, he--, she stopped before completing her thought. Kayla couldn't even bring herself to think about it, but she knew it happened. She saw the condom wrapper. Kayla pulled her knees up to her body and began to cry softly again.

Taea heard her stir and then begin to cry again. She was furious. *Damn it,* she thought. *I hope they find the bastard that did this, and cut his nuts off.* She walked into the bathroom and began to stroke Kayla's hair.

"Shhhh," Taea told her. "It's going to be OK. You're safe now. No one is gonna hurt you again."

Kayla stopped crying and looked at her friend.

"Is he mad at me," she asked softly, ready to cry again.

Taea was furious all over again. This bastard had Kayla thinking she did something wrong and Dezi was mad at her.

"Honey, he's not mad," Taea told her friend "He's worried about you. He wants to know who did this to you," she finished and waited for Kayla to answer her.

Kayla was looking down into the tub. She knew if she told Taea she would explode. She would tell Eric and Dezi and they would kill Chris.

Kayla thought about it hard. Chris hurt her so badly. He did the unthinkable to her, but did she want him dead?

Kayla looked at Taea.

"I want to talk to Dezi first," she told her. "Then I'll tell you both."

Taea didn't have an issue with that and told her okay, leaving to go downstairs and get Dezi.

● ● ●

"Why does she want us both there," Devastator asked her on the way back up.

"I don't know. I suppose she has her reasons. I just want to find out who the fucker is," Taea responded.

So do I, he thought, *more than she could ever know.*

"Hey baby," Devastator said softly.

Kayla was sitting on the chaise lounge. She looked up at him and smiled. Her eyes were still sad. He could see she was hurting. Devastator was going to thoroughly enjoy killing this dog.

"Before I tell you what you want to know," Kayla began quietly, looking at them both, but focusing on Devastator. "I want you to promise me you won't kill him."

Was she serious? What the hell was she thinking? Devastator was dumbfounded. How could Kayla not want him to get this asshole?

Taea wasn't surprised. She knew Kayla, and knew she held one helluva capacity to forgive almost anything.

"Promise," Kayla said again softly, looking directly at him.

Devastator wanted this man, wanted him badly, but he wouldn't hurt Kayla any more than she already was hurt, so he told her okay. Kayla looked at Dezi for a long time after that.

Devastator guessed she was trying to make sure he was telling her the truth. When Kayla was satisfied, she sighed deeply, looked past both of them, into the space beyond the bedroom door and spoke.

"Chris was the one who attacked me," Kayla told them quietly.

Taea reacted first.

"That slimy bastard! I knew he couldn't leave you alone!"

"Can I talk to Kayla alone for minute," Devastator asked Taea.

"Yeah, sure," Taea responded, excusing herself. "I'll be back to check on you in a few minutes."

Devastator sat next to Kayla on the chaise and held her.

"I love you and I'm sorry I wasn't there to protect you."

"It wasn't your fault," Kayla immediately spoke up.

Devastator repeated the same to her. Kayla smiled when he said that.

He asked Taea to bring Kayla something to eat and she arrived with the tray. Kayla started to protest.

"You have to eat to get your strength back," Devastator admonished.

She wanted to continue her protest but gave in and took the soup and juice Taea brought her. Devastator helped Kayla into bed, told her he loved her again and kissed her. He stayed with her until she fell asleep.

●●●

"She shouldn't wake up again for a while," Devastator told Taea in the hallway.

He supplied the drug to put in the soup. He didn't want Kayla up worrying or in pain.

"We'll be back later, we're going to take care of this business."

Taea stopped him before he could walk away.

"I don't give a damn what Kayla said," Taea told Dezi looking him directly in the eye. "You make sure that bastard doesn't draw any more breath, ever."

She was crying now.

He looked at her levelly.

"Count on that shit," Devastator replied, turning to get Dirty.

They called Monster on the way and he said he would meet them there. There was a score to settle and Devastator planned to see that it got settled now.

●●●

Chris was sweating bullets. *What the hell have I done*, he worried. He smoked a couple joints to calm his nerves when he got home. He was on his third drink right now. *I can't believe this shit*, Chris was still thinking. *I didn't mean to hurt her. I would never do that.*

Why couldn't he have just been a little more patient? Hell, he made her admit she didn't have a man and that she was just trying to hurt him. That was more than enough. He should have left well enough alone, but she was looking so damned good. When he kissed her, it felt incredible. Her scent was divine. Then she rejected him again and he lost it!

The knock on the door quickly brought Chris back to the present.

"Shit," Chris said aloud.

Did Kayla called the cops? Were they here to take him to jail? Maybe he should just pretend he wasn't home. They would go away. The knock came again, more insistent this time. They weren't going away. They didn't take stuff like that lightly, Chris figured.

"Just a minute!"

Well, he was about to face the music. He did it. Now, he would pay the price.

"Hey man, long time no see," Monster said, walking into Chris's apartment, Dirty and Devastator right behind him.

"Yeah man," Chris replied.

What did these guys want? He wasn't in the mood right now, not with all the stuff going on in his head. He paid them every cent of their money back.

"So umm, what can I do for you," Chris asked Monster, whom he recognized.

The other two he never saw before and guessed they were his helpers or something.

"Seems we have some unfinished business," Monster said again, looking at Chris levelly.

Dirty made his way to the kitchen, found himself a beer and was drinking it.

Devastator was simply looking at Chris, but the look was more than enough to trigger alarms and fear in Chris's heart.

"What business would that be man," he asked trying to sound confident. "I paid you back all that I owe."

Devastator walked over to the dining table in the apartment and was now sitting, slowly flipping through pages of the photo album he found there. It was filled with pictures of Chris and Kayla.

"Seems you have a new debt that has been brought to my attention," Monster told him.

What the hell was he talking about? Chris knew he wasn't at the track or the casino in weeks. Dirty took a seat on the other side of the table relaxing with his beer and watching Chris like a specimen under a microscope.

Devastator removed each photo, one by one, and placed them face down on the table. He looked up at Chris, took a deep breath and finally spoke.

"I would like for you to explain, make me understand, why you felt it necessary to rape Kayla today," Devastator posed.

Chris was speechless. Who was this guy to her? He knew he better say something and say it quickly. The man's tone was ice and the stare even icier.

Still, Chris wasn't ready to just roll over. He wasn't going to be intimidated by these fools. For all he knew, they were more goons Taea hired to beat him down.

"Man, who the fuck are you," he spat at Devastator.

He wanted to go ahead and kill this fool, but instead blew his breath from pursed lips and thought for a moment. That was actually a fair question he supposed. The man probably didn't know who he was. So Devastator decided to answer his question.

He looked directly at Chris when he spoke.

"I'm the man who's been teaching her to love again since she's been hurt by a little boy masquerading as a man. I'm the man who's been spoiling her and loving her like the queen that she is. I'm the man who showed her what it felt like to be made love to by a real man. And I'm the man who's here to pay you in spades for what you did to her this morning, you fucker," he answered.

Dirty was amused as usual. He loved it when Devastator messed with their heads before he killed them.

"Excellent," Dirty chuckled out loud. "Fucking excellent!"

Chris's mouth was hanging open. This was the boyfriend she told him about.

I'll be damned, he thought, *she lied to me this morning.*

Then he realized Kayla was scared. She would have said anything to get out of that room with him. He still couldn't quite grasp it though. What would someone as classy and sophisticated as Kayla be doing with this guy? Devastator, who watched Chris intently since he spoke, saw the question in his face.

"You're probably wondering why Kayla would be with someone like me huh," he asked, giving him a cold, deadly smile.

"She loves me you know," Devastator said, taunting Chris more.

Dirty was almost beside himself. He was trying really hard not to laugh. He could see Monster was about ready to pop, too. They both loved the talent Devastator possessed for getting under their skin.

"Whatever man," Chris replied, rather resentfully.

Devastator smiled again. He knew he struck a nerve. Then the smile disappeared and Devastator got deadly serious once more.

"But today, you hurt my baby in a most vile way. You took the smile from her eyes. So, before I close yours for good, I want to know why," Devastator told him.

Chris swallowed hard. He found himself forced to tell this guy what he wanted to know. He prayed he would get out of this with his life intact, beaten, bloody, possibly maimed, but alive. He took a deep breath and began.

"I didn't go there with the intention of hurting her man, please believe that," Chris said.

For the next fifteen minutes, he told them what happened, apologizing and begging forgiveness throughout. Finally, Chris was silent, waiting for whatever was coming next from the men who were in his house.

Devastator listened intently while Chris told his story. He wasn't impressed with either the story or the apology. He certainly wasn't hearing anything about forgiveness or mercy at this point. He was ready to do the deed and reached behind him for the 9 mm tucked in his waistband when Dirty interrupted with a question.

"Was she awake when you raped her?"

Devastator looked at Chris in earnest then. He knew what Dirty was getting at. It was bad enough that he violated Kayla, but at least if she were unconscious, she wouldn't have to remember the actual act. Chris was scared as hell now. The answer he would have to give to this question was definitely more condemnation for him.

"No," he said quietly, looking at the floor. "That was after I hit her and she was out."

Dirty leaned back in his chair, he was satisfied at least that she didn't suffer that much. Devastator posed a question of his own.

"Did you cum?"

Chris flinched. *Damn*, he thought. *What kinda fucking question is that? This guy is a fucking sadist!*

Chris really didn't want to answer that. He was breathing hard now and Devastator was getting impatient.

"Well," he asked again icily.

Chris's mind was racing. What the hell could he say? *Of course I came.* He hadn't touched Kayla in over a year and she felt incredible to him.

"Look, just do what you came for," Chris replied still not looking at any of them.

Devastator got his answer. He walked up to Chris and stood face to face with him, looking him in the eye while speaking.

"Well, I hope you enjoyed yourself because you will never, ever, touch Kayla again," he said with a finality that made Chris catch his breath.

Devastator hit him then. Chris steeled himself for what he knew would be the beating of his life. It seemed to go on forever in his mind when finally the guy seemed to have spent himself. Devastator returned to his chair and sat down, still looking at Chris hard and cold.

Dirty was admiring his friend's work. He thought Devastator did a fine job of beating this joker down. He looked like a tenderized steak in the face. One of his eyes was closed and he was drooling blood.

He was still conscious though. Devastator made sure of that. He wanted him alive and awake, so he could see himself die. Dirty laughed at that last thought and lit a joint. He took a drag and passed it to Devastator who hit it then passed it to Monster.

"I made her a promise I wouldn't kill you," Devastator said addressing Chris anew.

Chris was elated! He was actually beginning to think he might live through this. He knew Kayla couldn't stand the thought that his death was her fault or his blood was on her hands. Chris thanked her silently.

"And I'm going to keep my promise. I'm not going to kill you," Devastator said.

Chris visibly relaxed and let out the breath he didn't even realize he held. They were all quiet until Dirty emptied his beer can, placed it on the table and stood up. He stretched and then looked at Chris.

"Well me personally, I didn't make any promises like that. So guess that leaves me free to do whatever I want, now doesn't it," he continued, taking the 9mm out of his waistband and checking the clip.

"Your days of hurting people are over, sorry muthafucker," Dirty said as he unloaded two slugs into Chris's chest.

He felt the bullets enter his body. The burning was unbelievable. Chris sank to his knees. He couldn't catch his breath and he couldn't see. He knew he was dying. He thought about Kayla and about what he did to her. He felt Monster kick him, heard him say he's gone then everything went black.

●●●

Devastator tried to be quiet as he came in the room.

Kayla was already awake. She looked at him when he came in.

"Did you keep your promise?"

Devastator walked over to Kayla, sat down on the bed and began to stroke her hair. Her face was still a little swollen and her mouth held an angry purple bruise on it.

"Yes, I kept my promise," he gently told her.

Kayla was looking him in the eye when he answered. She believed him.

"How're you feeling?"

She smiled weakly,

"I'm OK, just sore," she started "And, of course, my face," she stopped, reaching up to touch it gently.

Devastator hugged her tightly. "It's okay baby, you can cry if you want."

Kayla broke down and he held her until the tears subsided.

Devastator lifted her face to him and softly told her, "No one will ever hurt you again baby, I promise, not ever."

Kayla could tell from the look in his eye, he was telling her the truth. If it were humanly possible, Dezi would be true to his word. She smiled and Devastator smiled back, kissed her, then lay down beside her and held her as they both drifted off to sleep.

A Deadly 18 Encounter

Three months passed since her attack and Kayla relocated her office. Business was good and she was busy. It was hard for them at first, but she and Dezi were okay again. She didn't give thought about Chris for a while and she didn't run into his friend Brendan anywhere. She was grateful for that.

She and Taea were going to Le Bistro today for lunch. They had not been in a while. Today was special. Adrian was leaving. This was his last day and his co-workers were giving him a party. Kayla grabbed the gift and met Tea at the elevator, headed out to the restaurant.

•••

"Hey heffas," Adrian quipped to Taea and Kayla as they hugged him.

He was glad they came. He was trying to be happy about his decision to leave. He knew it was what Monster wanted and he loved that man with all his heart.

"So, you finally caught that sugar daddy to keep you kept huh," Taea teased him.

Adrian smiled. *If she only knew*, he chuckled thinking of Monster.

"Well you two can't be the only ones landing ballers and stuff," he shot back, laughing.

They all enjoyed themselves, talking and trading stories about Adrian and his days at Le Bistro. Even Joe, the cook, told him he would really miss him.

"Awwww, that deserves a hug," Adrian replied, hugging the big man and embarrassing him even further.

The cake was finally brought out and everyone was enjoying it when "Well, I have to leave you all now," Adrian announced. "I have a hot date."

"Mmhmm, you make sure you still call us and come see us heffa," Taea and Kayla told him as he was headed out the door.

Adrian took one last look at his old job, his friends, waved and headed out the door.

Kayla and Taea stayed a little while longer talking to each other then headed out the door, each to their own plans for the evening.

● ● ●

The theatrical performance was good and he enjoyed it in spite of himself.

Devastator smiled and Kayla noticed.

"What's so funny," she questioned looking mischievously at him.

"Inside joke," he told her smiling back.

She gave him a look that said whatever, which made Devastator laugh even harder. Kayla reached over and began to stroke his chest.

"Someone got some needs tonight do they," Devastator teased.

"Yes, Big Daddy," Kayla replied, moving her hands sensuously down his body.

He was getting turned on.

"Girl if you don't stop, I'ma hafta pull this truck over and there's going to be trouble then," he told her looking at her lustfully.

She smiled and moved her hands even lower almost touching his growing erection, looked him squarely in the eye, and smiled again.

"I dare you," Kayla replied.

Devastator was still smiling contentedly as they got back onto the expressway.

That shit was damned good, he thought. He pulled the truck off at the next exit when she dared him and found a secluded place. They climbed into the backseat of the truck and made love. He loved how free spirited she was. He looked over at her. She was smiling and looking out the window. He loved this woman. Kayla was the one positive in a life filled with negatives. He could never lose her. Devastator didn't know why he was thinking that way. They just made love and everything was fabulous. He just couldn't shake the feeling that there was a storm looming on the horizon. He dismissed it instead speaking aloud.

"You want to stop for ice cream?"

"Mmm, that sounds good," Kayla answered him.

She could use a little ice cream, she giggled inside.

"I told you, you shouldn't dare me like that," Devastator told her laughing.

She looked at him and laughed.

"Am I complaining mister?"

They arrived at the ice cream shop and ordered. Kayla asked for her usual butter pecan scoop in a waffle cone. Devastator decided on chocolate in a sugar cone. They were sitting on the outside patio, enjoying their cones when his cell went off. He looked at the ID. It was Todd.

What the hell does this joker want, Devastator internally asked.

He answered.

"I apologize for interrupting your evening, but it's really important," Todd immediately spoke up.

Damn well better be, Devastator thought.

"What is it," he asked, finishing his cone and eyeing Kayla's.

"Beginning of possible trouble," Todd told him. "I got a tip from a reliable source that the alphabet men are looking at our business."

Devastator didn't like the sound of that at all. *What the hell is the damned FBI up to*, he wondered. He didn't need that kind of heat.

"Okay, anybody made any moves yet," he asked Todd calmly.

He couldn't get into this the way he wanted to right now. Kayla was with him and he made it a rule to never involve her in any of his business matters.

"No, everything is still in the paper chase stage," Todd told him. "They're trying to find a crack in the armor to get that inside look."

Devastator thought for a moment then assured Todd he would handle it. "That's fine, everything is fine on my end," Todd told him .

"Good, we'll talk tomorrow," Devastator told him and ended the call.

Kayla was just finishing her ice cream scoop getting down to the cone when he reached over and took it from her.

"Hey," she squealed and swung at him.

He laughed and devoured the rest of her cone.

"Oh you are *so* gonna pay for that mister," she fumed at him, laughing as they headed for the truck and on to the house.

Devastator was thinking about what Todd told him. He knew there were calls to make so he could get this situation handled before it ever got started.

A Deadly 19 Encounter

"I ran the test again," Dr. Merritt was saying. "The results are the same I'm afraid," he told Taea softly. "It's positive, you're pregnant."

She was crying softly.

"Do you need me to call someone for you?"

She shook her head no.

"Alright then, go ahead and get dressed," he addressed. "I'll write up your chart."

"Thank you," Taea agreed as he nodded and left the room.

●●●

"What have we got so far," Special Agent Robert Keller asked.

The organized crime task force was holding their morning briefing. There were three groups they were concentrating on, one of which was The Clique.

"Not much I'm afraid," Agent Donovan Black replied.

Black was a seven-year veteran with the FBI and organized crime families were his specialty. He was assigned this case two months ago. It was inching along painfully since.

The Clique covered themselves well and everyone was seemingly afraid to talk. He effectively hit a brick wall, but was still trying to find that crack in the armor.

"Well, if we don't get something in the next couple months," Keller said. "We are going to be shit outta luck because the senate committee is threatening to pull the plug on this thing. I don't want to see that happen gentlemen, so let's get to it."

His dismissed the meeting amid the groans and sighs of disgust from the agents.

"I don't want to see that happen either," Black told his partner, agent Maurice Collins, back in the office they shared.

Collins nodded in agreement. They put a lot of man-hours into this group because they were the deadliest and most vicious. He knew they were dirty. Black felt they were close to getting in. He just needed to find that opening.

•••

I can't have this baby, Taea thought as she dressed. She was still crying. Her cell went off, bringing her out of her thoughts. She looked at the number, pulled herself together and answered the phone. It was Kayla.

"Hello," Taea answered, sounding as much like herself as she could at the moment.

"Hey girl, you want to have lunch?"

"Sure," Taea told her. Give me an hour and we can meet."

After Kayla acknowledged the direction, they hung up.

Taea began crying again. How was she going to get through this lunch and pretend nothing was wrong?

Taea began thinking about her pregnancy. *Why now? Things were going so damn well and then ---*, she didn't finish her thought.

Taea couldn't allow herself to get attached to this baby. She wasn't keeping it. There was no way she could do that. She needed to make that appointment and do it quickly before she wavered and changed her mind.

•••

"Let me see the files again," Black said to Collins, reaching for the worn manila envelope stuffed with papers.

"Man, you been through that thing at least forty times already," he said, laughing and handing him the folder once more.

Black nodded and began to go through it yet again. He possessed all the mug shots and background information on Dezi Gianni aka Devastator, Eric Greene aka Dirty and Kevin Bradley aka Monster. He also held information on their lieutenants in the field. He gathered surveillance photos of all of them with their partners at various clubs, malls and other public places. He also obtained photos of them with what he discovered were their significant others.

They ran background checks on each of them and come up empty. They were all clean as far as the criminal system was concerned. He and Collins set up a sting operation for the three of them.

Collins was going to try and get close to LaTaea Everett, Agent Zachary Dobbins would try to get information from Adrian Roberts and he would deal with Mikayla DeWitt.

He was feeling pressured now by what Keller said. He needed an in and he needed it now. Black called the other two agents into his office and told them it was time to get into gear. They had to push for information, carefully of course, but quickly, too. Time wasn't on their side anymore.

•••

"Girl, I'm starved," Kayla said to her best friend, "I think I'm going to have a steak today."

Her friend smiled, speaking softly. "I think I'll just have a salad. I don't have much of an appetite today."

She's been like that since she got here, Kayla thought. She noticed that Taea was pensive, almost anxious the entire time. *What the hell is going on with her? This isn't like her at all!*

Their food arrived and they began eating. Her steak was great and she was quickly devouring it while Taea was arranging her salad on her plate. After watching her pick through the salad for the last twenty minutes, Kayla finally decided to get to the bottom of whatever was going on.

She sat back in her chair, eyed her friend carefully for a minute and then spoke. "What exactly is going on with you today?"

•••

Black was looking at the file compiled on Mikayla. He knew her history, educational background, and financial status. The one thing he couldn't figure out was, what someone who was obviously well cultured and held good position in society, doing with a cold-blooded killer like Dezi Gianni.

He had her followed and watched the last month so he could learn her habits. She was pretty normal from all appearances. The photos he received weren't the greatest. They were usually too far away or her head was turned. He looked at the file again. He noticed that she also frequented a restaurant called Le Bistro during lunch hour.

According to his records, she usually arrived between noon and 1 p.m. Black looked at his watch and saw it was 12:45. She would be there now he figured. This would be a much better venue to meet her he decided and got up to leave. He truly hoped he could get something from her. Black needed this case to catch fire. He needed to shut down The Clique before they could kill anyone else. He received information that they were involved in a multiple murder in South Carolina a few months back, but he couldn't prove it. Black was hoping she was going to be able to open that door for him. How was he going to approach her though? He was still in deep thought about that very thing when he pulled onto the freeway, heading for Le Bistro and his assignment.

●●●

Taea took another deep breath, looked her lifelong friend in the eye and opened her mouth.

"I'm pregnant."

What? I couldn't have heard that right, Kayla thought.

"You're pregnant," she asked to verify what she thought she heard.

"Yes," Taea said again softly.

"Are you sure," Kayla asked, still not quite believing what she was hearing.

"Positive," she replied.

Kayla was speechless and felt like she wanted to cry. When she looked across the table at Taea, she was already crying.

"You know I'm here for you, don't you," she asked, reaching across the table and taking her hand. "No matter what you decide, I'm here for you."

Still crying, Taea managed to nod yes.

Kayla didn't want to upset her further but asked one last question.

"Does he know," she asked looking Taea in the eye.

She didn't answer. The look on her face said it all.

"Come on," Kayla said getting up. "Let's get outta here."

Kayla hugged Taea. "I love you."

"Thanks girl, I love you too."

They left the restaurant and headed for home.

They walked by Agent Black just as he was about to enter the restaurant. *Something is going on*, he surmised. They were distracted and looked upset.

He took the opportunity to actually see his assignment since none of his photos were very good. She was very pretty from the glance he got while they were walking. He grudgingly admitted Gianni had good taste.

Well, Black thought, *I won't get a chance to talk to her today. Something else is obviously going on with them.* He was disappointed. He could hear the clock ticking in his head. *Collins isn't going to have any luck with the friend either. Whatever was going on, they were both involved*, he thought yet another time as he watched them walk away. They would have to hope Dobbins struck pay dirt.

•••

They arrived home and were sitting in the den. "Have you given any thought to what you're going to do?"

"I'm having an abortion," Taea replied flatly.

Kayla couldn't understand her on this one. This was something she wanted at some point in her life. They talked about it at length with each of them, admitting they wouldn't mind if it happened. So why didn't Taea want to have the baby?

"Are you sure you want to do that?"

"It's all I've thought about since the doctor confirmed it for me," Taea told her. "Now, is not the time for this to happen, for reasons I can't go into right now. It's just better if I do this, and move on with my life."

Kayla was quiet for a few moments.

"Like I told you at the restaurant," Kayla began. "I'll stand by you, no matter what. I just want you to do one thing for me, please. Wait three days. That's Saturday and if you still want to do it, I'll drive you down there myself."

Taea sighed.

"Okay. Not that it will make a difference but, for you, I'll wait."

●●●

Black was thinking about her again. *What the hell is going on with me*, he chastised himself. He only glanced the woman for a good two minutes, but she stayed with him. He just couldn't get the connection between her and Gianni. He was thinking again of how he would approach her and decided business interest would be best. The bureau gave him fifty thousand to make him look legit. He called her office after he left the restaurant and made an appointment for tomorrow.

Black would have to dig up some of the social skills unused in a while. The ones they all kidded him at the bureau about not having. That brought a smile to his face. He needed to connect with her on some level, so she would begin to trust him and let him into her world. It would get him one step closer to bringing Gianni and that whole murderous bunch down.

Black went to his closet to pick out something to wear to his meeting tomorrow. He decided on the dark blue Armani. He put the navy and powder blue accessories with it. Then he headed to the bathroom to shave off the beard he grew over the last two months when they started work on this case. Black got the impression she didn't like beards and he needed very much for her to like him. His case depended on it.

●●●

Kayla really didn't feel like going to work today. She thought about the situation all night. Unfortunately, the sunlight didn't make it any brighter this morning. She gathered her things and went downstairs to head out. Taea was already in the kitchen when she got there.

"Hey," Kayla spoke.

"Hey," Taea replied.

With neither of them really knowing what to say, the silence hung heavy in the kitchen.

"Will you call the clinic and make the appointment for me?"

Kayla eyed her for a moment before answering.

"I'm making it for Saturday. You did promise me that, remember?"

"I know and I plan to stick to it," Taea told her. "I just want everything in place and ready."

Kayla smiled weakly.

"Okay, I'll take care of it today."

They told each other goodbye and headed for their offices.

•••

"Good morning, Anne," Kayla said walking into the office. "Do I have any appointments today?"

Anne looked up, noticing her tone and saw she wasn't her usual self today.

"Are you okay?"

"I'm fine just got a lot on my mind today," Kayla responded.

Anne didn't believe her but told her that was fine just the same.

"You have a prospect coming in at 10:00."

"Thanks, that's fine," she responded again. "Please make sure we have coffee and pastries available."

I can do this, she told herself, *even with all that is going on*. She forced herself to pull it together. Life still went on.

•••

"I need the lease agreement for 3401," Taea's boss said to her.

Taea was trying to focus. Her mind was a blur. There was so much going on. She was busy trying to sort everything out.

"I'm sorry Leo, here it is," she replied, handing him the file he was looking for.

He looked at her intently for a moment. Something was off about her today. There was no fire, no spark like she usually held.

"You OK?" he asked. "You seem kinda out of it."

She smiled.

"I'm fine, just had a lot of things going on right now."

She chided herself silently, *Ok girlie, you gotta pull yourself together. You gotta function and get through this.*

Leo was talking to her again bringing her back to now.

"There's a new tenant coming in at 10:30. He wants information on 3403. His name is Maurice Collins."

She smiled at her boss trying to reassure him.

"I'll handle it," she replied, getting up to get doughnuts for the prospective tenant.

She would make the coffee when she returned.

●●●

Black walked into her office at 9:50 a.m. He made sure the wire was secure and the unit it was attached to wasn't visible. He greeted the receptionist and let her know who he was.

"Oh yes, please have a seat," Anne instructed. "I'll let Ms. DeWitt know you're here."

Black looked around the office as he waited. He loved the African artwork she placed. Anne made a quick call.

"Please follow me sir," interrupting his thoughts.

She led him to the office, knocking on the door and opening it, signaling him to enter.

"Good morning, I'm Kayla DeWitt," she announced, stepping from behind her desk and extending her hand.

Black wasn't as prepared for this as he thought. He was absolutely blown away when he looked at her, finally seeing her head on. She was gorgeous. Kayla was impeccably dressed in a pale blue blouse and navy skirt that stopped right above her knee. Her hair was pulled back in a professional bun and her jewelry complimented her attire. He shook her hand and introduced himself.

"Donovan Black," he said smoothly, still drinking in the wonderful sight in front of him. *No wonder Gianni guards her like he does*, he pleasantly concluded. *She is definitely a ten plus*.

"So, Mr. Black," Kayla began, motioning him to take a seat before walking back to her desk, allowing him to take in her shapely legs and backside. "What can I help you with today?"

She studied him the entire time. He was a very attractive man, creamy caramel with beautiful deep brown eyes, clean-shaven, beautiful smile, tall like Dezi, a little thicker, but all muscle. *Nice arms, great for hugging and lifting and seemingly well endowed*, she thought from the glance she stole as he spoke. Kayla smiled inside as she took her seat.

Black was still thinking about how beautiful she was when she finished talking. He shook the thoughts and got back to business. He pulled himself together and began telling her the story they concocted. They spent the next two hours going over his portfolio. After their meeting ended, they shook hands again.

"I'm pleased to have you as my new client, Mr. Black," Kayla spoke smiling.

"I am as well," Black responded. "I think I've made an excellent choice."

She smiled again at that statement and his heart skipped another beat. They said goodbye.

Kayla watched him walk away admiring the sexy butt attached to the powerful thighs he possessed. *You're a very naughty girl*, Kayla chided herself for the thoughts she was having about him.

●●●

Black thought he did very well. Kayla seemed very much at ease with him, but then again, they were only discussing business. Something she was obviously very good at, given her financial profile. He felt that he made some headway. They talked vaguely about a few personal things. On his way back to the bureau, Black couldn't help thinking about the way her eyes lit up when she smiled. There he was doing it again. He had to stop. This woman was an assignment, nothing more. Stay professional, Black told himself, but he got the feeling that was going to be a lot easier said than done.

A Deadly 20 Encounter

It was Saturday morning and they were standing in the kitchen having one last conversation.

"You're sure you still want to do this," Kayla asked Taea again.

She shook her head yes. They went through a lot together and as much as Taea knew how she felt, she understood how Kayla felt, too.

"Let's go then," Kayla said softly and they both headed out the door to go to the clinic.

●●●

"I'm telling you she's pregnant and she's having an abortion," Devastator was telling Dirty.

"How you know man?"

Devastator called him early this morning, much too early as a matter of fact. He was livid that Kayla was pregnant and getting ready to get rid of his baby.

"The damned clinic called back to confirm her appointment yesterday," he replied "She was in the shower when they called and I answered the phone."

Devastator was totally oblivious when the woman called and said she wanted to confirm Kayla's appointment for Saturday. He never even suspected she was pregnant. Why would she want to kill their child? He wanted this baby more than anything right now. Devastator's mind was racing.

"So what you wanna do man," Dirty asked, already knowing the answer.

"We're going to be at that damned clinic when she gets there. She is not killing my child," Devastator replied matter-of-fact.

He would do whatever necessary to ensure that. Even if it meant locking her in a room and keeping her there until she went into labor.

"Well, let's get moving then," Dirty told him. "It's already 8:30. You said her appointment was at 9:30."

Dirty was already in his truck headed to the clinic.

He knew his friend well enough to know from the beginning of the conversation they would end up at the clinic. He dressed while he was talking.

Devastator also made his way to his truck and was heading out to the clinic. They would meet there they decided and hung up.

"This shit is not happening today," Devastator growled as he sped down the highway.

●●●

They were all at the clinic in the parking lot. Devastator and Dirty arrived at 9:00, parking in the shadows, where they had a good view, but couldn't be readily seen. Agents Black and Collins arrived at 9:03.

They were tailing Devastator coming in from the other end to avoid being made. They were definitely curious why they were here at the clinic. Obviously the two men were waiting for someone. Maybe a meet was going down and they would get something on film that they could use against these guys. Black didn't know, but he was going to hang around and see.

Kayla and Taea arrived at 9:12. They parked in front, close to the elevator entrance. The building was carefully camouflaged as a podiatry office. There was a giant foot on the sign hanging above it, listing various foot ailments. It helped ward off the protesters, who without fail showed up every weekend like clockwork.

Devastator was angry and hurt seeing her arrive. He couldn't believe she was actually here. That she was going to actually go through with killing their baby, but there she was, sitting in the car getting ready to get out and do just that.

Inside the car, Kayla and Taea embraced. They looked at each other, but said nothing. It was what they didn't say that came through the loudest when they looked into each other's eyes, both trying hard not to cry.

Devastator and Dirty were out of the truck and almost to the car. Black and Collins watched the scene unfolding in front of them with interest and waited.

Taea was outside of the car and adjusting her clothes when she looked up and saw them. She didn't have time to react or warn her friend. Kayla was halfway out, reaching for her cell in the console, when she felt herself being pulled out of the car.

"What the hell are you doing here," Devastator screamed at her.

He pulled her from the car and pinned her against it. She was still trying to get her balance. Black and Collins were watching intently. Kayla was terrified. She never saw him like this. He was furious. His eyes were blazing. She couldn't get the words to come out. Her mouth tried to move, but nothing came out.

"Why would you do this," he was still yelling.

Kayla was crying now.

He continued to demand an answer as Kayla remained mute, too afraid to open her mouth and unsure what to even say.

Devastator was getting more frustrated.

She still wasn't saying a word. He wanted to get through to her. He wanted her to know how much he was against this.

"Why are you here," he screamed again, shaking her violently.

It took everything in Black not to get out of the car and take this guy down now, but he held himself in check and continued to watch what was going on.

Dirty saw the situation getting out of control. They didn't need the police to show up. Dirty ran over, grabbed him and pulled him off her.

"Man get a hold on it!"

Devastator was still looking at Kayla. She was sobbing now, holding onto Taea, who was trying to comfort her.

"You're gonna hurt her man, and the baby, too," he told him.

That seemed to calm him down a little and he started talking to her again.

Devastator pleaded with Kayla again for an answer to her being here at the clinic. She still remained mute, continuing to lean on Taea for support as Devastator fought desperately to control the rage he felt.

Black was surprised. She was pregnant? Black looked at her again. She stopped crying, but she wasn't getting anywhere near Gianni right now. She actually stepped back a couple of feet when he started to walk toward her.

Dirty was thinking while Devastator was talking. He brought a couple of the girls down here in the past. They got caught up, the condom broke, always some stupid stuff, but he remembered some of the things they told him. A new realization began to take hold of Dirty as he recalled some of the observations he made as Kayla and Taea arrived.

He stepped in front of Devastator, who stopped talking and looked directly at Taea.

"Kayla's not the one here for the abortion, is she baby girl?"

Everyone was silent.

Black and Collins were still watching intently from their car.

Finally, Taea looked at Dirty and quietly told him what he wanted to know.

"No, she's not the one," she replied almost inaudibly.

He was crushed. He couldn't describe the pain he felt when she said those words. Dirty loved this woman. He didn't understand, but he needed her to make him understand.

"Can we at least go talk about this, and you help me understand why," he asked her calmly.

Taea knew she owed him at least that much. Besides she loved him and somewhere in her heart she hoped she really could make him understand. She reluctantly agreed. She paused long enough to check on Kayla and be sure she would be all right.

"I'm fine, but please Taea, don't go with him," Kayla implored.

Taea smiled and hugged Kayla tightly.

"I love you, I'll always love you," Taea began. "But I have to be woman enough to face the mess I've made, and whatever happens I have to deal with that too."

Taea headed for the truck with Dirty and they drove off, headed to his place.

Devastator was speechless. She let him think it was her to protect her friend. She never even defended herself. He felt really stupid. He messed up this time and he knew it. He would have to work hard to make it up to her.

"Baby," he said softly.

Kayla turned to him. The look she gave taking him aback. She was livid; her face showed it plain and simple.

"I would never kill my own child," she coldly told him. "How could you even think such a thing of me?"

Turning, Kayla began to get into her car.

He tried to touch her. Devastator wanted to take her in his arms and hold her, but she wasn't having any of that.

"Get the hell away from me," Kayla said harshly breathing hard. "You put your hands on me, you were hurting me. I don't know if I can forgive you for that," she said starting the car.

Devastator was stunned.

"Baby, no don't say that," he told her quickly, pleading with her to stay and talk to him.

"I have nothing else to say to you right now. Please just leave me alone."

He stepped back from the car and let her leave.

I can't lose her! I just can't! Devastator thought.

He would drive by Dirty's and make sure everything was cool with him then head over to her house. He didn't care what she said. He was not going to give her the opportunity to decide she could live without him.

Black and Collins watched Kayla leave, knowing she was angry with Gianni.

"Looks like the perfect time for you to move in," Collins remarked to Black.

Black knew Collins was right. As low as it seemed, Kayla was ripe for a friend and he was determined to be that friend. He would give her a few minutes and he would call her.

•••

They arrived at Dirty's house about ten minutes ago. It was an expansive home located in a quiet, secluded community. She came over often and loved the layout as well as the professional décor. They were sitting in the living room on the massive leather sofa. The grouping was all black with white and burgundy accents throughout. The ceilings were vaulted and the room was laced with crown molding. Usually, she always felt warm and comfortable here, but today she felt completely alien. *Why won't he say anything,* Taea was wondering. He never uttered a word since they left the clinic. He was sitting across from her, staring and drinking his beer.

Dirty was trying to get his mind together. He was trying to figure out why she hid this from him and why would she be trying to kill their child.

"How far along are you," Dirty finally asked, not taking his eyes off her.

"About eight weeks," Taea replied quietly.

She was scared. She knew he carried a temper, but he never went off on her. Still, after what witnessed today with Dezi, she wasn't taking any chances. Dirty nodded thoughtfully after she answered then took a deep breath.

"So, make me understand why you were at that clinic," he told her, his grip tightening on the can he was holding.

Now, she was terrified. Taea knew he was angry. He was trying hard to control himself she could see, but he was pissed and she knew it. Taea started regretting her decision to come here, but it was too late now. She had to tell him the truth. She blew a long breath and began to tell him what he wanted to know.

•••

Kayla's cell was ringing.

"This better not be Dezi," she said heatedly, picking it up and looking at it.

The number came up unknown. *Hmm*, she thought, *might be business*. Some of her clients did call her on Saturday if they needed her immediately.

"Kayla DeWitt," she answered.

Black thought she sounded pretty good for someone who just experienced what she went through.

"Hi, I'm just checking with you because I haven't heard from you in a couple days."

"Everything is fine," Kayla told him. "You actually made a little money yesterday."

"Well, I have some free time if you would like to get together for lunch and you can show me then," he said.

He held his breath waiting for her answer.

She really wasn't in the mood for this now, but it was her job and maybe it was what she needed to soothe her frazzled nerves.

"That'll be fine Mr. Black," Kayla told him.

Black was elated, feeling like he was actually getting somewhere. "Cool, how about we meet at Le Bistro?"

"I know the place well," Kayla remarked, laughing, before disconnecting.

I have to make this work, he thought. He wouldn't get another perfect opportunity like this. She was definitely emotionally disadvantaged right now. He would play on it and use it to get closer to her. Sometimes Black hated parts of his job, but it was still his job. Personally, he thought Kayla was nice enough, but she held the key to what he needed; information on Gianni. Black would do whatever necessary, to get it out of her.

•••

"So you just snuck your ass down to the clinic, was gonna get rid of the baby and tell me what exactly," Dirty asked angrily as they continued to talk about this morning.

"It wasn't like that," Taea threw back still trying to explain.

"Yeah? Well let's see, you didn't tell me you were pregnant, you didn't ask me if I wanted the baby, you and your home girl just headed right on downtown. So you tell me what the fuck I'm supposed to think," Dirty yelled again as he flung the beer can in her direction.

Taea took a deep breath trying to calm herself again. She didn't want the situation to get out of hand any more than it already was. She knew Dirty was angry and most of the anger was from hurt.

"Please Eric, just listen," Taea tried again as the first tear escaped.

"Man, I don't want to hear no more lies right now. Tell me the fucking truth," Dirty ranted. "Tell me why the fuck you would kill my baby and not even bother to tell my ass about it. Just tell me that shit. It's all I'm interested in knowing right now."

He waited for her response.

Taea took another deep breath to push the fear away as she told Dirty about that night two months ago in South Carolina.

●●●

Stan was calling Taea another time.

"Look," he said, once he got her answering machine "I've been trying to reach you all day, so I'll just tell you what I want. I found that slime Gavin today and after I kicked his ass, he told the truth. You didn't sleep with him Taea. He lied. You passed out and he took your clothes off. Then let you think that the two of you slept together when you woke up the next morning."

He was about to hang up when he thought of something else.

"I love you girl. You know that. Call your big brother soon, will ya?"

He sure hoped she got that message. She was a wreck when he talked to her last. He had a bad feeling but dismissed it as nerves and headed back out the door to the spot. There was business to take care of.

He would call Kayla later and check on her, too. He was feeling something just wasn't quite right today.

●●●

Black arrived at the restaurant before her and got them a table off to the rear. He wanted some privacy with Kayla. He was wired up again. They didn't want any loopholes left for Gianni to slide out of when they finally busted him. Black was still deep in thought when his cell went off. He saw it was Collins.

He immediately broke the bad news to Agent Black. There was a major new development that depending on how it was played would either make or break their investigation. Black was stunned. He didn't expect this. Collins began to explain, as Kayla walked in.

"We'll talk later," he quickly interrupted Collins before disconnecting.

"Hi," Kayla greeted him smiling when she reached the table. "Sorry I'm late. I stopped by the office and got your files."

She sat down in the chair he pulled out for her.

"Would you like to go over your file now, or after lunch?

"After lunch will be perfect," Black told her.

"That's fine," Kayla smiled again.

Black did love the way she smiled, he thought again, taking her in from head to toe.

A Deadly 21 *Encounter*

Dirty was finishing the bottle of vodka, stroking her hair now as he held her. Taea was quiet. She remained so for a little while as his mind raced thinking back on how they met, the times they shared, and how great Taea made him feel.

His heart was void of love for a long time. Hell, Dirty didn't think he ever was in love like this before. Taea brought out things in him he didn't know were inside. He thought about her laughter and her sassiness, which attracted him to her in the first place.

She reminded him about their last visit to South Carolina together. He went to check on the operation and took her with him. They engaged in a huge fight because Taea wanted to stay a little longer and wanted Dirty to stay with her. Dirty angrily told her he didn't have time to babysit and left the house as she cursed him, throwing a vase at his head when he walked out.

She was still angry and feeling abandoned when he left. Dirty didn't want to leave, but the business here needed his attention. Looking back now, he supposed it would have been better if he said that instead of the insulting thing he did say. Taea told Dirty how she smoked and drank most of the night just to spite him. Her old friend, Gavin, came over supposedly to see Stan and found her there instead.

Taea told him that she and Gavin smoked and drank more, and ended up having sex. She said she didn't remember the actual act. She was too drunk and high, but she woke up naked with him the next morning, so they must have. Dirty was floored. He downed the rest of the liquor in his glass trying hard not to hit Taea right now.

So how the fuck am I supposed to feel right now," Dirty screamed at her.

"Eric I'm sorry, baby please," Taea tried again as Dirty threw his glass at her.

"Shut up! Just shut the fuck up with that shit!"

Taea began to cry as Dirty continued to glare at her.

"I'm sorry," she managed to get out in between the painful sobs.

Dirty sighed deeply as he watched Taea. He finally acknowledged his own role in the whole mess. He rose from his chair to go over to the couch and sit beside her. Dirty was still angry but trying to be reasonable. Still, he wondered how could she have done that to him? Dirty loved her with all his heart and she broke it today.

He asked her if she didn't get pregnant would she have ever told him. She was quiet for a long time, finally replying she didn't know. Dirty felt so betrayed and empty. He wanted a child and now Taea was telling him the one she was carrying may not be his. His mind was totally blown.

He got up again and made himself another drink. Taea asked him if he could ever forgive her for what she did. She told him she loved him and that she never wanted to hurt him or see the pain in his face she saw now because of something she did. She was still crying as he came back sitting down beside her. Dirty held her and they started to kiss.

"Shh, stop crying," Dirty told her in between the kisses.

Taea smiled slightly at him as he began kissing her again.

Dirty found himself becoming aroused. He wanted to make love to her, but then his mind begin replaying all the things Taea just admitted. Dirty tried as hard as he could to push them away as they continued to kiss and his hands roamed freely over her body.

Taea responded to his touch by pressing her body even closer to his own.

"I love you Eric," Taea told him softly as he kissed her neck, heading from her breasts.

The statement stung a little and Dirty returned to her lips, trying again to block out the darkness that was slowly overtaking him. All he kept seeing was her and Gavin making love. All he kept hearing was that the child in her womb wasn't his own.

Dirty didn't realize he was choking her until she started fighting back. He looked in her eyes as he killed her. Taea was trying to make him stop, hitting and scratching him. In the end, she gave up, closed her eyes and slumped down on the couch.

Dirty looked down at her again returning to the present. He was still holding her in his arms. He was in so much pain.

What have I done? Oh, God what did I do? He never meant to kill her. He was just angry and hurt. He loved Taea. He would never have done this to her. They could have made another baby. They could have tried again to be together. He should have been able to find it in his heart to forgive her. He was just too stupid. This was the kind of stuff Devastator always warned him about.

Now, Taea was dead and Dirty was hurting. The walls were screaming at him. He heard his mother telling him he was stupid and destined to fail. He heard his sisters and classmates laughing at him again, calling him slow. He saw Cobra laughing at him for crying when he was hurt. He thought of the pain he would cause Devastator and Kayla for what he did to Taea.

Dirty desperately wanted the pain to stop. He wanted to stop the screaming in his head. He kissed Taea on the forehead, tears rolling down his cheeks.

"I'm sorry baby," Dirty whispered. "I forgive you," he told her as he pulled the trigger on the 9mm he held pointed at his head.

•••

Devastator entered the subdivision when he saw the emergency vehicles.

What's going on, he wondered as he rounded the corner and saw they were stopped in front of Dirty's house. He began to get a sinking feeling in his gut. Devastator pulled up behind one of the other cars parked along the street where he still got a good view of Dirty's front door and waited.

"Shit, Dirty," he said aloud. "What have you done man?"

He wouldn't have to wait long for the answer. Devastator saw them bring out a stretcher with the body on it fully covered. It looked small, so he knew it was Taea.

"Oh, God," he said again. "Tell me you didn't kill her man."

They didn't need this kind of heat right now.

What the hell did she tell him to make him go off like that, Devastator sat thinking.

He was waiting on them to bring Dirty out of the house in cuffs. He would have to get their attorney to work on this fast.

He wasn't prepared for what happened next. They brought another body out of the house.

"What the fuck," Devastator asked, but already knew the answer.

He knew that the body in that bag belonged to his friend, his partner and the only family he claimed in years. His mind was reeling. What the hell happened in that house? Devastator was trying to comprehend that Dirty was really dead. That his best friend wasn't coming out with him to smoke, drink, and take care of business.

Dirty was gone and this time there wasn't any coming back from that. Devastator didn't know how to feel. He didn't know what to do with the deep hurt he felt in his heart right now.

●●●

Devastator took a deep breath, pulled himself together and prepared to get out of the car. The police and ambulance were gone now. Everyone was gone back into their homes. He was alone. The irony of that hit him hard and he started to hurt all over again. He got out of the car and walked up the sidewalk. He went behind the house to enter from the rear.

He used his key and went inside, coming in through the kitchen. Devastator came into the living room. It was filled with debris, papers, and the like. He saw the blood and brain matter on the wall. Devastator figured Dirty killed her, then realizing he messed up, killed himself.

"Why man," he whispered out loud to his dead friend.

He saw Taea's cell under the couch. *Musta fell there*, Devastator thought as he bent to pick it up. He scrolled through the calls she missed. Four were from her brother and one was from Kayla.

"Shit," Devastator said aloud again.

It hit him that he was going to have to tell her what happened. How the hell was he going to do that? He could barely believe it himself. He already knew that Kayla was going to lose it, but she had to know and he needed to tell her before the cops showed up. Devastator took one last look at the house, called the Front 5 and headed out the door to go find Kayla.

●●●

Kayla was speeding down the interstate, jazz pumping through her speakers, in deep thought. She was thinking about the scene at the clinic this morning. She was worried. There was no word from Taea all day.

"I hope you're OK," Kayla mumbled out loud.

She was scared for her friend. She knew the real reason Taea wanted the abortion. They talked about it the night before.

"Please girl, don't tell him the truth," Kayla said aloud again as she turned onto her street.

Kayla knew Eric would flip. He had a temper and she wasn't sure what he might do. She saw Dezi's truck when she opened her garage, which immediately put her in a worse mood.

"What the hell is he doing here?"

•••

Devastator heard her pull up. He smoked a little to try and calm his nerves. He wasn't looking forward to the task he was charged to perform now. He heard her come in and he walked toward the kitchen to meet her.

"Hey," Devastator greeted her.

Kayla gave him a frown in response.

"Why are you here," she asked testily. "I really just want to be alone, OK?"

She walked away from him.

Damn, he didn't want to do this.

"Can you sit down please baby? I need to talk to you," he told her.

Kayla stopped, looked at him hard and was about to say no when the look on his face told her something was wrong. She didn't think she wanted to sit so she didn't.

"What's wrong," Kayla asked him cautiously.

"Please, sit down baby," Devastator asked her again, a little more forcefully.

She was really starting to panic. *What the hell is going on*, Kayla asked herself.

She sat this time and waited for him to speak. Devastator's mind was racing. How was he going to put into words what he needed to tell her?

Kayla was staring at him intently and Devastator realized he was going to have to say something.

"Baby, Taea is gone," he said delicately.

Kayla sighed.

"Gone where," she asked him still not fully grasping what he was saying.

"Did she leave town? Go to her brother's or something," Kayla asked.

That wasn't so bad, so why was he tripping, she wondered.

Devastator walked over to her chair, kneeled down in front of her and looked her into her eyes.

"Taea is dead, baby," he said quietly.

Who is what, Kayla thought, looking at him like he was speaking Japanese. She could not have heard what she thought he said.

"What the hell are you talking about," she asked him, screaming and bolting from the chair she was sitting in.

Devastator grabbed her. She was hysterical.

"I'm sorry baby, I'm sorry," he said trying to get her to calm down.

"Where is she," Kayla was still screaming. "I want Taea! Where is she?!"

She couldn't, no she wouldn't accept this thing he was telling her. He was lying; he had to be, oh, God he had to be, Kayla thought, trying to reason.

She couldn't breathe. The room was spinning. This was not happening! Devastator caught her just before she hit the floor. He lifted her and carried her to the den and laid her on the couch.

He went to the kitchen to get her something to drink, deciding on juice and slipping in a Valium. Devastator needed Kayla to relax and to sleep. He needed to make some calls. He needed to inform people of Dirty's death and make arrangements. He was going to call Stan and try to explain Taea's death, too. Devastator returned with the juice, finding Kayla curled into a fetal position, rocking back and forth, still crying with her eyes tightly shut.

"Baby, please drink this," Devastator said gently, offering her the cup.

Kayla pushed his hand away.

"You need to drink this, please honey," he told her again, taking her in his arms and putting the glass to her lips.

Kayla drank this time and he made sure she emptied the glass before he put it down. Devastator held her and let Kayla cry herself to sleep. He laid her back on the couch and went into the living room to make his calls. It was going to be a long night.

A Deadly 22 Encounter

Black was thinking about his meeting with Kayla earlier and how well it went. He hoped she would call, but Black knew once she heard about Taea, she wouldn't be in any shape to call for a while. He hoped Kayla would be all right, finding himself genuinely concerned about her.

He read her file again. He knew that she and Taea were friends for many years. It was bound to be a tremendous blow to her. Black was finding it harder to be objective about her. Kayla was such a nice person. She seemed genuine and he had a hard time vilifying her or putting her on the same plane as Gianni, but Black was going to perform his job. That meant finding out all he could about The Clique. If Kayla held information, he would find a way to get it out of her. He picked up his cell and dialed Collins.

"Has anyone claimed Greene's body yet?"

"Yeah, the funeral home just picked it up," Collins returned. "The girl, too," he added.

He knew it must be Gianni. Black seriously doubted Kayla was in any shape to do any of that right now. He also wondered how she would react when she found out her man's best friend was the one who killed her best friend. Black was hoping it drove an even deeper wedge between her and Gianni and not just for the sake of the case either.

"Have you heard from Dobbins," Black asked.

"Yeah, we're meeting in the morning and he's going to tell us how it went," he told Black.

He was still sitting on the couch, nursing his bourbon and looking at her picture after they hung up. He truly hoped Kayla was the innocent. Black shook the thoughts and feelings he was developing for her and went to take a shower.

"You gotta stay objective man," Black told himself, knowing full well he was already fighting a losing battle.

•••

Agent Dobbins's day was extremely productive. He met Adrian earlier that morning as he was walking his dog.

"Hello there," Dobbins greeted him.

Adrian was startled. He never saw the man walking up to him. He was so lost in his thoughts and trying to control Master, the chocolate cocker spaniel puppy Kevin gave him for his birthday.

"Well, hello yourself," Adrian returned to the stranger.

The puppy was busy wrapping himself around Adrian's legs as usual and wagging his tail at the stranger.

Some watchdog! Didn't even bark at the guy, Adrian thought almost laughing aloud.

"I live in the house at the front of the subdivision," Dobbins told Adrian. "I bought it originally with my partner, but we're not together now, so it's just me, fending for myself."

"I know how that can be," Adrian replied sympathetically, letting out a huge sigh.

They walked together through the rest of the subdivision and Dobbins even managed to get an invitation to come to Adrian and Kevin's home.

"I will definitely take you up on that," Dobbins smiled. "Matter of fact you guys might get tired of seeing me."

"I doubt that," Adrian laughed. "I would welcome the company."

They smiled, waved and they each went their separate ways.

Adrian walked back to his house, excited that he made a new friend. Kevin was gone more these days and he was tired of being home alone.

"Come on Master," he told the rambunctious puppy as they both went inside the house.

Dobbins returned to the entrance of the cul-de-sac and got into his car. *That went very well,* he thought. He chuckled, thinking what a good job he did, started the car and headed home. Tomorrow was a new day and, with any luck, might bring some new leads to crack this case.

•••

Black and Collins were astonished at the number of people attending Greene's funeral some three days later.

"Looks like the damned crime family royalty has turned out in full force," Collins remarked.

Black nodded in agreement. They were everywhere. He knew it would be like this. They all came out to pay their respects.

He saw Gianni arrive earlier and knew he was in the chapel. Black didn't see Kayla. He actually didn't expect, too. He knew she wouldn't come. Greene killed her best friend. Black doubted Kayla would be too broken up over his dying.

•••

Devastator was greeting the mourners and accepting their condolences. The service was nice. He managed to find one of Dirty's sisters. She came to the services. He found her address when he went through Dirty's things after the Front 5 removed anything incriminating about their business dealings. She was a very nice woman. She and Dirty communicated regularly and formed a good relationship. Devastator found out she was a small child when Dirty's mother threw him out. She never really knew him, but always wanted to find him. Devastator gave her a cashier's check with some of the money from Dirty's investments and accounts.

Kayla wouldn't come. She was still hurting. Devastator couldn't fault her for that. He knew they still were flying to South Carolina for Taea's funeral.

Kayla agreed to Stan's request that his little sister come home to rest. It was a service he wasn't looking forward to, but Kayla would need him so Devastator would go. Devastator looked one last time at the fresh grave his friend rested in. Glanced at Eric's stone, said goodbye and walked slowly back to his truck. Black and Collins watched with interest.

•••

"Guess he does actually have some feelings huh," Collins remarked, half to himself.

Black was thinking the same thing. Greene's death seemed to have affected Gianni a lot deeper than they thought it would.

"Don't get too choked up for him," Black said aloud. "He's still a dangerous and vicious killer, probably even more so now. Grief has a way of doing that to some people."

Collins nodded in agreement as they started the car and left the cemetery.

●●●

Kayla and Dezi were to arrive in South Carolina, the morning of the funeral. Taea's body was flown back home a few days earlier. Stan was still trying to believe his younger sister was dead. Yet, here he was standing in this funeral home and looking into her peaceful face.

How could Eric have done this, Stan asked himself, tears threatening to come another time.

"I'm gonna get him Taea," Stan told her, knowing she didn't hear.

He made up his mind this was all Gavin's fault.

"That lying bastard!"

If he never told her that lie, she would not be dead. He didn't know about the baby. Taea didn't tell him that when he talked to her that Thursday night. Now, both his sister and her child were lying in this box because of Gavin.

Hatred, anger, and rage, stirred anew in Stan as he left the funeral home, to go and pick up Kayla and Dezi.

He thought about Kayla all the way to the airport. She was a wreck when he talked to her. He and Dezi ended up making all the arrangements. Stan hoped she was better. He knew she was lost. Taea was her lifeline for so many years that Stan really couldn't imagine either one of them without the other.

Stan saw them standing in the loading zone when he pulled up. Kayla greeted him with a small smile. *She is really trying,* Stan thought looking at her. He could tell Kayla was sleepless for a few days and looked like she wasn't eating much either. Stan hugged her and kissed her on the cheek. He and Dezi shook hands as they all got into the truck and headed for the service.

They arrived at the small brick church Kayla and Taea both attended when they were younger. Kayla smiled when she saw all the people who turned out to say good bye to Taea. *She would have loved this*, she thought and chuckled silently. Taea enjoyed being the center of attention. Kayla was seated on the front row with Stan and their sisters to her left and Dezi on her right.

The church had not changed much over the years. The wooden pews were replaced with new, red padded ones, Kayla noted. The same picture of Christ hung over the pulpit and the Sunday school banners still lined the walls. Today the church was filled with flowers and plants sent by various people to show their respect and say goodbye to Taea. Kayla knew the minister was speaking, but she couldn't hear what he was saying.

Kayla was staring at the soft pink coffin sitting in front of her, covered in cream and pink roses. Kayla was trying to wrap her mind around the fact that her friend, sister, the only family she knew for more than 10 years, was lying inside.

She thought about all the times they shared, the laughter, the pain and the secrets. Kayla thought about all the trips they took together and the plans they made. She thought about how protective Taea was of her. Kayla thought about how alone she was now. She closed her eyes. She didn't want to see that coffin anymore. Kayla didn't want to know her best friend wasn't coming back. The pain became even more unbearable and Kayla began to sob loudly. *Why*, was all she could think to ask.

Dezi took Kayla in his arms hugging her tightly and kissing her head trying to comfort her. Kayla clung to him, needing his strength just to breathe. It hurt so much. She didn't know how she made it through the service.

She asked Stan to have them open the coffin when they were at the cemetery. Kayla wanted to see her one last time. Stan reluctantly agreed. Kayla was standing beside it, looking at her friend. Taea looked peaceful, like she was sleeping, but Kayla knew she would never wake up again. The pink dress she wore was beautiful and made her look even more peaceful.

Damn Eric, Kayla thought angrily. *Damn him to hell!*

She placed a single pink rose inside the coffin, resting on Taea's crossed hands. Kayla leaned in and kissed Taea on the cheek and told her she loved her and that she would never forget her. Kayla's grief overtook her again and she began to cry uncontrollably. Stan pulled her gently away.

They closed the coffin and began to lower it into the grave they prepared. It was more than Kayla could take. She began to scream at them to stop. Dezi physically restrained her to keep her from running back to the open grave, finally picking Kayla up and taking her to the car.

She didn't remember passing out. She awoke lying on Stan's bed.

Stan stuck his head in to check on Kayla. He didn't hear her stir since they put her there.

"Hey," he said gently, speaking to Kayla.

"Hey yourself," Kayla replied trying to smile.

Stan came in and sat down on the bed beside her. They talked about Taea and about Kayla's life now. They shared a few tears and regrets, then embraced and promised to always be there for each other. Dezi came in just as they were parting.

"Sorry, didn't mean to interrupt," he told them gently.

"Its fine, just saying goodbye," they both told him.

"I'll take you guys to the airport as soon as you're ready," Stand now spoke.

"Thanks, give us about ten minutes," Devastator replied.

A Deadly 23 Encounter

Black was thinking about her again. He knew Kayla was back. His surveillance confirmed the fact for him. It took two weeks before she called him tonight. She said she needed to talk, so Black invited her over. He was glad Kayla was coming. Black also wanted to see for himself how she was. He knew her friend's death hit her really hard.

They were still trying to gather evidence for their case and coming up light. Dobbins was doing a good job with Adrian. He told them Adrian's tongue got very loose after about the third glass of wine, but he really didn't know anything. Black was hoping his meeting with Kayla would be a lot more productive.

●●●

Kayla felt pretty down most of the day; her thoughts constantly on Taea. Dezi called her numerous times, but she didn't feel like seeing him tonight.

She thought of Mr. Black and his offer after dinner when she was really feeling alone, so she called him. He remained true to his word and invited her over. Kayla was getting ready to go see him now. She needed someone to talk to. Someone who wouldn't patronize her or give her 'that look' like Dezi did since Taea's death. Her cell went off and Kayla looked at the display. It was Dezi of course.

"Hey you," she answered. "What's up," she asked, trying to sound upbeat.

"Hey baby," Devastator replied. "Whatcha doing?"

Kayla didn't want to lie, but she didn't want him to come over either.

"I'm going out for a little while," she replied which was the truth.

"So where are you going," he asked her nonchalantly.

"To Impressions," Kayla replied, asking silent forgiveness for the lie she told.

"Sounds like a plan," Devastator told her. "Have fun, I'll call you later on."

"OK, I will," Kayla replied. "Love you."

Kayla checked her reflection one more time. She was wearing a cute pair of low-cut jeans that hugged her curves, soft lavender, sleeveless, crosscut top and matching stiletto sandals. Her hair was up and she was wearing very little jewelry outside of her earrings. Satisfied that she looked okay, she picked up her keys and headed out the door. Black gave her great directions and she found the place easily.

"This is nice," Kayla said admirably, driving into the complex.

The property was beautifully landscaped with majestic trees and flowering blooms. There was a community tennis court and pool. Kayla loved the turn of the century gazebo and picnic area she saw adjacent to his building. After finding his unit, Kayla parked the Benz and got out.

● ● ●

Devastator's cell went off. He looked at the display and saw it was Todd. *Probably calling with some more information,* he thought as he answered.

"Yeah," Devastator said into the mouthpiece.

"I got some information from our source," Todd said.

The FBI was getting ready to have the IRS audit them. They were going to try and shut down some of the legitimate businesses and hoped the IRS would find some information to assist them with that.

"But, according to our agent, the IRS is in no hurry," Todd told him. "They may make a move in the next couple of weeks or so."

Devastator thought that was good news. It still gave them plenty of time to launder more money and to get their books and documents in order.

"Good, you and I will meet soon," he told Todd.

This shit is beginning to become a problem, Devastator irritably pondered. He was glad they secured the source at the bureau though. He paid good money to find himself one when he first heard that the alphabet boys were looking at him. Devastator chuckled.

Yeah, that was an excellent investment, he thought as he continued to drive. He decided he would swing by Kayla's. Probably wait on her to get home. Even though she went out to the club, he knew she wouldn't stay long. She planned to go into her office tomorrow and she took her work very seriously.

• • •

Kayla knocked gently on the door and waited for him to answer. She was nervous. Kayla hoped he wasn't just another guy trying to put the moves on her. Even though she thought Black was very attractive, what she wanted right now was a friend.

Black heard her knock. He double-checked the microphone's that were in place, took a deep breath and headed to the door.

"Hi there," Black greeted her when he opened the door and showed her in.

He took her in as she entered. Black loved the way Kayla looked in the low-rise jeans. *This is going to be a long night*, he thought, admiring every curvaceous angle of her body.

"Hi, yourself," Kayla told him, smiling.

Black showed Kayla to the couch.

"Would you like something to drink," he offered.

"Sure, something non-alcoholic," she replied.

Black brought her fruit juice.

"I really appreciate you letting me come over tonight, Mr. Black," Kayla told him after he sat down across from her.

Black wanted to sit next to her, but he didn't trust himself to be that close to her right now. He looked at Kayla intently.

"You are going to have to stop calling me that," he told her. "My father is Mr. Black."

Kayla laughed.

"I'm sorry, I'll call you Donovan," she replied.

"Just call me Black, that's what everyone calls me."

He wasn't very fond of being called by his first name.

"Well, how about Don? Or Van?" Kayla suggested, still smiling looking directly into his eyes.

She was teasing him, Black finally figured out.

"No, absolutely not," he smiled back.

Kayla laughed.

"OK, I'll call you Black."

They shared a good visit. Kayla talked to him about herself and Black found out a lot about her that his report didn't tell him. Black loved looking at her. He wanted to ask Kayla what the hell she was doing with Gianni, but he didn't.

Kayla looked at her watch. It was after 11. She needed to go. She was working tomorrow, not to mention, she was pretty sure Dezi was at the house, waiting for her.

"I'm sorry, but I'm going to have to leave you now," Kayla told him, smiling again.

Black wasn't ready for her to go yet. They were enjoying such a wonderful evening, but he knew he would have to let her go.

"Well, I certainly hope this is the first of many visits you'll pay," Black told her smoothly.

Kayla reflected for a moment. Black was the perfect gentleman. He didn't try anything, or say anything, that would lead her to believe he harbored any other intentions except being her friend.

"As a matter of fact, I think I will come back," Kayla told Black as she rose to leave.

He walked her downstairs to her car and gave her a short hug.

"Drive safely."

"Thanks again for listening and I promise to call soon," she told him getting into the car.

●●●

Black watched Kayla back out and drive away before returning to his unit. He made himself another drink and sat back thinking about the evening. *I could really get used to her being around,* Black thought. What was he going to do about this woman? He needed to keep seeing her. He was required to find out what she knew about Gianni's operation, but Black was falling in love with her. He knew it, just as sure as he knew Gianni was a killer. He drained his glass and headed for the shower. He needed to cool off.

● ● ●

Devastator heard Kayla drive up. *Right on time,* he thought. He knew she wouldn't stay out past midnight when she worked the next day. She said it made her groggy and not as sharp for her dealings. Devastator heard her come in, which interrupted his thoughts. He got up to go and greet her.

Kayla saw his truck when she drove up, sighed heavily, and got out. It wasn't that she didn't still care about him, she just felt smothered by him now. She thought about her evening with Black. She could just relax and enjoy herself. Something she wasn't able to do for a while. Kayla also thought how sexy he looked tonight in the tank and sweats he was wearing. Black was built very nicely. Kayla chided herself for thinking of him that way. She was very much involved with Dezi, but still, she felt something stirring when she thought of Black.

Kayla heard Dezi coming up to the kitchen. She shook her thoughts, took a deep breath, and walked in to meet him.

"Hey baby," Devastator told Kayla, greeting her with a kiss.

She felt so good in his arms, Devastator thought as he held her. He inhaled her deeply. She smelled good, too. Devastator began to kiss her on the neck, rubbing her back. In spite of what she thought earlier, Kayla found herself responding.

They began to kiss and Devastator undressed her there in the kitchen. He picked her up and put her on the counter as he kissed her. Kayla was turned on now, moaning softly as Devastator began licking her breasts.

He freed himself from his clothes and took her there in the kitchen. They made love at a furious pace, both feeling the others urgency. Afterward, they giggled at each other and picked up their clothing from the floor. Devastator followed Kayla upstairs to the shower where they made love once again.

• • •

She was sleeping now as Devastator called his source at the bureau. He needed more information. Agent Moss answered on the second ring. Devastator greeted him shortly and asked what news he could share.

Moss gave him details of the proposed dates the IRS was going to hit each of his businesses. It was all they released so far. He wasn't on the task force investigating him, so he would wait until they leaked something.

The information Moss gave would do nicely.

"Keep your eyes and ears open," Devastator advised him.

"Of course," Moss confirmed the request as they hung up.

It was good to have ears in all the right places, he laughed again, thinking of the agent and climbed back into bed with Kayla.

• • •

Adrian was angry. They were arguing for the last hour and he was sick of it. Kevin was out of town for the last month. Adrian understood with Dirty's death that Kevin shouldered a lot more responsibility, but he was tired of being home alone and being lonely.

"Don't go baby, please," Kevin tried again. "I promise I'll make it up to you."

Adrian grabbed his keys, headed downstairs as he yelled over his shoulder,

"You should have thought about that last night, I'm out. I'll be late, so don't wait up."

Adrian slammed the door behind him.

• • •

Adrian arrived at Caribbean around 11:30. The parking lot was packed, so he knew it would be jumping inside. Agents Dobbins and Collins followed him there from his house. They were keeping an eye on him, just in case he led them to something they could use.

"I am not going in there," Dobbins remarked to Collins giving him a look.

Collins laughed heartily. "You don't have too, not yet anyway."

That earned him another look from Dobbins, which sent him into another fit of laughter.

●●●

The club was indeed jumping. The music was pumping and the queens were out in full force.

Adrian was looking out over the room at all the people dancing when he spotted Trevor, his ex, on the other side. He seemed to be alone. Adrian didn't see Vincent, Trevor's current lover, anywhere. He felt an instant pang of guilt again. Adrian thought about how badly he treated Trevor when they were together and decided he wanted to try and mend fences. He got up and began to work his way across the room to where Trevor was. Vincent spotted Adrian as he got off the barstool.

"What the fuck is he doing here," Vincent grumbled.

He didn't like Adrian. He was still pissed about him taking Trevor from him the first time. He watched Adrian closely as he made his way over to their side.

"He better not be going anywhere near Trevor," Vincent fumed again as he continued to watch.

●●●

Monster continued brooding since Adrian left. He tried watching television, but it wasn't helping.

"Fuck," he groused, rising from the couch.

He was going to have to go down to this club and get Adrian to come home.

Monster went upstairs and put on different clothes. He grabbed his .9mm and put it in his jeans pocket. They were big and baggy, so you couldn't tell the weapon was there. He grabbed his keys and headed out to his truck arriving at the club about twenty minutes later and parking in the rear.

He sat there eyeing the entrance and scanning the parking lot for Adrian's car. He saw it finally, parked not far from his own. Monster decided he would smoke a blunt and relax a minute before going in. If he were lucky, maybe Adrian would come out.

● ● ●

Collins nudged Dobbins who was still watching the front of the club.

"Yeah," Dobbins answered him.

"Bradley just showed up," Collins replied, nodding in Monsters direction.

Dobbins turned to get a better view and saw him, too. He was sitting in the car smoking.

"Wonder what that's about," Dobbins returned.

He knew from his talks with Adrian that Bradley hated clubs. He didn't like to be out in public places flaunting his sexual preference.

"I dunno," Collins answered. "But we're gonna sit right here and find out."

● ● ●

Monster was watching the entrance, finishing up his smoke, when he saw Adrian come out and walk toward his car. Monster smiled. He put out the rest of his blunt and began to get out of his car. Vincent made it to the entrance and was coming up behind Adrian. He reached out and spun him around.

"Didn't I tell you to stay the fuck away from Trevor asshole?!"

Adrian was not in the mood for this tonight.

"Look, Vincent," Adrian began. "I only went to Trevor to apologize. I'm with someone now and I'm not a threat to you."

He turned to walk away.

"Don't you turn your fucking back on me," Vincent yelled again.

Adrian turned to face him again when Vincent swung and caught him hard with a right to his jaw. Adrian hit the ground.

Monster saw the guy come out of the club walking fast. He saw him grab Adrian and turn him around. He couldn't hear what they were saying, but he knew it wasn't good. He methodically made his way to the back of the crowd that gathered now and was slowly weaving his way up through it.

"Vincent," Trevor screamed. "Stop it! Don't start this shit again! Leave him alone, he didn't do anything!"

Vincent spun on Trevor, ignoring Adrian, who was slowly getting off the ground.

"Oh, so you still want this son of a bitch," he yelled at Trevor.

"Don't be stupid," Trevor yelled back. "He was just apologizing for Christ's sake! You are being such an asshole!"

He stared at Vincent hard.

Adrian was on his feet by this time. Vincent turned his attention back to him, ready to pound on him some more when he went down hard from the vicious kick to the back of his knee. Monster was directly behind him, taking him down. He was standing directly over him now.

"Who the fuck are you," Vincent bellowed, holding his knee.

Adrian saw Monster standing over Vincent and knew something very bad was about to happen. He tried to hurry and diffuse the situation.

"Kevin, please, let's just go," Adrian pleaded. "I'm OK, really."

Monster was still glaring at Vincent, who wisely chose to be quiet, once he figured out Monster was Adrian's man.

Monster reached into his pocket and pulled out the .9mm.

"Baby, no," Adrian screamed. "Please let's just go home!"

The crowd grew quiet. Everyone was waiting to see what happened next.

"You fucked up," Monster told Vincent coldly. "You put your hands on him." He quickly planted two slugs in Vincent's head.

The crowd scattered. Trevor and Adrian were both screaming. Dobbins and Collins held guns drawn as they ran toward the scene. Monster was calmly looking at the dead man lying at his feet.

"Drop the weapon Bradley, FBI," Collins was screaming. "It's over! Now drop it."

They had him. They witnessed him kill this guy. This was the break they needed to get to Gianni. They would offer him up a deal and get him to roll.

Monster, however, internalized other plans. He looked up at the two agents yelling at him. He scanned the crowd finding Adrian. He was crying and telling him to please give up. He looked at him long and hard. Adrian didn't like what he saw in Kevin's eyes.

Adrian looked at Dobbins holding his gun and realization took effect. *He wasn't some poor new neighbor, he was the damned FBI and he was trying to arrest Kevin.* Adrian felt terrible. This was his entire fault.

Monster raised his gun, pointing it straight at Dobbins.

Fuck! Collins thought, as he was forced to shoot him. Monster pulled the trigger, the bullet barely missing Dobbins. Collins fired four more times, hitting Monster with each bullet. Monster collapsed to his knees, looked at Adrian once more, and fell over dead.

People were running and screaming. Collins was on his radio screaming for backup. Dobbins was checking Monsters vitals. Adrian watched the scene unfold in horror. Then he slipped away in the crowd, remembering Kevin's instruction on what he should do in the event of his death.

• • •

Black's phone was ringing. He looked at the clock, 3 a.m.

"This is Black," he answered.

"Bradley's dead," Collins told him sounding frustrated.

Collins told him about the club and the shooting.

After they hung up, Black was thinking about the information he just received. What would Gianni do now? Both his first and second lieutenants were dead. Maybe this was what they needed to force The

Clique to fall apart. He hoped it would cause a small crack because right now they were empty.

Black knew wouldn't be able to sleep, so he dressed and headed to the bureau. He would go to the gym and work off some of the tension this case was continually giving him.

•••

Devastator's cell woke him. He looked at the clock. It was 3:30 a.m. *This better be real fucking good*, he thought, irritated at the interruption in his sleep. He got out of bed to go downstairs to take the call. He didn't want to wake Kayla who was still sleeping fitfully. The caller was Agent Moss, his source at the bureau.

"Your boy, Monster, was killed in a shootout at some gay bar downtown," he told Devastator.

"The Bureau is searching his house as we speak," Moss added.

Devastator was reeling again, *what the fuck was going on? Both his friends were gone. What the hell was he going to do now?*

"OK, thanks for the info," he coolly spoke, and hung up.

He called the Front 5 and told them they needed to meet. He went back upstairs and quietly dressed, kissed Kayla on the cheek, then left the house.

•••

Kayla felt him kiss her and heard him leave. She assumed he was taking care of business. Her cell went off five minutes later. She looked at the display seeing it was Adrian.

"Hello?"

She could hear him crying. Kayla was immediately alarmed. What was wrong, she wondered.

"Kayla," Adrian said softly. "Kevin's dead."

He burst into tears again.

What? Did she hear him right? Kayla jumped out of bed, now fully alert.

She rose and headed downstairs, where Adrian told her he was waiting on the patio. After letting him in, she offered him something to drink.

"Can I just have some water," Adrian requested.

Kayla went and got it for him.

"Here you go," she told him, handing Adrian the glass.

Kayla went to her safe and retrieved the letter Monster gave her to give to Adrian in case anything happened to him.

When she returned, Adrian told her of the events leading up to Monster's death. Kayla listened and let him cry before doing what Monster asked.

"He wanted me to give this to you," Kayla told Adrian softly, handing him the envelope bearing his name.

Adrian took a deep breath and opened it. He began to read, tears filling his eyes again. Monster gave him account numbers, keys and bankbooks for money he put away. He asked Adrian to take care of himself and always remember that he loved him more than anything in the world.

As a postscript, Monster asked Adrian to always remember the good times they shared, never the bad and to forgive him for any pain he ever caused him.

"You need to leave here," Kayla told him gently but firmly.

Adrian knew Kayla was right, but he needed to take care of Kevin. Kayla watched Adrian closely and read his thoughts.

"Dezi and I will take care of the arrangements for Kevin," she said. "It will be nice, I promise you that, but you know he wouldn't want you to still be here dealing with the drama that is sure to come, now don't you?"

She looked at Adrian evenly.

He took another deep breath and nodded. Adrian hugged Kayla.

"Thank you so much for being here for me and Kevin," he spoke wispily.

Adrian left and Kayla knew it would be the last time she ever saw him.

She went to the kitchen to make herself some tea. Sitting at the table sipping it, she thought about Black again. She needed to talk. She would call him again soon. Right now, she was waiting on Dezi so they could make plans for Monster.

●●●

Two days later they were once again at the cemetery for yet another funeral. Black and Collins looked out at the many people who gathered for this service also. They saw the same crime family royalty as before, but this time Black saw that she was here.

Kayla was beautiful in her tailored black dress. It was tastefully adorned with pearls. She wore her hair in a bun. Black liked it better down, but he only saw it that way once. Kayla was standing by Gianni's side as they greeted the mourners. It was a nice graveside service. Black knew Kayla was more than likely responsible for that. No one saw or heard from Adrian Roberts since the night Bradley was killed.

Black watched her intently. This woman was accomplishing something no other did in years. *Not since Sandra,* Black thought, thinking of a past love. Kayla was getting under his skin. He found himself jealous of Gianni standing there with his arm around her waist. Black felt his jaw clench when he saw him lean down to give Kayla a kiss.

I've got to get a hold on myself. He couldn't remain objective feeling like this. They retrieved nothing from Kayla yet, even though he saw her again right before Bradley's funeral. She needed to talk and he was more than willing to listen. Black was becoming more convinced that Kayla honestly didn't know anything. Gianni obviously effectively shielded her from his more heinous activities.

They turned up some documents at Bradley's house when they searched it. They were running those leads down now. Black was hoping they would shed some light on this quickly flickering case.

A Deadly 24 Encounter

Another month passed and they still didn't have much of anything. They were continuing to work on running down leads on the paperwork they found in Bradley's house. It was slow going, but they kept at it. Even with both Bradley and Greene being dead, The Clique seemed to be rolling right along like the well-oiled machine that it held the reputation for being.

Black was rushing to get out of there. Kayla was coming by tonight. He pretty much gave up getting any information out of her, but you never knew. At least that was the lie he kept telling himself to justify continuing to see her.

• • •

Devastator just completed his meeting with the Front 5, setting up new plans to get everything rolling smoothly again. He was getting sick and tired of this whole FBI nonsense. Devastator decided to call Moss and find out what the hell was going on. He dialed the agent's number. Moss answered on the second ring.

"What do you have for me," Devastator asked, a little more testily than he felt.

"They're still chasing their tails for the most part," Moss told him. "They haven't really found jack yet."

"Good, that's the kind of thing I like to hear," Devastator told him smiling.

"But, I do have something to tell you about your girlfriend's new friend," Moss said garnering Dezi's undivided attention.

• • •

Kayla arrived at his condo and Black invited her in. They were playing the new racing game on his PlayStation. He really sucked at it, Kayla thought, chuckling. Black's car crashed and was resting on the wall.

"You really do suck at this," Kayla began taunting Black.

"I think maybe you're cheating," Black laughed.

Kayla beat him easily five more times. Finally tired of the merciless beatings, Black asked her if she wanted to do something else.

"Sure, what did you have in mind," Kayla asked him innocently.

He almost laughed out loud when she asked that, looking her over in the hot pink capris and t-strap top she was wearing. Black wanted her. He wanted to kiss her, touch her, hear her scream his name in ecstasy while he made love to her. He was getting aroused, so he quickly cleared his mind and tried to get back to business. He was trying to think of something he might actually have a chance of beating her at.

"How about scrabble?"

"Sure bring it on," Kayla shrugged.

The game was intense, but fun. Black found out she was very competitive and he liked that about her. They were in the middle of arguing about a word he put down when her cell rang. Kayla was still laughing when she pulled the phone out and looked at the display. The smile instantly died on her face. Black was looking at her intently now. He knew the person on the other end of the phone was Gianni.

"Hi," Devastator said sweetly when Kayla answered.

"Hey you," Kayla answered back cheerfully, but cautiously.

Her mind was spinning, she didn't know why, but she began to get a bad feeling about this call.

"I'm outside," Devastator said again, picturing Kayla and how scared she was right now, wondering what he might do to her after finding her here.

He carried no intentions of hurting her. Devastator just needed to get her out of that condo.

Kayla's heart fell into her stomach. She was terrified, *Oh God*, she thought. Dezi was going to kill her when she came outside and she pulled poor Black into this mess. Dezi would kill him, too. Kayla knew Dezi was insanely jealous about her. When she didn't respond Devastator spoke.

"I want you to tell him good night and come downstairs now, alone," he said firmly but not unkind.

If I see that fucker now, I might blast his ass, agent or no fucking agent, Devastator thought.

Black was still watching Kayla. She was really scared. *What the hell is he saying to her?* Kayla was on the verge of tears.

"I'm not going to hurt you, I promise, but I want you to come down now," he told her again.

Kayla didn't think her legs would work. She was so scared. *How the hell had he found her? She didn't write Black's information anywhere. She didn't tell her secretary Anne where she was going. How did he find her,* she thought taking another huge breath.

"OK, I'm on my way," Kayla said quietly.

She wanted to hang up but she didn't. Devastator spoke again.

"That's my girl. And don't worry, I promised you I wouldn't hurt you and I won't. Now, get up and come on downstairs," he finished and hung up.

Devastator was still deep in thought. *She didn't know who Black was, or what he was up to, but thanks to his source he did. He wasn't going to let them get her all caught up in this bullshit. It was him they wanted, so it would be him they dealt with. Leave her the hell out of it.*

●●●

Black couldn't let Kayla leave. Gianni would kill her. He had to do something and do it now.

"I have to leave," Kayla told him as the tears fell.

What have I gotten myself into, she thought, worrying about Dezi waiting downstairs for her.

"I can't let you go back there," Black told her, "Look at you, you're a wreck!"

He stood in front of Kayla, looking into her eyes.

"Please stay here."

Kayla looked at him and smiled sadly.

"You don't understand. He's waiting for me downstairs," she finished quietly and headed for the door.

Black was bewildered. How the hell did he find her? Kayla didn't strike him as the type who left much to chance, especially considering she knew how Gianni was about her. No, something wasn't right. Kayla made it to the door and was opening it.

"Kayla wait," Black told her.

She paused.

"Will you please find some way, somehow, to let me know you're okay when you go with him," he asked her, feeling helpless.

Black wanted to go downstairs and handcuff the SOB, but he knew they didn't have enough on him yet, so he had to let her go. As much as he hated it, Black's hands were tied. He couldn't blow his cover, not yet.

Kayla hugged him and thanked him for everything.

"Take care," she told him. "I doubt I'll be over again."

Black didn't want that to be the case, he silently pledged to work harder to end this case.

"I promise I'll find a way to call or text your cell and let you know I'm okay," Kayla assured.

"I'm counting on that," he told her seriously.

As soon as the door closed, Black immediately went into his office.

●●●

He could see the parking lot well from here. Since the room was dark, no one would see him watching. Sure enough Gianni was there, leaning against the hood of his truck with arms folded in front of him. Black hated him. He wanted to nail him with a passion. He possessed even more reason to hate him now because he was with Kayla. Black desperately wanted her for himself.

Black saw Kayla walking toward Gianni. He rose off the truck and was walking to meet her. They met in the middle, fortunately for Black, under a one of the lights in the parking lot. He could tell Kayla was scared. She walked very slowly to Gianni when she got downstairs. Black watched intently. If the bastard hit her, that was all he would need. Black could throw him straight into a cell, but Gianni didn't hit her.

Instead he hugged her and kissed her forehead. Gianni said something to Kayla and she shook her head yes. Gianni leaned down and kissed her full on the lips, leading Kayla back to the truck. *What was he planning?* He couldn't believe Gianni would let it go that easily. No, he must be plotting something. Black just hoped Kayla would be okay. Black saw the other person now. He hadn't noticed them before. Obviously, they were sitting in the truck in the shadows. Gianni brought one of his boys no doubt, *but for what?*

He wouldn't have to wait long to find out. The guy inside got out and walked around to the driver's side, got into the truck and left. Gianni helped Kayla into the passenger side of her car, put her seatbelt on and walked around to the driver's side. Gianni looked up, like he could see Black looking out of the window, smiled, gave him the finger and got into the driver's side. He started the car and spun out of the parking lot.

"Please let her be OK," Black said to no one at all.

He could still only wonder what he would do to Kayla after finding her here.

A lot of stuff wasn't adding up and Black was going to find out why. He headed back to the kitchen, fixed himself a shot of bourbon and sat down to think.

● ● ●

Devastator looked at Kayla. She was still scared. She stayed quiet since they left the condo complex. He knew she was trying to figure out how he found her and what he was really going to do to her. There were a few things he wanted to know, too.

"How long have you been going to see him?"

Kayla jumped when he spoke. They were silent so long his voice took her by surprise.

"Maybe a month," Kayla replied guardedly.

He knew that much. The mole told him that. She confirmed it for him and she didn't lie.

"Did you enjoy spending time with him?"

Here we go, Kayla thought, *he's going to mind screw me now.*

"Yes, it was pleasant enough," she answered again.

I know he's working up to the mother of a big blow your mind question, I just wish he would get on with it, this is killing me, Kayla thought.

"Did he know about us," Devastator pressed again, knowing full well he did.

The dog knew everything about him, good and bad. He was just looking for a way to prove the bad.

"He knew I had a boyfriend," Kayla answered again. "We were just friends, so it wasn't a big deal."

Although lately, I think he was starting to see me less and less like a friend, Kayla thought, remembering some of the looks she caught Black giving her.

They were stopped at a light now and Devastator wanted to make sure he could see her face when he asked his next question.

"Did you sleep with him?"

Kayla looked at him. *I knew it,* she thought, *I knew this was coming.*

"No, Dezi, I didn't sleep with him," Kayla answered, rolling her eyes at him.

He almost laughed when she did that, but Devastator was satisfied with the answer. Now, he would tell her what she needed to know, but before he could begin, Kayla interrupted his thought with a question.

"What are you going to do to me, really," she asked full of fear.

They arrived at her house seconds later and were sitting in the garage. Devastator looked at Kayla long and hard before he answered, taking the time to reach over and stroke her hair.

"I'm going to take you upstairs and make love to you," he said simply.

Kayla looked at him like she didn't know him. She couldn't believe it was over, just like that. Devastator spoke again.

"Then I'm going to tell you some things you need to know about your new friend."

He got out of the car. Kayla sat there completely perplexed. Devastator came around and opened her door to let her out, then led her upstairs to the bedroom.

• • •

Two days later, Kayla was still trying to absorb what Dezi told her about Black. He was an agent for the FBI. Dezi told her about their investigation and how they were trying to find things to charge him with and coming up empty. So they were trying to intimidate and use everyone around him to destroy him, including her.

Kayla intentionally didn't call or text Black after finding out the truth. She was livid. How dare Black lie to her and use her like that. Dezi made her promise not to go back, but she did plan to go back. Kayla was pissed and she wanted to tell him to his face that she knew who he was and what he wanted; she wanted to tell him to go straight to hell. She picked up her cell and called him.

Black's cell went off right at the end of the mid-morning briefing. He stepped outside to answer it.

"Hi, it's me," Kayla said when Black answered.

He smiled and let go of the breath he held these two long days since she left with Gianni.

"Hi, I'm so glad to hear from you," Black told her.

Kayla looked at the phone and rolled her eyes. *I'll just bet you are*, she thought.

"I'm OK. I just couldn't get away to call you until now," Kayla returned smoothly, not betraying any of the anger or hurt she felt right now.

"I might be able to get away for a couple hours if you have time now," she said.

Hell yes he would make time! He needed to see her.

"Yeah, I'm headed home now as a matter of fact," Black told her. "Go ahead and leave and we should get there around the same time."

"OK, I'll see you soon," Kayla told him and hung up.

"I've got a little something for you Mr. Agent," Kayla fumed as she got dressed.

Kayla wanted to tell him how much he hurt her, but then she would have to admit she was in letting herself be attracted to him. No, she wouldn't give him that satisfaction. She would cuss him out though, that much she would do.

Kayla intentionally wore the sexy yellow mini-dress Dezi gave her last month. It was a wrap dress that plunged low in the front. The Lycra material clung to her and left little to the imagination. Kayla wanted Black to have a good, long look at what he would never have. She grabbed her keys and headed for the door.

●●●

Black beat Kayla to his house. He didn't think he would as fast as he knew she liked to drive. He smiled at the thought as he went upstairs to get everything in order. He purposely turned off the microphones in the room. Today, he wanted to talk to Kayla without anyone else hearing the conversation. Black needed to tell Kayla how he felt about her. He needed to tell her the truth about who he was and convince her that she needed to get away from Gianni.

It was all getting ready to go down. They finally found a potential source, which was willing to cooperate. He gave them information and they sent a team to South Carolina in hopes of verifying it. If everything went their way, they would take Gianni down by the end of the week. The doorbell rang, interrupting his thoughts. He went to let her in.

●●●

"We got a problem," Devastator was telling Stan.

He called him to give him a heads up on the agents coming there. Agent Moss tipped him off right after the team left the office heading for the airport.

"Yeah I heard rumblings about it," Stan told him. "They won't get shit from me."

"Good to hear," Devastator spoke. "I may be letting your take over for a minute until everything is straight again," he enlightened.

"You know I can handle my end, no problem," Stan told him .

"How is Kayla," Stan asked now.

"She's fine, I'm taking good care of her," Devastator told him.

"I appreciate that man," Stan answered. "She's just as precious to me as Taea was," he added.

Devastator acknowledged his understanding. They talked a few more moments before disconnecting.

She'll be fine now, he thought. Kayla was truly hurt when he told her about Black. Devastator recalled the pain in her face and the tears in her eyes after he told her the truth. *That bastard was pretending to be her friend to get information on me. She was vulnerable and he knew it and he used it to get close to her. She just lost her best friend for god's sake! What an asshole,* Devastator concluded. He effectively put an end to all that though. *Who says you can't still buy good help*, he chuckled, thinking about his mole at the bureau.

They were really trying hard to destroy everything he spent years building. *Lousy bastards!* He wasn't going to go without a fight though. He would never go to prison. He hated the idea of being locked up. If it came to that, he would do what needed to be done. He just hoped it didn't come to that.

●●●

"Boy, am I glad to see you," Black told her, smiling as he invited her in.

That damn dress is going to make me lose my mind, Black thought lustfully, as he watched Kayla walk inside.

I would like to slap that smile right off his face, Kayla thought as she smiled.

"It's good to see you too."

"Something to drink," he questioningly offered.

"Juice is fine," Kayla again requested.

He got their drinks and sat down across from her.

"Are you okay," Black asked, looking at her seriously.

"Yes, I'm fine," Kayla replied casually, still smoldering inside. "It wasn't as bad as it could have been."

Black looked at her quizzically. Did Gianni hit her? He wanted to press her about it, but she was looking at him like there was something on her mind.

"What's wrong?"

Kayla thought about what she wanted to say. She was looking at him, angry all over again. She found herself more than a little attracted to him and thought he was attracted to her, too.

"Well," Kayla began slowly. "I was wondering just what exactly was in your mind when you told me you could help me out of my situation," she paused for effect. "Agent Black."

She knew! But how? Did Gianni tell her? If he did, how the hell did he know? They never met. Black thought about the other night. How did Gianni know where she was? Obviously, Kayla wasn't responsible for the error, or she wouldn't be here now, looking like she wanted to kill him. A light went off in Black's head. He knew, but he would have to deal with that later. Right now he was about to deal with one very angry woman he was in love with.

"Kayla," he began.

She watched him intently him the entire time. *Surprise buster,* Kayla thought, satisfied. *Gotcha didn't I?*

"It's not what you think. Please let me explain," Black pleaded.

"Well, this ought to be good. So by all means, knock yourself out," Kayla said, crossing her legs and folding her arms in front of her.

Black knew he better sell the story of his life or he would lose her and that scared the hell out of him.

"Yes Kayla, I'm an FBI agent," he began. "Yes, I'm working a case involving Gianni," he continued. "It started off as just an assignment for me, but I quickly found myself genuinely attracted to you." Black told her.

Garnering no response, he plunged ahead another time.

"I just want to protect you now," he began anew. "There are some things about to happen and I don't want you in the middle of it."

"I never, ever, meant to hurt you. If you don't believe anything else, please believe that," he another time spoke looking into her eyes.

Kayla was still angry. She didn't want to be rational, and admit everything Black said made sense. She wanted to be mad. It didn't hurt so much then.

"You were using me," Kayla shot back at him. "I'm not some damned pawn! I have feelings! I'm human you know!"

She was yelling and crying now.

"What if he killed me the other night?! Did you think about that? Huh?!"

Black wanted to tell her of course he did. He didn't sleep these past two days, thinking about that very thing. Instead he got up and walked over to the couch to comfort her.

Kayla jumped up and slapped him hard across the face. He didn't let it deter him. Black wanted Kayla to understand how he felt about her. He took her in his arms, as she continued to fight and yell at him, until she was finally spent and fell into his arms. Black held her while she cried. She had every right to be angry. They were playing with her life.

They returned to the couch, sitting down. Kayla stayed quiet for a while and Black was deep in thought when she finally spoke.

"So, now what," Kayla asked, looking into his eyes.

Black looked back at her. He needed to get Gianni out of her life. He knew her survival and their future depended on it.

Black kissed her softly on the lips. Kayla pulled away, and looked at him.

"Is this part of your job too."

"Absolutely not," Black answered, taking Kayla in his arms and kissing her again.

He felt the desire inside him begin to stir. He wanted her. He began to touch her body, sliding his hand gently up her dress and inside it. Kayla's nipples were hard and he squeezed them. She let out a soft moan when he touched her. Black moved his hand lower, sliding it under her thong and caressing her gently there. He undressed her and looked at her body. *She is totally incredible,* Black thought, becoming aroused. He began licking Kayla gently all over her body, paying special attention to her breasts as she responded to his touch. He returned to her mouth after tasting her intimately and began kissing her again.

"I want you so much Kayla," Black told her softly, as he continued to kiss her neck.

She helped him undress. Kayla looked at Black's muscular body and was wholly aroused. They were both naked as Kayla eyed his firm manhood, wanting to feel it inside her. Black kissed her again, pulling her onto his lap. He stopped kissing her to look into her eyes, asking the silent question. Kayla looked at him and sat on his erection, allowing him to enter her, answering his question.

●●●

Where was she? Devastator was asking himself. He called her cell, no answer. He called her at home, no answer. Anne said she didn't come to work today. He drove back to agent Black's complex. She wasn't there. Where the hell was she? He was still thinking about that when his cell went off. It was Kayla.

"Hey you," Kayla said pleasantly.

Devastator was careful not to go off the deep end. Things were crazy all day and he didn't want to scare her or make her think he didn't trust her.

"Hey baby," he replied. "Where you been all day?"

Kayla smiled. *Oh, I've been making love to the FBI agent you warned me about,* she thought in her head.

"I was at the law library downtown. I'm working on a new project and I have to make sure I kept everything legal. After what you told me the other night, I figured I couldn't be too careful," she replied.

Kayla hoped he would buy this story. She wasn't looking at him, so it was easier for her to lie. She didn't want to lie to Dezi, but she knew now the full scope of the danger she was in and Kayla wanted to save her life.

If it were anyone else, Devastator would have said the story was a complete crock, but he knew Kayla did things like that. He admitted; he scared her pretty well the other night with all the things he told her.

"Are you coming over," Kayla asked.

He wanted too, but Todd told him they needed to get together tonight to put things on lock before the IRS paid them a surprise visit.

"Not tonight baby, I got some stuff to take care of," Devastator replied.

Kayla was elated. She didn't know how she was going to get through the night without Dezi looking at her and knowing what she'd done this afternoon.

"Oh, okay," Kayla said whining, knowing he liked that. "I guess I can get along this one night without you."

Devastator smiled.

"I'll be there tomorrow night baby. You just enjoy a movie or something and I'll talk to you later. Love you," he said and then hung up.

Kayla smiled as she thought about this afternoon, Black, and them making love. Black was an exquisite lover. Kayla stopped her thought. She didn't want to compare the two. It was bad enough she slept with him.

Black made her feel so different when he made love to her. He made her feel whole, complete, and safe. She couldn't really describe it. It was just wonderful and magical.

Then Kayla thought about the instructions he gave her and that made her scared. Black promised her this would all be over in a few days. She had to follow his directions to the letter though. Black promised he wouldn't let anything happen to her and she would be free of Dezi forever. Kayla hoped he was right.

●●●

Black was on a mission. There was leak and it needed to be plugged immediately. It all made sense now; the searches turning up nothing, Gianni showing up at his house, the businesses mysteriously shutting down for repairs and maintenance right before the IRS audit.

Someone was giving him information and keeping him one step ahead. Now, it was Black's job to figure out who, and fast.

He thought about this afternoon when he and Kayla made love. She was beautiful, and made him feel totally alive. The way she moaned softly and cried out his name, clinging to him when she reached her orgasm. The softness of her body as he held her and thrust into her, Black never wanted it to end. He told her honestly what Gianni did, even showing her crime-scene photos. Kayla was visibly shaken, and puked after seeing a couple of the more gruesome ones.

Black apologized, but he wanted her to know what this man was capable of. He couldn't leave anything to chance. Kayla was very important to him. He wanted more time to get to know her and maybe have a future with her, but right now it was about saving her life. Black got an idea for finding the leak in the bureau. He picked up his cell and called in a favor.

●●●

"Hey, everything is in place," Collins told him, once he arrived at the bureau.

They were setting up a scheme to find and plug the leak.

"OK everybody, it's show time," Black told the four other agents seated in the phone bank monitor room.

He sent Collins out into the main room of the office with fake information on the case.

"We just got a huge breakthrough in South Carolina," Collins told all the agents. "Seems the leader of the organization up there is willing to give us eyewitness testimony on Gianni and his role in the killings in exchange for a reduced sentence on the murder charge he is facing."

A large murmur consumed the office as all the agents began to speak amongst themselves.

"We're getting a warrant right and will be on our way to arrest Gianni in a matter of hours," Collins finished as several agents congratulated them.

He nodded, still smiling and left them heading back to the room.

"Now, we wait," Black said to Collins, when he returned to the booth.

● ● ●

"Come on Stan," the agent was telling him. "Give him up. We'll get you a reduced sentence."

Stan sighed before he answered.

"I don't know what you're talking about man," he replied coolly.

They were playing this game of back and forth for the last two hours, yet this guy was not budging. The local police arrested him on a murder charge. They found Gavin's body two days after Taea's funeral.

Stan already knew they were coming. He talked to Devastator before he was ever arrested for killing Gavin's punk ass. He told his wife he wouldn't drop dime, even if meant going down for life. She argued with him at first, but eventually accepted his decision. Now, here these jokers were trying to play him like he was stupid.

"Well, Stan," they started again. "You can't say we didn't give you a chance. Maybe we'll just go out there and talk to some of your business associates. They may not be as willing to do time as you are."

Stan said nothing.

"We done now? Can I go back to my cell," Stan asked the agents finally, sounding as bored as he could.

Disgusted, they called the jailer and sent him back to his cell.

"Let's go out here and hit the dirt. Something has got to come up if we turn over enough rocks," the agent said to his partner as they grabbed their briefcases and headed out the door.

● ● ●

They were an hour in and still waiting. Black was beginning to think he was wrong when the call went out. They saw the number come up on the screen. He was using a secure channel. Normally, they wouldn't have been able to see it, but Black called in his favor from an old friend with clearance to unscramble the channel. Not only could they see the number, but they could also hear and record the conversation.

"This is Todd," his machine answered.

Moss swore out loud but left a message anyway.

"It's me," Agent Moss said. "I got some real hot information to tell him, but not on the phone this time. I need to see him face to face. There are too many ears and eyes here for this one."

Damn, Black thought, *now they would have to set up a sting operation.* Moss told Todd to call him back when he got the message. Moss hung up and went back to work.

They began to plan how they would quickly wrap up this case. They were hoping for some good news from South Carolina, but time was quickly running out. Black excused himself and went to call Kayla. He wanted to make sure she was okay.

"Hi," Kayla answered.

He smiled in spite of himself.

"Hi yourself," Black responded.

"I'm just calling to check on you."

"I'm fine," she replied. "I really enjoyed being with you today."

"I'm looking forward to more days with you, Kayla," Black spoke honestly.

"I need to get back in here, but I'll talk to you again soon," he began anew. "I promise this is nearly over," he finished before disconnecting.

Things were pretty shaky right now. He hoped what he just told her was the truth.

A Deadly 25 Encounter

Devastator was making plans of his own for dealing with all the heat he was getting. He already transferred a significant amount of money from one of his offshore accounts to another of his private accounts. He was on his way to withdraw the money. For what Devastator was planning, he would need cash.

He was glad for his source at the bureau. He needed to know the exact moment to make his move, and of course, time to get Kayla. Devastator wasn't going anywhere without her. He started thinking of the time they were together. He really hurt Kayla on a couple of occasions. Devastator promised himself he would make it all up to her, once they were safe, and this storm was behind them. His cell rang and interrupted his thoughts.

"Yeah," he answered.

"Hi, I was just confirming the meet," Todd began. "And to let you know I managed to drop my phone in water, so my replacement won't be here for a couple days."

"OK, that's cool. I'll see you in a few," Devastator told him, and hung up.

He was glad to have Todd around. He kept everything running smoothly. Of course, Devastator knew Todd wasn't that strong, and might crack if they pressed him hard enough; which was why Devastator was going to tell him to leave town as soon as he possibly could.

Devastator knew a full out assault against him was coming, and they would take any prisoners. He was glad he got to Kayla before they lied to her, and turned her against him.

•••

Kayla was thinking about the pictures Black showed her. They were horrible. What kind of sane person could do the things she saw in those photos? Did Dezi really do all these things? They didn't have any evidence. Black told her they were still trying to link him to the crimes. Kayla was scared to believe it. *If he would do something like that to them, why wouldn't he kill me, too,* she wondered.

"Please," Kayla whispered softly, praying out loud. "Just let it be over soon and let me be all right."

She wanted to see Black and be with him. Kayla needed to feel safe, but she knew that would only put them both in danger, so she made herself a snack and watched television in the den instead. She did text him. That couldn't hurt, Kayla told herself.

●●●

Two extremely long and arduous days later they still weren't turning up anything in South Carolina. No one was willing to talk. It looked more like Gianni was going to walk if they didn't do something soon.

"Why hasn't that bastard called me back," Moss was grousing, quietly.

He left Todd the message two days ago! *He better be glad they didn't get the judge to sign the warrant yet,* Moss thought. He was about to call him again when Agent Keller asked to see him in his office.

●●●

"OK, what have we got on this scumbag that we can lock him up for, just to keep him on ice for a little while," Dobbins asked.

The three of them; him, Black, and Collins, were meeting trying to figure out a strategy since the agents failed to get the evidence they needed for the murder charge.

This sleaze can't walk, Black thought. *We need to take him down, but how?*

Collins came up with an idea.

"OK, let's grab that crooked manager of his, the one that handles all the legalities, what's his name?"

"Todd Reiner," Black said.

"Yeah, that's it," Collins continued. "He's not a hard-ass type. He's a collar, wears a suit. If we lean on him, lean on him hard, threaten him with about fifty years, which wouldn't be that much of a stretch, considering all the money laundering and fraud he is up to his neck in with this Gianni operation. He would crack and give us enough at least to pick up Gianni and hold him on federal charges for a while."

Black thought that was a fabulous idea. He called two agents in and gave them Todd's address, telling them to go pick him up and bring him in. *This just might work*, Black thought. If they could get this guy to roll, he could feasibly give them Gianni on a platter. They were sure they could get enough charges on Gianni to stick to keep him locked up for the better part of his life. This pleased Black more than anyone else in the room. He wanted Kayla to be free. Free to live her life again, and free to be with him. Black left the room to run information sheets on Mr. Reiner. He wanted to be ready when the agents brought him back.

●●●

"I'll hafta have at least one hour's notice," the man on the other end of the phone told Devastator. "Still gotta follow protocol ya know."

"That's fine, I've just got to know that you'll be ready whenever I call, day or night," Devastator told him.

"Sure, no problem, I told you that," the man replied. "You got the money, I got the time."

"I'll be in touch soon," Devastator told him and disconnected.

He was on his way to see Kayla. They were having lunch. She wanted to go to Le Bistro, but Devastator wanted to take her somewhere else. She put up a fuss but agreed in the end.

Stan called and told him the feds didn't get anything while they were there. They harassed half his crew, and none of them talked. He heard the agents finally gave up and left.

Devastator thanked him for being so loyal and told him he found an attorney there that was going to get him out of that murder charge. Stan thanked him, and asked about Kayla once more before they hung up.

●●●

Kayla wrapped up her last deal for the day when she saw Dezi pull into the parking deck. She didn't really want to go to lunch with him, but she agreed because she remembered what Black told her. She must appear as normal as possible. She couldn't give away that she knew all about him, or what was going on now.

Kayla thought about him even more. She missed Black so much. She wanted to see him, but he told her they couldn't risk it. Black was almost positive Dezi kept someone watching her and he wouldn't chance her safety like that. Kayla knew he was right, but she still missed him. Kayla took a deep breath and tried to relax, so she could be natural with Dezi. She didn't need to give him any reason to look at her sideways.

She heard her outer office door close. *He must be inside*, she thought, when she heard the light knock on her door. She willed herself to calm down and smile.

"Come in," she cheerily called out.

"Hey baby, ready to go," Dezi asked her smiling.

God, Kayla thought. *This is what got me into this mess in the first place, that beautiful smile, and those damned dimples.*

"Hey you," she replied, smiling as well. "Yes, I'm ready and I'm hungry. So this place you're taking me to, better not suck," she chuckled.

Dezi laughed.

"I promise it doesn't suck," he assured her as they walked out the door to his truck.

● ● ●

"And how are you this afternoon Mr. Reiner," Collins asked Todd, as he entered the room.

He could tell Todd was nervous but trying to play it cool.

"I'm fine," Todd replied, looking at agent Collins evenly.

"Good, glad to hear it," Collins sent back.

"What is this about," Todd asked him, still trying to sound cool and relaxed.

"It's about whether or not you spend the next 30 years of your life in a federal prison, Mr. Reiner," Collins replied smoothly.

He could see the change. He rattled the man. Todd began fidgeting and cleared his throat before speaking.

"Am I being charged with something?"

Collins took a few minutes before answering, making Todd even more nervous.

"Well, is there something you've done wrong, you would like to share with us," Collins answered.

Todd was silent. He wanted to get the hell out of here. He should have left the other night when Dezi told him to leave. Now, he was here dealing with these guys.

"I have no idea what you're talking about," Todd answered again.

"Hmm, well OK," Collins replied. "Let's see if I can help you out little."

Collins pulled out the folder compiled on Todd. It contained all his criminal history, which were basic misdemeanors such as traffic tickets. Then he pulled out the paperwork he filed on behalf of The Clique with his signature and the records from the bank accounts where he laundered the money. Dates, times, teller names and locations were all in the folder.

Todd asked for lawyer, and they allowed him to call one. A couple of hours later, Todd and his attorney Jonathan DuBois were conferring.

Collins and Black were now in the observation room watching the meeting.

"You need to save yourself here Todd," his attorney said.

"You don't understand," Todd replied. "If I give this guy up, I can kiss my life goodbye."

"We'll go for a deal that will guarantee you entrance into the witness protection program," Mr. DuBois told him. "That way you will be safe."

"That's no guarantee," he scoffed. "They already have a mole on the inside," Todd told his attorney.

"Well, hell that only sweetens the deal," Mr. DuBois spoke thoughtfully.

"We will offer up not only Dezi and The Clique, but the rouge agent, too," DuBois told him. "I'll get them to drop all charges against you in exchange for testimony and you can walk away from this mess a free man."

"Do you think they will really go for that," Todd asked his attorney.

"I believe they will," DuBois exerted. "It's not really you they want, its Dezi."

Todd thought about it for about 10 minutes, before agreeing with his attorney. DuBois stepped outside. "Could you get Agent Collins please, tell him we're ready to talk now."

Collins and Black exchanged knowing smiles after the agent delivered the message. Collins left to go get what they were waiting all this time for.

●●●

They ended up at Cole's Marina for lunch. It was an upscale bay front restaurant sitting directly on the water, specializing in seafood on the city's lower north side. Kayla loved the water, and she was glad they came. In spite of what she knew, she found herself very much at ease with Dezi like before.

"So, does this meet with your approval," Dezi asked her, slyly smiling.

"It's okay," she said playfully.

He laughed.

The server arrived at their table and they ordered. After she left, they sat back to enjoy the atmosphere while they waited on their food. There were several boats out on the water sailing. Kayla watched the colorful sails blowing softly in the wind. She was watching a couple trying their hand at waterskiing and failing miserably.

"I've missed you these last couple of day's baby," Dezi said softly, looking at her very intently.

Wonder what is going on in that mind of his, Kayla asked herself, turning her attention back to Dezi.

"I missed you too, you know that," Kayla told him. "We did talk though."

Dezi smiled at her, and then became serious.

"I promise to make up to you all the things that I've done to hurt you," he said gently.

Kayla was looking directly at him now, and felt the tears begin to come. *This could have been so different. They could have had a future, kids, and the whole nine yards. So many maybes and ifs*, Kayla thought sadly.

Dezi saw the tear roll down her cheek and reached over to brush it away. He also took the opportunity to kiss her.

He was looking into her eyes now.

"I love you more than anything in the world. Do you know that," Dezi asked her.

Kayla smiled but didn't answer.

"I promise you it's going to be better and you'll forget one day that any of this unpleasantness ever happened," Dezi told her.

That was too much. Kayla broke down. She just couldn't take anymore. Part of her loved this man still. Devastator held her while she cried. He knew he hurt her deeply. He just wanted the chance to make it up to her.

•••

Black was on top of the world! They just received everything they needed to get a warrant to pick up Gianni. Todd gave names, dates, times, access codes, documents, and even voice recordings, of all their dealings.

Now they were moving to freeze the private accounts Gianni hid offshore. Todd also gave up Moss, but they already knew about him. Agent Keller suspended him earlier that day. They were working as quickly as possible. They didn't want Gianni to slip out of the noose they placed around his neck.

Black and Collins were on their way to ask the judge to sign the warrant. Black thought about calling Kayla and telling her what was going on, but he decided against it. He wanted to have this guy locked up before he said anything. He wanted to be able to guarantee she would be safe.

Finally, Black thought, *he would have Gianni put behind bars where he belonged, and they would be free to be together.* He loved Kayla. There was no doubt in his mind about that. Black just hoped he could make her happy, and help her forget the nightmare she lived through these last few months.

"Let's hope his honor is in the mood today," Collins said, bringing him out his thoughts. "You know he has been real brand new here lately, making sure every 'I' is dotted, every 'T' is crossed. Damned crooks got more rights than the law has to arrest them."

Black knew he was telling the truth. Judge Adamson was known for being difficult when it came to signing warrants, and he was their only choice today. The other two judges were in court, and one was on vacation.

"He's got to sign man. We have all the evidence he needs," Black replied, hoping that was true.

Todd told them the location of the storage unit with all the evidence to back up his claims. They found everything he said would be there. It was being photographed and cataloged as they spoke.

They were running out of time. Black felt that in his gut. Gianni was making plans and whatever his plans were they definitely would include Kayla. He couldn't let that happen.

"C'mon man," Black told Collins. "Let's go see if we can pull a miracle out today."

They both smiled and got out of the car, saying a silent prayer that they could.

●●●

They arrived home from the marina and shared their meal together. Kayla wasn't crying now, she just seemed sad, Devastator thought as he watched her sleeping peacefully.

"I have put you through hell, haven't I," Devastator asked quietly, knowing she didn't hear.

Everything was almost ready. Soon they could just live their lives and enjoy being with each other. He left her to sleep and headed downstairs.

Devastator grabbed himself something to drink from the fridge and headed to the den. He found an old movie on and began to watch as he rolled himself a blunt and began to smoke. His mind wandered and he thought about all the events of the last few months. His best friend and his partner were gone.

Those slimy bureau guys killed Monster. Adrian skipped town. *Smart*, Devastator thought. He knew Monster left him well taken care of. He knew for years that Monster was gay. Even Todd's scary ass was gone. He was the only one still here. That was going to change though.

Devastator was waiting on one more phone call. Once he got that, they were out of here. *She's not going to understand*, he thought of Kayla, but he already made allowances to deal with that.

He smoked another blunt and found himself relaxing, and soon after was dozing. His cell went off and woke him up. Devastator looked at the display. This was the call he was waiting for.

●●●

"How did you come by the information," Judge Adamson was questioning the legalities of them coercing Todd into revealing the evidence they were gathering.

He didn't want this to come back and bite them at any trial that might take place.

"Mr. Reiner volunteered the information in exchange for not being prosecuted himself on the numerous money laundering and fraud charges we have evidence of, involving him," Collins replied, trying to stay calm.

He knew Black was as anxious and irritated as he was that Adamson was taking all this time to sign the warrant. The judge continued to read the affidavit and the charges. He leaned back in his chair, and eyed each of the agents carefully.

"I will give you a decision in one hour," he spoke dismissing them from his chamber.

He and Collins then left the judge's chambers. They managed to hold it together long enough to get outside when Collins exploded.

"Son of a bitch," he yelled, kicking the trash can sitting outside the courthouse. "If we don't move on that bastard soon, you know he is gonna be gone, right," he finished, still muttering curses under his breath.

Black was equally frustrated. He knew Collins was right. If Gianni left, he would take Kayla with him, whether she wanted to go or not. He couldn't let that happen, but right now his hands were tied behind his back.

Come on Adamson, he thought, *sign the damned thing*. He and Collins decided to go across the street to the coffeehouse and wait. They would try to calm their nerves, which were frazzled right now, while they waited for the green light to end this chase.

•••

"Everything is taken care of," Attorney Edwin Campbell said.

This was the news Devastator was waiting for. He was waiting until he was sure Stan was off the hook for that murder rap. He knew he owed Taea that much. Now, everything was straight. He would call Stan and give him instructions for running things.

Devastator congratulated him on his genius, and they both laughed heartily.

"Your money is on its way. It's being personally delivered," Devastator told him, "Along with a healthy bonus."

"Thank you, such a pleasure doing business with you, Attorney Campbell told him and hung up.

Devastator immediately called Stan.

"Hey man, wassup?" Devastator laughed when he answered.

"It's good to have friends in high places," Stan joked back.

They joked around a little more, and then got down to business. Devastator gave him names and contact numbers for the suppliers and told him where to deposit his portion. Stan took all the information and told him he would keep things running smoothly.

"You sure you and Kayla will be all right," Stan asked.

Devastator paused for a few moments before responding.

"Yeah, we'll be good," he assured.

Everything was ready and the bureau was still twiddling their thumbs. *There would be nothing to get in their way*, he thought.

"OK," Stan told him. "Be careful, and please don't let anything happen to Kayla. She is still my sister, blood or no blood, and I love her to death."

"I would give my life first," Devastator replied.

They double-checked information one more time, said their goodbyes and hung up. With that last piece of business finished, Devastator got up and began to ascend the stairs to Kayla's room. It was time.

●●●

They were outside Judge Adamson's chambers five minutes early. He made them wait every second of those last five minutes before allowing them to come in.

"Gentlemen, please don't make me regret the decision I've made here today," Adamson told them as he handed them the signed warrant.

It was all they both could do not to turn cartwheels right there in his office.

"Go do your job," he told them smiling wryly.

They both thanked him profusely and left the office. Collins was on his cell before they got out of the building. It was a go.

"Send agents and units to Gianni's house," Collins barked.

"Send some to Kayla's too," . Black told him.

His gut told him that's where he was.

Collins looked at him with an unspoken question between them. He knew if Gianni was there, he wasn't going to give up without a fight or without her. Black knew it was going to come down to this. He hoped that Gianni was at his home, but in his heart he knew he was at Kayla's. They called SWAT and tactical. Everyone expected this thing to get ugly. Gianni was not known for diplomacy, and he carried a passion for firepower.

It was still light and they needed darkness. They needed to be able to sneak up on him and catch him by surprise, but they couldn't afford to wait any longer. *She may already be gone*, Black thought, bringing a cold knot of fear to his gut.

●●●

Devastator entered the bedroom. Kayla was still sleeping peacefully. *Good*, he thought, as he pulled her bag from the closet and began to pack for her. They would only take a few things, just enough to get them through the trip.

His cell went off. Devastator looked at the display and answered quietly, trying not to wake Kayla.

"Yeah," he got the quick feeling he wasn't going to like this conversation at all.

"We're gonna hafta wait a few hours man," the pilot told him.

He made these arrangements days ago, and just called to let him know they were ready to go. Manuel owned a small private plane. For the right price, he would go anywhere, no questions asked.

"There's a big fire raging, FAA not letting anything fly until possibly nightfall," Manuel went on to tell Devastator.

"OK, it's cool man," Devastator answered. "Hit me up when it's a go, and we'll be on our way."

Devastator didn't want to have to wait. He wanted to leave now, but he didn't have a choice.

He heard nothing from Moss at the bureau, so that meant they were still chasing their tails. Devastator chuckled quietly. After he finished packing her things, he took her bag down to put it in her car. The feds weren't looking for Kayla. She wasn't a player in their game anymore since he broke up all that drama with her and Black.

"That son of a bitch was trying to get with my woman," Devastator fumed.

Devastator wanted to hang around and kill him for that alone but thought about Kayla. He could tell her nerves were on edge. She never experienced anything like FBI sting operations.

"You're lucky as hell," Devastator said out loud thinking about Black. "Well, guess I'll go get me a little nap my damn self so I can be sharp tonight."

He headed back in the house and into the den.

A Deadly 26 Encounter

They got a call from Keller. He was heading up their field operation tonight from the bureau.

"We hit Gianni's place," he spoke. "But he wasn't there."

Now, Black was sure he was at Kayla's.

"Damn," Black swore out loud.

Collins looked at him. He knew what Black was thinking.

"I also got an interesting piece of info from Moss," Keller told them. "You know he's trying to still save his skin from prison time," he went on. "Apparently, Gianni asked him about finding a pilot who would fly, no questions asked."

"Did he give him one," Black asked opening and closing his fist.

He didn't want to hear news like that.

"Yeah, guy named Manuel," Keller replied, "Two-bit hustler; locals have busted him a couple times."

"Thanks Keller, I'll get right on it," Black replied, his mind racing.

If that son of a bitch got to that airstrip, there was no stopping him. They needed him in a more controlled situation, like his residence, Black thought.

"No need, I already checked it out," Keller was saying, bringing Black back to full attention. "He tried to file a plan earlier, but they wouldn't accept. Fire and smoke, not letting anything go up until after dark."

"Excellent," Black replied.

He was ecstatic. Someone up there liked him. They knew where he was. They were graced with more time now, and they would have both darkness and the element of surprise on their side.

"I've already instructed FAA to clear his plans when he calls later," Keller said. "We'll bust him when he shows up at the strip. Look, I know Gianni has a penchant for violence, but can we try to bring him in alive? He's the last link we have to dismantle the rest of the cartels we've still got out here."

"I'll try everything in my power to see that happen," Black assured him.

He wanted to see the dog rot in jail, not die. *That was way too easy, but if he tries to hurt Kayla,* Black thought. *I'll plug him without hesitation.*

He and Keller hung up, and Black briefed Collins on their new good fortune. They called the squads together and began preparing for tonight.

● ● ●

Devastator woke to the smell of popcorn. Kayla was in the kitchen.

"Damn," he said as he stretched.

He didn't mean to sleep that long. He checked his phone. No call from Manuel yet. It was after nine now, and already dark. *It's cool,* he mused. They weren't on a time schedule. They could leave whenever.

"I want some," Dezi yelled to the kitchen.

He heard her giggle.

"It's only snack size, just enough for one," Kayla yelled back, chuckling. "How about I make you your own?"

"How about I take your bag, and you make another one," Dezi shot back.

She giggled again, but he heard her coming down to the den.

"Here, you big brat," Kayla told Dezi, handing him the bag and laughing.

He reached out and grabbed her, held her down on the couch with him and tickled her.

"Quit it," she laughed. "You're going to make me burn my popcorn!"

Dezi stopped and let her go. Kayla pushed him over and ran off to the kitchen.

This is what I'm talking about, Devastator thought, still smiling. It was a long time since they were this comfortable and close to each other.

He got up to go in the kitchen when his cell went off. He checked it. It was Manuel.

"We're set, meet me at the airstrip in a hour," the pilot told him.

"We'll be there," Devastator assured him.

He hung up and headed into the kitchen to find Kayla. She was already back upstairs, so he headed up to her, stopping at the fridge first to get her a juice.

•••

"Okay, everyone has their instructions. Let's move out and get into position," Collins said.

The agents watching her house told him they saw movement in the house, two people that they could make out. Black knew it was Gianni and Kayla.

Please, he prayed silently, *let us get her out without her getting hurt.*

"Use lights until we get within two blocks, then turn them off. No sirens at all, period," Collins told them, as they loaded up to go.

They wanted to surprise this guy and Collins knew Black was worried as hell about the girl. He didn't want to see her get hurt either. He just hoped they could pull it off without her losing her life.

Upon arrival, they all got into position. Spotlights were set up to shine into the house once they established contact with Gianni, or Kayla. Agents fanned out, surrounding the house. They evacuated the houses on either side of hers, and the one directly across the street. Snipers were positioned in top floor windows, and on rooftops. Now, they would wait. They needed to make contact and ascertain where they were in the house.

•••

"Hey baby, I brought you some juice to go with your popcorn," Dezi told her, as he entered the room.

She was watching a movie on television and shushed him. Kayla took the juice from him, looked at it, then looked at Dezi.

"I see you helped yourself to some of it too, huh," she asked, giving him a look.

Dezi laughed.

"Don't be like that. I only took a little."

"Mmm, hmm," she said, as she took to top off and drank it down.

Kayla was still watching the movie a few moments later when he began to stroke her hair and talk to her.

"Baby, we're going to take a little trip tonight," he began quietly.

Kayla was caught off guard. *What trip? Where were they going?* She remembered what Black told her. *"No matter what, don't let him take you anywhere out of town."*

"Where are we going honey," she asked, hoping the alarm didn't come through in her voice.

"Some place really nice. You'll absolutely love it," Dezi replied, still stroking her hair. "It's a surprise though, so I can't tell you where it is exactly."

Her mind was racing. *How the hell would she get out of here?* She didn't like where this conversation was going.

"Well, when would we be back? I do have a business you know," Kayla asked, again trying to keep her voice light.

She was having a hard time focusing. Something was wrong with her.

"We're not coming back baby, at least not here," Dezi told her gently.

Kayla was trying hard to shake the cobwebs out of her head. It was spinning right now.

"What do you mean we're not coming back," she asked again, slurring her words.

What the hell is wrong with me, Kayla asked herself.

"Dezi, I can't just up and leave my business. I have responsibilities. People who work for me," Kayla told him, trying to get him to see reason.

Dezi was still stroking her hair, and talking to her like she was slow.

"I've already taken care of that baby. It's all been done," he told her simply.

Okay, get a grip Kayla, she thought. *You're getting hysterical, and its making you lose your sanity.*

"What if I don't want to go Dezi?"

She was having a hard time staying awake now. She felt like she was falling. Dezi was holding her. She was almost out. The powerful sedative he put in her juice was taking effect.

"I promise you'll like it baby, and I'm going to take good care of you," Dezi was saying to her. "Now, stop fighting. Just close your eyes and relax. When you wake up, we'll be there, and everything will be all right."

He kissed her gently at the end of his sentence.

He drugged me, Kayla thought. She was slipping quickly, but she had to get out of here. She heard Taea in her ear telling her to fight. She must, if she didn't, she wouldn't make it out of here alive.

•••

They continued sitting outside for about an hour. They knew Manuel made the call already. Keller was holding him on ice at the airstrip. What the hell was Gianni doing? Why wasn't he headed for the strip yet? Black didn't like it. It didn't feel right. He tried to reel his nerves in. Black knew Gianni wouldn't hurt Kayla; not yet anyway. He wasn't backed into a corner. Things might be different then.

Black saw a shadow move across the window. It was Gianni; it was too big to be her. Black never saw Kayla move since he arrived here, and that worried him. What did he do to her? She should have at least gotten up to go the bathroom or something by now. Then Black saw her. She was moving slowly, like she was sick or hurt, he couldn't tell which. Gianni's back was to her. He didn't notice yet. Kayla was trying to get away.

"Come on baby," Black said quietly.

Collins looked at him and trained his binoculars on the window across the street. He saw her, too. They both signaled the agents nearest the doors to be ready. The hostage was trying to get out.

•••

Devastator went into the bathroom. Kayla was pretty much out of it, so he didn't think much of leaving her alone for a couple minutes.

Kayla watched him go. She could barely stand up. Her head was spinning, but she willed herself to get up. She tried to be careful, but she had to be quick. He would be out soon, and if Dezi caught her trying to get away he might hurt her. Kayla didn't want that. She made it to the dresser.

"Damn that was a long trip," Kayla said quietly.

She made it to the bedroom door he left open, easing out onto the stairs.

"OK Kayla, focus," she told herself, looking at the stairs swimming in front of her.

She did something that would have been comical if the situation weren't so grave. Kayla sat down on the first step and turned over on her stomach. She was going to slide down the stairs. She pushed herself and felt herself begin to move. Kayla had a hard time controlling herself and ended up tumbling head over feet down the last several. Devastator heard the commotion and stepped back into the bedroom.

"Kayla," he called out, heading to the stairs.

"Oh, God," Kayla cried out softly, starting to panic.

She managed, barely, to get herself off the stairs and around the corner to the hallway leading to the front door. It was closer than the back, she reasoned.

"He's going to catch me," Kayla said half aloud.

She was still dizzy, and the spill on the stairs didn't help. Devastator was coming down the stairs now.

"Baby, please answer me," he was calling to her.

He was worried that she really hurt herself. He knew she was still heavily under the sedative. Devastator saw that the runner at the bottom of the stairs was out of place. He knew she made it this far at least. He stopped to think. Now, would she head for the front or back door? He picked the back, since it led to the garage, and in her mind, her car and safety. Kayla held her breath, as she heard him walk by the closet she was in. She succeeded in getting herself inside just before he made it to the last stair. Kayla waited until she couldn't hear him anymore and figured that gave her enough time to make it to the front and get out before Dezi could catch her.

Kayla gingerly opened the closet door and peeked out. She didn't see him, so she slipped out, and began to slowly make her way to the door. Her head was still spinning, and trying to focus was a nightmare.

Devastator was at the back door. He saw the lock still secure and knew she didn't go out of it.

"Fuck," he swore out loud, turning and running to the front door.

●●●

Black and Collins were sitting on the edge of their seats. They were still upstairs in the house across the street watching the bedroom. They saw Gianni come out of the bedroom, and head for the stairs. They were both praying, and hoping, Kayla would make it out. The operatives downstairs told them they heard her, and that she fell. Evidently Gianni didn't discover her because they heard him still calling her, trying to coax her from wherever she was hiding.

"That's my girl," Black said under his breath. "You can do this."

Black instructed the agents to throw the spotlight the minute either of the doors opened. He figured it would blind Gianni long enough for one of the agents to grab Kayla, and pull her out of the way.

"I'm going downstairs," Black told Collins, calling Dobbins up to take his place. "Look, I understand you're worried," Collins told Black. "But remember you have to be an agent first, her man second."

"I know that, I plan to stay objective." Black told him. "I just want to be closer."

●●●

Kayla heard him coming. He was running, her heart starting racing.

"Please let me get this door open," Kayla was praying out loud.

She was fighting the lock.

"Kayla," Devastator was yelling again.

He would be on her in the next minute. She had to hurry! The lock would not budge. Kayla was crying now. She was scared! She knew if Dezi caught her, he would probably kill her. She didn't want to die tonight. Finally, the lock clicked, and Kayla threw the door open, almost making it to the front stoop.

Devastator saw her as he rounded the corner. He jumped the footrest, and grabbed her right as she was stepping out of the door.

Devastator held Kayla around the waist, and picked her up to carry her back inside when the spotlight hit him full force, temporarily blinding him and her fighting threw him off balance. Devastator dropped her.

● ● ●

Black saw the whole thing unfold like it was being shown in slow motion. The spotlight blinded Gianni long enough to throw him off balance, he dropped Kayla, and Agent Sheard grabbed her. Kayla was still screaming and hysterical. She screamed until he came and put his arms around her. Kayla looked up at Black, recognition flooding her face and passed out.

"Keep an eye on her until rescue gets here," Black told Agent Sheard.

"No problem sir."

Black was on his way to Dobbin's car where they put Gianni. He didn't have time to fight. Agents swarmed him as soon as they moved Kayla safely out of the line of fire. Gianni was looking past Black at Kayla, he knew. He didn't look up at Black until he stepped in his path, and blocked his view of her. Gianni's eyes were flat and lifeless; his voice, when he spoke, sent a chill through Black. That was no easy task, given some of the people he arrested in his career.

"I'm going to kill you," Gianni said simply, and quietly.

There was no one else around, so Black couldn't use it against him. Devastator knew that too, which was why he said it.

"You'll be too busy in prison to bother anyone, let alone kill me," Black returned calmly.

Devastator smiled. There was no warmth in it.

"Maybe, maybe not," he said.

What the hell was he talking about, Black thought, *they had this asshole, and he still thought he was selling tickets and calling the shots.*

"It's over for you Gianni. Now that woman over there can finally get some peace, and get on with her life," Black told him.

Devastator looked at Black again, colder and harder than before.

"Kayla will always be mine, and I will kill any man that touches her," he gritted through clenched teeth.

Black was amused. *He still thinks he is in charge doesn't he?* Black wanted to wipe that smug smile right off his face. He wanted to tell him right then and there about him and Kayla, but he wouldn't. Kayla didn't deserve that, and Black didn't give two damns what this loser thought about him.

"Go ahead and take him down and book him," Black told Dobbins, who walked over to his car by now.

He gave him the thumbs up, and got in the car to take Gianni down. Collins walked over to Black and asked him if he was okay. Black looked over at Kayla. Rescue had gotten there, and was placing her on the stretcher to go to the hospital.

"Yeah, I am now," he answered.

"Go ahead down to the hospital," Collins told Black, seeing the pain in his face as he watched them load her.

"This scumbag ain't going anywhere. Go make sure she's okay. She's been through a lot, but she seems to be a tough little lady," Collins told him.

"Thanks man," Black gratefully spoke. "Yeah, she hung in there like a trooper."

Dobbins and Collins headed off with Devastator. Black followed the ambulance carrying Kayla to the hospital.

Devastator watched Black from the back seat. Hatred and rage boiled inside him. He closed his eyes, and made an oath to spill the agent's blood, slowly and painfully.

●●●

Kayla woke up in the hospital room, and found herself restrained.

"You were a bit combative when you were brought in," the nurse told. "I'll take them off now."

"Where am I?"

"You're safe. You're at the hospital," the nurse answered smiling as she gently stroked her forehead. "You're going to be just fine."

"I'll check on you again in a little while," she added, before stopping her movement and speaking again. "You have a visitor, if you feel up to it."

Kayla grew immediately alarmed.

"Who is it?"

The nurse saw she was frightened and smiled again.

"FBI. Somebody's very own special agent I would say," she replied with a twinkle in her eye.

Kayla relaxed, and let out the breath she was holding.

"Sure, let him in."

The nurse went into the waiting room to find Black pacing. She walked up to him and spoke.

"She's awake now agent Black," the nurse informed him. "She said you can come in. But please remember she's not 100 percent yet. So try to be brief."

Black nodded and thanked her. He walked down the hallway to her room, and stood looking at her door for a few minutes. He took a deep breath, and got a hold on himself. Black didn't want Kayla to know how upset he was, or how worried he was about her. He pushed her door open and entered the room.

"Hey, Miss Kayla," Black said softly, smiling at her.

Kayla managed to sit up, and was propped on her pillows. She sported a couple of bruises on her face, where she fell down the stairs trying to get out of the house. The doctors assured Black she wasn't really hurt.

"Hi, Agent Black," Kayla said back, smiling at him.

Black came over, sat on her bed and touched her face lightly.

"You sure know how to give a brother a heart attack don't you," he told her, his voice full of emotion.

His heart almost stopped when Kayla walked out the door and Gianni caught her to pull her back inside.

"You did good Kayla, you really did," Black said, looking intently at her.

She knew he was worried and scared for her. She was just glad he was there, and kept his promise.

"Is he in jail," Kayla asked, referring to Dezi.

"Yes, and he'll stay there for a long time," Black told her.

"Now, you can get on with your life," he added.

Kayla looked at him, not really saying anything. She was thinking, trying to process everything that took place tonight. She was hoping that Black was right about Dezi being put away for a long time. She just couldn't shake the feeling it wouldn't be that easy.

"I'm not going to stay," Black told her, breaking her thoughts, as he got up to leave.

"Thank you for everything," Kayla said seriously, looking into his eyes.

Black looked at her, smiled and leaned down gently kissing her on the lips.

"You don't ever have to thank me for anything. Just allow me to be part of your new life. That's all I ask," he told her looking into her eyes.

Kayla smiled at him and Black kissed her again, leaving her alone with her thoughts.

A Deadly 27 Encounter

For Kayla, the last four months passed in a blur. Not long after she was released from the hospital, she sold her house, and was now leasing a small beachfront cottage. She and Black were spending time, and trying to put their lives back together.

Dezi was still in the federal prison they placed him. Kayla wasn't sure how long he would be there though. She was hearing rumblings about deals being cut, and strings being pulled. So far though, nothing happened, just a lot of talk. She certainly hoped it stayed that way. Dezi tried to contact her once or twice. She refused to talk to him. He didn't get angry like she expected him to. He just told her he loved her, and hung up.

She spent time trying to figure out how she really felt about Dezi now. She didn't hate him, but she wasn't in love with him anymore either. She was just relieved they were apart now. Although he made it very plain, he didn't see that as a permanent arrangement. *For once*, Kayla thought, *let the legal system work and keep him in there.* She looked at the clock. She had an appointment in about an hour. She headed in to the shower to get ready.

• • •

"You can't possibly be serious," Black was yelling at Keller, pacing back and forth, stopping to pound the table with his fist.

"Look, I know you're frustrated, but that's how things are done. It's still politics. You know that," Keller told him, running his hands through his own hair, just as frustrated.

Keller was trying to get Black to calm down. They just received word that the federal prosecutor was going to give Gianni the deal he asked for in exchange for the information he kept on other individuals deemed bigger fish than he was. Black was still trying to wrap his mind around the fact that this cold-blooded killer was about to walk out of federal prison a free man.

"This can't be happening man," Black said again, looking at Collins, who looked about ready to explode himself.

"I knew that slick talking son of a bitch would find a way to get outta this shit," Collins groused. "But there ain't no statues of limitations on murder, and I know he had something to do with that killing in South Carolina! Now, more than ever, we have to find a witness, someone willing to talk."

"I agree, and we need to start working on that right now," Black told him.

"He's got to be put away forever," Black told Collins again.

Black's mind was still reeling. How was he going to tell Kayla, Gianni was getting out? She just started getting her life back together. Now, the bastard was back.

"I'm going to find Kayla and tell her what's going on," Black told Collins. "She needs to be prepared."

Collins stopped him. "You know the bureau probably already called her."

It was procedure. They both looked at each other without speaking. They each knew what the other was thinking. *It has started again.*

"I'll be back," Black told Collins.

He left to go find Kayla, so that he could calm her down.

● ● ●

Devastator was on top of the world. His attorney did what he paid him to do. He got him off. Of course, he spent the last four months in prison, but that was nothing compared to what he was facing.

He thought momentarily about the implications of him giving up some of the other crime families, but quickly dismissed it. Devastator was a businessman, and the FBI would effectively eliminate his competition for him so he would have sole control of all the illegal activity in the city. *Street credit ain't worth shit if you're sitting in a jail cell,* he chuckled aloud pushing it from his mind.

Devastator couldn't wait to get out, have lunch, take a shower in his own tub, and of course, see Kayla. He needed to talk to her. He needed to explain things and make Kayla understand who he really was. Not the monster agent Black was trying to make him out to be.

Thinking about him, made Devastator furious all over again. The Front 5 was keeping an eye on Kayla for him and told him this joker was trying to put the moves on her.

I promised that fucker death, Devastator fumed. *I damn well plan to deliver.* Right now though, he just wanted to get out. He was waiting on his attorney and the prosecutor to finish the paperwork. His attorney told him it would be within the hour. Devastator was more than ready.

●●●

Kayla got the call as she was leaving her appointment. Her mind was reeling now. She knew he would come and get her. The restraining order didn't mean squat to Dezi. He would just come and take her away someplace where no one would ever find her. He probably hated her now, and would kill her. Kayla was scared. Her cell buzzed again. She looked at the display. It was Black.

"Hey," Kayla answered.

Black could tell by her tone, she already knew. He needed to play it down. He needed her to stay calm, so they could figure out what to do next.

"You okay baby," Black asked her.

Kayla thought, *Hell no, would you be?*

"I'm okay," she answered Black.

She was on her way to the store, and then she would go home.

"I'll meet you at the house in about an hour, OK," Black told her.

"Sure, I would like that, see you when you get there."

Kayla looked at the phone when she hung up. She was doing better at this lying thing. She just didn't want to make a habit of it. She already made her own plans for this day.

Now, she had an hour to put it all together. Kayla headed to her house. That would be her first stop. She made it home in about 15 minutes, grabbing the bag she kept packed, pulled out the two sealed envelopes she prepared, and laid them on the kitchen counter in plain sight.

Kayla took one last look around the house, and her eyes fell on the photo of her and Black. She walked over and took that, tears filling her eyes. She wished it never came to this. Why couldn't they keep Dezi locked up? Why couldn't she live her life? Her and Black together. Kayla loved him, and wanted to be with him, but not now.

Kayla knew Black would be hurt, but she was doing what was best for both of them. She knew Dezi would kill them both. She was sure he knew by now that they were together. That was an automatic death sentence.

Kayla wanted to call Black, but she knew he would try to talk her out of leaving, and he might succeed. She put the photo in her bag and headed for the door, stopping only at the landlords cottage to give her the key and final instructions for the rest of her things. They embraced and she told Kayla to take care of herself. Kayla told her she would and left. She looked at her watch. She had 20 minutes to get to the airport. She pushed the Mercedes to 100 mph, and made it in 10. Thankfully, she didn't get stopped.

Kayla made a call, gave instructions for the car and headed for the terminal. She managed to check in and get through baggage check with little time to spare. She boarded as they were making the final boarding call announcement. She found her seat and sat down.

The pilot came on and let them know they were cleared for takeoff. Kayla put her headphones on and turned them up. She knew where they headed. She closed her eyes and tried not to think. She was headed for a new life where she would be safe. At least that's what Kayla told herself to stop the shaking.

●●●

Devastator was finally home. He stretched as he got out of the cab, paid the driver, told him to keep the change and went inside. They were waiting for him when he got there; The Front 5, Big D, and the rest of The Clique. They provided drinks, weed, and women, for him to celebrate his release. Devastator smiled as he grabbed one of the bottles of champagne and opened it. *It was good to be home*, he thought, taking a huge drink from the bottle.

Devastator had a lot of work to do. Things were a little slack and, of course, the bureau was breathing down their necks at one point. They cost him a lot of money too, but he would get it all back. Right now, he was going to enjoy the party being thrown for him.

Devastator thought about Kayla for a moment. He planned to see her later after he relaxed and unwound. He picked out one of the girls and told her to come with him. She readily complied, following him into one of the ground floor bedrooms.

"Take your clothes off," Devastator told her, without much emotion.

She didn't waste any time complying. The rules were already explained to her before she got here. As sexy as this man was, she might enjoy it, she thought.

Devastator looked her over. She was cute, nice enough body.

"Undress me," he told her.

She again readily complied. Once they were both naked, Devastator pulled the condoms out of the drawer of the nightstand, put on a couple and began to punish the girl for his four months of confinement.

●●●

Devastator leaned back on the bed after she left him alone in the room. He would go see Kayla tonight, he decided. There was a lot of unfinished business. He thought about what the Front 5 told him about her and Black and how he kissed her. He was going to kill him too, agent or no agent. Black crossed the line when he touched Kayla. Devastator was going to make him pay.

Big D came to check on him.

"I'm going to grab a nap," Devastator told him. "Everyone can party until they get tired, then call it a wrap."

"Thanks man," Big D replied. "Damn, it's good to have you back again Devastator," he told him amiably as he left and closed the door.

Devastator closed his eyes and drifted off to sleep.

●●●

Black thought it odd he beat her here. She said an hour. He stopped by the bureau for a minute and got tied up. Black was half an hour late. He hoped nothing was wrong or happened. Kayla didn't call him to let him know she was running behind. He unlocked the door with the key she gave him and went inside. Everything looked fine. Nothing was out of order.

Then Black saw the envelopes on the counter. He walked over to them. One was labeled movers and the other showed his name on it. Black was beginning to get a very bad feeling as he picked up the envelope and began to open it. There was a letter from Kayla explaining that if he was reading this then Dezi was out of prison and she was gone.

Kayla explained that she wasn't going to risk Black's life by being with him. Kayla told him she loved him and wished they met under different circumstances. She asked him not try and find her and to please understand.

Black was furious, hurt, and in denial, simultaneously. Kayla couldn't be gone. He went into the bedroom, looked in the closet. He didn't see her bag. She was really gone. He sat down on the bed trying to absorb what was going on. The woman he loved, the woman he waited all his life for was gone.

"Fucking Gianni," Black swore out loud, knocking the lamp off the nightstand. *Where the hell could she have gone?*

"OK man, pull yourself together," Black said aloud again. "You're an FBI agent. Track her down."

He grabbed his keys, headed to the car, dialing his cell as he walked. Black instructed the agent who answered to get him phone, credit-card records, and bank information, for Kayla.

If she were using her credit cards, he would find her. He would deal with Gianni. He would make her feel safe again. They would have their life together. Black pushed the government issued car above the speed limit and headed back to bureau to bring his life back home.

●●●

Kayla landed two hours ago. She was headed to the house she bought last month. Kayla thought long and hard about her future. She knew she wanted to be with Black, but she also knew that depended on what happened with Dezi.

Now that he was out, she had to go. Dezi would be looking for her and if he found her, he would kill her. Kayla was certain of that. She found Taea's diary when she cleared out the house. It contained conversations Taea indulged with Dirty and all the things he told her Dezi and he did, including what Dezi did to Sasha, the woman he claimed to love. Kayla was determined to stay one step ahead of him. She wasn't going to end up like that woman.

Kayla looked at the house and took out the keys the real-estate agent sent her, opening the door. The house was right on the water. Kayla hoped she would enjoy many days sitting out on her deck relaxing.

"Well," Kayla spoke aloud. "Might as well get started and get groceries in here."

Kayla called a cab. Her car wouldn't be here for a few days. She was having it halfway shipped. Then a private driver that she hired would deliver it to her. Kayla wasn't taking any chances on anyone finding her.

She thought about Black. She knew he found her letter by now. He was probably beside himself right now. *I could call him on my cell*, Kayla thought, *he wouldn't know where I was*.

She pushed the thought out of her mind as her cab arrived and she told the driver to take her to the nearest fresh market.

• • •

Devastator woke from his nap feeling refreshed. He was in a very good mood. *Sleeping in your own bed will do that to you*, he thought, smiling.

Devastator went out into the living room where the party was earlier. Everyone was gone, except Big D. He was cleaning up the remnants of the guest's trash.

"Wassup man," Devastator asked. "You applying for housekeeper now," he joked.

Big D smiled.

"No, just trying to clean up a little."

Big D looked at him, and Devastator knew there was something on his mind.

"Spit it out man," Devastator told him.

Big D thought about it. He wasn't sure how his boss was going to handle what he was about to tell him.

Big D had a friend who worked for a moving company. They received a call to come clear a house. They could keep whatever they found. He called Big D to see if there was anything he could use. When he got there his mouth fell open in disbelief. Big D saw it was Kayla's house. He found out from the landlord she was gone, but left no forwarding address. He had to tell Devastator now. He just wasn't sure of the reaction.

"I, um, got something to tell you about Kayla," Big D began.

He garnered Devastator's full attention as the man continued looking at him hard.

"She's gone, she um, moved," Big D told him nervously.

Devastator took in what Big D was saying.

"What do you mean she moved," Devastator asked evenly.

"She left the state. The landlord says she didn't know where she went," he braced himself for what he knew was coming next.

Devastator was quiet for a moment, taking in what Big D just told him. He hurled the glass in his hand against the wall and stood up.

"I've been waiting to see her for four fucking months, and she's gone?!"

"I want her found!" Devastator said between clenched teeth. "Get me a private dick."

He held at least some idea of the areas to look. Devastator knew Kayla and certain areas that were more appealing to her than others. He hoped she was in one of those areas.

Devastator called Stan. He knew Kayla loved Stan like her brother. She would call him. Maybe not right now, but she would call him eventually. Devastator needed him to be alert, and get Kayla to tell him where she was.

Devastator was livid. Not at Kayla, no, this wasn't her fault. It was that Agent Black. He was the one. He told her so many bad things she was scared of him now. Kayla probably thought he wanted to hurt her, which was the farthest thing from his mind.

He would find her though, he would go to her, and tell her how much he loved her. He was going to kill that Agent, oh yes sir, he was definitely going to do that, and soon. Big D brought Devastator out of his thoughts, telling him the detective was on the phone. Devastator took the phone to fill the detective in. He told him he would send a photo of her, instructing him to call him as soon as he found anything. Then he hung up. Devastator looked at Big D.

"I got a debt to pay after I find her," he told him flatly.

Big D didn't even have to ask. He knew Agent Black was a dead man.

●●●

Kayla was starting to feel right at home. The market was a delight. She wanted a light salad for dinner, but decided she should have something with a little more substance.

She was eating for two now, Kayla thought. She went to the doctor this morning, which was the appointment she told Black about. The test came back positive. She was pregnant. They weren't very careful that first week after she got out of the hospital, and of course, she and Dezi were together the day he was caught, which was a week earlier.

Kayla thought about when she conceived. She just didn't know for sure which of them fathered her child. She briefly considered abortion, but knew she couldn't go through with that. She planned to sit Black down tonight to tell him about the baby and her uncertainty the baby's father, but then the call about Dezi came. That sealed it for her.

Dezi was already furious with her. If he found out there was a chance this baby wasn't his, he would have killed her on the spot. Kayla couldn't allow that. She was thinking of her child now. She wouldn't let anyone hurt the precious life she carried. Kayla hoped that it was Black's child. Kayla loved him and she wanted her child to be conceived in that love; but she just didn't know and wouldn't until the baby was born.

"Tomorrow I'm going out," Kayla said again. "I need to find something to occupy my time."

She thought about how lonely she would surely get with no friends here and no Black to hold her and make love to her. Kayla felt herself getting down and near tears. She flipped on the television, hoping to find something to help her mood. She didn't. She picked up her cell. She needed to talk to someone, but who? Kayla thought for a moment, smiled and began to dial.

•••

Black continued working frantically all afternoon. It was night now, and he was still clueless where Kayla could have gone. Black was frustrated. He missed her already. Why didn't she call? He just wanted to hear her voice and know she was all right. He knew why she didn't though. Kayla knew he would try to find out where she was and bring her back. She also knew she wasn't strong enough to tell him no right now. Black was still thinking when his phone rang. The caller was blocking the number.

Please, please be Kayla, Black hoped, as he answered the phone.

"Hello," Black said as evenly as possible, trying not to let his nerves show.

"Well, hello agent Black," the voice said.

He knew this voice. He was trying to place it.

"I see you've succeeded in costing me something very precious to me," Devastator said coldly.

Black recognized it then, Gianni! *This guy has some balls on him, calling me!*

"What do you want Gianni," Black asked, annoyed that it wasn't Kayla.

"I want Kayla back, but you've run her off. So that shit won't be happening now will it," Devastator growled back at him.

Black was more angry and offended than frightened. *How dare this bastard call me, and accuse me of being the one to run her off.*

"If anyone made her leave it was you, you sick bastard," Black shot back at Devastator.

Devastator thought about how much he hated this fool. He wanted him dead in the worst way, but he wanted to know if the dog had any idea where she was first.

"So did you set up your little witness protection shit for her," Devastator asked Black.

He's fishing, Black thought, *he wants to see what I know.*

"Yeah, we put her in it, so she wouldn't have to run from scum like you for the rest of her life. You'll never find her, so give it up Gianni," he replied, satisfied that he successfully threw him off balance.

At first he couldn't make out what he was hearing and then he listened closer. The bastard was laughing, softly at first, but now he was laughing loudly.

"What the hell is so funny?"

The reply came back low and cold.

"You have no fucking idea where she is do you, you fucker," Devastator asked. "But I'm going to find her, and I'm going to take her far away from all this bullshit. And I'm still going to keep my promise to you."

Devastator disconnected.

Black was livid. He wasn't worried about Gianni and his threats, but it did bother the hell out of him that he was looking for Kayla, too. Black knew he better find her before Gianni did. He picked up the phone and began to work again, saying a silent prayer as he dialed.

A Deadly 28 Encounter

After five months, the detective was yet to turn up jack. Devastator was beyond angry. The only reason Black wasn't dead yet was because he wasn't faring any better in finding Kayla. There was always the off chance she would get in touch with the joker. Devastator kept someone watching Black. If he took off anywhere, Devastator would know and he would be right behind him.

He admitted that Kayla did one hell of a job of hiding herself. She wasn't working, so they weren't able to track her that way. He knew she was using the money he left in her car. That was fine. Devastator loved her, and it was for them anyway. He also knew Kayla would have more than enough to stay hidden for at least the next two or three years. Devastator couldn't wait that long to find her. He called the detective.

"Have you found anything," Devastator asked, instead of a greeting when the man answered.

"I might have something for you later tonight or tomorrow," he said. "I got a hot tip from one of my skip tracers. I'm just waiting on them to get back with me."

Devastator was getting mildly excited. This was the kind of news he wanted to hear.

"OK, but you call me the fucking second you hear from them, got it," Devastator said in a deadly serious tone.

"I'll do that man, I'll do that," the detective quickly replied and hung up.

Devastator rose and made himself a drink. He was thinking of holding and kissing Kayla again which filled him with a longing absent from him for a long time. Devastator missed her, more than he could ever put into words

"I'll see her soon," Devastator said out loud.

He was hoping that the detective got a hit this time.

● ● ●

Kayla couldn't believe how fast time flew. She settled down and got into her new surroundings. She joined a book club and spent time at the local boys and girls club. She kept a couple new friends she made at arm's length, only seeing them when she was at the center. She couldn't afford to let anyone get that close to her, not only for her sake, but for the baby's. Kayla felt the baby kick.

She found out she was having a girl during an ultrasound in her fifth month. Kayla was excited. She always wanted a little girl. She and Taea talked and joked about having little thems.

Kayla was also thinking of what she wanted to name her. She finally decided on the names of the two people she loved the most in the world. Her name would be Mariah LaTaea after her grandmother and her best friend.

Kayla began to worry as the due date neared. She knew once the baby was born that she would know who the father was, and she would have to deal with that. She made up her mind even if Dezi was the father that she would tell him.

Despite the monster that he was, he still had a right to know his child. Even though Kayla didn't want him to be a part of her life, she wouldn't keep him from his daughter. If Black was her father, well, Kayla hoped that she would have much more from him than just the occasional weekend visits. She missed him more now that she was close to delivering the baby. Kayla struggled a minute, but finally got out of the chair she was sitting in. She made her way to the kitchen.

Her cell was on the kitchen counter. Kayla picked it up and dialed.

"Hello," the male voice answered.

"Hey, it's me," Kayla replied.

"Well, hey stranger," he said. "It's good to hear from you again, everything alright?"

Kayla smiled thinking how lucky she was to still have Stan in her life.

"Yeah, I'm fine," she answered back.

"And how is my niece today," Stan asked her.

He was glad she called. He was worried about her. She called him when she first left and he tried to get her to tell him where she was. Kayla wouldn't tell him. When he pressed her more, she got angry and threatened to hang up and not call back. Stan stopped pressing her. He wanted to hear from her and know that she was all right.

Kayla was quiet for a moment, reflecting. She knew Stan still did business with Dezi. Kayla was scared Stan would tell him about the baby, but he promised her he wouldn't.

"Stan, have you kept your promise about the baby?"

"Yes, I told you that," Stan assured her.

He was grateful to Devastator for setting him up and keeping him in the money, but Kayla was family. Stan wouldn't do anything to put her or the baby at risk.

"Well, I'm really tired," Kayla was yawning as she talked. "I'm gonna go lay down now."

"OK, but you call us the minute little Miss Mariah LaTaea makes her grand entrance," Stan told her softly, his voice full of the love he felt for his little sister.

Kayla smiled and touched her belly again.

"I promise," she told him and hung up.

She was heading for the bedroom when she felt the gush of fluids from her water breaking. She called her doctor who told her to head to the hospital. She called Mary, her friend from the book club who lived across the street. She promised to drive her to the hospital.

"I'm on my way, be ready," Mary told Kayla.

"OK, I will, thank you so much Mary," she relayed and hung up.

This is it! Kayla thought, the first pain of labor hitting her hard.

●●●

Collins laid the manila envelope on Black's desk, stepped back and smiled at him.

"What's this," Black asked him sourly.

He wasn't in a good mood today. He was thinking about Kayla all day. Five months in the book and he found nary a trace of her anywhere. She just vanished.

"Open it and see," Collins replied, snapping him out of his thoughts, and still smiling.

"I'm really not feeling the games today," Black replied irritably.

Collins knew once he opened the envelope his mood would change, so he kept at him.

"Just open the damned thing would you," he asked, faking exasperation.

Black looked at Collins standing there grinning. *What the hell was he so happy about*, he wondered then picked up the envelope.

"If I open this will you go away," Black asked him, still grouchy.

"Absolutely," he replied.

Hmph, well what have I got to lose, Black thought, and tore open the envelope. He dumped the contents onto his desk and gasped. Collins took a little bow and sat down. He waited for his friend to grasp what was in front of him.

Black was staring at the contents of the envelope in disbelief. He picked up one picture and looked at it. It was Kayla. *Oh my god,* Black thought. It was really her. Kayla was alive and she was well. She looked beautiful. She was at a market it appeared. Black saw lots of fruit and vegetables.

He looked at the next picture. He knew immediately why she left. Kayla was smiling and touching her very pregnant stomach. Black felt his emotions begin to churn. She was carrying his child and he wasn't there with her. She looked about eight months or so in this photo.

Black looked up at Collins who was watching him intently right now. He couldn't speak. He just looked at him questioningly.

"I had some friends looking for her at the other bureaus," Collins explained.

He remembered Black telling him how much she loved water, so Collins asked every contact he knew on every coast looking for Kayla. Then he got these pictures and an address from one of the agents.

Black got up and shook his hand, embracing Collins.

"How can I ever thank you enough?"

"By going to her and making things right," Collins told him.

"In the meantime, I'm still working on getting Gianni for that South Carolina murder."

He left Black alone to think.

Black dialed the airline. He wasn't wasting any time. He finally found her and he wasn't going to let any more time go by without him seeing her. Black booked his flight and hung up. Then he called and asked for some time off. He took a negligible amount of vacation in his seven years there. Keller cleared him for leave. Black grabbed his coat. He planned to make a quick stop at the house for his bag and then he would be on his way.

"I'm on my way Kayla," Black said aloud. "I'm on my way."

●●●

The pain was getting worse. Mary got her here to the hospital in plenty of time. She even insisted on staying with her. Kayla was secretly grateful for that since she didn't want to be alone now.

"You're doing good Kayla," Dr. Densmore told her. "You're already dilated six centimeters, only four more to go."

Easy for you to say, Kayla thought, as another contraction gripped her. She wanted Black. *She wanted him here now*, Kayla thought, as the pain eased up.

She couldn't wait to see her little bundle though. Even with all the pain, she was excited. She knew there would be a lot to face once the baby got here, but right now she just wanted her to be born healthy and safe. Another pain hit her and she screamed. Mary was holding her hand.

This is a lot harder than it looks, Kayla thought, bracing for another contraction.

●●●

Devastator answered his cell on the first ring. He was anxiously waiting for this call.

"Yeah?"

"You got a fax machine," the detective asked.

"Yeah, I got one," Devastator told him.

"Well, walk over to it, and give me the number," the detective said.

Devastator complied. Seconds later, images began to come out the machine. The first one was a photo. Devastator snatched it out, and looked at it. It was Kayla. A smile immediately spilled into his face. She looked like she was at an ice cream parlor. She held a cone in her hand. Devastator smiled even wider.

The next photo almost made him drop his cell. It was another picture of Kayla coming out of the ice cream parlor, but that wasn't what caught his attention. It was the perfect roundness of her stomach that held his stare. *She was pregnant. That's why she left*, Devastator thought. *I'll be damned!*

He never even considered the possibility, but once Devastator thought about it, it made perfect sense. They made love the night he was locked up, the math was there. Who else could be the father? He knew that Kayla never slept with Black. The last page was her address.

"Good damned work man," Devastator thanked the detective. "I have a serious bonus on its way to you."

"Thanks for that," the detective spoke. "Just sorry it took so long."

They hung up and Devastator sat there looking at the photos.

Kayla looked so beautiful pregnant. She looked about eight or nine months in the picture. Devastator had to get to her. She may have already given birth. The thought filled him with a happiness Devastator never thought he could experience. He made reservations to leave tonight, and then called the Front 5 to tell them where he was going.

Devastator left them in charge. He told them to call his cell, but not for any drama they could easily handle themselves.

He went upstairs and threw some stuff in a suitcase, then called a real-estate agent. He needed a house close to the address he gleaned from the detective.

"Certainly, and I'll have the information waiting for you at the hotel upon your arrival," she pleasantly responded.

Devastator looked at the address again. *Damn baby*, he thought, *you did good at this hiding shit. Virginia Beach? Who would have ever thought to look for you there?* He knew that's exactly what Kayla wanted.

He was going to her now and they would be a family. Devastator set his security alarm in the house, picked up his keys and headed out the door to the airport.

"I'm on my way baby," Devastator said softly out loud. "Big daddy is on his way."

●●●

"OK, Kayla," the doctor said. "You're complete and ready to push."

Thank you Lord, Kayla thought. She was more than ready to get on with this.

"Now, when you feel the next contraction, I want you to bear down and push, OK," Dr. Densmore explained.

"OK," Kayla managed to get out as the contraction gripped her.

She took a deep breath and pushed with all her might. The nurse counted while she pushed. It seemed like she was counting in slow motion. After Kayla let that breath go, they told her to push again. She took another deep breath and pushed again.

"Very good, the head is out," the nurse was telling her.

All that pushing, and the head was the only thing out, Kayla thought wearily. Another contraction rocked her and she delivered the baby's shoulders.

"Give me a moment, let me suction," the doctor told her.

The next contraction, she pushed again and the baby slid out.

"Here she is mommy," Dr. Densmore was saying excitedly, still smiling.

Mariah was screaming. Kayla was laughing and crying at the same time.

"She has great lungs," Kayla said, as she continued to cry.

They laid her on Kayla's belly for a brief moment, but she really couldn't see her for the tears in her eyes. They took her and told Kayla they would bring her back after they cleaned her up and weighed her.

Dr. Densmore helped Kayla deliver the afterbirth.

"You're fine Kayla, and everything went very well," he told her.

Kayla was happier than she ever thought possible.

"I promise they'll bring the little one back in a few moments," Dr. Densmore assured her. "In the meantime, you should rest."

Kayla smiled tiredly.

"Thank you for everything Dr. Densmore," she tiredly spoke, laying back on her pillow and closing her eyes.

●●●

Black already made hotel reservations on his cell as he drove to the airport. He just landed and was looking for his rental car. His nerves were on end. He wanted to go straight to her house and see her, but he needed to get himself together first.

Black knew their meeting was going to be as traumatic for Kayla as it was for him. There was also, of course, the baby to consider. Black didn't want to upset her and cause anything to happen to the baby. He couldn't believe it. He was going to be a father. Now, he truly understood the depth of her love for him. She left because she wanted to protect him and their child.

Black made a mental note to call Collins when he got to the hotel. He sure hoped he was making some progress on that murder charge. The sooner they got Gianni on ice, and out of their lives permanently, the better off they would all be.

Black arrived at his hotel and went to the desk to check in.

"Oh, yes sir your room is ready," the desk clerk said, handing him his key. "Do you need anything else?"

Black thought for a moment.

"Are the rooms Internet ready, he queried.

"Yes sir, fully," she told him.

"Thank you," he replied with a small smile as he turned to go find his room.

Black switched on the light after he opened the door. It was a nice room with a view of the water. Black was still rolling around the idea of going by her house tonight, but decided against it. He would take tonight to get everything together. Then he would go see her first thing tomorrow. Black headed to the shower, stopping at the phone to order room service. He would eat and hang out in his room tonight. Tomorrow would be the day he would finally get his life back.

● ● ●

Kayla woke with a start. She never meant to fall asleep. Kayla thought about her baby and began to smile. She reached up and pushed the nurse call button.

"Yes, may I help you?"

"Yes, I'm awake now. Would you please bring my baby," she asked the nurse.

"We'll bring her in a few minutes."

"Thank you," Kayla replied.

She was both excited and apprehensive. She would finally get a good look at Mariah and know who her father was. Kayla was still thinking about each of the men she was with and how different they were.

Please God, she silently prayed, *don't let my daughter suffer for my mistake.*

She heard the door open and looked up. The nurse was wheeling in the neonatal bed with her daughter in it. Kayla was getting more excited by the moment. The nurse stopped beside her bed. Kayla looked over at the sleeping bundle lying inside. The nurse handed Kayla the baby.

"I'll be back to collect her later and take her back to the nursery," she advised.

Kayla thanked her without looking up. She couldn't tear her eyes away from the beautiful little girl, lying in her arms. Kayla unwrapped her gently, looking the baby over from head to toe. She counted all her fingers and toes.

"All there," Kayla giggled as she looked at her intently, trying to decide who she looked like. After about fifteen minutes, Kayla smiled.

"God does indeed have a sense of humor," she murmured.

Mariah resembled her. There was nothing she could really pick out that looked like either of them. Mariah was blessed with big beautiful locks of hair like Kayla; her nose and mouth. *Great, just great*, Kayla thought as the baby stirred. It was feeding time and Mariah was waking up. She opened her eyes and Kayla saw she had her same light brown eyes. Kayla sighed deeply. There was only one more thing, Kayla thought as she picked up the bottle to nurse the baby.

As Mariah began to suckle, Kayla saw them and then she knew. The baby showcased a big, deep dimple in each cheek. This was Dezi's child. Kayla began to cry softly. She knew this was going to destroy Black and any chance of them ever being together again.

It was her mistake though, not Mariah's. Kayla wouldn't let her baby suffer for it. She finished feeding Mariah and rocked her back to sleep. She was so beautiful and such a good baby. It wasn't her fault who her father was. Kayla could not have loved this child more. She sighed as she thought about the task of calling Dezi to let him know about the baby. Kayla dreaded it and decided it could wait a few days.

The nurse returned and took the baby back to the nursery.

"I'll bring her back later for her feeding," she told Kayla.

"OK, thank you so much," she returned, closing her eyes and drifting back off to sleep.

A Deadly 29 Encounter

Devastator arrived at the hotel later than he intended. His flight was delayed, which pissed him off. He wanted to see Kayla and find out if his child was born yet. Devastator looked at his watch. It was after midnight. He wouldn't disturb her now. He would wait until tomorrow. Devastator walked up to clerk at the desk.

"I have a reservation," he posed, giving her his name. "Is my room ready?"

"Yes sir, here you are," the clerk replied and gave him the key.

After Devastator settled in, he made a few calls. He called home to check on his operation. Then he called Big D to check on the girls.

"Everything is straight man," Big D told him. "If anything comes up I can't handle, I'll call."

He called Stan to check on things in South Carolina. Devastator was close enough to drive down and check things out. He thought he might do that later in the week after he saw Kayla.

Devastator lay back on the bed and thought about her and the child she was carrying. Devastator wanted to see her. He wanted to know if it was a boy or a girl. He wanted to assure Kayla he would be there for her and the baby. He wanted to plan their future together. He knew he was going to have to do a hard sell to her, especially after all the lies she was told, but Devastator was determined. He would do whatever it took to make his family a reality. Devastator eventually drifted off to sleep still deep in thought.

•••

The phone ringing woke him up.

"Hello," Black answered sleepily.

Collins winced. He forgot about the time difference. He wanted to give Black the news as soon as he heard it.

"Sorry man, I forgot about the time thing," Collins explained.

Black looked at the digital display on the clock and saw it was 7 a.m.

"It's OK man, what's up?"

"I got a lead, a good one," Collins told him. "I'm on my way to Florida."

"I think we may actually have found a witness to that whole thing in South Carolina. If this pans out, we can finally nail Gianni for good," Collins finished the explanation.

Black was fully awake now and the thought of them getting this guy filled him with excitement, especially now.

"Keep me informed man. Let me know the minute you find out anything," Black said.

"You know I will," Collins assured him. "Have you seen Kayla yet?"

"No, I got in late last night, so it's on my list first," Black told him.

"Good luck man," Collins genially wished him.

"Yeah man, you too," Black returned as they hung up.

Black got up and walked to the window. The waves were softly breaking on the shore. The sun was starting to come up and it made the whole sky sparkle. He was thinking about Kayla again, wondering if she were awake yet. Black decided he would leave around nine or so to go see her. He changed his clothes and went out to take a run on the beach, thinking about Kayla and what he would say when he saw her.

●●●

Collins arrived in Miami early in the morning. He grabbed a few hours sleep on the plane. He was keyed up. He wanted to talk to this guy the agents were holding. Collins hoped this time they wouldn't run into a dead end again. He saw the agent standing by the waiting car and waved to him. He signaled back and Collins began walking toward the car.

Once Collins was inside, they all exchanged pleasantries about the trip, the weather, their families and the bureau. Then they got down to the discussion of their potential witness. They told Collins the man was initially arrested on federal fraud charges for cashing and forging

Social Security checks of a dead relative. He was a known drug abuser and been in and out of the system since he was 16.

"So how did the South Carolina murders come up," Collins asked them.

"He was high when we picked him up," the one agent began. "He tried to bargain almost instantly."

"He told us he had information we could use to put away a lot of people," the second agent began. "We dismissed it as the delusional ramblings of yet another crackhead, until he mentioned South Carolina and a hotel killing rampage."

Collins was intrigued. It certainly sounded like their case, but he didn't want to get too excited. They were still 15 minutes from the Miami office. Collins knew this would be the longest ride of his life.

•••

Devastator woke bright and early, despite his late night and the time change. He was hungry, so he ordered room service then walked to the window and looked at the beach. It was stunning. He loved the water. Something else they held in common. He smiled thinking about Kayla.

The hotel was eight blocks from her house, so he could pop around whenever he wanted. Devastator opened his door and saw the package. *Should be from the real-estate agent,* he thought as he opened it. She sent him photos of several houses near Kayla's. He decided to look at them later, tossing them on the bed and heading for the shower. His food arrived shortly after he got out.

Devastator was still clad only in a towel when the server brought it in. He smiled seeing how uncomfortable the young woman was while setting everything up for him.

He purposely walked close to her, gently grazing her body as he did. She jumped slightly and he noticed her nipples were hard. Devastator looked her over. She was nicely shaped, not unpleasant to look at. He might want to have some fun with her, he thought.

Devastator got close to her ear and whispered, "Do you approve of what you see," as he kissed it softly.

The girl shuddered. He knew he would have her undressed and in his bed in a matter of minutes. *Good thing he packed the condoms*, he thought. He smiled again.

"I definitely approve of what I see," he told her reaching down to cup her breast.

She was his at that point.

After the sex he got her name, which was Olivia, and told her she was great and he hoped she would come back and see him again while he was there. *Why mess up a good piece of ass trying to find a new one every day*, he reasoned behind the smile she saw on his face. Olivia smiled back.

He kissed her softly for good measure, and sent her on her way. *His day was starting off pretty good*, he thought chuckling. He grabbed the brochures and began to look at the houses. He decided to find a house first, get settled in and then go see Kayla.

●●●

Collins walked in the room, saw the young man sitting at the table and thought this could be anyone walking the street. The man showed none of the usual signs of gang or drug life. He was clean shaved and he spoke eloquently when he talked. *Just goes to show what happens when you don't choose your friends wisely*, Collins thought. He sat down across the table from the man and opened one of the two folders he brought with him. Joe, the potential, was watching Collins closely.

The other agents told him this was the man who would decide on the deal. Joe desperately wanted to make this deal. He was in big trouble, looking to do at least ten years in a place like the federal pen. Joe was sure he owned something to bargain with. It ought to be worth something besides the nightmares and excessive drug abuse it drove him to these last few months.

Collins, feeling that he gave the man enough time to get worried, looked up and addressed him.

"So, I understand you feel you have information pertinent to an investigation we are conducting," Collins said to him.

Joe looked at him for a moment before answering.

"Yes, I believe I do," he said softly.

Collins went on to tell him of all the charges pending against him, then sat back and folded his arms.

"What do you want out this whole thing," he asked Joe calmly.

Collins didn't have to wait long for the answer. Joe obviously already made up his mind.

"I don't want to do any time in prison."

Collins eyed him again.

"Well then Joe, you better open your mouth and tell me something that's going to blow my socks off."

He waited.

Joe took a deep breath, sighed, but before he could begin, Collins interrupted him telling him he needed to tape their conversation. Once the tape was set up, Collins dated it, stated his and Joe's name, and then signaled Joe to begin talking. Joe took another deep breath, and then began to tell Collins what happened that night at the Desert Inn in South Carolina.

●●●

Black returned from his run, showered, and finished dressing. He picked up the directions he printed from map quest, grabbed his keys and headed out the door to her house. Black was nervous and apprehensive the entire ten minutes it took to get there. He parked outside about a house away from hers.

What if Kayla didn't want to see him? What if she asked him to leave, Black asked himself. He was really nervous.

Finally getting out of the car five minutes later, he walked toward her house. Black knocked gently on the door after he was unable to find a doorbell. He waited a few moments and got no answer. He knocked again, a little more forcefully, in case she was sleeping or in another part of the house away from the door. After a few more moments, still no answer. *She must not be home*, Black thought dejectedly, and turned to leave.

●●●

Mary watched the well-dressed man since he drove up. She knew Kayla lived alone. She was very protective of her young neighbor. Even though she never said anything, she knew Kayla was running from something or someone. She wondered if this was the baby's father. Kayla never mentioned him except to say that things didn't work out between them.

Maybe he was trying to reach out to her now, Mary thought.

She got up and headed out her door, across the street to the man walking down the sidewalk.

"Hi," Mary addressed Black as he reached his car.

He looked up at the woman. "Hello."

"You're looking for Kayla," Mary asked him cautiously.

Black didn't want to alarm her. She obviously knew Kayla and that she lived alone. So he smiled brightly and told her yes. Mary walked up to him. She looked at him long and hard. He seemed like a nice guy. She didn't feel any alarms going off, so she decided to tell him about the baby.

Black was elated. He had to get to the hospital. He needed to see his child and Kayla.

"Thank you so much Mary, for being there when I couldn't," Black told her yet another time.

Mary gave him directions to the hospital. He jumped in the car. Black was halfway there before he remembered he didn't ask whether it was a boy or girl.

"Who cares," Black laughed out loud as long as the baby was healthy and Kayla was okay.

●●●

Collins was blown away. Joe finally put the missing pieces together in a puzzle they were working on for months. He gave him explicit details of how each man was killed, who killed them and who was witness to the killings.

"Can you identify them if you saw them again," Collins asked.

"Yes," Joe responded. "I can never forget them."

Collins then unfolded the second file folder he brought into the room with him. First, he laid out the photos of the Front 5: Marvin Gaines, Sammy Jones, JePaul Moyer, Gilbert Reid and Dontavious Hart; all vicious killers.

"Are any of these, the men you saw that night?"

Joe looked at the pictures and felt a chill.

"Yes, all of them," Joe replied. "They beat the first three guys to death."

It was coming together, Collins thought, taking out more pictures. *If he identifies these three we're in business.* He then laid down the other pictures inside the folder of Dirty, Monster and Devastator.

"What about these three?"

Joe picked up each one individually, thinking as he looked at each one, and then laid them back down.

"Yeah, all of them were there," he replied again.

Collins was rounding third, heading for home, when he asked the next question.

"Which of them killed the other three men?"

Joe took another deep breath, thinking back again to that night. He thought back to the men screaming, human guts, blood spilling, men laughing and that crazy one; the cold, heartless, soulless one, taking a bow before putting his finger on the picture.

"That one. He killed all three of them," Joe replied, shuddering again at the thought.

Collins smiled for the first time since he arrived. Joe placed his finger on the picture of Dezi Antony Gianni, aka Devastator.

• • •

"And this one has the master suite downstairs as well as two more bedrooms upstairs," the real-estate agent was telling Devastator.

They were touring one of the three houses she sent him.

He wanted something cozy; something that he and Kayla could be a family in. Devastator smiled at the thought. He drove by her house on his way here. He couldn't help it. The agent took that route.

"And here is your spacious deck," she said, bringing Devastator back to the present.

"Thank you so much for the tour," he spoke. "Do you think you have time to show me the other two houses?"

"Why yes of course," she assured him.

Of course, Devastator thought, *the commission check calleth*. He laughed under his breath at that one. The agent looked at him, but she didn't comment.

His plan was to go to the hospital to see them once Kayla delivered. Then he would convince her to come home with him.

Devastator knew it was a long shot, but having a baby changes a lot of things, he reasoned. Kayla had to be more willing to listen. Devastator was definitely counting on that. Twenty minutes later, they were on their way to the final house. So far, Devastator liked the first one best, but he remembered there was a baby now. Maybe stairs weren't such a good idea. Fortunately, the third house was ranch style. Devastator liked it more than he thought he would.

It's perfect he mused. It was cozy with that homey feel even empty like it was now.

"I love this one," Devastator told the agent. "I think this is it."

"Excellent choice," she clapped her hands and smiled. "Let's go back to the office and sign the contracts."

"How long are we talking until close," Devastator asked.

She thought for a moment before answering his question.

"Well, since you already have your financing in order, from start to finish and barring no unseen circumstances, it should be about two and a half weeks."

He thought about it. Three weeks was a long time. What if Kayla already gave birth? Well, then he would just rearrange his original plan. He knew where she lived, so he could always find her. Devastator wanted everything to be ready and perfect when he went to her.

"OK then, let's go to your office," Devastator told her, smiling.

She smiled back and they headed for her truck.

●●●

Black arrived at the hospital. He was walking to the elevator when his cell went off. He looked at the display, seeing it was Collins and stepped back outside to answer the call.

"Hey man, what you got," Black asked him, right after hello.

Collins told him the entire story, from start to finish. The witness identified all of them, including naming Gianni as the killer.

"That's the second best news I've heard all day," Black told Collins.

"Yeah," Collins said. "What's the first?"

Black chuckled.

"Kayla had the baby."

Collins was genuinely happy for his friend.

They talked about the case, and what their next move was. Collins told him he already called and was having warrants issued.

"Well, call me as soon as you get those five. Something tells me that they can help us a lot more with Gianni," Black said.

"I'll do that, and I'm sending agents to South Carolina to pick the ones up there the witness named," Collins told him.

They hung up and Black felt better than he had in a long time.

Finally, he thought, *we can put this slime away and my new family can live in peace.* Black smiled and pushed the button for the fourth floor. When the doors opened three minutes later, he was looking at the entrance to the maternity ward. Black stepped out and headed to the nurses station.

He stepped up to the nurse's station and asked for her room. The nurse gave him the room number and directions. Black thanked her and headed down the hallway. He gently pushed her door open and walked in.

"Oh my god," Black said softly, looking at Kayla again for the first time in five months.

She looked beautiful and was sleeping peacefully. He walked over and carefully put the roses down on her nightstand. Black looked over on the other side of the bed and saw the baby. He looked at the child for what seemed like forever before he finally walked over to where she was.

Black looked at the tag on the bassinet; DeWitt, girl, it read. He had a daughter! His mind was going a thousand miles an hour. He wanted to see her. She was lying on her side, propped up by a little pillow. She had so much hair he could barely see her face.

"Like mother, like daughter," Black chuckled softly as he gently lifted her into his arms.

She didn't cry. She slept peacefully while he held her. She was perfect.

She looks just like Kayla, Black thought. *She is beautiful.* He sat in the rocker and rocked her gently, admiring her. She began to fret and he tried to soothe her. She got louder. Black was getting alarmed.

"She's hungry," Kayla said softly.

Black looked up and she was looking at him, tears slowly rolling down her cheeks. He brought the baby over and gave her back to Kayla.

"Hi," was all Black could say right now.

He was so full of emotion, looking into those beautiful brown eyes of hers again.

"Hi, yourself," Kayla replied, smiling through the tears now.

She began to feed the baby who began to protest rather loudly.

"How did you find me," she asked Black.

"We had every friend we knew in other agencies looking for you," Black told her. "I was so worried."

"I never meant to worry you Black," Kayla told him. "It's just that when Dezi got out, I was scared, especially after I found out I was pregnant."

"She's beautiful, Kayla," Black said softly, looking at Mariah.

How could she break his heart? How could she tell the man she loved with all her heart that the child he adored wasn't his? Kayla took a deep breath, needing to get this off her chest now before he got in too deep.

Before she could speak, Black interrupted her.

"What's her name," he asked, holding her again now that she was full and sleeping contentedly.

"Mariah LaTaea," Kayla told him softly, not looking at him.

She explained about the name and Black told her he liked it. It seemed to suit her very well. She mustered the strength to tell him now before she lost her nerve again. She didn't want to, but she steeled herself and looked at him.

"She's not yours," Kayla said as gently as she could.

She waited for Black to react, but he never moved since she said the words. He was still holding Mariah and looking down at her. Kayla held her breath. Black finally stirred and looked at her again.

"How do you know that," Black asked her, the pain in his eyes more than she could bear.

She couldn't look at him anymore, so she looked at her hands instead.

"I slept with Dezi the day he was arrested, so I wasn't sure until she was born who her father was," Kayla replied.

Black was quiet again for a long time. Kayla was slowly dying inside as she waited for him to say something.

"So, what made you determine she was his," Black asked Kayla again, still calm.

Kayla explained that at first she couldn't tell because Mariah looks so much like her. But when she fed her, she saw the facial trait she shared with Dezi, her dimples. Black was silent. He still never took his eyes off the beautiful little girl resting in his arms. He spoke slowly and deliberately.

"I'm not upset with you for sleeping with him. I understand the circumstances surrounding that. I'm past that. I want to talk about here and now and about Mariah. I want two things from you at this point," he told her, taking another slow breath before continuing. "I want a paternity test, for one."

Kayla interrupted.

"Why," she asked quietly.

Black didn't answer for a minute and she thought he wasn't going to.

"Just because I do," he said finally. "Then, secondly, however that test turns out, I want you to know, I'm still going to be Mariah's father for the rest of her life." Black caressed the baby's face.

Kayla was stunned. She couldn't believe what she just heard. Black still wanted to be a part of her daughter's life, even after she hurt him like she did.

"All right," Kayla replied. "I'll ask them to do the test. As far as you and Mariah, words can't explain the happiness I feel that you'll still be a part of her life. I'm so sorry I hurt you Black. I never meant to do that. I'm just sorry it turned out this way. I never wanted to lose you as part of my life."

Black rose and took Mariah back to her. He handed her the baby and looked directly into her eyes. She looked away. He saw the tears begin to well. Black gently cupped her face, lifted her chin, leaned down and kissed her passionately. He turned to leave the room, but stopped at the door.

"I'll be back later today to see you both," he told her.

Kayla nodded, but wouldn't look at him.

"By the way," Black began.

This time Kayla looked up at him.

"I don't ever remember saying you lost me."

A Deadly 30 Encounter

It was a long three weeks for Collins. He spent the majority of his time rounding up suspected criminals that Joe fingered for him. The bureau devoted a lot of time and manpower. It was all starting to pay off. They managed to grab two of the Front 5, Dontavius Hart and Sammy Jones, by surprising them at their girlfriend's homes. The third, Marvin Gaines, opted to shoot it out with them and they killed him. They were still looking for the final two, Gilbert Reid and JePaul Moyer.

Collins questioned Jones and Hart extensively, neither of them giving up any information. They were going out to a location today. One of their informants told them that they could find Moyer there. They were trying to do this quickly without tipping Gianni off. They didn't want him to flee before they arrested him.

"Agent Collins," he answered after his phone rang.

It was one of the other agents in the South Carolina office. He was telling him they picked up three more men that Joe identified.

"We, haven't found Stan Everette, the named leader," the agent informed.

"Lean hard on the ones we have," Collins told him. "Maybe they will give up Everette."

"Call me later with any developments," he told them as a final thought, and hung up.

Collins made a mental note to call Black to update him on the case. Collins was glad things were working out between Black and Kayla, especially now that they shared a child. Collins just hoped they got to Gianni before he could find out about her and the baby, and then try to make a move on them both. Collins grabbed his shield and gun, motioned the two other agents in the office to come with him and headed out to find Moyer.

They arrived at a remote location outside the city, an area with an abundance of run down apartments and duplexes. The informant told them they could find Moyer in unit 607. After locating the unit,

Collins and the other agents fanned out. They secured both exits and the windows in case Moyer tried to flee.

Collins approached the door carefully; making sure the agent with him was at his back.

"This is Agent Collins, FBI!" he said loudly. "We have a warrant, open the door!"

He heard a lot of commotion and a woman scream. Collins kicked the door open, just as Moyer was running toward it gun drawn.

"Freeze," Collins yelled at him. "Drop the weapon!"

Another agent came in the back door, yelling for him to freeze, as well, weapon pointed at the suspect.

Moyer stopped for a moment as if contemplating whether to try and shoot his way out. Finally, after what seemed like eternity, Moyer dropped the weapon and went down to his knees in surrender. Collins kept his gun trained on him while the agent who was behind him came up and handcuffed him. Once they placed him in the car, they returned to the apartment to conduct a search.

They recovered multiple weapons, which they would send to lab to compare with other unsolved homicides, and a large storage box containing what appeared to be personal items from multiple contributors.

Maybe they kept souvenirs, Collins thought. He sure hoped so. That would even further tie them to the killings and extend their sentences. They headed back to the bureau. Collins planned to call Black to let him know what was going on.

• • •

Devastator was still working with the real-estate agent to close the deal on the house. They were having trouble with the title search, further delaying the sale. He was getting anxious, not only because of Kayla, but he got the feeling that his business wasn't going well. He was unable to reach the Front 5 for days.

Devastator reached Big D who told him everything was fine. He still didn't like the fact that he couldn't reach the others, but he told Big D okay and hung up. He called South Carolina, but no one could tell him where Stan was.

What the fuck is going on, Devastator thought. He decided to drive down there since he was close. He called one more time reaching Gilbert, the veteran of the Front 5, this time.

"I've been trying to reach you for the last four days," Devastator told him. "Everything is fine man, why you tripping," Gilbert replied. "I just saw the others a couple days ago."

It was a lie, because Gilbert was hanging out with his girlfriend hitting the casinos for the last week.

"I made the collections last night, everything is cool," he said.

"Well, damn," Devastator began again. "Don't let my ass have to chase y'all down again like this."

"Sorry about that man, real talk," Gilbert apologized, making a mental note to himself to find the other four, and cuss them out.

"I'll call you later this week," Devastator told him, and hung up.

"Well, at least that shit is off my mind," Devastator said out loud.

There was a knock at his room door. *Who the hell could that be,* he thought as he opened the door. It was Olivia, his morning room service girl. She didn't come around this morning, and he was still pissed about that.

She wasn't dressed for work today. She was clad in a dangerously short skirt and see-through shirt. Devastator admitted he was already getting aroused. The girl smiled, seeing that her outfit turned him on.

"I'm sorry about this morning," she apologized, going on to tell him of her new schedule.

Devastator's mind was still on his business however;.

"It's straight," he replied calmly. "I'll see you tomorrow," he finished, opening the door for her to leave his room.

He asked the desk clerk to send him directions to South Carolina. Devastator was going down to check on his operation and Stan. He paid his room for the next two weeks. He grabbed his keys and made a mental note to pick up some firepower once he got there. Devastator headed to the parking lot to get his car.

●●●

Kayla was completely enjoying motherhood. Mariah was a wonderful baby. Kayla loved the fact that Black was still there. He was true to his word when he came to pick them up to take them home. Black adored Mariah.

They never spoke again about Mariah's true parentage. Kayla knew Black received the test results, but he never mentioned them, she didn't either. She didn't want a copy, so he was the only one who got them.

Kayla was so grateful that Black didn't leave her. She loved him and still felt guilty about hurting him. She thought about Dezi during the last few weeks. Kayla knew she still needed to tell him about Mariah. She was still torn and until she straightened it out in her own mind, she wouldn't call Dezi. She looked at them again, Black and Mariah, both sleeping peacefully. Mariah was lying on his chest and Black was cradling her in his arms. Something clicked inside her at that moment. She made up her mind that Dezi would never know about Mariah. Never get the chance to destroy her or hurt her like everyone else he ever touched, including her. Kayla walked out to the deck, leaving them lying there together.

●●●

Collins called Black after they returned to the office, but got his voicemail. He left him a message to call, and then headed off to interrogate Mr. Moyer.

Collins hoped that this one cracked. He needed more information and someone to support the things Joe told him. They ran checks on some of the personal items they found at his home today. Several of them came back belonging to four of the six men killed at the hotel in South Carolina that night. Collins hoped it would be enough leverage to get Moyer to talk. He adjusted his tie, said a quick prayer and entered the room.

For the next five hours, Collins grilled Moyer with questions and accusations. He told him he would do at least 50 years before they even thought about asking about a parole hearing. Collins told Moyer he would see to it that they locked him in the toughest, maximum-security federal pen they could find, and that he didn't have to go down alone. He told if Moyer if he cooperated he could get out of prison while he was still a young man.

After the sixth hour, Moyer broke. He gave them names, addresses, dates, times, and places, including the club shooting they did here. Moyer named Gianni as the person who hired them to do at least four multiple murders over the last six months. Moyer agreed to have his statements taped and also agreed to testify against Gianni at trial.

Collins told him he wouldn't walk free, but they would guarantee no death penalty and he would serve no more than 20 years. For Moyer that was a done deal, considering he was looking at being executed at least six times over.

Moyer took the deal. They took him back to his cell. Collins was almost ready.

●●●

Black dialed Collins cell, and he answered on the second ring.

"Took you long enough," Collins said, trying to sound irritated.

"OK, so I'm calling now," he said. "Spill it."

Collins laughed. He gave him a recap of what Moyer told them. He since received word that the agents in South Carolina obtained statements from two of the three they picked up there. All of them were telling the same story.

"We located and detained Stan Everette, the leader of the operation down there." Collins told him. "So far though, he isn't talking."

"What's next," Black asked

"We still have to get Reid, but we have a sting in place tonight," Collins told him. "After that, we will leak the story we put together and flush out Gianni," he added.

"Sounds good. Keep me updated," Black told him and hung up.

He was silently hoping it would be over soon. They were doing well together, and he was ready for them to have their life. Black wanted his family, his wife and his daughter, to be together and safe. Black wanted to marry Kayla. He wanted too for a long time. He knew exactly when he was going to ask her. Black smiled and went to find Kayla.

A Deadly 31 Encounter

Collins was making sure the sting didn't fall apart this time. Reid canceled on them last time and they were forced to wait another week and a half for this meet. They were setting up a buy between Reid and another supplier. The supplier was actually an agent. The meet was going to go down in less than an hour. They had to get this right or they would lose him. Then he might tip off Gianni. They knew Reid started asking questions and looking for his other four partners. How they managed to keep the information under wraps this long was a miracle. Collins grabbed his jacket and headed to the meet.

•••

Devastator was on the road headed home. He arrived in South Carolina and found things in shambles. FBI had arrested Stan and half his crew. They shut down his operation and he couldn't find agent Moss's ass anywhere. Shit was going bad quickly. Devastator needed to get home long enough to get to the safe where he kept his cash. He and Kayla would need it. Devastator was going to have to take them out of the country now. They weren't going to be safe, not even in Virginia Beach. He knew he could slide right in and right out. They didn't know about the other entrance to house. *Almost home*, Devastator thought, as he hit the state line picking up the car's speed.

•••

Collins called Black on his way to the sting.

"Hey man," Black greeted him "Is it set?"

Black wanted to be there, but Collins told him to come in a couple days when they were getting ready to take down Gianni. Collins knew that was what Black lived for all these months. Black agreed, besides he didn't want to leave Kayla and Mariah right now.

"Yeah, I'm on my way now," Collins said. "I sure hope this goes down smooth. This one, Reid, is as seasoned as Gianni. He may decide to die instead of surrender."

Black knew exactly what he was saying, but he hoped for the best anyway. The more testimony they gathered against Gianni, the better.

"Call me after it's all said and done," Black said.

"Of course," Collins replied as they disconnected.

He watched her for a while before he finally spoke.

"I'm going to have to go back for a little while," Black told her quietly.

Kayla sighed. She knew this was coming, sooner or later.

"Have you found what you need to arrest Dezi," she asked, looking directly at him.

"Yes," he replied. "The warrant is going to be issued tomorrow. I'm going back to arrest him personally."

Kayla knew he hated Dezi, and she understood why, but she was afraid for him. Black watched her while she thought. He saw the tears come to her eyes. He reached out for her, holding her.

"I'm going to be fine Kayla," Black assured. "And I'm coming back."

"Promise," Kayla asked him, looking at him intently again.

"Yes, I promise," Black told her, as he kissed her.

He took her hand as they went and lay down together.

Later, Kayla woke with a small scream, jumping up to check on the baby. Mariah was sleeping peacefully in her crib. Black, who heard Kayla cry out, put his arms around her waist and held her.

"Everything is okay baby," Black spoke turning her around to face him. "You and Mariah are perfectly safe."

"And you already know I will do everything in my power to keep it that way," he added, kissing her again.

Still, Kayla had a very bad feeling.

● ● ●

This was not happening, Collins thought, as they listened to the police scanner. Reid was pulled over by LAPD on his way to the meet for a minor traffic infraction. They ran his license and warrants came back.

In the process of trying to arrest him, Reid shot an officer and was now involved in a high-speed chase.

"This is so not happening," Collins yelled.

They didn't want him dead. They wanted him to testify against Gianni.

"Shit," Collins exclaimed, thinking about Gianni.

He would surely hear about this and go into hiding. They had to get to him before that. Collins picked up his cell and began to dial.

●●●

Devastator's cell went off. He was still about 10 miles from his house. He looked at the display. It was Big D.

"Yeah," Devastator answered, wondering what bad news he was going to hear now.

"Yo man, we're out," Big D told him. "FBI hit our spot, I managed to get four of the girls and we slipped out. It's bad man, real bad. I don't know where you're at, but you need to be up outta this piece, too."

Devastator swore and pounded the wheel. Then took a deep breath trying to calm himself.

"Thanks for the update man," he replied. "Do what you need to do. It was a good run, but we gotta do our own thing now."

They wished each other well and hung up.

He had to be extremely careful now. He knew the FBI would be watching his house and waiting for him. He would find someplace to lay low until dark; then he could slip through his private entrance and get what he needed. Once he grabbed the money, he could slip back out and head to his woman and his child.

Devastator thought about his empire crumbling, all the friends he lost, and the FBI. This was their entire fault.

"Especially that fucker Agent Black," Devastator growled. "I still owe that bastard."

He was even angrier because he knew he didn't have time to take care of that debt.

"I'll just owe him one," Devastator said. "I gotta go get Kayla, and the baby, and get the hell out of the country."

He turned into a rundown motel at the edge of town.

"This will do until nightfall," he said, as he drove into the parking lot, found a tree and parked under it.

•••

"I'm on my way to the airport now," Black was telling Collins as he grabbed the bag he packed earlier.

Collins called to tell him about Reid, and that they had to move on Gianni now or they would lose him.

"Did they apprehend him," Black asked Collins, referring to Reid.

"No," Collins replied. "He started shooting at officers; they returned fire and killed him."

Damn, Black thought.

"We still have a good case though," Collins told him. "We have at least four that are willing to testify against him. We can still get the death penalty easy."

Black agreed. Neither of them wanted to see Gianni walk free again.

"I'll be on the ground in a few hours," Black said before hanging up.

He went to the bedroom to find Kayla and Mariah. She was sitting in her rocker holding the baby who was studying her intently.

"Hey," Black said softly, looking at her. "I'm leaving now, but I promise you I'll be back."

He leaned closer to kiss her. He called a cab. He didn't want her to go to the airport.

"Please be careful," Kayla told him, ready to cry again. "I can't lose you again."

They embraced. Mariah, squashed in the middle of them, began to complain. They both laughed and Black kissed the protesting baby. He kissed Kayla again and walked out the door to his waiting cab.

"Please God," Kayla prayed quietly, watching Black go. "Protect him and bring him safely back to me."

•••

Devastator was taking care of a little business while he waited for dark. He called the real-estate agent in Virginia to tell her there was a change of plans and he wouldn't be buying the house. She was disappointed, but she understood. She told him she would have his check waiting for him at the hotel when he returned. Devastator thanked her and told her to keep her commission anyway.

Devastator called Big D again. He needed some information.

"Yeah man," Big D answered his cell, knowing who it was.

"Where are the Front 5," Devastator asked him.

Big D knew he was out of town, so he probably didn't know about everything that transpired in his absence.

"Two of them are dead," Big D began. "Moyer cut a deal."

Devastator was livid. He had been good to all these jokers and now they were turning on him. He took another deep breath. He couldn't worry about that now. He had to get his money, and get the hell out before they caught him.

"Thanks man," Devastator said to Big D, who was always been loyal

"No problem, man," Big D replied.

Devastator told him thanks again for his help and they hung up. It was dark now. He wanted to be back on the road before light again. He needed a head start. He was driving and it was going to take more than two days to get back to Virginia. He could have flown, but he wouldn't risk it. Devastator was sure they plastered his picture up everywhere. Not to mention all the cash he would be carrying. He started the car, heading toward his house.

•••

Collins was waiting for Black when he landed. They greeted each other as Collins began to brief him on what they were about to do.

Black's mind was racing. This was what they were waiting for. He was excited, but cautious. Gianni escaped them before. Black didn't want that to happen again.

"Are we sure he's there this time," he asked Collins.

Collins told him they were sitting on the house all day. They couldn't really tell if he was there or not. It was the first place they had to check before they could issue an All-Points Bulletin, or APB, on him.

Black understood.

"I get it man, I'm just anxious to get this over with."

Collins nodded agreement and they both headed out to the SUV loaded with agents pulling out headed for Gianni's house.

•••

Devastator was pleased with himself. He made it to the house without being seen. He thanked his private entrance for that feat. It was perfectly camouflaged with the trees he attached to the wrought iron gate. You couldn't tell there was an entrance there, which was one of the reason's he bought the house.

Once inside, he looked around at the magnificent home he once lived in. Devastator was saddened at the thought of leaving it, but it wasn't the same anymore for him here. Dirty and Monster were gone, his empire now crumbled, and the woman he loved was in another state. Devastator walked into his dining room, pulled out the massive china cabinet, revealing the wall safe behind it. Devastator opened the safe, and began to load the cases he brought with money.

•••

Collins and Black were both deep in thought as they got closer to the house. They hoped he was here. They wanted this done.

"Do you think it'll be as easy as last time," Collins asked him hopefully.

Black looked at him, then shook his head.

"Hell no," he said plainly. "He is going to fight tooth and nail, you know that."

Collins knew he was right. They possessed evidence and testimony this time. Gianni knew he would spend the rest of his life in prison, and that was the very least sentence he would get. They turned onto the street, still about half a mile from his house.

"OK, everyone let's get ready to do this," Collins instructed, as they all put their vests on.

The convoy of agents and SWAT arrived at the house. They got out, and everyone set up position. They had a warrant, so Black and Collins, accompanied by six other agents, went to the door and knocked.

"We have a warrant," Collins shouted. "FBI! Open the door!"

They waited. No response. Black gave the signal, and they rammed the door, entering the house. SWAT came in first, clearing each room. Finally, after 15 minutes, they announced the house was clear. Gianni wasn't there.

"Damn," Black swore out loud.

He wanted him to be here. There were other possible locations, so they assigned two agents to stay there and sift through the stuff in the house for any evidence. Black and Collins headed back out to the truck to go to the next location.

● ● ●

Kayla was giving Mariah a bath when the phone rang. She picked the baby up, wrapping her in a towel and went to answer it.

"Hello?"

Black smiled. It was good to hear her voice again.

"Hey baby," he replied.

Kayla was elated, and relieved. She was so worried when he didn't call.

"Are you all right," she asked.

"I'm fine," Black told her. "We're still looking for Gianni," he continued. "I just wanted to check on you and Mariah."

"We're fine," Kayla told him. "We just had our bath."

"Well give her a big kiss from her daddy," Black told her. "And I'll call you back soon."

"I will, please be careful Black," Kayla told him.

"I promise baby," he assured as they said their goodbyes and hung up.

A Deadly 32 Encounter

Devastator was thinking about Kayla again. He held his cell in his hand. He wanted to call her. He procured her number while he was in Virginia at the hotel. He thought about it, but decided against it. He didn't want her to leave. He knew she was still afraid of him.

He would wait until he got back to see Kayla. Then he would make her understand. He would show her he loved her, and tell her he would never hurt her or their child. He had to find them a way out of the country. He still possessed a couple of contacts and he needed to get in touch with them. Devastator scrolled through his phone and found a number. He began to dial.

•••

Two days and they turned up nothing. Black was frustrated. Where the hell was Gianni? They hit all his spots. They even hit places they got call-in tips about. Gianni was nowhere to be found and it was already halfway into the third day. The longer they took to find him, the harder it was going to be.

"Agent Black," the agent entering his office spoke.

"Yeah," he answered, not looking up.

"Here is a file folder we found at Mr. Gianni's house the other day during the raid. It was put on the wrong desk by mistake," he apologized and left.

Collins came into the office immediately after the young man left.

"What's this," he asked, picking up the file bearing Gianni's name.

"Some file they found at his house when we raided it," Black answered, still studying the map on his desk in front of him.

"Why is it just now turning up," Collins asked.

"Some brilliant person put it on the wrong desk," Black told him.

"Well, just damn," Collins said, opening the file. "It could be some useful information in here. I swear, good help is --," he stopped midsentence, which made Black look up at him.

"What is it," he asked, when he saw the look on Collin's face.

Collins laid the file down on the desk for Black to see. His heart sank. The pictures of Kayla were staring him in the face. Black saw the report the detective sent Gianni. He knew where she was.

"Oh my God," Black said, realization hitting him.

That's why they weren't able to find him. Gianni was on his way to Virginia to get Kayla. What if he was already there? They lost almost three days looking for a damned ghost. Collins was way ahead of him. He already called and secured them a plane.

"Let's go man," he yelled at Black, shaking him out of his thoughts.

Black grabbed his cell. He would call Kayla on the way and warn her.

●●●

Devastator was excited having just gotten back to the hotel.

"Whew! Shave and a shower," he laughed, talking to himself.

He was going to clean up and rest for a couple hours. The trip was long and tiring. Devastator couldn't relax too long though. He still had to get over to Kayla's; collect her and the baby. He opened his room door and walked in, dropped his bag and headed straight for the shower.

"That was wonderful," Devastator remarked afterward, walking back to the bed for his nap.

He set the clock on the nightstand next to him for 5:00, three hours from now, closed his eyes and slept.

●●●

Why the hell wasn't she answering the phone? Black was beside himself now. He was continuously trying to call Kayla for the last half hour before they boarded the plane.

"Don't panic," Black reassured aloud. "Maybe she took Mariah out for a walk or something."

It wasn't a far-fetched idea. Kayla often took the baby out or over to Mary's for a visit. Black boarded the plane and took his seat. Collins was seated next to him. They were on a mission to end this thing, once and for all. Black closed his eyes and said a silent prayer for his future wife and his daughter, then fastened his seat belt for takeoff.

•••

Devastator woke with a start at the scream of the alarm clock. He rubbed his eyes to clear the sleep then shut off the clock.

"OK, time to do this," Devastator remarked, as he rose and stretched.

He was going to Kayla's to get her and the baby, then drive to the port and board a ship. He set it all up already and the money was with him to pay for it. He mapped out her house during his first visit and knew he could access to it from the rear.

Devastator hoped after they talked, she would understand and leave with him willingly. Devastator gathered all his belongings, threw them in the bag and headed to the desk to check out.

•••

Black was trying Kayla again for the third time. Still no answer, he called Mary, getting no answer there either.

"What's today," Black asked Collins.

"Wednesday," he replied.

Book club day, okay, Black thought, relaxing now. Kayla went to that club meeting every Wednesday, and she started taking Mariah lately, so all the ladies could fuss over her.

Black smiled, thinking about the beautiful little girl they created together. She didn't have her cell. She must have left it at home. Damn! He needed to warn her and tell her to be careful. Black just hoped they would get there in time. They were still four hours away.

•••

Devastator slipped in the unlocked back door. He carefully walked inside, and listened. He quickly discovered that he was alone. He began walking through the house, exploring each room. It was a nice place. He knew that it would be. Kayla had great taste. Devastator saw pictures of her and the baby. He picked up the larger of the photos, and held it up. He had a daughter.

She is beautiful, lots of hair and my dimples, Devastator thought, smiling. He looked through some papers he found on her nightstand, finding one bearing the baby's name.

"Mariah LaTaea," he repeated out loud. "Very nice."

Devastator left the bedroom, and went into the kitchen. He was hungry, so he figured he would make himself a sandwich or something while he waited on them to come home. Devastator wondered where Kayla and the baby were. *Probably an appointment or something*, he surmised. He hoped she would be home soon. They still had to make it to the port to get on their boat. Devastator walked back out onto her rear deck and sat on one of the lounge chairs. He decided he would wait here until he heard Kayla come in. Devastator closed his eyes and was soon asleep again.

• • •

Kayla was telling Mary goodbye and heading for the house. They were still laughing and talking about their meeting. She didn't hear the phone ringing inside the house. Devastator did as he woke with a start. He looked at the I.D. Donovan Black.

"What the fuck," Devastator growled aloud, eyes going cold and flat, when he heard them.

He quickly gathered himself and went back out to the deck to wait.

"You have enjoyed an exciting day haven't you missy," Kayla laughed, talking to Mariah, who was cooing at her.

"Come on, you need a nap and mommy needs something to eat," she continued, as she took the baby and put her in the swing.

"Do you wanna eat, too," Kayla asked the baby, who smiled at her. "Guess that means yes."

She laughed again, heading for the kitchen.

• • •

Devastator walked back into the room and saw his daughter in her swing. He walked over to her and knelt down.

My god, she is beautiful, he thought, as he lifted the baby out of her swing. This was the first time he ever held his child. She smelled good.

"Like a baby," he chuckled.

Mariah was perfect. Devastator couldn't believe he made something this wonderful.

"Did you fall asleep on mommy," he heard Kayla saying, as she walked toward them.

"I've got someth--," Kayla stopped, dropping the bottle in her hand, as she saw Dezi holding Mariah.

"Hey baby," Devastator spoke gently, looking into her eyes.

Oh my god, he's really here, she thought. She was speechless and terrified. Dezi was here, and he was holding her baby.

"How did you find me," Kayla asked him finally.

He walked over and picked up the bottle, rinsed it, and was now feeding Mariah, who was resting comfortably in his arms.

"It took me a while, but I finally did," he said.

Her mind was racing. What was she going to do? How was she going to get her and Mariah out of here?

"She is just beautiful Kayla," Devastator said to her again, watching her intently.

"She has your dimples," she told Dezi, trying to sound friendly and get him to give her the baby back.

He smiled.

"Yeah she does. Look," he began, looking at her evenly. "I know you've been told some real bad stuff about me Kayla. I know you're probably scared to death right now as I'm sitting here, but I want to let you know, I'm not here to hurt you or our daughter. I came to get you both, so we can be a family."

Kayla was really scared now. Dezi wanted to take them somewhere. She couldn't let that happen. She had to protect her child. He was rising with the baby now, heading to her bedroom. She followed, wanting to keep an eye on him.

Devastator was totally enamored with his child. He put her down gently for her nap, and then turned his attention to Kayla.

"I've missed you so much," he told her, as he bent to kiss her.

Kayla forced herself to not pull away. That would have been very bad, and right now she needed to keep things good for her and Mariah's sakes.

"Dezi, I'm not sure what I feel right now," she told him, backing away from him. "It's been a long time, and so much has happened."

Devastator understood, and he could accept that. There were a few hours to spare, he would talk to her, and try to help her understand. He took her hand, and they headed for the den to sit and talk.

●●●

They finally landed and Black was trying to call Kayla again.

"We're out of range for your cell," Collins told him, as he saw the disgusted look come across his face.

"There are payphones inside," he continued. "Use one of those."

Black nodded, and they headed inside to the terminal. He prayed to reach her. He was scared for her and Mariah. Who knew what was in Gianni's head right now. Black didn't think he would hurt them. He still was obsessed with Kayla. Black wanted to talk to Kayla and hear her voice. He reached the phone, dropped in his coins and dialed.

Kayla heard the phone and got up to answer. Dezi followed, and looked at the I.D. It said unavailable.

"It's probably my neighbor, Mary," Kayla explained.

Devastator knew Kayla didn't know the FBI was looking for him, so he let her answer, as he went back and sat down.

"Hello," Kayla answered.

Black breathed a huge sigh of relief.

"Hey baby, where've you been all day?"

She was never so glad to hear a voice in all her life, but she had to be smart about this. She needed to tip him off without Dezi getting suspicious. Kayla needed his help, and she needed it now.

"Oh, hi Mary," Kayla replied.

Black immediately got it.

"Fuck," he swore under his breath.

Gianni was there with her. Black began to question her.

"Is he there with you?"

"Yes, you know that was an interesting interpretation the author used," Kayla replied.

She heard Dezi chuckle. She knew he was listening, but so far so good. Black mind was moving warp speed. He couldn't keep her on the phone too long, but he wanted to glean some information they could use.

"Is Mariah in your bed? Are you in the same room with her? Is he armed," Black asked her, all at once.

Kayla thought for a minute.

"Yes, she that was quite a steamy bedroom scene, but no, they shouldn't have painted it in the same room, and I'm not sure about the last one they did," Kayla answered.

Hearing Dezi chuckle yet again, he was looking at her doing and impression of her. Kayla forced a smile and stuck out her tongue at him. She faked normal, her mortality on her mind. Dezi laughed harder and Black heard him.

"OK baby, I got it. Stay calm, you're doing great, we're here and we're on our way. Don't let him get you in the car, do you hear me?"

Kayla knew this drill. She also knew not to drink anything Dezi gave her either.

"Yes, Mary I enjoyed it too, but I do have to go now," she sensed Dezi was getting restless. "I'll talk to you soon."

"Hang in there baby, I'm own my way," Black told her as they hung up.

● ● ●

He yelled for Collins and briefed him. They called the local bureau, and told them what they needed. They were headed there now and then they would head over to Kayla's.

Black was in a race against time. He knew Gianni was planning to take them somewhere. He couldn't let that happen. *This time, he's not walking away*, Black thought, as they sped toward the Virginia bureau.

● ● ●

"Come sit next to me," Devastator said to her, as she walked back into the den.

You can do this, Kayla thought, as she sat down beside him.

"I've missed you so much, all this time we've been apart," Devastator said softly, stroking her hair and looking into her eyes.

"I'm not a monster Kayla," he continued, "I've done some stuff in my life I'm not too proud of, but that has nothing to do with you. I've never let what I do, get in the way of us, and I never will."

Devastator began to kiss her, and she sensed where it was going. *He wants to have sex*, Kayla thought. That's the last thing she wanted, but she couldn't upset him. Kayla thought of her baby. She let Dezi kiss her and touch her everywhere he wanted.

"I want to make love to you," Devastator told her huskily, starting to undress her.

"Dezi, this is so fast for me," she told him, almost tearfully. "I haven't seen you in almost a year, and there is so much I've heard. Now, you're here, and I just don't know how I should feel right now."

Kayla prayed that he would believe her.

Devastator was looking at her again, thoughtfully, as if he were trying to figure out whether to believe her or not. Kayla held her breath. Finally, he kissed her gently again.

"I understand baby, it's okay," he said. "We have plenty of time to get reacquainted."

Devastator pulled her to her feet and hugged her.

"You need to go and get your things packed," he said. "We need to leave soon."

He'd told her about the trip, and Kayla protested mildly, as he expected. Finally she quietly agreed after he explained it was best for them and their child.

"OK," Kayla told him softly.

Devastator lifted her head and kissed her again. Kayla left for the bedroom, and he went back into the kitchen to get himself something to drink.

●●●

They expeditiously set up the perimeter, evacuated all the neighbors and surrounded the house. They were quiet, and stealthy. Gianni was clueless they were outside. Now, they needed to get Kayla and the baby out of the house. Black and Collins went around to the window of her bedroom. It was high off the ground and they needed a ladder. Once they secured it Collins went up to get the baby out of the room. They could see the windows were up. That was good. The plan was to get Mariah out safely. Then grab Kayla as she and Gianni came out the back door to get into the car. Collins was at the window. He carefully peeked inside and spotted the baby sleeping on the bed. He also saw Kayla. She turned and caught herself before she could let out a scream. Kayla was so relieved to see him there.

Collins motioned for her to give him Mariah. She readily complied, handing him the still sleeping baby.

"Stay put, I'll be right back for you," Collins whispered.

Kayla nodded; too scared to talk for fear Dezi would hear and come into the room.

●●●

Devastator was getting his juice when he knocked a magnet off the refrigerator. He bent to pick it up, and saw the picture under the bottom of the unit. He pulled it out and turned it over. It was a picture of Kayla, but she wasn't alone. She was with Black. She was sitting on his lap, smiling. Devastator was livid. She lied to him. Devastator took a deep breath. He tried to be reasonable. She was lied too. *This fucker made Kayla think he was going to kill her. That he was a fucking loose cannon just running around killing people at will. She was probably scared, and she was alone while she was pregnant. He was trying to understand,* Devastator thought. He went to the den, and called her name.

Collins just made it down with the baby, when he heard Gianni call her.

"Shit," he said aloud.

He wouldn't have time to get back up to her now, he thought. Black heard him call Kayla, too. He didn't like the tone of Gianni's voice. They put Mariah safely inside one of the trucks. Now, it was time to flush out Gianni, and end this nightmare for all of them.

Kayla heard the edge to Dezi's voice. *What now,* she thought, as she went into the den to see him.

"Explain this to me," he told her.

She could see he was trying hard not to lose control. Devastator laid the photo of her and Black down on the table, and looked at Kayla hard. She was scared all over again. She knew Mariah was safe, but she was still here. He could kill her at any time.

"I went out with him a couple times," Kayla answered cautiously.

Devastator was still looking at her, hard and annoyed

"Why?"

Kayla knew the question was anything but simple, and she better make her answer damned good.

"I was lonely. You were gone, I was alone," she said softly, the tears coming now. "I didn't want to be by myself, and I was afraid."

She was crying quietly.

Devastator felt like a jackass again. He was out of control. No wonder she was afraid of him. He got up and went to her. He put his arms around her, telling her it was okay.

Devastator kissed her again, as he got up and pulled her to her feet.

"Go ahead into the bedroom and get your bags. We need to go," he told her.

Kayla smiled slightly and began walking to the bedroom. He watched her leave, smiling to himself at how lucky he was to find her again and that she would give him another chance. Kayla brought her bag out, and set it on the floor for him. Devastator pulled her to him.

"This is going to be a whole new start for us baby," he told her, in between kisses.

Kayla giggled.

"Stop or we'll never get out of here," she playfully returned, still in character.

He laughed and grabbed the bags.

"I'm going to put these in the car," he told her over his shoulder, as he was getting ready to go out the door.

"Did you hear me," he asked, when she didn't respond. "What is that woman doing," Devastator chuckled, heading for the bedroom.

●●●

Black just helped Kayla onto the ladder, when Devastator charged him. They landed on the bed. Kayla screamed, losing her balance as Collins grabbed her, and pulled her down the ladder.

The fight was extreme, each man trying to kill the other. Devastator caught Black with a hard left knocking him off balance. Black quickly recovered and threw a hard right of his own connecting with Dezi's nose, drawing blood. Devastator wasn't giving up though. He lunged at Black again as the fight continued. Black used a tactical maneuver and slammed Dezi to the floor. Devastator swung wildly as he went down and caught Black in the mouth bloodying his lip.

The blood was flowing freely from both men and the blows were raining just as fiercely as they continued to struggle. Devastator pushed Black hard and he flipped across the bed. Black was right back up and they were at it again. Devastator was trying to grab the gun Black carried from his shoulder holster. Black continued to fight the man knowing if Dezi got his hands on the weapon he would kill him.

Devastator hit Black with two more rights as Black countered with another hard left of his own.

"I promised you death fucker," Devastator said coldly, still struggling with the man intent on getting his gun.

Black pushed Dezi off him once more and tried to gain his footing. Devastator reached out and grabbed Black's ankle tripping him as he jumped onto his back and began raining down blows again.

Black covered his head with his left arm to protect himself and lifted his body from the floor with his right, throwing Dezi once again off of him onto the floor. Turning to face Dezi, Black lunged at him as they continued to grapple. Finally through some twist of fate, Dezi managed to remove the gun from Black's holster. Feeling his weapon being taken, Black tried desperately to wrench it from Dezi's hands.

The two men continued to struggle each with a portion of the gun in their hand, when the first shot went off. The burning he felt was indescribable. Devastator shot Black in the shoulder. He was bleeding heavily. The bullet managed to enter above his vest. Still Black hung on tenaciously knowing his existence was on the line. Devastator wanted to finish it now. He knew Black was wounded and at a disadvantage. He tried once again to aim the gun at the agent, who was still fighting back.

Black managed to once more get leverage and flip Dezi over. Still Devastator hung onto the gun and they were once again fighting for control of it, when it went off again. Black felt the weight crushing down on him as he struggled to breath. He heard several voices and shouts coming from the other room as he tried to stay conscious.

"Get me rescue," Collins shouted to another of the agents.

Black felt the weight being lifted from him as he gasped for air. Finally able to breathe he looked to his partner and spoke.

"Is he dead," Black asked nodding toward Gianni's motionless body.

Collins looked over at the agent, who was checking the still man's pulse and confirmed the death.

"Yeah, he's dead," Collins told Black, looking once more at the dead man lying on the floor, then returning his attention to his friend, missing the sly look exchanged between the answering agent and another that was present in the room.

The ambulance arrived and they brought Black out of the house. Kayla ran to him, Mariah in her arms and kissed him as he lay on the stretcher. Black reached up and caressed her face.

"You did good baby," he told Kayla weakly. "You did real good."

They loaded him in the ambulance and took him to the hospital.

EPILOGUE

The Clique was finally dismantled, as well as several other crime rings that were intertwined. Kayla finally found out what happened to Isabella and who she really was.

Dezi committed her to an asylum with instructions to keep her heavily medicated when she threatened to tell Kayla who he really was. Once he stopped paying her bill, they finally released her.

Isabella called, seeing the story of Dezi's death in the paper. The breaking of his cartel was front-page news. Isabella claimed his body and planned his service.

Kayla attended his funeral. She felt she needed to for closure and for Mariah's sake. He was still her father. Black never protested. He simply told her they would talk when she got back. She remembered thinking how peaceful he finally looked lying there in the coffin. He looked very different somehow, not completely like himself, but she dismissed it as post mortem change and thought no more about it. Now, he was finally free from the torment that was his life. She left right after the service, she and Isabella saying a tearful goodbye.

They were celebrating tonight. Black was home from the hospital and he received his transfer to the North Carolina office. He wanted them to move close to his parents and the rest of his family, so they would always feel safe.

He asked her to marry him that night in front of everybody. She was so embarrassed, but she said yes.

"I want to talk to you for a moment," Black told her, catching her alone in the kitchen.

He was looking very serious when they went to sit outside on the deck.

"What's wrong," Kayla asked him, fearful he was going to say something she didn't want to hear.

Black didn't say anything for a moment. Kayla guessed he was gathering his thoughts.

"I want you to look at these," he told her, handing her three documents.

Kayla looked at him apprehensively.

"What are they," she asked him, still fearful.

Black looked at her evenly.

"You'll understand once you look at them," he told her, still looking at her.

The envelopes were numbered, so Kayla opened them in sequence. The first envelope contained a photo of a very nice looking woman, holding a small baby about Mariah's age now. Kayla wasn't sure what she was supposed to see.

Kayla sighed gently, and then opened the second envelope. It was an adoption certificate for Black. Kayla looked up in surprise. She never suspected he was adopted and he never told her.

"I don't understand baby," she told him pleadingly.

Black still didn't say a word, just kept looking at her. Kayla opened the last envelope and saw the paternity test results. She didn't want to look at these. Why was he showing her this? Kayla started to fold it back up when Black finally spoke.

"Really look at it," he said softly.

Kayla looked at him quizzically, sighed again and looked back at the results. 'Female infant DeWitt. Test subject: Donovan Black; Test results: 99.93% biological relationship.' Kayla was stunned. She must have read this wrong. Mariah had Dezi's dimples. She was his. Kayla looked at Black with confusion and disbelief in her eyes.

"I don't understand," she pleaded with him.

Black smiled a tad.

"This is my natural mother," he told her, and Kayla looked at the photo again.

This time, she saw that the woman possessed one big, deep, dimple on each cheek. Now, Kayla understood. That's why he insisted on the test. The tears were flowing as Black hugged her and told her he loved her. He got up to go back inside, giving Kayla a chance to digest what she just learned. Mariah was Black's child, not Dezi's.

She heard Taea laugh. *"You did good Kayla, you got it right!"*

Kayla smiled, closed her eyes and mouthed a silent thank you to God for answering her prayers. She dried her eyes and walked back into her house a free woman.

About the Author:

K.R. Bankston is an established Romantic Suspense author with some 40 published works to her credit, including the highly successful Thin Ice and Gianni Legacy series. KR is the CEO of Kirabaco Media Group, LLC which houses her works. In addition to being an author KR is a Mentor, and Public Speaker. KR is one half of The Literary Evolution specializing in empowering Authors in the literary marketplace. Quietly taking the industry by storm, KR also pens drama filled contemporary romance under the pen name, Kay Raneé.

KR's "BookOpera" series Thin Ice was voted Serial Novel of the Year and Urban Fiction of the year. Her other series The Gianni Legacy has been touted as The Godfather of modern day. Her novel, Christian was voted #75 of Top 100 Books of the year. Her novel X-Mafia was voted Urban Fiction of the Year.

You can find the Author on the following networks:

https://www.facebook.com/KRBankstonAuthor
https://www.patreon.com/KRBankston
https://youtube.com/@KRBTheAuthor
https://www.amazon.com/author/krbankston
https://www.instagram.com/bookoperalegacy

Also, check out these other offerings from the Author KR Bankston available www.krbankstononline.com and other online retailers: Amazon.com www.amazon.com/author/krbankston, BN.com, and more.

THE GIANNI LEGACY:
A Deadly Encounter
Sins of the Father
Smoke & Mirrors
Life After Death
Aftermath
Sinister Alliance
Requiem

THIN ICE – THE SERIAL:
Thin Ice
Thin Ice 2- Hide & Seek
Thin Ice 3 – Armageddon
Thin Ice 4- Resurrections
Thin Ice 5 – Checkmate
Thin Ice 6 – Hangman & Socrates
Thin Ice 7 – Echoes of Reckoning
Thin Ice 8 – Separazione Finale
Thin Ice 9 – Epiphany
Thin Ice 10 – Ambition
Thin Ice 11 – Homecoming
Thin Ice 12 – Siren Song

NOIR FROST SERIES:
Shattered
Evolutions
Darker Shades of Light
Crosshairs
Reawakening

THIN ICE GENERATIONS:
Blood Legacies
Dark Confessions
Malevolence
The Wedding
Eldest Son

OTHER BOOKS:
X-Mafia: The Rise of Pirate & Creeper
Unholy Empire (pt1 & 2)
Christian
Atomic
Shattered Peace
Interception
Three The Hard Way
Now You're A Star
The Agency
The Master Orchestrator
King of the Game
One of the Boys
No Take Backs
Gold Plated Dreams

www.ingramcontent.com/pod-product-compliance
Lightning Source LLC
LaVergne TN
LVHW091531060526
838200LV00036B/564